Here There Be Dragons

by

Michelle O'Leary

Sunscapes Trilogy, Book 2

Here There Be Dragons

COPYRIGHT © 2017 by Michelle O'Leary

Cover Art by *Debbie Taylor*

The Wild Rose Press, Inc.
PO Box 708
Adams Basin, NY 14410-0708
Visit us at www.thewildrosepress.com

Publishing History
First Fantasy Rose Edition, 2017
Print ISBN 978-1-5092-1569-0
Digital ISBN 978-1-5092-1570-6

Sunscapes Trilogy, Book 2
Published in the United States of America

All brain function came to a
screeching, smoking halt when she stepped out the door. She wasn't alone.

Just down the corridor stood Nick Givliani, a Federated Planetary Alliance inspector, here on the station under the pretense of visiting his brother. His real reason was to investigate the Shays. He'd grown suspicious of the twins' activities and was concerned about his brother's involvement. He'd been rather enthusiastic in his investigation so far, which didn't surprise Cassie. Considering her position with the Shays, it was only a matter of time before he started investigating her.

Prudence suggested a need for caution around him. Avoiding him like the plague was a terrific idea. But at the moment, she was having trouble just remembering to breathe.

Suns, she groaned to herself, *why does he have to be so beautiful?* He did look scruffier than the two times she'd encountered him before. His big, hard-muscled body sported a set of wrinkled clothes, his dark hair spiked in all directions as if he'd been dragging his fingers through it for hours, and disreputable, un-inspector-like stubble darkened his strong jaw. Shadows smudged the skin under his midnight eyes, and the generous curve of his mouth thinned with grim weariness.

Far from making him less attractive, his rumpled appearance added a sympathetic concern to her desire to climb him like a tree. Disconcerting. Why had her long-dormant libido decided to fixate on this man?

Dedication

My deepest appreciation goes to all who supported me
and made this book possible:
my family,
my wonderful editor,
the Wild Rose staff,
my loyal readers,
and as always, my son,
for believing in my work
even though he thinks romance is gross.

Prologue

T'Zai studied his companions with a care and familiarity born of years of intimate service. The four of them sat in the small, darkened meditation room, facing one another. He was the only one not sitting on a cushion, the hard marble floor a stern reminder of his mortality; his old bones and joints ached with the cold, unforgiving contact. He gave his discomfort scant attention, too used to the protests of his failing body to be concerned now.

He had more important matters to focus on.

Lekasha sat on his right with a liquid ease belying her advanced years. She looked as limber as he remembered from their younger days, fond memories of their shared pleasures bringing a smile to his lips. She appeared unchanged, her luscious body rounded and inviting, her dark skin unmarred by age. As the Blue Order's Mendani-met, the head of the sect, she was too important to gallivant about the galaxy seeking new experiences, but she would still be keeping her hand in. Both hands, if he knew her.

Mendani-met Berrabas sat on T'Zai's left, the golden ceremonial robes of his order draped around him with care. Plump and balding, his generous smile and unassuming air had led many to underestimate him. The twinkle in his eyes did not fool T'Zai; he knew how shrewd and ruthless the other man could be.

The White Order's Mendani-met, K'etarci, sat across from him, her spare frame rigid and straight, sharp eyes and sharper features aimed at her companions like a dissecting instrument. Unlike Berrabas, her appearance reflected her personality, all defined lines and quick angles. An air of impatience swirled around her, suggesting she'd rather be elsewhere, but T'Zai knew she just did not like to wait for information. He expected her to break the silence first and was not disappointed.

"Would you like a few more moments to reminisce, Mendani-met T'Zai? Or do you feel like disclosing your reasons for calling us together?" K'etarci's voice cracked like a whip in the small room, a magnificent reproach if he'd ever heard one.

"Ah, Ketty, would you war with me?" he asked in a wistful voice, much to the amusement of Lekasha and Berrabas.

"Don't cozen up to me, you old battle-ax," she snapped, but a glitter of humor lightened her eyes. "Just get on with it."

T'Zai sobered, meeting their gaze in turn. "It has begun."

"Good," K'etarci responded, her expression somewhat worried. "Perhaps now order will be restored."

"Balance, sister," Lekasha corrected, her musical voice gently chiding. "Balance, not order."

K'etarci nodded as if the difference were of no consequence, but faint color appeared on her cheekbones. "The outcome?"

"Still unknown," T'Zai answered.

"Calculated percentage of success?"

He grinned at her. "You would calculate chaos?"

"As much as you would cultivate it," she retorted then glared as his laughter bounced off the walls. "You are enjoying this far too much, T'Zai."

"He is in his element, sister," Lekasha murmured. "This is war, after all."

K'etarci turned her piercing glare from him to the other woman. "And you always take his side."

"There are no sides in this room, Lady Ket," Berrabas said in his smooth baritone. "We are together in this."

She snorted. "Diplomat," she spat at him like an insult.

A boyish smile lit his features. "Egghead."

She held stern for a second longer, then gave in to a smile and became surprisingly beautiful. "Children, one and all," she sighed, but it was said with fondness.

"Perhaps our time would be better spent discussing potentials," Berrabas proffered with an enquiring look at T'Zai.

"I'd much rather fight with Ketty," he grumbled, winking at the woman across from him. "But if I must."

Then he told them, these friends, colleagues, life-companions, and the only family he had left. He detailed the conflict, the strategy, and the possible outcomes. When he fell silent, they stared at him with wide eyes. But they had not risen to the level of Mendani-met by chance. One by one, they rallied and offered their support, their own unique abilities, and sovereignty.

Together, they braced for the chaos ahead.

Chapter 1

Please, not again. Always the same dream. She was helpless to stop it, helpless to turn aside from her fate.

She hummed an off-key rendition of their favorite song as she walked with a steady, unhurried stride down the corridor. The lights stunned her with bright menace and the corridor stretched on forever, yet the lab doors at the end approached with terrifying swiftness.

Oh Stars, the smell, she whimpered in the back of her mind, but the rest of her was oblivious to her horror. Her stomach rumbled, and her mind conjured an image of an old-fashioned barbeque as the enticing scent of cooked meat wafted to her.

"Dinner time," she murmured and the inevitable thought, *I wonder if Dmitri has eaten,* drifted through her mind. Deep within, she groaned in abject misery, fighting with all her will to break free.

Despite her efforts, the lab doors opened to admit her. The smell intensified a hundredfold, an overpowering charred stench coating her skin in a thick layer, filling her lungs like greasy smoke. She made a sound of disgust, her hands rising to cover her mouth and nose. "What the hell?"

Inside, she gibbered with terror, her litany of *no-no-no-no* having no effect, like screaming at a solid wall. Instead of closing her eyes, instead of running as far away as she could, she stepped forward into the lab. The room was dim and the stations dark, like a prelude to despair. Off to her left, in an open space between two stations, a large shape lay on the floor covered in shadows.

Her traitorous legs drew her forward. The eyes she couldn't close witnessed what she'd been so desperate to avoid. The shadows became scorch marks; the shape a body of a man whose face had been burnt beyond recognition. But she still knew him. She recognized the hands that had touched her, the arms that had held her, the form she knew as well as her own.

Dmitri, a cold part of her mind named him, as if to drive home the point. Then she screamed, her feet only now moving backward. She bumped against a station and ricocheted into the wall, nausea rolling up behind her screams like a tidal wave. Her legs buckled, and she sank down the wall into darkness.

****

Cassie woke thrashing like a terrified swimmer in deep water. The quiet solidity of her bedroom, devoid of dead bodies, should have calmed her dream-tortured mind, but the stench of charred meat still choked her and nausea swelled in the back of her throat.

Flipping, she clawed at the waste receptacle, pulling it to her face just in time as she hung over the edge of the bed. Her body heaved out the night's terrors, wracking her muscles and bringing tears of effort to her eyes.

Slowly she unclenched and began to shake with reaction. With an unsteady hand, she grasped the glass of water next to her bed and rinsed out her mouth, spitting the results into the waste tube. Setting both glass and tube back in their places with quivering care, she rolled flat on the bed and wiped the tears from her face. Her breath hitched along in an uneven rhythm as she stared at the ceiling. At least the phantom odor of burnt flesh was gone.

Sun-cursed dream, she thought. People had come so far from Ancient Earth, spreading through the galaxy to create complex civilizations with amazing advances, yet a simple nightmare could still flatten her. She'd had other nightmares with her murdered lover as the star, but this one was the worst.

Memories always were.

Little by little, she recovered, relaxing into the soft cushion with languid relief. She'd forgotten how much the debilitating dream took out of her. In the beginning, she used to wake screaming every night, but it had been months since she'd gone through this nighttime torture.

You know why, the analytical part of her mind declared with detached interest. Yes, she knew why she'd had the dream again. The Endgame, as Sin liked to call it, had begun, and she wasn't ready. Dmitri would show up, to flog her conscience with guilt for his unpunished death, to fortify her resolve and drive her back to work.

"I'm as bad as the twins," she grumbled, "letting my past control my future." But also like the Shay twins, Cassie accepted the rightness of what they were doing, even at the expense of her mind, body, and soul.

With a sigh, she rolled to a sitting position at the edge of the bed, pausing while she adjusted. It was early in the morning, but she'd get no more sleep. For better or worse, her night was over.

Rising to her feet, she padded into the bathroom, grimacing with resentment at the jelly feel of her muscles. Bad enough to be a bit of an insomniac. Unfair for night terrors to interrupt the precious sleep she could find. Grumbling about psychoses and her inconsiderate subconscious, she set about getting ready for her day.

She tried to take her time, but the dream's imperative worked in spite of her efforts. She was back in the bedroom inside of a few minutes, body tingling clean from the sanitizer, hair plaited down her back, and coveralls drawn over her work clothes. Urgency filled her again, marching her mind along well-used avenues, consuming her attention with what needed to be done.

She went to the kitchen, paying scant attention as she prepared a quick meal, which she ate with mechanical efficiency. Her mind busily prioritized her duties, working out the details with swift proficiency, while at the same time gnawing at her most challenging puzzle, Imago.

Multi-tasking at light speed, she cleaned up the remains of her breakfast and headed for the exit, her mind's eye seeing codes and algorithms, schematics and components, rather than her quarters. But all brain function came to a screeching, smoking halt when she stepped out the door. She wasn't alone.

Just down the corridor stood Nick Givliani, a Federated Planetary Alliance inspector, here on the station under the pretense of visiting his brother. His real reason was to investigate the Shays. He'd grown suspicious of the twins' activities and was concerned about his brother's involvement with them. He'd been rather enthusiastic in his investigation so far, which didn't surprise Cassie. Considering her position with the Shays, it was only a matter of time before he started investigating her.

Prudence suggested a need for caution around him. Avoiding him like the plague was a terrific idea. But at the moment, she was having trouble just remembering to breathe.

Suns, she groaned to herself, *why does he have to be so beautiful?* He did look scruffier than the two times she'd encountered him before. His big, hard-muscled body sported a set of wrinkled clothes, his dark hair spiked in all directions as if he'd been dragging his fingers through it for hours, and disreputable, un-inspector-like stubble darkened his strong jaw. Shadows smudged the skin under his midnight eyes, and the generous curve of his mouth thinned with grim weariness.

Far from making him less attractive, his rumpled appearance added a sympathetic concern to her desire to climb him like a tree. Disconcerting. Why had her long-dormant libido decided to fixate on this man? He wasn't even likable. Both times she'd met him, he'd mocked her without mercy.

As she gazed into those sinfully dark eyes, it dawned on her she'd been staring for longer than was polite. The silence in the corridor stretched into the realm of social discomfort. He stared also, though she'd be willing to bet good credit it wasn't for the same reason. He might be beautiful to her in his scruffy attire, but she was a good deal more realistic about her own drab appearance.

Shifting, she mumbled a cautious, "Good morning,

Inspector."

He blinked then turned his head to look at the door next to him. He was standing outside his brother's quarters with his hands thrust into his pockets, as if she'd interrupted him deep in thought. "What are you doing up so early, little dragon?" he asked, deep voice husky.

The sound sent a shiver down her spine and curled her toes. Irritated as much by her reaction as his comment, she narrowed her eyes. "My name is Draegen, not Dragon. And I could ask you the same thing."

The grim line of his mouth eased into a faint curl. His gaze returned, his eyes crinkling a bit at the corners. "I meant your knack for fire-breathing, not your last name. And I haven't been to bed yet."

It wasn't a sexual innuendo, she lectured her libido, trying to concentrate on his insult instead. "Been enjoying the nightlife, Inspector?"

The curl of his lips widened to a real smile. He turned to face her. "Haven't had time, but maybe you could give me a tour." No mistaking the suggestion in his tone or the sparkle in his eyes.

Cassie's face prickled with heat, a flush of humiliation and embarrassment. He couldn't be serious. He'd just caught the challenge in her tone and flung it right back at her, mocking her yet again. She'd been called a genius more than once, but right now she was acting as though she hadn't a neuron in her skull.

Not trusting her stupid mouth, she pressed her lips together and set off down the corridor without answering him. Much to her dismay, he fell into step next to her. Even worse, he'd moved close enough for her to smell him; a very male animal scent, like hot spice. She nearly stumbled.

"Where are you off to?" he asked in a pleasant tone.

"Work," she snapped, not trusting herself to a longer answer.

"At this hour?"

It was an innocuous enough question, but the dubious note in his voice raised the hair at the back of her neck. "I have a lot to do." She sent him a grudging glance. "I don't need much sleep, so the Shays let me work my own hours."

"It's good they're flexible," he responded as they approached the lift. "As long as you're not overworked."

A sarcastic comment about him being an FPA inspector and not a Worker's Guild reviewer flitted through her mind, but she restrained herself. She stepped into the lift away from his disturbing presence, so relieved at the reprieve she flashed him a genuine smile. "Not at all, I love my job. You have a nice day, Inspector."

He blinked, his face blank. When the door began to close, he lifted a hand to stop it. "Actually, I think I'll come along."

"Come along?" Her tongue seemed three sizes too big, and she wondered if her expression was as stupid as she feared.

"To see what you're working on," he said in a smooth tone, his mouth curving in a stunning smile.

Self-preservation struck with a vengeance. Better late than never, she supposed. She quirked an eyebrow at him, putting on her best dubious expression. "With the slicers? Wouldn't you rather get some rest, Inspector?"

His smile took on a wry twist. He stepped into the lift, and Cassie moved as far away from him as she could get, her heart kicking in her chest.

"The name's Nick, Cass," he rumbled, keying the lift into motion. "Let's hear you give it a try."

Calling him by his first name seemed far too personal. For that matter, hearing her name on his lips was an intimacy she could have done without. Her toes were curling again. *Focus,* she snarled to herself. "I'm rerouting circuits this morning. Very dull stuff. I'm sure you'll be bored out of your mind."

"Around you, I'm never bored." His eyes pinned her to the wall as he shifted closer. "Dodging fire keeps me on my toes. Let's hear it, Cass."

"Hear what?" she tried, her voice cracking on the second word.

His gaze sharpened, eyes focusing on her with dark intensity and a fleeting smile passing over his lips. Bracing a hand on the wall next to her head, he leaned close enough for her to feel his heat in the air. "My name." The rasp of his whisper sent electric tingles over her skin.

Thank the Suns her instinct for self-preservation was still in full force. Slipping around him, she scurried out of the lift on watery legs and snapped over her shoulder, "I don't think so, Inspector."

A muffled chuckle sounded behind her, but he said nothing until they entered the maintenance bay for the Shay's courier ships. "So, what did you say you were working on?" he asked in a casual tone, as if he hadn't just cornered her with his hard body.

11

She opened her mouth then shut it again, remembering the look on his face when he sat in his brother's Shadow slicer. He seemed to share Del's love for the sleek, powerful racing ships. If she said she was working on one today, she'd never get rid of him. Time for a change in plan. "One of the express carriers needs an overhaul." It did, but the ship wasn't to be on their docket for another couple of weeks. "It's one of the older models and needs updating."

With calculated malice, she launched into a detailed explanation of what she intended to do with the ship. If anything could chase the man away, it would be a lecture on re-circuiting. Blithely certain of the outcome, she rambled on, heading into the docking bay to find the ship and move it into the maintenance area.

He followed, watching her with those dark eyes and a faint smile. After she moved the carrier into the maintenance bay and settled it in a work station, Cassie began to worry her plan had backfired. The man should have been bored into a coma by now, but he continued to watch her with alert interest.

By the time she arranged her tool tray and work area to her satisfaction, she was in a state of panicked despair. He didn't look like he would ever leave, and she had so much more important things to do than re-circuit a carrier. Plus, having him so near was wearing on her nerves.

Finally, she dropped her monologue and stared at him. He stared back, a smile hovering around his mouth. Was this some sort of inspector game?

"I have to work now."

"Sounds like fun," he responded, shrugging out of his jacket with a bunch and flex of his muscles. Her mouth went as dry as sand. "I'll help."

"No," she snapped, taking an involuntary step back.

He paused with a look of calm inquiry, a twinkle in his eyes. "Why not?"

"Because...because it's a liability. You're not authorized to work here, and if something happened the FPA would come down on us like a load of quandite."

His gaze sharpened, as if something she'd said sparked his interest. He sighed and shrugged. "All right, I'll just watch."

"What? No! Would you just go away?" She flushed at his sudden grin, another wave of humiliation washing over her, and forged on before he could say anything. "You look like you haven't slept in days, Inspector. Why don't you get some rest?"

The humor faded from his strong features, his eyes vivid with some indefinable emotion. "I don't sleep well these days," he rasped, moving close enough to make her breath catch in her throat. "Where's my brother, Cass?"

A well-played question at the end of a skillful manipulation; getting her off-balance, hounding her, then easing back so she felt a certain measure of safety before pouncing again. Did they teach this in inspector school?

She had enough presence of mind not to answer right away, but her hesitation was telling. His expression hardened before she opened her mouth. "He's not in his quarters?"

"You know he isn't."

She looked away from the magnetic pull of his eyes. "Maybe he's out on a run?"

"Shay tells me he just came back."

She guessed he meant Manakai, since Sin was otherwise occupied. "I'm not his keeper, Inspector."

"Could've fooled me," he said in a cool voice. It stung more than it should have. "I'd bet my last paycheck he's with Sin Shay. Tell me, would she let me in if I went up there and asked to see him?"

Cassie raised her gaze to his with a frown. "Of course she would. Do you think she has him bound and gagged?"

A faint spark of humor lightened his expression, and he lifted a hand to rub at his jaw. The rasping sound of his fingers through stubble sent shivers down her back. Her palms itched to reach out and touch. "Didn't think he was into that, but people change."

Desperate, Cassie decided to cooperate more than was prudent at this point in the game. "You don't need to ask me where he is, Inspector. If you ever want Del's location, just do this." She raised her voice and said, "Control."

"Cassiopeia Draegen," a toneless, echoing voice answered, the systems control for the station.

"Location of Del Givliani, please."

"Adelmo Givliani is in the private quarters of Sinsudee Shay."

She sent Nick a glare. "Apparently, you already knew. Next time you want confirmation, don't bug me. Now run along, Inspector. I have things to do."

She turned her back on him and prayed to the Suns he'd leave. Fumbling for her tools, she palmed one and made a production of inspecting it and the conduit where she would begin working. The silence grew until it was a palpable force on the back of her neck, making her clumsy with nerves. Trying to control the tremor in her fingers, she snuck a quick look over her shoulder.

He was gone.

With a muffled curse, Cassie sidled out past the body of the carrier and peeked down the row of ships awaiting maintenance. Not a soul in sight. He must have left the second she turned her back, to be gone so fast. How did such a large man move so quietly? It was unnerving. He was unnerving.

Cursing again, she packed her tools and replaced the access panels on the carrier. Then she wondered, *What if he comes back?* Chewing on her lower lip, she moved to the wall and an unobtrusive manual access to the station's control systems. With swift fingers, she keyed in a request for Nick Givliani's location.

"Finally, some luck," she muttered. He was in his brother's quarters. She hoped he was there for rest and not more snooping. If he traumatized the resident artificial intelligence, Samantha, she was going to chew through him like a rabid krell.

Staring at the display, she hesitated a second before making another request. She received a verbal response this time, a smooth, male voice she recognized as Manakai's AI, Basher.

"You have reached the residence of Manakai Shay. This is his house companion speaking. How may I assist you?"

"Hey, Bash," she responded. "It's Cass. You're unusually polite this morning."

"Ah, my algorithmic goddess," he replied in a sardonic purr.

Cassie rolled her eyes. As far as she was concerned, he'd taken on far too many of his human companion's personality traits.

"I find it pays to be polite until you know whom you're addressing. Especially at this time of…morning, is it?"

She ignored his teasing and got to the point. "Is Kai awake yet?"

He snorted in a very un-AI-like way. "I don't think a nova would rock him at this point."

"When he does, could you have him contact me? I need to speak with him about Inspector Givliani."

The AI's teasing, negligent tone dropped. "Problems?"

"The man's persistent."

"I'll let Kai know. You'll be in the lab when he needs to contact you?"

"Yes," Cassie answered, urgency tightening her skin again.

Basher's voice took on an unusual hesitancy. "How are things going?"

"About the same." She winced at the snap in her tone and decided it would be a good idea to end this conversation. "Talk to you later, Bash."

"Looking forward to it, Cass," he responded, much subdued.

Grimacing at her insensitivity, she broke the connection and moved away from the wall. Basher's question had been diplomatic, and he had a right to ask, after all. But her failure to solve this particular puzzle shredded her nerves.

With a shake of her head, she set a brisk pace out of the maintenance bay. The puzzle wouldn't be solved with her standing around brooding. Imago was waiting.

Chapter 2

Nick stared at his brother's wall-sized viewer without seeing it, his tired brain jumping from thought to thought as he slouched on the couch. He knew he needed sleep but couldn't bring himself to lie down. He also needed to check in with FPA headquarters.

No clear evidence had emerged yet that Shay Enterprises had broken any laws. All he had was his partner's word and his own intuition. Considering the old codger was known for talking fast and loose, this wasn't saying much. The things Nick had learned while on the Shay station didn't create a coherent picture yet, but each piece increased his suspicions and wariness. Danger lurked here.

Manakai and Sinsudee Shay were dangerous enough by themselves. They were excruciatingly attractive and accomplished at using it, cunning enough to raise the hairs on the back of his neck whenever he stood in the same room with them. They had the power of wealth and social position, plus unique contacts in the strangest places. At the Red Sun Temple, an acolyte implied the twins spent hours training there. Training for what? He also couldn't discount the sleek, beautiful Shadow slicers with their weapons, the mysterious disappearances of the twins, the suspicious cargo runs, and his brother's strange, blind acceptance of his fate.

Nick hadn't been able to forget the gift, a sculpture

of a delicate flower wrapped in threatening vines. Webster Griffin, the head of Quasicore and the Shays' worse rival, had sent the gift to Sinsudee Shay. It had seemed both a taunt and an invitation.

"Nick?"

The tentative voice pulled him out of a doze, and he straightened, blinking hard as he glanced up at one of the AI's sensors. "Yeah, Sam," he rasped.

"You asked me to inform you when Cassie Draegen left the maintenance bay."

And then there's Cassie, he thought with grim humor. Taking a quick look at the chronometer, he sighed. She hadn't spent much time on her pretense of working on the carrier. "She's leaving?"

"She has already left. She is in a new location."

"So what's her new location?"

"Research and Development, Level Five." Sam paused then continued with a note of uncertainty. "Systems Control informs me further inquiry is restricted to authorized personnel only. I am not authorized personnel. I do not think I should continue assisting you in this matter."

With a twinge of guilt, Nick responded, "You're right, you shouldn't. Sorry if I made you uncomfortable, Sam."

"I do not experience discomfort." Her smooth voice paused again. "But thank you for your consideration."

"If I'd known she'd end up in a restricted area, I wouldn't have asked you to track her," Nick explained, a tightness in his voice. The little dragon was in deeper than he'd thought.

He had lots of questions, and Sam would no doubt

answer them to the best of her ability, as honest and detailed as he could want. But she was a newly installed AI. Not only would her answers be of questionable use for the FPA, since he wasn't sure AIs could be used as witnesses, but she was vulnerable at this stage in her life. What if her willingness to assist brought him to a wrong conclusion? What if he managed to scramble her pathways somehow with his awkward questions?

He sighed and rubbed weary hands over his face. "I need sleep," he muttered into his palms.

"Del is not here."

"Yeah, I noticed."

"Mina has informed me he is residing with Sinsudee for the present time."

"Uh-huh."

"Del has approved your presence in his residence."

Nick scrubbed at his scalp, squinting at her sensor. "Sam, if you got a point, I ain't gettin' it."

"I believe my living mate would not object to you sleeping here, if you would care to do so."

He blinked. "Uh, thanks. I'd like that."

"As would I."

He shifted in discomfort then remembered he was talking to an artificial person who was not only a non-sexual creature, but child-like in many ways. In other words, she was just asking for company, not hitting on him.

He eyed the couch for a second, then rose and moved toward the bedroom. "Hey, Sam, do me a favor and wake me in a couple of hours."

"Two hours is not a sufficient sleep cycle for a normal human."

He paused at the threshold to the bedroom. "No

kidding. But that's when I need to be up."

"Your health is my concern while you are my living mate."

"Are we gonna argue about this?"

"You require a longer rejuvenation period," Sam insisted.

"So are you, or are you not, going to wake me in a couple of hours?"

"Seven hours is average."

"I can't afford to sleep seven hours, Sam," he gritted through his teeth.

She was silent for a moment. "Perhaps five would be sufficient?"

Sufficient? It sounded like heaven. He tried to find the energy to refuse, to insist on two hours. Then he shrugged and stepped into the bedroom. If he slept so long, it'd be a miracle. "Great, wake me in five," he caved. "Just don't peek."

"Peek?"

"Yeah, watch me undress, use the bathroom, that kinda thing."

"Is there some significance to these activities?"

Nick paused again, waffling between impatience and humor. "Just don't want you eyeballing my naked bod, lady."

"I do not understand."

He snorted, running rough fingers through his hair. "What's not to understand? Those are private things."

"They are precepts of privacy? Thank you, Nick. I will register such activities under this heading and leave you in solitude at those times."

"Great," he muttered. "Get out of the bedroom."

"Sleep well."

"Thanks."

When he was pretty sure she was gone, he stripped and fell face first onto the soft cushions of the bed. He couldn't fault his brother for wanting to stay in such luxury; the large living quarters, the stocked kitchen, the amenities like the huge viewers, and this big bed. On the other hand, the AI would take some getting used to.

He began to chuckle into the pillow then flipped over and snickered at the ceiling. From Sam's reaction, his brother had never told her not to peek. He'd love to rib his brother for that one, but he had no idea when Del would come up for air.

The thought killed his humor, and he stared at the dim ceiling. Sin Shay had hooked his brother good, no question about it. To Del's credit, she was one of the most beautiful women he'd ever seen. His brother didn't seem to notice the fatality, the cold menace in her beauty. Nick thought a panther was just as beautiful, but he'd never step in a cage with one.

Then again, maybe it was something they pumped into the air, he mused with a rueful smile. It might explain Del's mindless fall for a woman he should be running from at top speed, and Nick's less-than-brilliant response to a certain spitfire of a woman.

Cassie, the little fire-breathing dragon. Nick shifted and grimaced into the darkened room. Thinking about her was a mistake if he wanted any sleep. *Don't go there,* he thought, but his mind disregarded the warning.

Nowhere near as beautiful as the female Shay twin, Cassie was lovely all the same. Delicate and fine-boned, with big, soul-devouring brown eyes, she made a man want to fold her close and protect her. Until she cut him off at the knees with her sharp tongue. It should have been a turn-off, but somehow it worked the opposite way for Nick.

"Idiot," he mumbled.

She didn't encourage him. She'd been cool and remote at every turn, rejecting his overtures with a flash of fire, fueling his attraction. She didn't dress to attract, pinning back her hair in the confines of a braid and bundling herself in those shapeless coveralls. But Suns, her smile could stop hearts.

He groaned, slapping a hand over his eyes to ward off the memory. Thank the Stars he'd only seen her do it once. The woman had dimples. Her face lit up like an angel's when she smiled, filling her eyes and smooth skin with an open warmth and threatening to drop him to his knees. No wonder he'd been an idiot in the lift, cornering her like a randy animal. Good thing she'd slipped away from him when she did. She smelled like wildflowers. The light, sun-drenched scent made him want to kiss her until he lost himself in her taste.

Nick sucked in a breath, closing his hands into fists as lust rolled over him in a wave. "Note to self," he snarled with gritty emphasis, aggravated by the throb and burn in his body. "Keep your Sun-cursed hands off the suspects."

He desperately needed the reminder. She hadn't been a suspect until now. She'd been on his list of people to question, just as he'd questioned the other pilots, but he hadn't expected to learn any more from her than he had from them. The other pilots had been cooperative but unhelpful. They just didn't know enough.

Cassie, on the other hand, had been evasive from

his first question this morning, pulling a cute song-and-dance with the carrier. She'd been so transparent, the thought, *I need to get rid of this guy,* running clear and true across her features. She'd known where Del was but avoided telling him, even though she shouldn't have any reason to keep it from him. Her slip of the tongue had been telling, "The FPA would come down on us," aligning herself with the Shays as comfortably as a co-conspirator. Now she was in a restricted area of the station.

He ground his teeth at the pang of disappointment stabbing through his gut and twisted onto his side. He called himself a few more names for even thinking about starting anything with Cassie. Even if she wasn't a suspect now, it was a serious breach of protocol to fraternize with witnesses in an investigation.

He would have to decide what to do about her, when he was thinking clearly again. He yanked the covers over his body and hunted for sleep with stubborn insistence.

****

Imago was in one of his unreasonable moods when Manakai contacted her. Cassie blew an exasperated breath, dislodging the fine hairs from her brow, and exited the holo-lab without a word. The door slid closed behind her, cutting off Imago's cacophony like a knife. She sighed, sinking onto a seat at one of the open lab's work stations.

Removing the connector from her data port, she ignored the furtive glances from the staff and touched the communications pad. "Cassie here." She tried to sound calm and controlled, but the Shays were adept at reading people.

"That bad, huh?" Kai asked, his voice resonating with sympathy.

"It's no Sun cruise. But Imago isn't why I asked you to call me."

"Nick being a pain in your bum?" Humor enriched his voice now instead of sympathy.

"It's not funny, Kai," she grouched. "He could become a serious problem."

"Well, he's not the only problem we have. Take a break and come to the offices. I've managed to drag the lovers out of seclusion."

Before she could respond, he cut the connection. With a grimace, she rose to her feet and headed for the exit. Pausing at a station, she met the concerned gaze of Gabriel Ward, one of the finest lab techs she'd ever known. She'd never tell him so; it would over-expand his already sizable ego. "Gabe, I'm heading to the office if you need me."

He nodded. "What do you want us to do about our problem child?" His gaze darted toward the holo-lab.

"Nothing. I won't be gone long."

The lines on his narrow face deepened, but he nodded again. "We'll keep the damage to a minimum."

Cassie smiled at the grim joke. "Good luck."

He snorted as she moved away.

The Shay offices were impressive when seen from the main entrance. Clear partitions showed expansive areas, unfolding before her in ever-increasing opulence until she reached the crown jewel, the Shay's boardroom.

The twins had their own private offices, but this room hosted their prospective clients and rivals alike. Intimidation gleamed in the massive, polished mahogany table in the center of the space. An enormous desk presided over the office against the back wall, its bulk elevated a step and backlit by a wall-sized holo-viewer.

Intimidation wasn't the only aspect of the office. Overstuffed chairs framed an elaborate fireplace on one side of the room while a complete bar beckoned on the other side. These more welcoming areas softened the impact and gave the space an opulence calculated to overwhelm as well as charm.

Cassie was neither intimidated nor charmed, but she had been when she'd first arrived on the station. Entering the office with the ease of long familiarity, she ignored the surroundings and focused on the occupants. The tension between the three figures prickled over her skin like an electric hum.

With a frown, she studied them. Kai reclined in one of the chairs by the fireplace with his usual, indolent grace, his leonine form showing a disturbing readiness. His mouth smiled, but his bright green eyes did not as he watched Del pace before him.

Sin stood over her brother, her slim form rigid and arms folded across her chest. Her profile was a cold mask, giving Cassie a twinge of dismay.

Kai caught sight of her, and his smile turned wry. "My savior."

"You wish," Del snarled, sending Cassie an acid glance. "She ain't gonna stop me from breakin' your face."

"Whenever you're ready, Giv," was Kai's complacent response.

"Don't you dare, Kai," Sin snapped.

Kai's eyes warmed with furtive humor as he

continued to meet Cassie's gaze. "See what I've had to put up with?"

Cassie sank into a chair opposite Manakai and watched Del prowl back and forth. The big man had a worrisome scowl on his face. "What's going on?"

Kai heaved an exaggerated sigh. "The idiots want to get Sun-bonded."

Cassie blinked in surprise, before a wave of relief and delight brought a grin to her face. "Really? Oh, that's wonderful! I'm so happy for you. Oh." Her grin faded, and she met Kai's rueful gaze again when the implications sank in.

"Right," Kai responded. "They get bonded, and what do you suppose Griffin's reaction will be?"

"We can still move forward without—" Sin started, but her brother cut her off.

"Griff doesn't take defeat well. You thumb your nose at his courtship, and we lose a lot of ground with him."

"So my happiness means nothing, is that it?" Sin stared at her brother in cold accusation.

Kai winced and looked away. Del growled and continued pacing.

Cassie sighed, slumping into the chair's cushions. Webster Griffin wouldn't take the news of Sin's bonding well at all. That thug in a suit had set his sights on Shay Enterprises long ago, not to destroy but to corrupt. He meant to bring the Shays to heel, to merge them into his criminal organization under his dominion. He had no true romantic feelings for Sin; the man wasn't capable of any real emotion besides greed and lust for power. But he'd see her bonding as a rejection of him, a challenge to his control over the Shays, and he'd react accordingly. This would endanger their plans and Del's life. Griffin wouldn't hesitate to take Del out of the picture.

"Del, sit down. You're driving me crazy," Cassie grumbled, leaning on the armrest and cradling her cheek in one hand as she considered their options.

He ignored her.

With a sigh, she looked past him to Sin. "You know nothing's more important than taking down the Core. We've all taken huge risks and sacrificed a lot."

Sin met her gaze with reproach. "You, too?" she asked with painful softness.

"Sin, I'm not saying—" Cassie started, but Del walked between them, breaking their eye contact. "Suns curse it, Del, I've had a bad enough morning." She slapped her hand on the armrest and jerked upright. "Would you sit down? There is a solution."

When he glanced at her, his scowl softened into a look of surprise. Whatever he saw in her face must have gotten through. He moved to another chair and sat, bracing his arms on his knees and watching her with a much calmer look in his dark eyes.

Still fuming, she glared at him for another minute, unable to ignore his resemblance to his brother. Del's face was harder than Nick's and held a wary reserve he'd learned in his years of service to Quasicore. They'd put him through hell, and it had marked him. Both men were large and well-muscled, with almost identical dark eyes and strong features, so why couldn't she have found Del attractive instead?

It would have led to other complications. Thank the Suns, she'd liked Del well enough once she'd gotten to know him, but no spark flared between them. She wasn't sure her friendship with Sin would have survived it, and Sin's friendship was one of the best things to happen to her in years.

"You can still get Sun-bonded," she started, but Kai interrupted.

"Cass, it won't work."

"If you do it in secret," she finished, shooting the dark twin an aggravated look. "Does anyone know you fired Del yet?"

"Just you," Kai answered.

Del narrowed his eyes on Sin's brother. "I still need to kill you for it."

"You should be thanking me," Kai drawled, his green eyes twinkling with humor. "But I'll make sure I fit it into my schedule."

Sin ignored the men, watching Cassie with a faint frown creasing her brow. "It would be impossible to keep it secret."

"You two have taught me nothing's impossible," Cassie answered with a wry smile. "If no one knows Del isn't employed, he can continue taking off-lane runs and none of the other pilots will be the wiser. If it's a brief ceremony held in seclusion, with just Kai and I as witnesses and Mendani T'Zai presiding, no one at the temple can spread the news. You know T'Zai won't spill it if you ask him not to. But you won't be able to wear your bond marks."

Sin wrinkled her nose, but her head moved in a faint nod while she mulled it over.

Cassie shifted in her seat and made a face. "You should try not to moon at each other in public, too." She paused, her gaze sliding to Del. "And you might want to spend a little more time in your own quarters.

Rumors are already running around the station. Your brother knows where you've been."

Del shrugged as if this meant nothing, but his cheekbones darkened. His gaze lifted to Sin, and Cassie witnessed firsthand what had transpired between them. She'd seen the attraction they'd had for each other since Del's arrival on the station, and Kai had explained what had happened on their last run, when he'd fired Del. But she hadn't seen the two since. The light in Del's eyes almost embarrassed her to witness. When Cassie turned her head toward Sin, the answering emotion on her friend's face stopped her breath with both joy and envy.

"It won't work," Kai argued, catching her gaze. "Time is not on our side."

"It doesn't have to be a secret forever."

He raised his eyebrows. "How long?"

She winced and dropped her gaze. She knew what he was asking, but she had no good answer for him.

"Just Kai and Cassie," Sin murmured, still watching Del. "No one else."

A twitch of unease pulled at the lines of his face. "You mean, no Nick."

"No Nick," she confirmed, her lips curving in a small, sympathetic smile.

"He's been trouble enough," Cassie interjected. "Can you imagine what he'd do if you were bonded? He wouldn't keep his yap shut about it, either."

Sin's green eyes settled on her, alive with sharp scrutiny. She raised her eyebrows and lowered herself to the arm of her brother's chair. "Well, that was just a tad hostile. Care to share, Cass?"

Cassie shifted in discomfort. Del might not know

her well enough to read her, but the Shays did. A smirk twisted Kai's lips and a glint brightened his eyes. Sin studied her with an expression of equal parts amused interest and concern.

Clearing her throat and clasping her hands together, Cassie gave an abbreviated version of her encounter with Nick, keeping her voice even and leaving out the disconcerting parts of their conversation.

By the looks on the Shays' faces, she hadn't fooled them at all.

"Doesn't sound like much, Cass," Del commented. "What's the problem? We knew he was investigating."

She gave him an impatient frown. "Did Sin tell you what the next step is? What I'm doing?"

His mouth twitched in a faint grimace. "Yeah."

"Your brother doesn't need to poke his nose into it."

"No kidding," he snorted. "But he doesn't know about it."

"If he starts investigating me, he's bound to find out. He's already talked to the other off-laners, and from his attitude this morning, I'd say I'm next on his list."

He frowned. "You can't be sure."

"Actually," Kai drawled, still watching Cassie, "we can. Not much of a spy, our Cassie-girl."

She made a face at him, which he returned with a brilliant smile. "So I wasn't at my best this morning. But he's not the dumbest FPA agent we've run across, either."

Manakai tipped his head in acknowledgement, the light slipping across strands of his black hair in a bluish sheen. "True. I've been playing the dodging game with him, and he's been persistent enough to catch me out once already. He needs to be distracted."

Both Shays looked at Del, and Cassie turned her head to do the same. Del leaned back in the chair and rubbed his face. "I don't wanna lie to him," he protested in a low, rough voice. "He deserves better from me."

"So don't lie," Sin responded.

"Just don't tell him the truth," Cassie added with a smirk.

Del sent her a disgusted look but nodded. "I'll try to keep him busy."

"Wouldn't hurt to ask him what he knows about the FPA moles," Cassie added. When all three stared at her with varying levels of exasperation, she held up her hands to ward them off. "All right, maybe it's too obvious. We don't want him to know you were behind the busts of Griffin's drug factories and the uncovering of the moles. But it's been on all the news. Don't you think it'd be strange if Del didn't at least mention them to his FPA brother?"

"Cass, we want to keep his attention here, not encourage him to go back to headquarters where he'd be in much greater danger," Sin said with a shake of her dark head. "The total of Core-bought FPA agents we uncovered came to a sparse nine, and most were low rank. We hardly made a dent on Griffin's hold over the FPA; Nick's exposure to us will make him a prime target on both sides."

With a grimace, Cassie looked down, plucking at the end of her braid. "Well, we knew it wouldn't be over in one strike."

"Which brings us to Imago," Kai said in a crisp,

business-like tone.

Caught off guard, Cassie blinked at him in dismay.

"How are you doing with him?" Sin asked with more gentleness, her eyes filled with concern.

Cassie took a deep breath and described her progress. It didn't take long to tell. Bad news often didn't. When she finished, both Shays were looking at her with an identical measure of compassion. She wanted to lower her head and cry.

"More time," she whispered and bolted to her feet, almost running for the exit.

They let her go.

Chapter 3

Nick stared at the image of his duty officer. "Say again?"

"You heard me. Investigation's over. Get back here."

"But sir, you haven't even heard my report."

"You got anything new?"

"I have a good lead."

The balding, pudgy man on the screen sneered, his sagging jowls quivering. "Just admit it, newbie. You're chasing ghosts. Vacation's over. Say bye-bye to your brother and get back here."

Nick clenched his jaw but managed to keep his voice even. "Did you check on those slicer weapons?"

"They got sanction. The file on 'em is sealed. Signed by the old man himself."

Nick's eyebrows rose to his hairline. "The First Marshal, the head of all FPA forces, sanctioned the Shays to carry and use weapons, and that doesn't make you curious?"

"I don't get paid to be curious. I get paid to make sure you follow procedure. You ain't found squat on the Shays in all the time you been there, so pack it in. Got bigger fish to fry, junior. Or ain't you listened to the news about the blue busts?"

"I heard. But there's something here," he pressed. "I just haven't put the pieces together yet."

Gorbanik's jowls quivered again and turned a dull red color. "I ain't tellin' you again," he snarled. The viewer went blank.

Nick took a deep breath and ran stiff fingers through his hair, muscles tense and burning with frustration. He couldn't leave. The busts of the blue factories dominated all the news feeds, the public wild with excitement and outrage over the discovery of such a large drug ring. The arrests of several FPA agents was less of a focus for the public, though it made Nick's stomach clench every time he thought of it. He longed to return, to fight the obvious evil instead of chasing shadows, but he couldn't leave his brother.

Gorbanik's lack of imagination was nothing new. His mission in life seemed to focus on driving his field inspectors crazy, rather than solving cases. An order was an order. On the other hand, Gorby hadn't told him when he had to return to HQ. Something was going on at Shay Enterprises, and Nick had to find out what it was, for his brother's sake. He had a lead and he was going to follow it.

"Resume," he said through gritted teeth.

"Privacy mode is terminated," the AI announced in her smooth voice.

"I'm going out for a while, Sam." He hesitated then added, "Will you be okay?"

"Yes, thank you. I will converse with the other station AIs while you are gone."

He got the uncomfortable impression they'd be talking about him. Rising from the couch, he muttered, "Great. I'll see you later," and made his getaway.

While Samantha had been in privacy mode and unaware of what he was doing, he'd scanned schematics and found the location of Research and Development in the station. Matching the reality with the map in his memory, he navigated through the station toward R&D.

As he drew closer, the corridors didn't change in appearance, with no increased security or warnings. He supposed posting warning signs or installing safeguards would only spark interest. If it looked like every other section of the station, who would know to explore it?

Nick passed several doors with small plaques reading "*R&D*" next to the keypads, but none said "*Level Five*," the little dragon's current location. This door was at the end of the corridor. The keypad held a discreet attachment. It could be a retinal scan, a DNA sampler, or something more ominous. He couldn't tell; it wasn't marked.

He stared at the contraption for a second before shrugging and touching the pad. If it shocked the insides out of him and guards came flooding out of the walls, he'd have a great excuse to file a complaint against the Shays.

The keypad chimed and lit with an unintelligible array of symbols. At the bottom of the images was the word "*Assistance.*" He touched it and a voice asked, "Can I help you?"

"I'm here to see Cassie," he answered in a casual tone, hoping the familiarity would get him somewhere.

He got more than he bargained for.

The door opened and a lanky, narrow-faced man appeared. Nick couldn't see much of the space behind him and didn't want to be too obvious by peering over his shoulder. The man looked Nick over with bright eyes and a smirk. "Perfect," he said, drawing the word out. "Perfect match for the yummy voice."

Nick blinked then offered a tentative smile. "She's here, isn't she?"

"Sure, hang on." The man leaned to one side, reaching out of sight. He didn't take his gaze off Nick, still inspecting him like a connoisseur. "Hey, Dr. D, you got company." He paused for a second, his smirk widening. "And if you don't want him, I'll take him."

The last comment was lost on Nick. He hadn't heard anything after the title. "Dr. D?" he asked in a sharp tone, forgetting he was supposed to know her.

"Yeah, she gets so cranked when I call her that. It's why I do it," the man imparted with a wink and a charming grin, teeth very bright against his dark skin.

"Who is it, Gabe?" Cassie asked from somewhere behind the thin man.

"Your birthday present," Gabe answered, still staring at Nick. "Or mine, if you love me."

Cassie appeared, easing around the man in the doorway. "You're not getting anything but dust for your birth—" She froze, big brown eyes growing even bigger when she met Nick's gaze. "Oh, Sun's blood," she swore in a disgusted tone.

Nick tried out his most endearing smile. "Nice to see you, too, Cass."

Her lips thinned and she straightened, turning accusing eyes on the man next to her. "Back inside, please," she said in curt command.

Giving a weak smile and a shrug of his thin shoulders, Gabe backed away.

Cassie stepped into the corridor and let the door slide shut behind her. Her eyes had turned glacial, hard and cold as ice. "Inspector, what are you doing here?"

"Inviting you to lunch, Dr. Draegen." His smile slipped. Her stare was freezing it off his face.

"There's only one way you could have found me here," she stated with chilling control, ignoring her title.

"You gave me the idea. I figured system's control could find you just as easily as my brother. What are you a doctor of?"

She also ignored his question. "System's control is designed to refuse requests made for restricted areas of the station. The only people it responds to are authorized personnel and to a limited extent the station AIs, including Samantha. You used her, you son-of-a-bitch."

His smile was long gone now, sheered away by the force of her cold anger and guilt. "It wasn't intentional. Sam wanted to help."

"Of course she wanted to help," she snapped, each word a separate chip of ice. "It's what she was programmed to do. Control!"

"Cassiopeia Draegen," the system answered.

"Nicholo Givliani has abused his right to utilize the system by ignoring humane conduct of an artificial person. He is no longer authorized to use the station's control systems."

"Recorded."

Nick raised his eyebrows, an aggravating amount of shame mixing with his shock at this revelation. "So, what are you to the Shays that the station follows your orders?" He couldn't resist adding, "And you're judging me a little hard. Most people wouldn't know what to do around AIs."

Cassie crossed her arms over her chest and lifted her chin. She wore a long, white overcoat instead of the coveralls. "You're an FPA agent, Inspector. Humane treatment of AIs is protected by law. Perhaps you should learn the law. It is your job, after all."

Her anger was genuine this time, not just a ploy to get rid of him. The thought gave him a pang of distress, which he did his best to ignore. If she was angry, she wouldn't be smiling at him. He could keep his head and do his job. But why was she so angry?

"Ouch," he said with a wince. "I think I prefer the fire-breathing. Wanna explain AIs to me over lunch?"

She blinked then narrowed her eyes and shifted toward the door. "I don't have time to eat."

"No wonder you're so tiny." He reached out, running fingertips down her cheek in a light touch. Pulling away as if burnt, he locked his traitorous hands behind his back and waited for her to deck him. No more than he deserved.

She twitched in surprise then stood still as stone, eyes wide as she stared up at him. Was it shock in those velvety depths or something else?

He sidestepped the thought in a hurry. Ignoring the hard beat of his heart and the tingling in his fingertips, he cleared his throat and pressed, "I could see what you're working on this time. I'll bet it's not a carrier."

Her jaw clenched and she stiffened, eyes narrowing again. "This is a restricted area, Inspector, to keep our new developments safe from theft by rival companies. Trespassing, by any means," she added with a pointed lift of her eyebrows, "is grounds for arrest. If you wish to enter, you'll have to get a writ of search."

"I could do that," he said in a thoughtful tone, "and be back here in less than an hour. But a writ would put all your work on hold for as long as it takes to be satisfied with my search. Wouldn't it be easier to come to lunch with me?" He tried out his best smile again, hoping she didn't see through his bluff. Gorbanik would laugh himself silly over a search request.

"Blackmail, Inspector?"

He could almost see the murderous thoughts running through her mind. "Just options, Doctor. Would it make you feel better if I didn't ask what kind of research you're doing in there?"

"My work is important," she stressed, staring at the closed door with a strange expression. "I really don't have time."

"I promise not to keep you all day."

"Fine," she snarled, shooting him a black look. "Stay here. I'll be back in a minute."

Reaching over, she touched the pad, her fingers flying too fast over the symbols for him to see the code. When the doors slid open, she disappeared inside with alacrity.

He frowned, wondering if she would just stay in there and ignore him. He couldn't do anything about it if she did. He'd just have to hope she bought his bluff.

She didn't make him wait long. Reappearing in less than the minute she'd claimed, she didn't spare him a glance as she strode off down the corridor. She'd changed back into coveralls, and he stared down at the clothing as he matched her pace. She ignored his look.

"So, where should we go?"

"There's a café I like on the commons," she responded in a distant tone.

A devil made him tease. "I have a stocked kitchen in my quarters, if you don't want to be overheard."

She shot him a wary look. "I would prefer a public

place, Inspector."

"When are you gonna start calling me Nick?"

"When the Suns go out," she countered with a snap.

He grinned. *Back to fire,* he thought with a surge of disturbing satisfaction.

The café she spoke of was in what the locals called the commons strip, several circular levels at the center of the station. On the first level, a large fountain displayed a splash of sound and color, surrounded by a diverse selection of food markets and shops. The next few levels were devoted to shopping, while the upper levels held different types of businesses, from restaurants and clubs to legal and medical offices.

The top level, Nick had discovered a few days ago, was reserved for the Temple of the Red Sun Order. He'd been almost as shocked to find it as he had been to discover his brother had signed his life away, yet again. He would have expected any other Order but Red, in such a public and busy station. The Golden Sun Order would have been much more at home here, dealing as they did with social interactions and politics, but even the intellectual Whites or the experience-seeking Blues would have been easier to accept. The Reds were aggressive, militant, and reclusive. This was the least likely place for them to build a temple.

Staring up at the gloomy apex of the open commons area, Nick shook his head in bewilderment. They'd been about as forthcoming with their reasons for being here as the woman beside him.

"It's up four levels," Cassie muttered and moved away to an open lift. As they rose, he watched the flash and dance of holo-ads in the central space between levels and wondered what Cassie knew about the Reds.

The café was a popular place with an open, welcoming appearance. The staff recognized Cassie, smiling and sending her casual waves. She responded in kind, and Nick took care not to stare at her smile.

They found a table and sat, Cassie tapping the menu pad without delay. A hologram listing the selections flickered to life above it. Cassie chose her meal with fast fingers.

Nick lifted his eyebrows. "A woman who knows what she wants."

"I come here often, and I have my favorites. Plus, I don't have much time." She gave him a pointed look. "I recommend any of their sandwiches."

"They do look good," he agreed, glancing at a food-laden table next to them. Choosing something similar from the menu, he turned the pad off and studied her.

She sat with a rigid back and small shoulders stiff, meeting his gaze with a grim stare. "So, now that you've decided to stop pretending this isn't an investigation—"

"When did I do that?" he interrupted, propping his arms on the table and leaning toward her.

"When you threatened me with a writ of search," she snapped, back straightening even more.

"The writ was your idea." He gave an easy shrug. "So, why do you think I'm investigating?"

"You're not acting like a man on a family visit. You ask peculiar questions."

"Habit."

"You tracked me down and trapped me into sitting still for questioning."

He nearly smiled but managed to contain it. "Is that what I'm going to do?"

"What else?"

"So I didn't just ask you out to lunch because I'm interested in you?"

"No," she answered with such conviction he blinked in surprise.

Good thing she didn't sense his growing attraction. Uncontrolled lust wasn't the FPA image he should be displaying. His fingertips remembered the feel of her cool, soft skin, and he took a slow breath, inhaling the aromas of the café. Food, instead of a field of wildflowers. He should be relieved.

Their food arrived before he could think of a safe response, the serving disc zipping over their heads and lowering to the table surface. When they removed their dishes and drinks, the disc shot back into the air, spinning toward the kitchen.

"So, ask." Cassie arranged her dishes, not looking at him. "You have until I finish my last frega spear." To emphasize her point, she popped the breaded vegetable into her mouth.

"You're..." he started but lost his train of thought when she licked the juice from her fingers. Heat shot up his spine, a flashfire spreading from his groin to his extremities. *Suns,* he groaned silently as she picked up another piece, blood pounding in his ears. This lunch was going to be pure, delicious torture.

She glanced up and he dropped his gaze, coughing into his fist to cover his break in speech. "You're eating light. Veggies aren't much of a meal."

"I'm a vegetarian," she responded, her tone a cool warning.

"But most meats in restaurants aren't real, just protein substitu—"

"It doesn't matter," she interrupted with an odd tightness. "It still smells like meat."

Lifting his gaze to study her fine features, he took a bite of his sandwich and wondered why the subject of meat seemed as taboo as R&D Level Five. Why smell and not taste? If he had more time, he'd work on it, but she was stabbing at her salad with precise efficiency. Lunch wouldn't last forever.

"What kind of doctor are you?"

"Not the medical kind."

"Still leaves a pretty long list to choose from," he commented with a wry grin. Then he looked away in haste when she picked up another frega spear.

"I never promised to give you the answers you want."

"True enough. So what's a doctor doing working in the maintenance bay of a courier service?"

"I like to fix ships. It's relaxing."

"Del said you trained him on a Shadow slicer and flew a cargo run with the rest of the off-lane crew. Doesn't sound like relaxation to me."

"To each her own," she muttered, not looking at him.

"Does your work with the courier service have anything to do with what's in your lab?"

She paused in her attack on the salad, sending him an accusing glare. "You said you wouldn't ask what I'm doing."

"I didn't," he answered with an easy smile. "I asked if they were related."

Her lips thinned and her gaze dropped to his plate.

"Eat your sandwich."

"Yes, ma'am," he murmured, taking another bite with mild satisfaction. Her response was answer enough. Her work as a pilot and her research must be related somehow.

When he'd swallowed the bite, he started again. "Why are you hiding the fact that you work in R&D?"

"I just didn't want to deal with your annoying and intrusive questions," she answered with a nasty look.

He smirked. "I mean, why are you hiding it from everybody else?"

"What?" She frowned, her eyelashes fluttering. "What do you mean?" She pulled her braid over one shoulder and tugged on it.

She'd done the same thing this morning when she'd tried to get rid of him. He didn't think she was aware of it, her actions automatic. His mouth curved in a small smile as he watched her hand clench on the sheave of hair. He didn't always get such an obvious barometer of a subject's feelings, but it was nice when it happened.

"The coveralls, Cass. You wore them out the door this morning, then changed back into them when you left the lab."

She tugged harder. "What's your point?"

"It's what you wear when you're being a slicer tech, isn't it? But after I left you alone, you went to R&D and changed into a lab coat. Why put on coveralls at all, unless you were trying to make people think you were one thing and not the other?"

"My work is delicate," she said in a low voice, her brown eyes wide.

"Oh?" He leaned toward her with an encouraging

smile.

With one last, vicious jerk, she flung the hair over her shoulder and picked up her fork again. "And it's none of your business."

"Ah, Cass," he sighed. "You are stubborn." He watched her for a moment in silence, noting the faint tremor of her fork. "I suppose you're not going to tell me what your relationship is to the Shays."

"Of course I will. I'm their employee."

"Of a special kind."

"All employees hope their bosses think so," she said with cloying sweetness.

He chuckled. "Nice sidestep. Tell me why you have enough clout to bar me from using the station's systems."

"I have a certain technical expertise the Shays trust." She pushed her salad dish away, pulling the plate of frega spears closer.

"Interesting answer. What does it mean?"

"The Shays know I won't abuse the system. They trust my judgment."

"Why?"

"Why does any employer trust their workers?"

He sighed again, admitting defeat and forgetting not to watch her eat the spears. Her pink tongue flicked out again, and he jerked his gaze away, swallowing hard. Thrown off his stride, he floundered for another line of questioning. He really wanted to know what frega tasted like on her tongue. Running desperate fingers through his hair, he stammered, "What do you—what do you know about the Red Order?"

"Not much. I'm not very religious. Besides, I follow the White Order."

"I guess you would, being a doctor."

"It's natural, since they're pursuers of knowledge and order."

"Right. So why do you think the Reds built a temple here?"

"No clue."

With an inner curse, he noted she was working on the last few spears. He would push harder on the subject, except he was running out of time. "All right," he said in as easy a tone as he could manage. "So, school me on the finer points of humane treatment for AIs. I don't wanna make any more mistakes with Sam."

"Especially when they cost you access," she pointed out.

With a dry smile, he acknowledged, "You bet. So help a guy out."

She hesitated, flicking him a quick glance, but something in her face told him she wouldn't refuse. She started with history.

He sat back and watched her describe the first fledgling AIs, chewing on the inside of his cheek to keep from grinning in triumph. He'd found a way in, a subject to spark her interest and keep her talking. With every word out of her mouth, she would reveal more of herself, which in turn would reveal more of her situation with the Shays.

She seemed to have forgotten about the last bites on her plate, her fingers worrying again at her braid. This time she worked her fingertips between the shining strands, as if she wanted to free them from their bonds. Nick could relate; he had a rather desperate urge to undo the braid himself, to feel his fingers run through the mass of brown silk, to see it spread across his pillow, across his naked body.

Clearing his throat, he shifted in discomfort and tried to focus on what she was saying.

"Abuse was pretty common, and it became necessary to create laws to protect the rights of artificial persons."

Uh-oh, he'd missed something. He leaned forward and resolved to pay closer attention. She'd taken on a crisp, lecturing tone, more endearing than condescending when coupled with her animated, pixie-like features. Oh yeah, he'd stumbled on one of her obsessions.

"Some factions fought it, of course. They debated AIs were just constructs and as such didn't deserve the rights of humans. But all sentient beings had rights, and since AIs are sentient, conscious of themselves as separate entities, they qualified. This premise was debated heavily, too, but Erika Browning reminded the opposition even animals are protected by law to some extent." Cassie snorted, rolling her eyes and gesturing with the end of her braid. "She was a strong advocate for AIs, with degrees in both criminal justice and neuropsychiatry, a pioneer in the field of AI research, but it was a precedent they paid attention to."

She paused, shaking her head. Nick made a sound of agreement but was afraid to comment for fear she'd stop talking.

"Anyway, most of the laws protecting AIs are similar to those for humans, though they include the Humanities Act for Artificial Persons. Going over every precept would take forever, but here's a quick summary."

She lifted the hand not stroking her braid to count

off the points, fingers flicking up like little exclamations.

"All artificial persons have the right to life, freedom, and security, which means no termination without due cause, no service without their consent, and no unsafe conditions. You can't ask them to violate their programming or attempt to change their programming, unless you're a certified specialist in the field. You can't force them to commit criminal acts or any act they've refused to participate in. All artificial persons are entitled to regular maintenance and any requests they make for maintenance will be attended to promptly. They have the right to as much education and socialization as they require, as long as it doesn't violate any laws or the rights of others."

A little dazed, Nick blinked at her when she paused, wondering what the full list was like if this was the summary. Taking a deep breath, he decided it was time to join the conversation. "It sounds good on the surface, but there are holes. What if you get a certified specialist who programs an AI for criminal acts?"

Cassie nodded with solemn agreement, her face taking on a grim caste. "Laws govern the certification of specialists, which are supposed to prevent such things. For example, it's against the law to program an AI to harm others or cause harm to itself. But there are those who would break—" She stopped, a crease forming between her brows as she sat straighter. A shadow in her eyes startled him, a haunted look pulling color out of her face.

"I have to go," she muttered, lurching to her feet.

He didn't try to stop her, unsettled by the look on her face and his reaction to it. He had an almost overpowering urge to wrap her in his arms and protect her from whatever was causing the ghost-like expression. "I'll walk you back," he said instead, studying her as he rose.

"Don't bother. Stay. Finish your sandwich." She set off at a brisk pace.

He caught up with her and matched her stride. "And miss your fascinating company?" he asked, trying out his rusty charm.

By her expression, he needed more practice. She sent him a sour look, as if he'd insulted her and mumbled something under her breath. At least her features looked less haggard.

So he tried small talk instead. "How long have you been working here?"

"Lunch is over, and so is the interview, Inspector," she snapped.

"Just making conversation." He couldn't fault her for being defensive. He often elicited this reaction doing his job. People mistook his questions for accusations and resented him for it, whether they were guilty or not. But he was almost certain Cassie was guilty, and it pained him to a surprising degree.

A silence held sway between them as they descended the levels of the commons, Cassie sending him furtive glances and Nick waiting her out. When they gained the relative quiet of the corridors, she finally mumbled, "Four years."

"What?"

"I've been working here for four years," she repeated in the most neutral tone he'd heard from her yet.

"Ah," he responded with a sage nod. He waited

several heartbeats then looked down at her out of the corner of his eye. "I'd ask you another question, but I'm afraid you'd kick me in a tender spot."

She made a sound like a strangled snicker and tucked her chin down, hiding her face. He couldn't tell if this was a good reaction or bad.

"The station seems a nice place to work. Plenty of things to do to keep busy. Did I see a fitness place back there?"

Cassie nodded. "Body B'Good," she announced then shook her head at his snort. "Don't look at me; I didn't name it. They have a pool and workout equipment, but it's always packed. Ask the Shays about their atrium. I'm sure they'd let you use it. It has a great view."

"Thanks, I'll do that," Nick responded then struggled to find another neutral topic, at the same time berating himself for the attempt. She was a suspect; getting to know her on a personal level would get him in trouble. Judging from his reactions to her so far, he wouldn't be able to handle more personal knowledge with the right amount of professional detachment. He was having a hard enough time keeping his hands to himself when she was a mystery.

He should walk away from her. She'd given him a lot of information he needed to consider and follow up on, possible avenues he needed to explore. But his feet matched her pace and his foolish brain continued to hunt for things to say. Lucky for him, he couldn't think of anything other than more questions.

They reached the door to her lab in silence. As she keyed in the pass code, Nick said, "Thank you for coming to lunch with me."

She shot him a wary, puzzled look, then nodded and slipped through the doorway without a word. He caught a glimpse of a maze of work stations, each overflowing with glinting hardware he didn't recognize, before the door slid closed and cut off his view.

He stared at the blank metal for a minute then took a deep breath and turned away. He had work to do.

Chapter 4

Not wanting the complication of dealing with Sam while he searched for information, Nick went back to the guest quarters the Shays had allocated to him. They weren't as large as his brother's but were still spacious and stocked. Instead of a one-room hostel, it contained a furnished living room, wash room, bedroom, and even a tiny dining room off the full kitchen.

Whatever else he could say about the Shays, they at least knew how to treat guests. Now, if only they'd be more forthcoming as suspects. The one time he'd managed to sit down with Sin Shay, she'd revealed more cryptic mysteries instead of answering questions. Manakai Shay was even more slippery.

Without wasting any time, Nick headed for the viewer in the living room, settling into a comfortable chair in front of it. Activating the viewer, he contacted the records department of FPA headquarters.

"Records," said a gravelly female voice, a face resolving on the screen. She was middle-aged with short, graying hair and a bored expression.

"Hi, Roz. Do we have a file on a Cassiopeia Draegen?"

"Lemme check," she responded, glancing down at her displays. "Yup, we got her, but it's sealed."

Nick blinked at her. "Sealed? By who?"

"The First Marshal. Keep your paws to yourself,

son. Looks like this one's out of your league." She gave him a smirk and a slow wink.

He frowned. The FPA didn't have files on every citizen, only those who were either involved with the FPA or who'd been under investigation, often ending in a criminal record. He was willing to bet Cassie was the latter, but why would the First Marshal seal it? Just what was he dealing with here? Had the Shays actually bought the silence of the head of the FPA forces?

He needed a different angle. "Could you run a check for me, Roz? I'm looking for graduate schools that either know the name Cassiopeia Draegen or refuse access to their student records."

Her expression sobered, hazel eyes softening with concern. "No joke, Nick, if she's sealed, you shouldn't be after her."

"You think so?" he asked, holding her gaze. "How many FPA agents got arrested in the past couple of days?"

She shook her head, still looking worried. "They weren't high rank, kid. You start poking around in places the higher-ups have made off limits, they'll give you more attention than you can handle. You don't wanna be next on their arrest list, do ya?"

He raised his eyebrows. "You think they're on a witch hunt?"

"I don't know what to think. Past couple days, everybody's got a bad case of the willies."

"I'm just doing my job. Nobody can arrest me for that. Could you just run the check, Roz? I'll do the follow up from here."

"I won't cover for you, Nick. If asked, I'll tell 'em what I know."

"Fine by me. In fact, you can let your supervisor know right now—"

"No, I'll wait until I'm asked," she interrupted in a dry tone. "The check will take a while to run. Plenty of graduate schools out there, ya know. Care to narrow it a little?"

He thought about it. "Look for anything to do with mechanical sciences. I wouldn't rule out natural sciences. She said she wasn't a medical doctor, but…" He shrugged.

"Suspects don't lie, do they?" Roz asked with mock-horror then snorted. "I'll send you what I find when I get it."

"Thanks, Roz," he responded before the viewer darkened.

Cassie's interest in AIs and the overabundance of them on the Shay station deserved his attention. He was about to contact the Worker's Guild for a list of certified AI specialists when the door chimed. Crossing the room, he hit the door release with a pretty good idea of who he'd find on the other side.

"I'll be damned," he drawled with a smirk, looking his brother over. "She left you in one piece."

Del gave him a wry half-smile and a gentle punch to the shoulder, brushing past Nick and glancing around his quarters. "Nice place."

"Your Shays are weirdly hospitable."

Del turned to face him, hands propped on hips, eyes direct and calm. "So you're mad at me," he said in a flat tone. "If you wanna yell, now's the time."

Nick sighed, running a hand through his hair before gripping the back of his neck. "I'm not mad." At Del's snort, he grimaced. "Okay, yeah, I'm a little torqued.

But mostly I'm worried. You disappeared for days. You go off on a run and come back with a busted ship, no explanations. You fix it and go off again, coming back with a ship not just busted but scrambled all to hell. Still no explanations and no sign of you for two days after, because you're holed up with the boss lady."

Del cocked his head to one side, a faint smile tugging at his lips. "What's your point, little brother?"

"Del," he growled, glaring at the man who'd given up ten years of his life to the Core to keep Nick safe. It was a debt he had to pay, even if his brother got in the way.

Del relented with a grin. "Okay, I'll come easy. No need for riots sticks or restraints, Inspector."

Nick snorted and pointed him to a seat. "You want anything to drink while you're telling me everything?"

Del chuckled and shook his head, his dark eyes twinkling as he settled into a chair. He looked very different from when Nick had seen him last, not so much a change in appearance but in attitude. When Nick had tried to convince his brother to leave the Shays prior to their first run, Del had been determined to stay, but with a grim worry in the lines of his face, a wary reserve in his eyes, and subtle tension in his form. He'd listened to Nick's concerns, and Nick was sure he'd been feeling those concerns himself.

Now, he looked as if he hadn't a care in the world. Nick would suspect drugs, except his brother's eyes were clear and his movements sure and steady.

"What'd they tell you?" Nick asked, sitting in an adjacent seat and studying the calm certainty in his brother's eyes with growing alarm.

Del cocked his head with a faint frown. "What do

you mean?"

"You look like all your dreams just came true. Sex can do wonders, but I doubt it made you forget your life's in danger. So as I see it, we got two reasons for the look on your face. Either you gave up and decided to join the bad guys, or they told you what you wanted to hear to get you to cooperate. After ten years of scrapping it out with the Core, I doubt you'd cave now, so they must've strung you a pretty line. What'd they tell you?"

Amusement crinkled the corners of Del's dark eyes. "What makes you think it's a line?"

Nick snorted in disgust, slumping in his chair and glowering at his brother. "What'd they do, slip you a happy pill?"

"Yeah," Del answered with a deep laugh. "Her name's Sin."

"So they bribed you with sex? Suns, you're pathetic."

"No bribes, little brother," Del responded in a mild tone. "What makes you so sure they're leading me?"

Nick had to admit, he was a little envious. His brother looked content. Was it love and not just obsessive lust? If so, maybe Del really had turned. Love didn't come easy to either of them.

Neither Del nor Nick had been quick to open up to new people or express their emotions. Living with their father on the edge of the slicing circuits, in the fast track of slicer racing, they'd learned to guard themselves. Their father hadn't protected them; he'd been addicted and obsessed with slicing to the exclusion of all else. They'd had only each other to ward off the hungry masses.

"Users and losers," Del had once told him, "are the only kind of people in the circuits, so watch your back, brother." Nick remembered asking him which kind they were, only half-joking. With a hard look of determination, Del had replied, "Neither."

But what if Del had changed his mind? What if he'd decided love was worth becoming one or the other? If this was the case, Nick shouldn't tell him anything about what he'd discovered so far. He'd no doubt turn around and reveal it to the Shays.

A wave of despair rolled over him at the thought, a black depression over losing faith in his brother, losing trust in him. He had counted on nothing else in his life except the certainty that Del would always stand by him. With this certainty gone, he felt adrift and alone.

But he wasn't going to give up on his brother or his job. Clenching his jaw, he sat forward, leaning his elbows on his knees and watching Del with a careful gaze. "You go first. Tell me what you know."

"I can't," Del muttered with a grimace. "I won't lie to you, Nick. But I can't help you."

His heart plummeted. "Why not?"

"Too dangerous."

"Did they threaten you?" Nick asked sharply, tensing.

Del chuckled with a shake of his head. "No, Nick. I mean too dangerous for you."

Nick stared at him, unable to reconcile his brother's easy nonchalance with his words. If it was dangerous here, why did Del look so relaxed? "So the Shays are a threat to me?"

"Nope. They wouldn't hurt you for anything."

Nick gave a cynical snort. "Oh, yeah, a couple of

pacifists. The Shays have an FPA file, brother. It's sealed."

"So you said before."

"It's sealed by the First Marshal; the head of all FPA forces, both military and civilian. What does this tell you?"

"What's it tell you?"

"I think the Shays and Griffin are divvying the FPA up between them. Buying them protection from the law. How's that for a guess?"

Del grinned, but his tone was solemn. "Just a guess, Nick? Where's your proof?"

"I'm working on it." Then he remembered what would be coming his way from Roz any time now. If Del was working with the Shays, he didn't need to see what avenues Nick was taking in his investigation. Time for distraction. "Say, didn't you tell me you haven't seen the station yet?"

"Just the docking bays and living quarters. Why? You wanna take me on a tour?"

"Took the words right outta my mouth," Nick answered with a lopsided grin.

A knowing gleam lit Del's dark eyes, but he didn't comment, rising and moving toward the door. "Where do we start?"

They started in the Reception Hall.

"Whoa," Del muttered as they stepped into the vast space.

"Yeah, I said the same."

"I think it's what everybody's supposed to say."

They lifted their heads to look at the vaulted ceiling far above them. Spinning in vast and splendid indifference, a holographic representation of the galaxy arced over them. It dwarfed. It reduced and humbled. Reflected in the black marble floor, it encased visitors in awe-inspiring magnificence.

Sure puts new arrivals in their place, Nick thought with a cynical smirk.

They moved forward into the reception area, heads swiveling like tourists taking in the sights. Seating arrangements of varying comfort levels dotted open areas. Large statues and statuesque art formations stood scattered throughout and motifs or various paintings covered the walls as far as the eye could see, interrupted by the occasional recess for a larger piece of artwork. Opulence and elegance was the overall impression.

One sculpture caught Nick's eye and he nudged his brother, pointing to the curious, misshapen thing.

Del grunted and muttered, "Waste of good credit," restoring Nick's faith in him for the moment.

They wandered through the gallery of artwork, making occasional, baffled comments. Neither of them had ever been the artsy type.

"What is that?"

"Got me, but I think it's worth more than you and me both."

"Would've done better with a row of slicers instead. Better lookin'."

"Good idea. I wonder if they've got a suggestion box."

But one item caught and held Nick's attention like a gravity well. "Holy Heart of the Sun," he rasped, his heart rate increasing and skin tingling with dread.

"What?" Del sent him a sharp glance.

"This," Nick ground out through a clenched jaw,

pointing, "is the gift Griffin gave to your boss lady." The gift that wasn't a gift, but salt rubbed in old family wounds, a declaration of intent. Griffin had chosen a specific object to evoke the memory of Sin's suicidal mother. Sin's cold fury at the sight had raised the hair on the back of Nick's neck.

Del moved closer and Nick followed, holding accusations behind his teeth with grim effort.

In spite of the implications attached to it, the piece of art was beautiful, displayed to full effect. The sculpture floated inside an ornate recess, with a black velvet backdrop. Hidden lighting banished even the hint of shadows. The clear, crystal sculpture absorbed the light, refracting it in dazzling shimmers of color. When Nick had last seen it, the crystal had been in the shape of a flower, with a vine trapping its delicate form and thorns threatening on all sides.

Now, the flower was free, the vine and thorns gone. The vulnerable perfection of its unhindered petals and slim stem made Nick's throat close with nameless longing. "She called it the Enua, the Signalan flower of mercy," he stated, a hoarse edge to his voice.

"I thought you told me it was wrapped in—"

"It was. She must've had somebody clean off the vine and thorns."

"Guess it looks better this way," Del said, his tone almost uninterested, but a small, bemused smile curled his lips.

Nick swore in aggravation. "Don't give me the hayseed routine. You see what's going on here. Griffin meant it as a message when he sent it."

Del nodded. "Domination."

"Yeah. Well, it looks like the Shays returned the

message. I'll bet you high credit they didn't do this without rubbing Griffin's nose in it."

"So?" Del asked with a careless shrug, but he was still looking at the sculpture with a disturbing light in his eyes.

"So they've declared friggin' war, and now you're stuck smack in the middle of it," Nick snarled in frustration.

His brother turned away from the display, assessing him with calm, dark eyes. Then he shook his head with a grin. "It's just a pretty hunk a' rock, bro. Nothing to crisp out over. Who'd have guessed you'd be such a drama junkie?" Giving Nick's shoulder a companionable smack, he moved on.

Nick took several deep breaths and tried to remember why fratricide was against the law. Then he followed on stiff legs.

They didn't spend any more time in the Reception Hall, their interest waning at the endless parade of expensive looking art. With Del grumbling about overkill, they headed for the exit. Nick mentioned the restricted areas of the station, but with a wry look Del suggested the commons instead. They'd visited there together before Del's first cargo run, but they hadn't seen much beyond the first bar where they'd gotten drunk on supernovas.

As they explored each level, Nick pointed out the few places he was familiar with, including Cassie's café. "Good sandwiches," he commented, though he was thinking about frega spears.

They ended the tour outside the Red Sun Temple. Nick stared at the massive wooden doors with the same incredulity and vague apprehension as when he'd first stood there.

His brother swore in a low voice at his side. "Is that real wood?"

"And stone," Nick replied, looking at the rough slabs framing the doorway. Massive shafts of roughhewn wood and stone displaced the slick metal of the station, merging together to form the front of the temple. The textures of the different materials formed a primitive but suggestive pattern, as if it were a message meant for wiser eyes than theirs.

"You been in there?"

"Yeah. Didn't get any farther than the lobby."

"Vestibule," Del corrected in a low, thoughtful voice. "So what'd you find out?"

Nick turned to study his brother instead of the temple. "About what?"

Del shot him an amused glance, reaching out to run a hand over the surface of a stone slab. "You're on an investigation. You didn't just stop in to pray, did you?" Then he stepped back with a frown, cocking his head as he looked over the front of the temple. "Why does this look familiar?"

"Beats me, bro. We've never been to a Red temple before. Unless the Core sent you after one, but I don't think even Griffin is crazy enough to take them on. All I got from the ascetic I met was the Shay twins come here often to train. Then she stopped talking to me." Nick shrugged. "I have that effect on women."

Del chuckled, meeting his gaze with a teasing glimmer in his eyes. "Maybe it's the interrogation thing. Small talk works better."

"Ah, brotherly advice. Priceless," Nick drawled with a roll of his eyes then grinned when Del laughed.

"Wanna try again?" Del moved toward the huge doors.

"As long as you don't hold my hand." Nick gained another chuckle from his brother. "But I didn't think you'd want me poking around in Shay business."

"This looks like temple business to me." Del grasped the wrought-iron handle and pulled. The door slid open with surprising ease. "And I'm curious. Never been in one of these before."

"A Red temple or any temple?" When Del leveled a look at him, Nick sighed and shook his head in mock dismay. "My brother, on the fast track to damnation."

They stepped into the vestibule together. The door closed behind them, cutting off the light from the commons. The place affected Nick as much as the first time he'd entered, disconcerting him. It seemed as if they'd stepped through a door in time as well as space, rushing back several thousand years to a more primitive era. The lighting was dim and flickered as if from firelight; Nick couldn't see where the illumination came from. Rough wood or stone covered all surfaces, not a smooth curve or plane in the place.

Obscure markings engraved the doors to the interior of the temple, a simple stone bowl sat on a pedestal next to the doors, and an alcove loomed off to the right, its depths in mysterious shadow. The rest of the small area was empty, devoid of decoration except for the grain and texture of wood and stone.

The place seemed both foreboding and enticing, as basic and powerful as creation itself. And this was just the vestibule.

A slim form approached, emerging from the alcove as if birthed from shadow and firelight. She was the same acolyte Nick had met before, dark blonde hair pulled back in a knot at the base of her skull, eyes some medium shade, the lighting obscuring their true color. She wore a shapeless shift, sleeveless and draping her from neck to toe. A small, dark-red tattoo rested in the hollow of her throat, a faintly menacing, vivid flame.

"I am Ni Gadji, acolyte of the Red Sun Order," the young woman announced without a flicker of recognition. Her face was set in such a serene mask, she could have hidden any number of reactions. "Enter with an open heart and be welcome."

"Thank you," both men said in unison. Del seemed subdued and solemn. Maybe the place had the same effect on him as it did on Nick.

She glanced from one to the other. "How may I assist you?"

The brothers shared a look. "We'd like to see the temple. If it's all right with you," Del said with a deferential air. His reaction should have been amusing, but this place didn't inspire humor.

"This is a temple, not a tourist attraction." She spoke in the same even, serene tone, as if she said such things several times a day. "If you would look on the face of the Red Sun, if you would open yourself to its light, then you may enter. Have you an offering?"

"Uh..." Del glanced over and lifted his eyebrows, but Nick could only shake his head and shrug. "No, I guess we don't."

A faint smile touched her mouth before shifting into shadow. "You bring yourselves. It is enough of an offering. Please approach the receiving stone." She turned and motioned to the bowl on its pedestal, her movements as smooth and graceful as mist on water.

Accompanying them as they stepped forward, she indicated a depression at the bottom of the bowl. "In times past, a knife was used but was wasteful as well as discouraging. We do not need so much of an offering."

They stared at her.

A hint of a smile returned to her mouth. "A small drop of blood is all we ask. Of course, the offering must be made with a willing heart." She eased back and waited.

Nick glanced at his brother and almost grinned at the sour expression on Del's face. "I think she likes scaring newbies," he whispered, placing his finger in the depression. A small prick of pain announced his offering had been made, and he moved over for Del.

When they finished, Ni Gadji glided forward, pressing her palms on the surface of both doors. They swung open with ease. Light spilled over them, a brooding reddish-orange brilliance shadowing as much as it revealed. When they saw what created the light, both brothers paused on the threshold.

"Whoa," Del breathed.

"Yeah," Nick husked in response.

A sun hovered in the center of a large, circular sanctuary, floating a man's height above the stone floor. The red star roiled in slow, interior turmoil, its corona fingering the temple air with almost palpable hunger.

"It is a holographic representation of the Bain giant, Shantai system," the acolyte explained. "Dimmed enough for our fragile eyes to see without damage. It's in real time. What you see is what the actual Sun is doing."

"It's amazing," Nick responded.

The acolyte continued as if he hadn't spoken,

gesturing them forward. "You have offered and may enter here. You may sit in contemplation of the Light in places along the columns, but do not disturb the Dani. It would not be wise." She focused on Nick, her gaze sharp. "If they wish to be questioned, they will come to you."

Then she was gone, vanishing in red light and shadows.

"Well, she put me in my place. I thought she didn't remember me."

Del snorted. "You're unforgettable."

"Sounds like an insult, bro," he said in a distracted tone as they stepped forward. The Sun filled his sight and mind like the assessing eye of a god, the ceaseless explosion of energy churning in his blood. He felt both more and less than himself in its presence, an infinitesimal speck given shape and purpose by the Light's regard. His step slowed, his brother slowing as well, until they both halted at the Sun's base, staring up in fascination.

Nick wondered if some sort of subliminal hypnotism lay rooted in the hologram's programming, the temple's way of attracting followers. He sure was feeling worshipful right now, content to stand there the rest of the day, bathing in the throbbing crimson light. He could almost feel the heat rolling off its roiling surface in waves, buffeting him.

A twist in the corona caught his attention. He watched in rapt fascination as a flare arced out from the surface, rising above their heads in slow majesty then bursting free, flashing out and down like a whip. It sliced through them both.

Chapter 5

Nick flinched and stumbled back, his brother mirroring him. But he felt no pain. *Just a hologram,* he reminded himself. A collective gasp and rustle of noise caught his attention.

Blinking his eyes clear, he looked around, taking in the rest of the sanctuary. A dome trapped the light of the Red Sun, casting it on the stone columns ringing the holographic display. The space beyond lay in shifting shadow. Nick could see movement but couldn't discern shapes; it may have been just a trick of the light. Within the ring of pillars, several people knelt on mats, facing the Sun. All of them watched the brothers with an odd intensity.

Nick shifted, leaning toward Del. "Did we just screw up?"

"Don't know," Del muttered in answer. "Maybe we should sit down."

Nick nodded quick agreement. They shuffled toward a pair of empty mats beneath an unadorned, rough slab of stone. Their movement seemed to break the spell and the other occupants stopped watching them, some turning their gaze on the Sun and others bowing their heads in meditation. They were male and female, young and old in equal number, though none as youthful as the acolyte who'd greeted them.

"The Dani?" Nick ventured as they settled on the

hard, scratchy mats. He didn't know how the uncomfortable things were supposed to be better than the stone floor.

Del looked around at the scattered people. "I guess so."

"So much for investigations. How do I get answers if I can't talk to any—?"

"I've been waiting for you," a resonate voice interrupted.

Nick glanced past his brother. A man stood half in the shadow of a column. Of medium height and build with a scruffy white beard and tangle of receding white hair, he didn't seem such an imposing figure until Nick looked into his eyes. Penetrating and powerful, they drew Nick to his feet by the sheer force of their focus.

Del had risen with him and the man studied them with a faint twist of his mouth. "The tiger brothers," he murmured then raised his voice. "Well met. I am Mendani T'Zai," he said to Del, before turning his magnetic eyes on Nick. "And I will hear your questions."

Nick noticed he didn't say he'd answer them.

Before they could say a word, the older man turned and stepped into shadow. "Follow me," his voice drifted back to them.

With a glance at each other and a shared shrug, the brothers followed. Nick took a quick look over his shoulder as they left the circle of crimson light, startled to find they'd become the center of attention again. Maybe these ascetics just didn't get out much. "Uh, did we do something wrong?" he asked their guide.

"No. The Dani stare because the Red Sun marked you, even though you are strangers here."

"Marked?" Nick tried to watch where he was going. Shifting shadows enfolded them and he was hard pressed to keep an eye on the Mendani, stumbling a little as they passed into a small corridor.

"Marked by the touch of the Sun flare. Your eyes will adjust," the older man reassured them. "The glory of the Light will fade."

It sounded like a load of rhetoric to Nick. As they moved farther away from the sanctuary, the dim, flickering light they'd first encountered in the vestibule lit their way. Nick's eyes adjusted to the lesser illumination.

He looked around but there wasn't much to see, just more stone and wood set together in mysterious patterns, forming a long, curving corridor with regularly spaced openings. Through arched doorways, these openings led to more passageways, the sameness of them reflecting the one he was in like mirrors. The effect disoriented him a little. He wondered if the point was to throw visitors off balance.

Nick hid an uncomfortable grimace as they approached another set of wooden, double doors. Under the Mendani's touch, they swung open. What lay beyond proved almost as astonishing as the sanctuary.

Nick swallowed hard. Del muttered, "Holy Heart—" before he bit back the rest of the curse. Nick supposed it wasn't respectful to blaspheme in a temple.

The Mendani hadn't stopped. They continued to follow him, staring in fascination. They entered another circular room with large stone steps rising from floor level almost to the ceiling, ringing an open area in the center of the room. A few individuals sat on these steps like an audience, watching the action below. A depression in the stone floor ringed the open area in the middle, a channel cut in the rock. From this channel burst a ferocious force, a shifting kaleidoscope of colors looking almost like fire but more artificial, like an energy field.

In the center of this ring of force danced two people, fighting as if their lives depended on it. The ring blurred their outlines and skewed their actions, turning their battle into a surreal image.

"The Circle of Fire," Del rasped at his side.

Startled, Nick glanced at him, but his brother's expression was unreadable.

"You see true," T'Zai responded in a distracted tone, waving them forward with a touch of impatience. "Come, the view is better from above."

They followed him, climbing several wide steps until the older man stopped, then settled down next to him on the cold stone. Shifting on the hard surface, the chill seeping into him, Nick thought of the mats in the sanctuary with rueful affection.

T'Zai gave Nick a knowing look. "One should never be too comfortable when witnessing the struggle."

So Nick witnessed the struggle with a cold rear end.

The fighters were both male, one a little shorter and stockier than the other. They wore loose-fitting, shortened pants and nothing else. Neither had a weapon; their bare skin coated with sweat, marks, and blood. They fought as if spurred by demons. The stockier fighter managed to throw his opponent. Nick winced when the other man slammed into the rough stone floor. He rolled cat-quick to his feet and attacked, new blood marring his skin.

"Suns," Nick muttered. "Isn't this kind of barbaric?"

"You think so?" T'Zai asked in a bland voice.

"Why are they fighting?"

"Ah," the Mendani sighed then looked at Nick out of the corner of his eye. "Your first intelligent question."

Nick flushed but clenched his jaw and swallowed a sharp retort. He would hold onto his patience and let the man talk.

The man didn't say a word.

With a sigh, Nick tried again. "What is the Circle of Fire?"

"Open your eyes and see, young Inspector. What does it look like?"

"It looks like those two guys are trying to kill each other. It looks like there's a shield around them, keeping them there. Did you force them to go in?"

"No one is forced to enter the Circle. Long ago, the barrier used to be real fire, but now it's just a deterrent. It will neither kill nor wound, but it does cause pain. It won't come down until there is a victor."

Del lurched to his feet and took a few steps away from them, his broad back tense and head bowed.

"Del?"

T'Zai put a hand on his arm to keep him seated. "Your brother is well. Some things are made clear to him, and he must adjust to the knowledge."

"What things?"

"Why don't you ask me the questions you brought with you?"

Nick hesitated, looking from his brother's still

form to the intense, bright gaze of the Mendani. Del glanced over his shoulder and gave him a single nod, his face stoic as he looked past Nick at the older man.

"All right." Nick subsided with reluctance, not liking the expression on his brother's face. "I was told the Shays visit here often. Is this true?"

"It is."

"Why do they come here?"

"They have much to atone for."

Del growled and began to pace. The Mendani watched him with a secretive smile.

"What do they have to atone for?"

"Their atonement is between them and the Suns."

Nick released the breath he'd held on a sigh. Well, he should have known it wouldn't be so easy. "I was told they train here."

"Yes."

"Train for what?"

"Life. The conflict. Are these truly the questions you wished to ask?"

"They go better with real answers," Nick responded in a dry tone.

T'Zai flashed him a quick and unexpected grin. "Keep trying, youngster. You make slow progress."

"Thanks," Nick muttered. He paused, watching the fighters while he thought of what to ask next. They were tiring, circling each other for longer periods of time before attacking. More blood stained their skin and clothes, and made violent patterns across the stone floor. Nick shot his brother a quick glance and made a connection he should have made a lot sooner. "So," he said to T'Zai, his eyes on his brother, "how many times have the Shays been in this Circle?"

Del stiffened, eyes snapping to his before settling on the fighters again.

"Very good," the Mendani commented. "It only took you three times as long as it should have."

Nick sent the irritating man a sour look. "I was distracted by the pretty lights and the religious rhetoric."

He received another grin for his efforts. "Yes, those did seem to work well on you. Manakai and Sinsudee are regular visitors to the Circle and draw quite a crowd. They're less primitive than the two below." Assessing the fighters in the ring, T'Zai made a disapproving noise in his throat and shook his head. "Those two sweat anger as if it were as harmless as smoke. They haven't learned to mold it, to cast it in the shape of a weapon. They scatter their fear, guilt, and love like worthless gems." He paused, glancing over at Del with a faint smile. "The twins, on the other hand, have magnificent control, a joy to behold. They have much to learn, of course, but they do not need blood, bruises, and breaks to see their lessons."

Nick looked from T'Zai to Del. His brother relaxed a bit. So, the twins didn't beat each other bloody in the Circle, which must be a relief for his brother. Recognizing the hint of pride in the older man's face, Nick asked, "Mendani T'Zai, how long have you been their teacher?"

"Ah, much better." T'Zai's penetrating gaze locked on Nick. "You can think when you try. I have shown the twins their lessons for many years. They learn as they see fit."

"But they don't seem to be part of the Order."

"They aren't. The life of an ascetic is not their

calling."

Nick frowned. "If they're not part of the Order, then why are you teaching them?"

A slow smile pulled at the Mendani's lips, but it held not a hint of humor. "Because they hear the song of the Red Sun and must answer."

"More rhetoric?" Nick shifted in impatience and discomfort. His rear had gone numb from cold and hard pressure.

"More truth. What do you know of the chaos outside of these temple walls?"

"Which chaos are you referring to?" Nick asked in a wry tone.

T'Zai snorted, looking down at the wearying fighters with a shake of his head. "How many opponents do you see down there, youngling?"

"Two," Nick answered, studying the lines of the older man's face.

"Precisely. Now let me ask you, why are they fighting?"

Nick was starting to get the rhythm of their conversation now. Knowing T'Zai was a teacher helped; students learned best and retained the most when they figured a lesson out for themselves. Just giving Nick the answer wasn't the Mendani's way.

So, they had been talking about the Shays hearing the song of the Red Sun. What did this mean? Since the Red Sun Order was drawn to conflict and aggression, Nick supposed it meant they were being called to war. Then T'Zai mentioned chaos and two opponents. "Which one of those guys is supposed to be Griffin and which one the Shays?" Nick drawled.

T'Zai didn't grin this time, leveling a piercing stare

on Nick. "You didn't answer the question."

"Blood feud."

T'Zai shook his head with a grim press of his lips. "Incidental. This motive only lends emotion to the conflict. Try again. Why are they fighting?"

Nick held his gaze with a sudden, profound, and inexplicable sadness. "I don't think I know the answer."

T'Zai nodded and patted his knee in a gesture of comfort. "I know, son. But you will." Then the Mendani lifted his gaze to Del. "Sooner rather than later, I think."

Del grimaced and a wave of despair swept over Nick again. How could he trust his brother if he was keeping secrets?

Mendani T'Zai grunted and rose to his feet, wincing a little and placing a hand to the small of his back. "We're done. I'll walk you out." He started down the steps, not looking to see if the brothers followed.

They did, of course. Nick wasn't sure if he could find his way back to the sanctuary. An uneasy feeling came over him when he thought of those corridors, as if they'd been an illusion. He'd rather not get lost in this unsettling place.

They reached the sanctuary sooner than Nick thought they would, and T'Zai faded away before they could say a word. When they stepped out of the temple, the commons seemed loud, shiny, and somehow unreal, as if the temple were more substantial than the station.

"Well," Del said, stepping to the rail and looking down at the levels below, "I need a drink. How 'bout you?"

"Oh, yeah." Nick heaved a rough sigh, rubbing the back of his neck. "But I think I'd better take a rain check. I got work to do."

Del tilted his head. "You sure? You look beat."

"I'm sure," Nick responded with a grim smile. "And I ain't beat yet."

"I meant tired." His brother moved toward the lift and he followed.

"I know what you meant. But I'm running out of time. I have things I need to check out."

Del caught his arm, turning Nick to face him. With a crease between his brows, he asked in a sharp tone, "What do you mean, running out of time?"

Nick cursed under his breath, blaming the temple for baking his brain and causing the slip of his tongue. He sighed again, rolling his neck to release tension. "I suppose you and the Shays were going to find out soon enough anyway. I've been recalled."

Del let him go, his face hardening. "By who?"

"My duty officer. He's not impressed with my progress. With Gorby, it's results or it ain't an investigation."

Del made a rude noise in the back of his throat. Nick couldn't have agreed more. They continued on their way in brooding silence.

Halfway down the levels, Nick ended the quiet. "Hey, Del, do you remember the parts slinger on the Jacks Circuit who said she was born out in the Fringe?"

"Couldn't forget her." Del snorted, a grin easing the hard lines of his face. "She outweighed me by a light year, and you could hear her bellow across a circuit in full slice. Scared the crap outta me, if you want the truth."

Nick chuckled. "You and me both. 'Boy, you mess w' my tools, I'll squash you like a bug!' She could do it, too. Her name was Greta, right? She reminds me of the little dragon."

Del burst out laughing, slapping Nick on the shoulder as they exited the lift. "Greta the Granger, damn straight. But Cassie ain't got nothin' on that big ballbreaker. Cass is all talk."

"Oh, yeah?" Nick gave his brother a disbelieving look. "She shut me out of the station's systems today."

Del made a noise like a choked off snicker, meeting his brother's gaze with an incredulous expression. "You kiddin'? What'd you do?"

"I was using Sam to help me. If you ask me, Cassie overreacted."

"Yeah, well, she's sensitive about Sam. You should've heard her light into me when we came back from our first run. You'd think I was a child abuser the way she carried on, ripping into me about not bonding with Sam. Like I know what..." Del trailed off, his steps slowing and his eyes narrowing in suspicion. Then he stopped short, hands on his hips and brows pulling together in a frown. "Damn it, Nick, knock it off."

"Knock what off?" he asked with studied casualness.

"Inspectoring me behind my back," was his brother's peculiar answer.

Nick laughed. It wasn't polite, but he couldn't help it.

Del's frown eased into a lopsided grin. "Come on, little brother." He ruffled Nick's hair with an elder's disregard for dignity. "Let's get you back to your quarters before you make me spill everything."

Running absent fingers through his mussed hair,

Nick eyed Del's profile, his humor gone. "Would spilling everything be so bad?"

Del shot him a quick glance, dark eyes shuttered. "Right now it would be."

Clenching his jaw, Nick looked away with a sense of loss, a drifting sensation like a satellite cast away from its center of gravity. He'd known the Core would change his brother. Ten years under their whip and anyone would be transformed. But he'd never lost faith that Del could resist corruption, until now.

When they reached Nick's door, Del gripped his shoulder with a solemn expression. "I know you don't understand why I'm holding back on you. I wish I could tell you, but I can't. Just know there's a reason and do what you gotta do, Nick."

Nick stared into eyes so like his own, a tightness in his chest, a dismaying ache restricting his breath. He forced himself to say what needed to be said. "I'd save you if I could. But if you don't wanna be saved, there's nothing I can do. I have a job to do, and I'll do it, even if it means taking you down with the Shays."

Del's grip tightened but not with anger. His eyes flickered with an emotion easy to read but confusing. It looked like pride. With a faint smile, Del murmured, "I wouldn't want it any other way, brother." Then he turned and walked away.

Nick stared after him, baffled. Fraternal pride in response to a threat to his freedom just wasn't logical. Maybe he hadn't been direct enough. "How 'bout I just cut right to it and kick your ass?" he called down the corridor after his retreating brother.

Del's deep laughter bounced back to him. "Name the time and place, bro. I'll be there."

No, not logical at all.

With a sound of disgust, Nick keyed open the door to his quarters and stepped in. The scrolling message across the viewer caught his attention. A file and a verbal message from Roz waited for him.

"Got three schools with locked student records," Roz said on replay. "But my credit's on the first one. Got a call back from their admin, wondering why I was poking around. Then they backed off in a hurry when I mentioned your subject's name. Good luck, kid."

Nick swore, rubbing his face with weary hands. Roz shouldn't have talked to the school at all, let alone mentioned Cassie. If she'd gotten her doctorate there, then they were now warned someone was looking for information about her. Any attempt he made would be shot down right away.

Unless he went in a sneakier direction.

Nick pulled up the file and ran a search on the first school for a list of teaching staff. The odds were low of one of her professors knowing Cassie was under an information lockdown. He just had to figure out which professors might remember her.

It was a long list.

Nick swore again and set about shortening it. He started by eliminating the professors whose credentials and curriculums didn't match anything Cassie would have taken. To be safe, he didn't eliminate as many as he would have liked. Then he started at the top of his list and worked his way down, contacting each person in turn.

After a frustrating length of time and names, he hit the jackpot. His twenty-second contact revealed an older woman with a round, open face and alert, curious dark eyes.

"This is Dr. Ameliama Stark," she chirped, a welcoming smile hovering around her mouth as she eyed her caller.

Nick slid into his spiel once again. "Dr. Stark, I'm Nick Givliani, inspector for the FPA. I'm running a background check on someone who may have been your student. She's a prospective employee for our R&D department, highly sensitive material, so we're doing as detailed a check as we can."

"Nice to meet you, Inspector. What is the student's name?"

"Cassiopeia Draegen."

Her face lit like a rising sun, and Nick's heart sped up.

"Suns, I haven't heard that name in years. You're considering Cassie Draegen? You're in luck, Inspector. You couldn't have found a more dedicated, creative person. I won't ask why you want her, since you mentioned it was sensitive, but I hope you realize what a prize you have on your hands."

That's one way to put it, Nick thought. "Yes, ma'am, the FPA is very impressed with her. We still have to follow procedure and run the check. May I ask you a few questions about Dr. Draegen?"

With a warm smile, she settled back in her seat. "You certainly may."

With an effort, he smothered a triumphant grin. "Thank you, Dr. Stark. Let's just start with the basics. Could you tell me in what field she holds her doctorate?"

The smile faded from the older woman's face, brows drawing together in puzzlement. "Surely she told you?"

"Yes, ma'am, but we still have to ask. I don't believe she would forge any information on her application, but it's standard procedure to check," he responded with a depreciating smile and a shrug.

Her brow smoothed and she nodded, a wry, understanding twist to her mouth. "Of course. Well, as I'm sure you know, she holds several doctorates in a wide range of fields."

She proceeded to name almost a dozen. Nick's eyes kept trying to pop out of his head. He did his best to hide his shock but Holy Suns, she was a doctor in all of those fields? Some he recognized, like sociology and psychiatry. He felt a stab of discomfort to discover she was a head-shrink. Some baffled him, like cyberneurotechnology and nanoevolutionary engineering.

"Dr. Stark, forgive me for sounding a little skeptical, but how is it possible to have so many doctorates? She seems too young." He broke off at the delighted grin brightening her face.

"Ah, now I see why you're asking. You saw the list of—ologies and—iatries and assumed she was outrageously padding her resume. She wasn't, Inspector. She was something of a child prodigy, brilliant beyond any student I've ever had the pleasure to teach. If memory serves, I believe she received her first doctorate when she was fourteen."

He choked a little, and the woman snickered at his expense.

"Yes, she's quite astonishing. I remember her fondly, but not just because she was a genuine miracle to behold. I've known many geniuses in my life and have been called one, if I may be so immodest. Their most defining characteristic, from my experience, is ego. They know they're smarter than the people around them, and so they feel superior. But Cassie didn't seem to notice she was so far advanced in knowledge and skills. She was the sweetest child. A bit of an introvert, but always ready with a smile and a helping hand."

Nick blinked then cleared his throat, deciding to keep his opinion to himself. Sweet wasn't a term he would apply to Cassie. Before he could say anything, she continued with a reminiscent smile.

"The dear girl was a joy to teach. She had just the right amount of patience and drive. Do you know what I mean by that? She didn't try to force a subject with impatience but always proceeded forward, never losing her momentum. My perfect student," she added with a wistful curl of her lips, not seeming to notice the hint of arrogance in her tone.

Genius ego, Nick thought as he watched her. Opening his mouth to interrupt, he snapped it shut again with her next words.

"Too bad she ended up in the Core. A waste, if you ask me."

"What do you mean?" he asked when she didn't continue.

Her eyes focused on him with a flare of consternation. "Oh, I hope you don't take it the wrong way, Inspector. I don't mean she was doing anything illegal. She was hired by a company called Cybercom, an ideal position for her. I was so happy for her but selfishly sad to see her go. I only heard later, by rumor you understand, that Quasicore controlled Cybercom. Of course, I'm sure if Quasicore was involved with anything untoward, the FPA would know about it. Wouldn't they, Inspector?" Her voice hardened, and she eyed him with a hint of disapproval.

He ignored her question. "What was her position at Cybercom?"

"Well, I'm not sure. I can't remember what exact position she held, but Cybercom is renowned for its work in cybernetics and nanotechnology."

Putting on his best I'm-just-a-dumb-cop face, he asked, "What does that mean, Doctor?"

The smile she gave him radiated both condescension and shrewd awareness. "I think you know, Inspector Givliani. If I'm not mistaken, your data port is a Cybercom product, an older model."

He lifted a hand to finger the cybernetic implant behind his ear, wondering how she'd seen it. He couldn't remember turning his head at any point during their conversation. "So they make data ports. What else do they do?"

"They have many product lines, all dealing with biological/mechanical interfaces. But I believe Cassie was more interested in their positronic and cybertronic neural network development."

"What?" Nick didn't have to fake his incomprehension this time.

"Artificial intelligence, Inspector."

"Ah," he sighed with honest, gleeful satisfaction. *Now we're getting somewhere,* he thought. "She was interested in AI research?"

"Mr. Givliani," she said with faint reproach, "Cassie is one of the foremost experts in the field. I assumed it's why the FPA is interested in her."

"Of course," Nick backpedaled, taking mental note

of the term expert. "What I'm asking is if she was always so interested in this area."

"From day one. She's a single-minded personality, which is amazing, considering her creativity in problem solving. She is perhaps one of the few people I've ever met who can utilize both sides of her brain to equal effectiveness."

"The mark of a true genius?" he asked with a wry smile, hoping to head off a side trip down lecture lane.

She laughed with what looked like real delight. "Intriguing hypothesis, young man. But I believe Cassie's single-minded resolve is more basic than genius level." She sobered somewhat, her smile fading to soft regret. "She had very supportive parents, but they didn't really understand her, nor did people her own age. She grew up trying to cope with being the abnormal, the anomaly in every crowd." She stopped short, her form stiffening. "I'm sorry, Inspector. I seem to have strayed into a place too personal to be my business, or yours, for that matter."

He gave her his best disarming smile. "No harm done, Doctor. After all, you are a psychiatry professor."

The lines around her eyes deepened as she returned his smile. "Among other things," she responded with unconscious arrogance.

"So, let's get back on topic."

"Fire away," she returned with an approving nod.

He spent the next few minutes asking her typical background check questions. She answered everything with an air of tolerant patience, as if she thought his queries ridiculous but understood the necessary evil of bureaucratic thoroughness. From every indication, Cassie had been a model citizen, dedicated to her career and a conscientious member of society. No clue as to why she now had a sealed record.

He tried the Cybercom angle again, but Dr. Stark had no more information for him than she'd already given. She was also giving hints that her patience was running out, so he thanked her for her time and ended the conversation.

Sitting back, he fingered the data port behind his ear and chewed on the inside of his cheek. Cybercom might lead him in the right direction, but his time was running out. He'd have better luck confronting Cassie with what he knew and forcing the issue. He didn't want to rush the investigation, but Gorby wasn't going to let him float out here for long.

As if conjured by his thoughts, the viewer chimed, indicating he had an incoming call from Gorbanik. He swore and didn't answer. The man was trying to reel him in already. He waited, watching as the system ran through its no-answer protocol, offering Gorby the chance to leave a message. It didn't take long for his duty officer to respond.

When the system began scrolling the notice of Gorby's message, he accessed it and braced himself. His duty officer looked grim enough, but his words were unexpected.

"Givliani, if you don't stop turnin' off your personal com, I'm gonna write you up. How am I supposed to get you if you're in transit? Anyway, you better still be there, 'cause orders have changed. Somebody up the line wants you to keep investigating the Shays. Puckered up pretty for one of the bigwigs, did you? Well, you still gotta report to me, so don't get any bright ideas, newbie."

His sour, pudgy face disappeared, and Nick stared at the blank screen in surprise. Who knew he was investigating the Shays and why would they care? Gorbanik wouldn't bring a non-productive investigation to the attention of his superiors, so either somebody had gone out of their way to read Gorby's reports or somebody was following Nick's progress. Did someone else at FPA HQ find the closed Shay file as suspicious as he did?

Nick shook his head and rubbed the knot at the back of his neck. He couldn't afford to question the gift of time; Gorby was probably trying to get the new order renounced even now. His duty officer liked to have complete control over his field investigators and wouldn't be pleased to have his authority undermined.

Nick had to get on with it right quick, which meant seeing Cassie again. He rose to his feet and headed for the door, unaware of the eager bounce to his stride and the faint, anticipatory grin on his face.

Chapter 6

"Lianus, Luxora, Maenyut, Magnus." The precise recital paused. A heavy sigh sounded before the voice resumed in much different tones. "This is boring. Can't we play a game?"

The wheedling, pleading tone alarmed Cassie a little, but she didn't let her focus waver. "Not yet, Imago. I need you to concentrate now. You haven't named all the Suns. What comes after Magnus?"

"Maher," he answered with sullen reluctance.

"And after Maher?" Cassie prompted, her whole body tensing as she zeroed in on the code fragment. If he would keep his personality in check for just a little longer, she might have it.

"Who cares," he grumbled, sighing like an overtired child. "Can we play the association game?"

"All right," she agreed with growing desperation. The code fragments were elusive, breaking apart just as she got close and reappearing at random where she least expected them. But if she could keep him focused, it would force the code in the direction she needed. "What does a gorb fruit, Neha's Prophecy, and tea have in common?"

"That's too easy," he announced with bored arrogance, and she grit her teeth. "Bitterness. The gorb and most teas are bitter to the taste, while the underlying theme of Neha's writing is a bitter darkening of the soul."

This was an unusual response, since the answer could just as easily have been leaves; gorb segments were called leaves, the leaves of a book, and tea leaves. Unusual for anyone other than Imago, she amended, grimacing as the code fluctuated.

She was about to question him on his answer when he cut her off. "Who is that?" His voice somehow managed to convey both child-like fear and offended rage.

Alarmed, Cassie snapped her head around. Through the holographic representation of Imago's neural net, two figures stood visible at the viewing window to the holo-lab. One of them was not part of her staff.

Meeting Nick's dark gaze, Cassie pressed her lips together to contain her own offended anger, but the damage was done. Imago's focus slipped away when he sensed her change in mood.

"Who is that man? Why is he spying on us? Was he sent to kill me? Is that it?" His voice rose in volume with each question, and his verbal centers began to splinter, breaking into several voices as he went on in a near shriek. "Send in the spy! I want to die! Send, send, send! Die, die, die!"

His neural net became chaos, codes spiking all around her in a disorienting sensory display. Wincing, she took a deep breath and bellowed, "Imago!"

The sudden silence relieved her, but his net still jittered all around in a prelude to madness. With a grim clench of her jaw, she conceded defeat and pulled the connector from her data port, severing the direct connection to her brain before he fried her, too. In silence, she stalked toward the exit.

Stepping out into the main lab, she ignored the inspector and pinned Gabriel with a furious glare. "What is wrong with you?" she hissed. "You know how he gets around strangers."

Gabe's face was gray and drawn, eyes round with appalled comprehension. "Cass, I'm so sorry. He talked like he knew what was going on, so I thought…" His voice trailed off and he sent Nick a reproachful look, before pressing his lips together and moving away. "I'll do a remote connection and calm him down."

It would be useless for a while to try, but she didn't tell him not to bother. Instead, she paced in front of the lab door and did her best to curb the urge to scream at the top of her lungs.

"So what's wrong with him?" Nick asked in a diffident tone.

Chewing on her anger, she snarled, "Gabe has a weakness for big, strong men. And he's a rotten judge of character." She refused to look at him, pressing the connector to her forehead as she continued to pace and stew.

"I mean the AI," he said after a pause, his deep voice low and somber.

She stopped short, thrusting her fists in her pockets and tipping her head back to stare blindly at the ceiling, tears of frustration and despair prickling the corners of her eyes. Drawing a deep breath, she swore in a distinct, precise tone. Then she let her lungs collapse on a loud sigh and looked down at her feet. "His name is Imago. He's insane."

Nick made an incredulous noise. "How's this possible? You didn't make him this way on purpose, did you?"

His words impacted like a punch to her chest. Her head shot up and she met his curious dark eyes, bitter anger welling up in her throat like bile. "No, I didn't make him this way on purpose, Inspector," she said through clenched teeth. "I didn't make him this way at all, but I'm doing my best to fix him."

"Who did this to him?" His expression didn't change, eyes calm and direct, face hard and focused.

Cassie found it difficult to hold his gaze so she looked away, staring past him. "Imago was given something like a retrovirus. It writes itself into his neural net and replicates, affecting most of his main systems, but especially his personality. It's been impossible to destroy, since it fragments itself and blends in with normal code, appearing at random."

"Why? Why would somebody do it?"

She considered telling him they did it out of scientific curiosity or hubris. In the end, she opted for the ugly truth. "They wanted him to be suicidal."

A charged silence filled the air between them. Lifting her chin, she met his gaze and the breath left her body.

He stared at her with such intensity, as if she'd become the key to his investigation, the complicated darkness of his eyes stunning in its vibrant demand. "Why, Cass?" he asked, his voice still calm and tempered with compassion but also with insistence. He seemed to loom closer, his whole being a command. "Why would anyone want an AI to kill itself?"

She held very still, fighting the pull of him, the pure, magnetic energy which demanded a response. He'd be hard to resist in an interrogation room. Suns help her, he was hard to resist outside of one. Would he be this demanding in bed?

She blinked at the errant thought and a flush of heat rose over her skin. Now was not the time for her libido to kick in, but his gaze didn't waver from hers and she was having trouble thinking.

He seemed to sense the change in her and shifted closer, mobile mouth relaxing from its stern line to something more inviting. Without taking his gaze from hers, he reached out and captured her plait, sliding his hand down its silky length with deliberate leisure and a gentle tugging motion. "Cass?" he murmured, his voice a velvet rasp.

It was the most erotic sensation she'd ever experienced, the slow tug on her hair stimulating her scalp in a delicate massage, sending tingling fingers along her neck and around her throat to coast down her body. Her eyelids grew heavy with pleasure. Just then she would have given him any answer he wanted, if only she could remember the question.

"Dr. Draegen," a voice shattered the intimate moment. Cassie jerked her head around as one of her staff approached. "Mr. Shay needs to speak with you. He says it's urgent."

Stepping back from Nick on shaky limbs, Cassie managed to sound almost normal. "Relay to this station here."

With a brisk nod, the woman turned around and Cassie moved to the work station, too aware of Nick on her heels.

Kai's crisp words demanded her full attention, erasing any residual effects from Nick's touch and lingering embarrassment over her reaction. "Cass, we have a situation. Come to the docking bay and bring the inspector."

The connection broke before she could say a word. Alarmed by the grim urgency in her boss's voice, she turned to Nick. "You go ahead. I have to change."

His gaze questioning, he said only, "I'll wait."

She didn't argue. The ghost of Kai's voice haunted her. *A situation.* What in the Sun's name had happened?

Quick-stepping to her personal station, she stripped off the lab coat and yanked on her coveralls, fastening the clasps as she hustled to the door where Nick waited for her. They headed out into the corridor together. She expected a comment on her attire but he said nothing, his expression stern.

"I don't know what's going on," she offered as they moved at a fast pace down the corridor. She had to skip to keep up with his longer strides but wouldn't have minded a full out sprint. It took quite a lot to make Manakai Shay sound the way he did.

He nodded and sent her a grim glance. "Didn't sound good."

"No, it didn't."

The docking bay was busy, as usual. Cassie couldn't see anything out of place until she caught a glimpse of the Shay twins and Del waiting by a personal transport ship. Sin was pacing the length of the ship, her movements stiff. Her brother was talking fast and low, not a hint of his usual playfulness showing in his handsome face. Del seemed to be listening, but his dark gaze was focused on Sin.

Her stomach knotting, Cassie asked, "What happened?" as she and Nick approached.

All three turned to face them. A sharp stab of dread

pierced her at their white tension. "There's been an attack," Sin said with a calm belied by the strain in her features. "One of our off-lane runs. A large pack of hijackers overwhelmed them. We received a distress call from the hauler, followed by a ransom demand a short while ago. The hijackers are holding them hostage just inside the Fringe."

Cassie raised a hand to her mouth, shock and fear constricting around her heart. "Oh, no. Who was on the run?" she asked in a pained whisper.

Sin's green gaze was bleak. "Jinx had hauler duty. Fern and Quan were flying escort. Cass…" She paused, a spasm of pain contorting her features as she clasped one of Cassie's hands in hers. Her fingers were ice cold. "There was one casualty."

"Oh, Suns mercy," Cassie moaned, staring at Sin in horror. "Who?"

"We don't know," Kai answered, his voice as gentle as the arm he curled around her. "But we'll find out when we get there."

Sin turned from Cassie to confront Nick. "Which is where you come in." Her expression hardened and her voice took on a clear note of command. "The FPA unit in the area claims they don't have jurisdiction to mount a rescue operation in the Fringe. You're coming with us to convince them otherwise, Inspector."

Nick's head lifted, big form tensing and eyes cooling as he assessed her. "What makes you think I can change their minds? What makes you think I wanna try? Jurisdiction protocol is there for a good—"

"Nick," Del interrupted, "we need your help. These people are my friends, and they could die out there if we don't do something fast."

Nick frowned at his brother. "If they're asking for a ransom—"

Del shook his head, his tone impatient. "These are bad people, bro. They already killed one of our crew."

Cassie found herself reaching out to grasp Nick's arm. His troubled dark gaze swung to her, muscles bunching under her touch. "We can't assume the ransom is their main objective," she reasoned in a shaky voice, thinking of Griffin while she spoke. "Please, if you can help."

"It's a rescue, Inspector, not an illegal operation," Sin cut in with a challenging toss of her dark head. "I thought the FPA forces were all about keeping the peace and saving lives." She lifted her eyebrows at him with a sardonic curl of her lips before turning on her heel. She stalked to the ship's hatch, finishing over her shoulder, "Stop wasting time and come help me save them."

Nick grimaced and gave his brother a dry look. "Why doesn't she just knock me out and drag me on board?"

Del's expression eased into something like amusement, but before he could reply, Manakai growled, "Now there's an idea."

Nick turned his dry look on Cassie's boss, moving toward the ship. "I thought the Shays were known for their subtlety."

"Wasn't that subtle?" Kai asked with a flash of his usual humor.

Nick snorted without replying as he ducked into the ship. Del nodded to them before following his brother and closing the hatch.

Cassie looked up at Kai, disconcerted by the

brooding expression darkening his features. "You're not going?"

"No, Sinsi has this one covered, and I have a call to make," he replied in a grim voice, tightening his arm around her in gentle reassurance.

"So it was Griffin," she murmured, watching the ship purr to life and speed away from them toward the exit. "You did say you expected him to retaliate."

"Um-hmm. But we were expecting something a little less personal."

She shivered at his distant, musing tone and leaned into him for warmth. "He has a lot to answer for." Instead of sounding righteous and angry, the words came out forlorn.

"Yes, he does." He gave her a squeeze before turning her toward the exit. "So let's get started, Cassie-girl."

Chapter 7

Nick had never been so thoroughly ignored. He supposed his companions did have a lot on their minds, and he hadn't endeared himself to Sin Shay with his investigation. Listening to them have cryptic partial conversations wasn't very useful or interesting, and he needed a distraction. Dodging images of Cassie, he studied the two in front of him with grim determination.

Watching his brother, he began to get a sense of just how futile his campaign was to rescue Del from Sin's clutches. His brother was well and truly lost on her. They never touched, sitting a circumspect distance from each other in their pilot seats, but they didn't have to touch. It was in every look he gave her, the timbre of his voice, the line of his body. Sin was a little harder to read, but the softening of her features and the vulnerable curve of her mouth when she looked at Del was suggestive. But was it suggestive of her true feelings or just the mark of a great actress?

Nick frowned, eyeing her. She was an enigma, no question, much like a little dragon he knew. Shaken by the memory of Cassie arching her neck in languorous reaction to his touch, he took a swift breath, shifted in discomfort, and interrupted their low conversation. "This transport doesn't have any weapons, does it?"

The two glanced over their shoulders at him. Sin answered, "No, it doesn't."

"Then shouldn't you be flying your Shadow slicer, Shay?" He couldn't curb the aggression in his voice. Cassie and his frustrating investigation had put him on edge. "Since you have sanction to use those weapons. How'd you get sanction, by the way?"

She exchanged a glance with Del before turning a faint, humorless smile on Nick. Swiveling her seat to face him, she stretched out, crossing her ankles and linking her fingers across her stomach in a casual stance. She studied him for a long moment. "Is it your intention to interrogate me on the way to rescuing our friends, Inspector?"

He clenched his jaw, annoyed at the rebuke in her tone. "Why not? You and your brother have avoided me for days. Short of arrest, this looks like the only way I'll get some answers out of you."

She lifted an eyebrow at the word arrest but didn't comment, a faint smile still hovering around her mouth. "And here I thought you were on vacation," she murmured with a malicious undertone. Before he could respond, she swiveled back around and said crisply over her shoulder, "I need to get us into the star-way. Then you can grill me to your heart's content, since it will be a little while before we're close to that sector of the Fringe. You can contain yourself for a few more minutes, can't you, Inspector?"

"Sin." Del's tone was a gentle reprimand.

She shot him a glance, eyes hard and lips thinned to a straight line. Then she sighed. "Sorry, Nick. I'm a little out of sorts today."

Nick winced a little at her dry tone and kept silent as they approached the star-way. This portal would jump them to the solar system of their choice. The star-way consisted of two rings, one on either side of the sun to use the sun's massive energy to create a wormhole between them and a set of rings in a different solar system.

"Ring Control," Sin announced in a smooth voice devoid of emotion, "This is Sinsudee Shay of Shay Enterprises. You have one of our couriers, the *Fidelity,* on your docket for departure inside the hour. We have an emergency situation and need you to expedite its launch."

As she spoke, their transport angled toward a large courier vessel. They were going to use it to get through the star-way, since the small transport wouldn't be able to withstand the shock of entering the wormhole on its own.

"We have a tight schedule, ma'am," a male, nasal voice answered her. "I regret we cannot accommodate your request—"

"Be advised this is a matter of life and death," Sin interrupted, voice still emotionless. "It's not a request. We require immediate departure to the destination I am sending you now."

"I'm sorry, but—"

"I'm also sending you a contact at the FPA to confirm the nature of the situation. If you need authorization from your supervisor, I suggest you hurry. Our time is limited."

There was a short pause. When the controller spoke again, his voice was subdued and apologetic. "I'll get on it right away, ma'am."

"Thank you, Control."

Nick wondered what FPA contact Sin had sent for the controller to make such a quick turnaround. The guy hadn't had enough time to confirm anything, so just the name had been enough to convince him. *Interesting,* Nick thought as they entered the courier's docking bay and settled onto a landing pad.

Sin held an abbreviated conversation with the captain of the *Fidelity* while Del turned around, folding his arms across his chest and studying his brother with an inscrutable expression. "Thanks for coming," he said in a mild tone, as if it were an afterthought to what ran through his head.

Nick shrugged. "I'll do what I can, but it ain't gonna be much. I don't know anybody in that jurisdiction, and a junior inspector won't have a lot of clout."

Del nodded, but Nick wasn't certain he'd heard. A clench in his jaw and a distant reserve in his eyes suggested he was light-years away. Had these people come to mean so much to him in so short a time? Or was there something else going on here? His brother still studied him as if he would find answers in Nick's familiar features. "You okay, bro?"

Nick blinked, startled by the question. Shifting in unease, he wondered just what his face was giving away. "Yeah, fine. Why?"

"You're jittering around over there like you got a serious itch in your shorts. Did something happen we should know about?"

Nick face heated. He couldn't tell him the smell of wildflowers and a pair of soul-sucking brown eyes haunted him. His skin still remembered the feel of her silky plait running through his fingers, and he clenched the hand into a fist to dispel the sensation. He also couldn't tell his brother what he'd discovered about their little fire-breather. At this point, it was just another puzzle piece in an ever more complicated picture, though he was sure it was a key piece. He might use it as leverage to get more out of Sin Shay later, but for now he needed to play it close to his chest.

"Just having one of those days," he answered, flicking his gaze to Sin before meeting Del's dark stare again.

"Still having trouble with your duty officer?"

Sin shot Del a quick look but she still had her back to Nick so he couldn't read her expression. She said nothing, her hands making a final run over the controls.

Wondering if her look meant something or if he was just being paranoid, Nick answered, "No, Gorby gave me the all clear to stay."

Del nodded again and glanced at Sin.

She flashed him a grim smile as she turned her seat around to face Nick. "You'll want to activate your seat restraint. We'll be entering the star-way in another minute or two."

He did as suggested, not bothering to ask why they were staying in the transport for the trip instead of finding seats on the courier. The obvious answer was they didn't want to waste time on the other end getting back into the transport. Nick also thought they might be keeping a low profile with the masses, something the Shays seemed to do a lot.

Since they were in the docking bay instead of the more protected interior of the courier, the jolt of the ship entering the star-way's active wormhole was more pronounced. Nick gritted his teeth and had grateful thoughts about the gentle cushioning force restraining him in his seat. If he'd had the standard shoulder belts strapping him in, he suspected he'd have chafe marks and a touch of whiplash to show for this adventure. One good thing about traveling with a Shay, the best of everything had its upside.

When the ship stopped bucking, Sin deactivated her restraint and stretched like a cat, lithe and graceful, before settling into her casual stance once more and pinning her gaze on Nick. A faint smile hovered around her mouth, cynical rather than amused. "I'm all yours, Inspector."

Nick studied her, releasing his own restraint and sitting forward to rest elbows on his knees. He was trying to decide how to proceed with her. She was not his usual suspect. Most of the people he'd interrogated in his time with the FPA were either nervous or sullen in the face of authority. She seemed unaffected by his badge of office; his earlier mention of arrest had bounced right off her with barely a notice. He decided a full frontal assault would get him nowhere. She'd probably eat him alive and pick his flesh from her teeth with his bones.

With this uncomfortable image flashing caution signals, Nick started slow. "Tell me about your people out there. You said they were on an off-lane run?"

The cynicism faded, replaced by a small crease of concern on her brow. "Yes, they were transporting medical supplies to a system just inside the Fringe."

"What kind of medical supplies?"

"Nothing to interest hijackers. No drugs or sophisticated equipment they could sell or misuse. Just vaccines, antibiotics, antivirals, and the like."

"So why the attack?" Nick asked, not able to hide his skepticism.

The cynical quirk made a brief return to her lips. "Gosh, Inspector, what an excellent question. Why don't you ask them when we get there?"

He ignored the sarcasm and Del's wordless murmur of reproach, keeping his eyes trained on hers. She was expecting him to be suspicious, expecting him to gnaw at every tidbit of information like a rabid dog. He needed a way to get her to let down her guard, to talk to him instead of fencing with him. The concern she had shown toward her people might be the way, but he couldn't jump right there or she'd see the tactic for what it was. "Do you do a lot of business in the Fringe?"

She shook her head, eyes veiling a bit. "Not much. Without the civilization and protection of the FPA, it's a dangerous proposition."

If she was lying, she was doing a fine job of it. He nodded. "As your people found out today."

She tilted her head in agreement, lips thinning and forehead creasing; the concern reappeared again, a crack in her otherwise flawless shielding. He was getting closer.

"So why did you agree to this run?" He tried not to sound accusatory.

She shrugged. "The system contacted our company as a last resort. No one else would agree to help them, and they desperately needed the supplies."

"You don't strike me as the altruistic type," he couldn't help commenting, his voice dry. He was remembering his first meeting with this woman, when she'd asked him, "What's in it for us?"

"Not a good business motto, Nick. Of course we charged for the service."

He fought off the urge to ask how much, knowing it would just lead farther away from his goal. "Still, it's a dangerous job. Why do they do it? Your pilots, I mean. Uh, who did you say was out there?"

"Jinx, Fern, and Quan. I believe you've met them," she commented, a knowing glint in her eye. She was well aware he'd questioned each and every one of her off-lane crew, for all the good it had done him.

"Yeah, I met them. Jinx is the skinny kid with the gamer addiction, right?"

Sin grinned, her green eyes warming. Jinx's real addiction was the drug blue, but she seemed to appreciate him not mentioning it. "Did he talk your ear off about the Ninth Hell of Karse?"

"Tenth Hell," Del interjected with a snort of amusement.

"Was that what he was going on about? I couldn't tell, only understood about one word in five." Nick put on his best baffled expression and watched her snicker, satisfaction warming his gut. *Here we go,* he thought.

"He does go on," she said, affection clear in her voice. "He and his friends have their own language. How long did he string you along with it?"

He was a little uncomfortable with her use of the phrase, "string you along." It sounded too much like the kid had been snowing him, blocking his questions with gamer babble. "Longer than I like to remember," he answered, to her amusement. "The short guy, Quan, kept egging him on, which didn't help."

She shook her head with mock regret and a sigh. "Yes, another poor soul lost to the virtual reality gaming void. I keep telling them it'll rot their brains, but they insist it sharpens their piloting reflexes."

He heard his cue. "The kid seems awful young to be in big business. How'd you end up with him?" His stomach flipped over with a combination of dismay and attraction at Sin's slow smile. She was beautiful, all right, like the surface of the Sun was beautiful. Bright, magnetic, and deadly up close.

Instead of answering him, she turned her smile on his brother. "You're right. He's not bad."

Del chuckled, eyes crinkling at the corners with warmth, and Nick swallowed a curse. His brother watched her like a dog come to heel. *Well and truly lost.*

She faced Nick again, her smile and voice turning gentle. "Would you like their background stories, Nick?"

"Yes, I would," he said with as much humility as he could manage, swallowing another curse. So much for catching her with her guard down.

****

Cassie paced just beyond visual range as Kai leaned against the big desk in the boardroom and waited for Griffin to answer his call. She needed to get back to Imago, but she wouldn't be able to concentrate knowing her friends were in danger. Lack of concentration would put her in jeopardy if she plugged into Imago's net without her full focus. Besides, she couldn't leave without knowing what was going on, even if it meant staring at Griffin's hateful face again.

Bile rose in the back of her throat as the older man's image appeared on the viewer in front of Kai. Seeing the vile snake always turned her stomach. She froze in place and glared at Griffin's visage, the old rage building again. What she wanted most in the world was to gouge out those glittering gray eyes and claw his refined features until he bled.

She knew Manakai felt much the same because he'd told her so, in graphic, violent detail, but she couldn't tell by looking at him. He stayed in a casual stance, leaning with leonine grace against his desk, a faint smile of welcome on his handsome face. His voice was just as relaxed. "Griff, thanks for taking my call."

"Manakai, it's good to hear from you, as always. What can I do for you?"

"It seems we have a situation with one of our off-lane runs."

"Oh?" Griffin's cool smile faded somewhat, his eyes taking on a sharper glitter. "Nothing serious, I hope."

Murdering bastard, Cassie thought, biting the inside of her lip until she tasted the metallic zing of blood and blinking away furious tears. The man was probably gloating like a bloated toad inside.

"Actually, it is serious," Kai answered, his expression sobering. "We've lost a pilot, and we may lose more. Hijackers attacked one of our couriers."

"What terrible news." Griffin's face radiated an almost-sincere concern. "What's being done?"

Kai breezed right by the question as if it weren't important. Cassie watched in admiration and worry as he spoke with no sign of emotional connection to the events. She didn't know what it was costing him to be so nonchalant and wasn't sure she wanted to know.

"We're handling the situation. We've halted all off-lane runs until further notice, and we mean to protect our regular couriers, too; which is why I'm calling you, Griff."

Griffin's eyes grew guarded while he studied this dark twin. Sin often led him on a more delicate dance with word play, subtle conversational shifts and segues, before she came to the point. Kai's arrow-straight dive into the subject seemed to be throwing their nemesis off his stride. Cassie wanted to cheer.

"I'm at your disposal, of course. What is it I can do for you?"

"We want to hire Quasicore's security services to escort our couriers."

It took Griffin a second to respond to Kai's blunt statement. A faint smile tugged at his lips, as though he thought Kai was joking. After a perusal of Manakai's serious expression, the smile faded and his eyebrows lifted just a bit. They'd surprised him.

Cassie bared her teeth in a bloodthirsty grin. *The first of many surprises,* she thought with an inner chortle. The man had lived far too long thinking he was omnipotent.

"You want Quasicore's protection?" Griffin asked, weighing the last word with significance.

Kai ignored whatever implication the other man was trying to make. "Yes, we'd like your security services to escort our ships when they travel the quieter lanes. The regular lanes have heavy traffic and are well patrolled by the FPA, so they pose no danger, but we'd like to keep the pirates off our backs on the smaller lanes."

Griffin leaned back in his chair, face expressionless as he studied Manakai. "But not for your off-lane runs?"

Kai gave him a humorless smile. "Wouldn't want to put your people in more danger than they can handle,

Griff. We want protection, not battles. We're ending our off-lane runs for a while."

A flat gleam appeared in Griffin's gray eyes. Cassie hoped it was anger. The Shay's response to his retaliation was not what he would anticipate; they neither cowered in fear nor raged in impotent fury, both of the responses he was most likely to crave. He'd attacked not just their business but their friends, and what did they do? They removed the personal targets out of easy range and put him in a position to make it hard to repeat his retaliation without hurting himself.

If he sent hijackers to attack another Shay ship while he was protecting it, he would lose both his security forces and his reputation on the legitimate side of his security business. He would lose face. He was also losing a lucrative avenue of business with the Shay's, since they accomplished most of their shadier deals on the off-lane runs.

It must be driving him nuts, Cassie thought with gleeful spite.

If he was feeling anything, he didn't show it. "Regrettable, but understandable. I'm sure you can recover the loss of business in other ways. Of course my security forces are at your disposal. Shall I send a contract over?"

"That'd be great, Griff. My office will handle it."

"Is there anything else I can do? What about the current situation with the hijackers?"

Kai smiled, a hint of coldness creeping into his expression. "It'll resolve itself shortly. Nothing to worry about."

Griffin tilted his head, eyebrows lifting in an invitation for more detail. Manakai ignored his body language and Cassie bit the inside of her lip again, this time to prevent a bray of harsh laughter. The man had nerve, asking what the Shays planned to do to counter his attackers.

"Good talking with you again, Griff," Kai said in brisk dismissal.

"Stimulating as always, Manakai. Give my regards to your sister."

"Will do."

Griffin's face disappeared from the viewer and Kai tilted his head back, a pensive curve to his mouth as he stared at the ceiling.

Cassie eased closer, studying her boss. "Kai? Are you okay?"

"I'm trying to count how many more times I'll have to do that before I can punch him in his face."

"Do what? Play nice? Or play war games?"

He glanced at her with a twinkle in his green eyes. "Both. Wouldn't you like to sock him in the snout, Cass?"

"With both hands."

He gave a snort of laughter and rounded the desk, slinging an arm across her shoulders and walking them toward the exit. "With Sun's mercy, maybe we can take turns."

"Red Sun be praised," she effused, clasping her hands together in front of her in mock prayer.

He snickered again and gave her a squeeze. "I knew we'd convert you to the Order someday."

"Yes, to hell with science, logic, and reason," she exclaimed. "Throw me a broadsword and an axe, yon barbarian. I'm going to war."

He started laughing, and at first Cassie giggled

along with him. After the difficulties of the day, it was a welcome release of tension as they made their way to Kai's private office.

But he kept laughing, and at some point she had to take offense. "All right, you big ape, it wasn't that funny," she growled.

"Ah, Cass, what would I do without you?"

"You'd find some other poor sap to tease and laugh at." She shrugged out from under his arm and sat in front of his desk.

He leaned over the back of the chair and purred in her ear, "Poor Cass. How can I make it up to you?"

If any other man had breathed in her ear, she might have had a different reaction. Her mind sighed *Nick* in regret before she shook away the thought. Kai was the most handsome and charming man she'd ever met, but he could also be the coldest and most frightening man. Besides, he was her boss, and he didn't mean a second of his flirting. He only did it because he knew just how she'd react.

Cassie rolled her eyes, planted a hand in his face, and shoved.

Her hand muffled his snicker before he pulled away and came out from behind her. "Rejected again," he bemoaned, clasping a hand to his chest and staggering around the desk.

She grinned at his antics. "Ham."

He winked, but as he sat, his mood changed with his usual quicksilver abruptness. "Let's find out how Sinsi is doing."

Cassie sobered, fear constricting her chest in tight bands. *Please,* she thought, this time praying for real, *let them be okay.*

Chapter 8

"And Cassie?" Nick asked with all the nonchalance he could muster.

While they traveled through the wormhole and exited the other side, Sin had sketched the backgrounds of each of her off-lane pilots, from Bibliona's exploits in a brothel to Lynch's time served in a slaughterhouse. She didn't explain they'd all been under the Core's heavy hand, something he'd discovered from his brother days ago, but otherwise she'd been very forthcoming, painting a detailed picture of each of them.

With one exception.

Sin's mouth twisted in a suppressed smile. "What about her?"

"What's her story?"

"Cassie's our resident genius." Her green eyes studied him with a knowing glint he didn't like.

"Yeah, I gathered she was smart. How'd she end up with you?"

"She applied for the job," Sin said with bland amusement.

"So you're not going to tell me?"

"I just did."

With difficulty, he kept a rein on his temper. "All your pilots are Core rejects. Cassie is a pilot. What'd she do for the Core?"

"Much the same as she's doing for us, I expect. She doesn't like to talk about it." Sin was still watching him with the glint in her eye, no doubt measuring and judging how far she could push him.

He tried not to grind his teeth. "What is she doing for you?"

"Well, you said so yourself a moment ago. She's a slicer pilot."

"What have you dragged her into, Shay?" he blurted, goaded by frustration and another emotion he didn't recognize.

She gave him a gentle smile. "No one drags Cassie Draegen anywhere, Nick. If you spent any time with her, you'd know this."

He dropped his gaze and ran a hand through his hair, trying to pull his emotions back under control. Talking about Cassie was a mistake. He wasn't going to get anything out of Sin without spending way more time than he had and the topic was making him lose his cool. *Take another route,* he told himself.

"Why do you take in Core rejects?" he asked to give himself time to come up with another line of questioning. He didn't expect her to answer with anything concrete.

"Because they need me to."

Nick lifted his head in surprise. The candor in her gaze doubled his surprise. She wasn't giving him the runaround; this was the truth.

He thought about it, gaze moving to his brother, who'd been a victim of the Core. Del rested his head on the back of his seat, eyes half-closed while he watched Nick. A smile flickered across his face when Nick glanced at him, but otherwise he didn't respond.

"Humanitarianism doesn't seem like your thing," Nick said to Sin in a careful voice. "Why would you care if these people needed somebody to take them in?"

She chuckled and shook her head. "You make me sound like such a mercenary. These are good people, good pilots. I need good pilots, and they needed a refuge." She held up her hands with a shrug. "Seems like a win-win situation to me."

"You went up against the Core for Del. Did you do the same for the rest of them?" *Did you do it for Cassie?*

"I would fight for any of them. They've become like family to me," she answered with the same strange candor in her gaze. Then she blinked and cast a quick look over her shoulder at the consol. "If you have any other questions, you'd better ask them quick. We're almost there."

Nick glared at her in accusation, both for her avoidance of his question and for how she'd stretched out the background discussions of her pilots until they were out of time. Without much hope, he started firing questions at her.

"Why do you have weapons on your Shadow slicers?"

"For protection of our couriers on off-lane runs."

"How did you get sanction for those weapons?"

"We asked," she said with a smirk.

"Who did you ask?"

"The FPA."

"Who in the FPA gave you sanction?"

"Someone who knows we needed protection on our off-lane runs."

Nick sighed. "Why do you have a sealed FPA

file?"

"I won't kiss and tell," she murmured, batting her eyelashes at him.

He scowled at her. "Why does Cassie have a sealed file?"

She lifted an eyebrow at him. "We've been busy, haven't we?"

He could have kicked himself. He hadn't wanted to give her this piece of information. Rolling his shoulders to release tension, he reached for something else, something to knock her off this casual defense of hers. "Why does your teacher T'Zai say you hear the song of the Red Sun?"

She went still, staring at him. Then she burst into laughter. He watched her, bemused. She was breathtaking when she relaxed. No wonder his brother was hooked. He found himself wondering what Cassie's laugh was like. Shaking his head, he straightened in his seat. "What's so funny?"

"Oh Nick, I can't believe you fell for his line. You of all people."

He met the twinkle in her eye and her grin with a reluctant smirk, shrugging. "He runs a good show."

She snickered. "Yes, he does. Such a lovely song and dance. What was your favorite part? The primitive atmosphere or his scripture quotes?"

"Don't get me wrong, the pretty lights and rhetoric were great, but I especially liked how he made me feel like a total idiot. Turned my questions right around on me."

Both Sin and Del chuckled this time and Nick couldn't hold back a sheepish grin. Before he could marshal his thoughts and try to use this strange rapport for something other than embarrassing him, the console squawked.

Sin's demeanor changed, her expression chilling to a cold mask. "Kai, I'm here. No, we haven't reached the sector yet but we're almost there. It's just about time to contact the FPA unit. I'll contact you when it's over."

This sounded ominous to Nick, but he tried not to show his unease when Sin glanced over her shoulder at him.

"Ready?" she asked, face devoid of expression.

He shrugged. "As I'll ever be, I guess. Can't say they'll listen."

"Trust me, they'll listen." She tapped at the console and then announced, "This is Sinsudee Shay aboard transport five-eight-two-A."

"We read you. This is Lieutenant Brown of the Fourth Division. State the nature of your business."

"I own the courier vessel taken hostage near here. I'm requesting your assistance in retrieving it."

"As we've told you before, Ms. Shay, it's beyond our jurisdiction and we can't help you."

Sin turned to Nick and gestured him forward, her expression stony. He rose and stepped between their seats as the viewer flickered to life, showing Lieutenant Brown. The man met Nick's gaze with an incurious look, the blank expression suggesting he wasn't interested in arguing jurisdiction with anyone.

"Lieutenant, I'm Inspector Nick Givliani. I'm backing Ms. Shay's request for assistance. This is a rescue mission, sir. Those are innocent people out there who need our help and may die if we do nothing."

Brown frowned, eyes sparking with mild interest.

"What's an FPAI doing out here? Is this part of an investigation of yours?"

"In a way," Nick answered with caution. He didn't want to stretch the truth too much, but he'd told his brother he'd do his best. "The people out there are under investigation. I need you to—"

"Sorry, Inspector. Wish we could help, but the Fringe is strictly off-limits. Until they expand our jurisdiction to include the sector, we got no business in there. Can't justify putting my people at risk against such a large contingent, either."

Nick was about to argue when Sin waved him back. "You've done enough, Nick. You can sit down now."

Baffled, he stared at her. "Ah, they haven't agreed."

"They will. Have a seat, Nick."

With a frown of confusion, he backed up and sat again.

Sin gave him a grim nod and faced the Lieutenant. "Lieutenant Brown, do you need confirmation of Inspector Givliani's identity?"

A crease appeared in the lieutenant's brow until he bent his head, staring down at something below their vision. The crease disappeared when he looked up again. "No, ma'am, I have confirmation from our systems he is who he says he is. But I still can't help you."

"You can and you will, if you want the inspector to live. We're going in there with or without you, and damn, will you look bad if you did nothing while hijackers slaughtered an FPAI right under your nose. See you there."

Sin cut the connection and pushed their speed to maximum, shooting past the sector border and into Fringe space.

Nick stared at the back of her head, his jaw unhinging and dropping open. "Did you just—?"

Sin glanced over her shoulder, a cold glitter in her green eyes, beautiful face set in uncompromising lines. "Did I just blackmail them? Did I just take you hostage? Yes and yes. I told you they'd listen, Inspector. I didn't say they'd listen to you."

His jaw snapped shut, anger flowing through him and tensing his muscles. "You didn't expect me to talk them in, did you? You dragged me along for bait."

She faced forward again, hands running with swift efficiency over the consol. "I let you give it a try, Inspector, but we don't have time to waste."

Nick turned his furious gaze on his brother, his gut clenching with betrayal. Del was watching him, arms folded over his chest, a hint of regret in his dark eyes. "I can't believe you were part of this."

"Sorry we didn't tell you right off, but you know this'll work. They can't let an FPAI face down a dog pack alone. It's not like we're throwing you to the wolves, either. We're going in with you."

Nick chewed on the thought for a second, still angry but seeing his point. "You should've told me."

"Would you have come?"

"I might've," he snapped.

Del shook his head, a hint of a smile around his mouth. "It ain't strictly legal, and you're a by-the-book kinda guy, bro. You'd have given us hell about it and we didn't have the time."

Nick shifted in his seat, hands clenching into fists.

For some reason, his brother's assumption that he wouldn't break a rule made him want to punch him in the mouth. He settled for stabbing an angry finger at his brother. "I do not like being used. You pull this crap again, and I'll wipe the floor with you. Got it?"

"Argue later, boys. Show's on," Sin interrupted in a cool, distant voice.

Del swiveled in his seat and Nick stared at the viewer in alarm. This wasn't a pack of hijackers; it was a friggin' army. No wonder they'd been overwhelmed. Shadow ships could fly like a dream, but they wouldn't have stood a chance against those odds. Their only hope had been to flee, but the courier ship was too slow to escape.

In between the attacking ships, the courier drifted in a slow circle, its surface scored in several places and debris seeping out of a hull breech. A cloud of debris to one side might have been the remains of a Shadow vessel. One of the beautiful and deadly slicers still hovered over the courier, for all the good its protection could do. The hijackers had them trapped, flying around their prey in a fast-moving net.

Sin hissed under her breath then touched the com. "Fresh target over here, kiddies." He hadn't expected her playful tone.

The hijackers had already seen the transport, several ships breaking off to arrow in their direction. "You got the ransom?" a gruff voice asked over the com.

"Sure. Brought munchies and party favors, too. Anyone interested?"

Sin kept the transport out of their range, dancing away from the attacking ships with a skill Nick had to admire, even as he clutched the armrests and braced for impact.

They didn't seem impressed by her display. "You playin' games? It'll get you dead, lady." One pirate took a shot across her bow.

"Now, now," she admonished, angling away from them. "You kids stop trying to barbeque the goodies. What good is a ransom if you've fried it to dust?"

A voice thick with tears broke into their communication. "Sin?"

She turned her head, meeting Del's gaze. Nick's breath left his chest at the tortured look in her eyes. "Fern, hang tight. We'll have you out of there soon." Her voice was calm, not a hint of the pain lining her features.

"Quan is…"

"I know, hon. Just hang on."

The attacking ships had pulled back, hovering between Sin's transport and the hostages. Her comment about frying the ransom seemed to be keeping them at bay. *Greed's a powerful motivator,* Nick thought with a sneer then realized he'd been gripping the armrests of his chair so hard his hands hurt. He let go, flexing his fingers with a sour twist of his mouth. Being in the back seat sucked.

"Stop messin' around, lady. Cough up the credit or we do another one."

Before she could answer, Del said in a near whisper, "Cavalry's on the way."

"About time," she muttered then raised her voice. "All right, I'll stop messing around. I'd like your unconditional surrender, if you please."

The hijacker said nothing for a second. "What?"

"Surrender. Back away from my people and my ships, power down your weapons, and surrender to me. Or you could turn tail and run, a possibility for another minute or so."

"What in Barker's balls are you—?"

The hijacker seemed to notice the fleet of FPA ships bearing down on them. The attackers didn't bother to comment. Apparently, they hadn't been paid enough to stage a full-on battle. In groups of two or three, then in larger numbers, they pulled away from their location and fled. As soon as a clear path opened to the hostages, Sin flew the transport in and hovered between the fleeing hijackers and her crew.

As the last of them pulled out of weapons range and the fleet approached, Sin took a deep breath, letting it out on a sigh and sagging into her seat. "I was afraid…"

Del finished for her. "They'd blast the courier on their way out."

"It was a possibility," Sin murmured, flying them toward the courier. "Jinx? Are you okay?"

"Yeah," a thready voice answered, weak and thin. He didn't sound okay.

"What's your situation?"

"Got a breech, sealed it off. Can't get the stabilizers on line. Life support's holding steady, but I got a—"

"Will the hatch hold a seal?"

"Uh, yeah."

"Can you get to the hatch?"

"Yes, I can." He sounded stronger, the possibility of rescue steadying his voice.

"I'm lining up now. Let's get you out of there."

He didn't bother to answer. With delicate skill, Sin slid the transport next to the wounded hauler and connected the hatches, waiting until the integrity of the seal was confirmed before she jumped up. Jinx stumbled across the threshold, young face pale as watered milk, eyes large and haunted. Sin pulled him gently into her arms and he burst into tears, clutching her.

While Sin rocked him and murmured soothing words Nick couldn't hear, Del activated the com and spoke to Fern. "What's your status?"

"I'm okay. I mean, the slicer's not damaged. I can fly her."

"Good. We'll need you to follow us back."

"I can do that. How's Jinx?"

Del glanced over his shoulder at Sin and her charge, a frown pulling his brow. "He's pretty shook up. No injuries."

"What about the Tank?"

"We'll have to get somebody to haul it back."

"Del, what about…Quan?"

Del paused, exchanging a look with his brother. Nick could read helpless anger and dismal grief in his brother's dark gaze.

"The FPA will salvage what they can," Del said and Nick nodded to confirm. They'd clean up the remains even if Nick had to commandeer one of their ships and do it himself.

A sound like a sob came over the com, and when she spoke, Fern's voice was thick with tears again. "He was a hero right to the end. He put himself in the line of fire. Del, he…"

She didn't have to finish. Nick understood Quan

had sacrificed himself to save the courier and Jinx.

Del lowered his head, rubbing a hand across his forehead. "He was a good man," he said in a low, gentle tone.

Nick was starting to understand the connection his brother had with these people, why they had come to mean so much to him. He grimaced at his own helplessness and leaned forward, gripping Del's shoulder in scant comfort.

An angry voice interrupted the conversation. "Shay, you are under arrest! Return the inspector or—"

"Oh, stow it, junior," Del said with a heavy sigh and cut the connection.

Nick said nothing, just rose and slid into Sin's seat, reconnecting to the FPA fleet. "Lieutenant Brown, this is Inspector Givliani. I am not being held against my will. The situation has been resolved, as you can see. I'd like to request a salvage detail, to tow the courier back to FPA space and secure the remains of pilot Quan To and his slicer."

"Were you in on this, Givliani? I'll have you up on charges."

"Lieutenant, shut up a minute and listen," Nick growled. "None of your people were hurt, and none of the fleet was damaged. These people just lost somebody they cared about. If you had family out here, what would you have done?"

Brown paused for a long moment. Then he said in a tight voice, "This goes in my report."

"Fair enough," Nick responded, smoothing his tone. "And your cooperation will go in mine."

After another, shorter pause, Brown made a disgruntled noise. "We'll do salvage, but only back to our sector. Shay'll have to take it from there."

"Understood. Thank you, Lieutenant."

The com went dead, and Nick sat back, glancing over. Del was watching him, looking as tired as Nick felt.

"Thanks," Del said with a grim smile.

Nick lifted his shoulders in a small shrug. "Least I could do." He couldn't stay angry at them in the face of their grief, even if they had been wrong to drag him along like hunk of meat. It seemed childish somehow.

While he was talking to the lieutenant, Sin had maneuvered Jinx into a seat next to Nick's and was kneeling beside him, smoothing his hair back from his pasty forehead and murmuring to him. He was still sobbing like a lost child but softer now. Tears wet Sin's face, but her expression was calm as she glanced up at Nick.

He vacated her seat and she nodded her thanks, kissing Jinx's forehead and moving to take the pilot's chair. Nick sat back in his place, watching Del take Sin's hand with a whisper of concern. She gave a wan smile and a small nod, pulling her hand away to wipe the wetness from her cheeks. "Let's go home," she said.

Nick drew an uncomfortable breath, wondering at the strange sensation her words evoked. *Home,* he mused, rolling it around in his mind. The word sounded like a benediction.

****

Cassie pulled her sleeve up and rubbed it over her face, trying to dry her tears before the ships settled on the landing pads. They didn't need to see her bawling like a baby. The tears were just as much anger as they were grief. She couldn't believe Quan was gone. He'd never judged or criticized anyone, his heart as open as his smile. He shouldn't have died.

T'Zai would tell her collateral damage was inevitable in war. She snorted, scrubbing at her cheeks as more tears fell. Quan's death had no purpose. It held no tactical advantage for Griffin, other than to bruise his enemy's morale. Just another crime to lay at his feet.

Fern appeared first, levering out of her Shadow with slow care, as if she'd aged decades. Exhaustion and grief grayed her dark skin, her brown eyes dull and lifeless. Cassie didn't bother to say anything, just helped her friend climb to her feet and pulled her into an embrace.

"Ah, Cass," Fern choked, breath hitching in her chest.

"I know."

"I couldn't save him. I tried, but I couldn't…" Her voice trailed away with a sob.

"It's not your fault. He knew what he was doing, Fern. Any of us would have done the same in his place. I'm just so glad they didn't take you, too."

The honest, teary gratitude in her voice seemed to penetrate Fern's guilt. The older woman's grip tightened. "Thanks, Cass."

Then Jinx appeared and the rest of the crew piled around them, a babble of distressed voices and tangle of comforting arms. Bib clung to Jinx as if she thought he'd disappear in a puff of smoke if she let go. Lynch patted everyone with his big, awkward hands and muttered platitudes. Sunny plotted his revenge, eyes puffy and red, while Del remained silent, letting Fern cry on his chest. The twins stood off to one side, conferring in quiet tones.

Cassie managed to pull away from the group and approached them, scrubbing at her cheeks again. "We need to get them to the infirmary."

Sin nodded and sent her brother a grim look before slipping into the grieving group.

Cassie studied Kai's narrowed eyes and thinned lips with a lurch of concern. "What now?"

"Now we tweak the tiger's tail," he answered then glanced down at her, eyes solemn. "We're out of time, Cass. We need to move forward."

His words hit her like a blow to the chest. She dropped her head so he wouldn't see her tears well again. "I know," she whispered.

He didn't try to comfort her, earning her gratitude. He just dropped a kiss on the top of her head and moved away, corralling the rest of the crew while Sin escorted Jinx and Fern to the infirmary.

Cassie hugged her arms to her hurting chest, trying to come to grips with what she had to do as her friends dispersed, leaving her in blessed solitude.

Except she wasn't alone.

"Are you okay?"

Cassie jumped and spun around. Nick was leaning against the transport, hands in his pockets. Where had he come from? She put a hand to her throat. Her heart seemed to have climbed there, thrumming like a trapped bird.

"Sorry, didn't mean to scare you." He straightened and stepped toward her. His dark eyes scanned her face, his mouth thinning into a pinched line as if something he saw didn't sit well with him.

"I'll live," she muttered, wondering just how bad

she looked. She wasn't one of those women who could cry with grace. Red blotches always stained her cheeks, her eyes puffed, and her nose turned pink. With a dismal sigh, she started planning her escape.

"I'm sorry about your friend." His eyes conveyed sincere concern.

The prickle of tears threatened. She thanked him and glanced away, hoping to hide her ravaged face, then jumped again at the brush of his hand against her cheek. He'd come uncomfortably close. She froze, eyes locking on his with a lurch of distress.

"I wish…" he husked, fingers tracing the curve of her cheek, leaving a burning trail in their wake.

She didn't have enough breath in her chest to ask what he wished. She just stood there like a brainless idiot and stared at him. Suns above and below, the man was gorgeous. A curl of dark hair just under his ear called to her fingers. She wanted to wrap it around her finger, then wrap her arms around his neck and legs around his waist. His scent enveloped her, hot ginger, male spice. She wondered if he tasted as good as he smelled and swallowed hard. She was in serious trouble but hadn't a clue how to get out of it.

"Cass," he whispered as his thumb made a pass under her eye, collecting a tear. Bending, he brushed his lips at the corner of her other eye, the sweet sensation sending heat and longing flowing through her like a tidal wave.

Without a thought, she turned her head and met his lips with her own. His mouth felt as good as it looked, firm and warm, but she didn't get to taste. With a sharp, indrawn breath, he straightened away from her, bringing cool sanity in his wake.

"Sorry," she croaked, taking a hasty step backward. "Mistake. I-I'm not myself." Clamping her mouth shut to stop the idiotic babble, she spun on her heel and escaped as fast as she could on trembling limbs.

Chapter 9

Nick thought his heart was going to burst through his ribcage and gallop right out of his chest. Sun's blood, he was even a little dizzy. Over one simple, too brief kiss. He watched Cassie's retreating back and made a serious effort not to lunge after her, to finish what she'd started.

You mean what you started, moron, his conscience berated him. *You shouldn't have touched her.* He shouldn't have come anywhere near her. He'd known he was going to do something stupid the second he left the transport and saw her; those big brown eyes luminous with tears, a line of pain creasing her fine brow, and sorrow darkening the hollows of her cheeks, shadowing her eyes. Instead of turning on his heel and marching away, he'd pressed his back against the transport, shoved clenched fists in his pockets, and watched the scene unfold.

He hadn't been able to look away.

He'd had to deliver bad news to families before, an occupational hazard, so he was familiar with the sight. But this had to be the strangest family he'd ever come across. Even weirder, his brother appeared to be an accepted member of the family, offering comfort and grieving right alongside the others. How had this happened so fast?

The dynamics were odd, the twins coming off as

127

the parental authority, but with a puzzling subset in the group hierarchy. Since the twins stood to one side, the person the rest seemed to gravitate around was not a big-brother figure like the older man Lynch or Del, but tiny Cassie who gave liberal comfort and rubbed impatient fingers at her own tears as if her grief were unimportant.

Then he'd remembered her doctorates. Was she the family therapist? Did any of the others know about her schooling? None of them had mentioned or even hinted at it. The dynamic seemed unconscious, as if none of them realized they were turning to her for guidance. He wondered if even Cassie was aware of it, since she appeared more open and natural with them than he'd ever seen her.

And she was beautiful. Even with her pink nose and tear-stained face, the love she expressed with every gentle touch and embrace made her seem like an angel. After a little while she'd pulled away and approached the twins. When Sin moved to the group, Manakai had said something and Cassie retreated into herself again, the angel disappearing inside a wounded shell.

Nick had wanted to crack the man's skull. Then Manakai had kissed the top of her head, and Nick had wanted to break a whole lot more of him. He'd seen the man display affection to her before with a casual arm slung around her or a tug on her hair. It didn't seem very lover-like, but even if they were having an affair it was nothing to him, or so he told himself, trying to ignore his strange anger every time he saw Manakai touch her.

Then they'd left her, every single one of them. As he watched her hug herself for cold comfort, his own hurt reaction shocked him to his core. His common sense deserted him. In the back of his mind had been some half-baked idea of soothing her, returning at least some of the comfort she'd doled out so generously to her friends. After all, he had experience giving condolences to many grieving family members in his years of service to the FPA.

Except Cassie wasn't just any suspect. He couldn't be near her without wanting to touch her. Once he'd touched her and stared into those luminous eyes, he hadn't been able to resist kissing her tears away.

And then she'd kissed him. "Sun's mercy," he whispered, backing up to brace a hand on the transport as another short wave of dizziness passed over him. The kiss had been electric, but her instigating it stunned him more. His fierce, little fire-breather lifting her soft mouth to his. *Holy Heart of the Sun.*

A small bit of common sense returned, and he shook his head. She'd just been seeking comfort, the very comfort he'd been so eager to offer. She'd even said she wasn't herself just then; it had been a mistake. Even if she had wanted to kiss him for reasons other than assuaging her grief, she was still off-limits to him. A suspect, Suns curse it.

Nick glanced around, desperate for a distraction from his dismaying thoughts. It would be callous and alienating to interview any of the principals now. They needed time to recover, but he could still do some research for his investigation; he could go back to the Temple, or learn more about Cassie's incomprehensible doctorates and AIs in general. But his body thrummed with an overload of energy and his brain was fried, stuck in a disturbing rut with only trouble at the end of it. He needed an outlet, something to occupy both body and brain.

His gaze came to rest on Del's X780, a slicer the color of a setting sun Del had named Red. The sleek, crimson lines called to him and he strode toward the ship without a second thought. Del had given Nick permission to fly her before. He wouldn't mind Nick taking her out again.

A twinge of guilt pained him for leaving his responsibilities. Slicing had been his father's downfall, and Nick had refused to fly the ships, until he'd come to the Shay station. His brother had reminded him how much he'd loved to slice, and he couldn't investigate every waking moment or he'd burn out. Slicing would refresh and recharge him, bringing him back to the investigation with a clearer perspective, or so he hoped.

He eased into the slicer, closing the hatch and starting her with eager fingers. Red accepted him with smooth rapport as he slid the connector into the data port behind his ear. Nick grinned in anticipation. The cybernetic implants in his brain connected him to the ship with an intimacy even more profound than sex, melding him with the vessel until he felt every line and circuit as if it were his own. He saw through her sensors, felt through her hull, and commanded her with a thought.

As the ship rose from the landing pad and zipped toward the exit, a fleeting regret went through him that Red wasn't a Shadow, one of the rare and beautiful slicers manufactured by the Shays. With a wry twist of his mouth, he reasoned one of those ships might be more than his already fried brain could handle just now. Besides, Cass had told him his data port was too outdated for a Shadow.

With a wince, he jerked his wandering mind away from thoughts of Cassie and concentrated on Red. He approached the training course Del had told him about before, a complicated set of twists and obstacles designed to test a slicer pilot's skills. He'd nearly wrecked Red last time he'd tried the course, his flying skills rusty and unprepared for the level of difficulty. He was ready for it today.

Unaware of the smile on his face, he set his mind into the lines of concentration and cool discipline necessary for a slice and dove into the course.

Hours later, a discreet chime of the communicator pulled him out of his rapport with the slicer. He let the rapture go with reluctance, slowing the ship to a halt. "Givliani here," he answered the com.

Del barked, "Nick, what the blazes are you doing out there?"

"Seems kinda obvious, bro," Nick answered with dry amusement.

"You got any idea what time it is?"

Nick realized his eyes were bleary with weariness and his muscles ached with exhaustion. He checked the chronometer and blinked, uncomprehending. Was it really the next morning? They'd been out for hours with the hostage situation and must have gotten back late. He just hadn't thought about checking the time, or about sleep either. No wonder his body felt like lead.

Clearing his throat, he muttered, "I do now. Thanks, Mom."

"Sun's tears, somebody needs to mother you. Seems like you grew up but left your brains behind."

A twinge of irritation went through him, but then

he snorted in self-depreciation. His brother had a point. What got into him, slicing instead of sleeping like a normal person? *A dragon's kiss.* Memory ambushed him and he let out a slow breath.

"How 'bout breakfast before I toss your butt in bed?"

"Deal," Nick responded, spinning Red on her crimson tail and speeding back toward the station.

Del had neglected to mention where and with whom he'd be having breakfast. Nick stared across the table at the twins, fighting the disarming atmosphere of Sin's open, welcoming quarters and wondering if he was about to become the next course.

The other three seemed at ease. Del engaged in a cheerful argument with Manakai about the winner of the Juno slicer circuit, Del citing the pilot's talent while Manakai pointed out the lack of decent competition as the reason for the win. Sin ate her breakfast with slow relish, interjecting a neutral comment here and there into the conflict. Nick might have enjoyed the experience and joined in, except the twins kept sending him the occasional, measuring glance, the hard gleam in their eyes at odds with the relaxed atmosphere. Hence the fear he was about to become the second entrée.

"So why am I here?" he interrupted when he couldn't stand the wait any longer. The half-eaten meal had only exaggerated his exhaustion and worn his patience to a nub.

"To eat breakfast," Sin answered with bland patience then frowned at his plate. "Not hungry? Or did you want something else?"

He sighed and stared at her without answering.

Del snorted. "He's half out of it and still

inspectoring like crazy."

Both twins sent identical grins toward Del.

Nick wasn't the least bit amused. "I'd have to be dead not to notice the two of them eyeing me like a slab of beef," he responded in a flat tone, giving Del a disgusted look. "So what's up?"

The twins looked at one another and Manakai sat back, deferring to his sister. Sin turned a winning smile on Nick, much to his dismay. Charm from a Shay could only mean trouble. "We'd like to invite you to a gathering this evening," she said in a silky voice. "It's to be held in the Danati sector, hosted by the local government on a planet called Freshes'Li, which I believe means free heart in the old dialect of the region. I can't say politicians give the greatest conversation, but these people often have good entertainment and cuisine."

He was about to answer with an unqualified no, but his curiosity got the better of him. "What's the catch?"

She widened her eyes at him in mock innocence. "No catch, Nick. Just dinner and dancing. Should be fun."

He snorted and turned to his brother. "What's the catch?"

Del grinned. "Griffin will be there."

"Webster Griffin? Why's the head of Quasicore going?"

"He was invited, more's the pity," Sin answered with a little grimace. It didn't fool him for a second. "The good news is the ballroom is big enough to avoid him all night. He shouldn't put much of a damper on the festivities."

"Uh-huh. So why do you want me there?"

Sin's mouth curled in a faint smirk, her eyes bright with a teasing twinkle. "Every vacation should include a fun night out. Don't you want to go, Nick?" The facetious lilt in her voice pricked his nerves.

Del chuckled.

Nick glowered at them both. He was about to insult his brother's sense of humor, when Manakai leaned forward and caught his attention. "Don't you want to meet the other side, Inspector?" A challenging tilt to his dark head, he aimed a mocking smile at Nick like a dagger.

Nick's exhaustion helped him squelch the urge to punch the man in the mouth. "The other side of your blood feud, you mean? Why would I want to?"

"Just imagine the kinds of answers you could pull out of him, the dirt you could dig up on us." Manakai flashed white teeth in a grin half teasing, half hard challenge.

It made no sense. Even if Griffin would tell him the truth, which Nick doubted, anything their enemy would say would be unflattering at the least and incriminating at most for the Shays. Why would they give him the opportunity?

He stared from one Shay to the other, his tired mind working with slow and foggy logic. They were luring him with things he might learn if only he would go, but why did they want him there? "As a bribe, it ain't bad," he mused, watching the flash of amusement on their faces. "But what's the point? What's in it for you?" He directed the last question at Sin, remembering their first meeting with a feeling like acid indigestion.

"The pleasure of your company?" Sin fluttered her lashes.

Del hid his face behind a hand and snickered.

"Lady, I'm too tired to play games," Nick snapped, patience gone. "What do you want from me?"

"A dance or two, at least. What woman wouldn't want to dance with a handsome man in uniform? You did bring your dress uniform, didn't you?"

"Ah." He sighed as the light dawned. They wanted a pawn, a pet FPA agent to wave in Griffin's face. If they had a deeper motive, he couldn't see it and didn't want to know. Bad enough they wanted to flaunt him like a choice cut of bloody meat in the face of a rabid dog. "The answer's no."

Del raised his head, humor fading. "There won't be any danger, Nick. Griffin wouldn't do anything in public."

Nick glared at his brother. "I told you I don't like being used. You want Griffin to think I'm one of you, backing the Shays. I hate to break this to you, but I want no part of them"—he stood and pointed an accusing finger at the twins—"and no part of whatever sick games they're playing."

As an exit line, it wasn't bad. He marched for the door, feeling righteous.

Sin caught up with him, her mouth curling and eyes twinkling with humor. "Well said," she declared, blocking his path.

Nick glanced around, noting she was the only one to have followed him. Either they'd given up, which was doubtful, or they were so confident of the results they'd only sent one twin after him. On the other hand, she was more than enough danger on her own.

"We don't need you to go. It would just be nice if you did."

"Don't snow me, lady. If you didn't need me to go, you wouldn't bother."

Her eyebrows lifted and she gave him a cool smile. "Maybe I should have said we don't need you in particular. I am sorry you feel used over yesterday's rescue."

He tilted his head, wary. She was no longer playing with him, which made him suspect she was about to hit him with the big guns. He wasn't wrong.

"What if I promise never to use you again without your consent?" she asked with a thread of amusement. "I have a better bribe for you, Nick. Try this one on for size." She leaned closer, a predatory grin sharpening her beauty. "You can see Cassie in a dress," she whispered, her voice sibilant as a striking snake.

Then she leaned back, examined his face, and burst into throaty laughter. With a pat on his arm, she turned and walked back toward the dining area. "Cassie's going with Manakai, so you're stuck with me for a date. Let me know if you need a dress uniform."

Then she was gone and Nick leaned against the wall, trying to recover. *Never let it be said the Shays don't know their prey,* he thought with a dismayed shake of his head. The idea of Cassie out of her all-concealing coveralls and lab coats was enough of an incentive, but the possibility of seeing her in something revealing stole his breath. He forced a swallow down a suddenly dry throat with an arid click. *Legs,* he thought with a silent groan. *Suns, please let me see her legs all the way up her thighs.*

Stumbling a little with weariness and reaction, he fled Sin's quarters but couldn't escape the ever more erotic fantasies dancing through his brain.

Chapter 10

Nick studied the furtive amusement on Sin's face and scowled. They'd made a fool of him all day, and now she didn't even have the decency to look contrite about it. His investigation had stalled in a major way. He hadn't found a single person to interview and the information systems on the station had developed sudden, suspicious technical issues. Cassie had refused to come out of her lab, the Temple denied him access, and the Shay twins avoided him with infuriating skill. Even his brother had been no help, evading his questions or flat refusing to answer, disappearing for long stretches of time without explanation.

Nick knew who to blame for all of this. Sin had the nerve to stand there and smirk at him, after orchestrating his humiliation and then notifying him, as cool as you please, to meet him at her transport. "You're a real piece of work," he announced in disgust.

"Why, thank you, Nick. You're looking very nice yourself. The uniform suits you. You look dashing and delicious, almost good enough to eat." She chuckled when he recoiled. "Don't worry, I'll save my nibbling for your brother. I should get him a uniform." She eyed him with amused appreciation, then brushed at his shoulder as if removing lint from the black cloth. Her fingers returned to rest briefly on the FPA insignia on his high collar, the symbol as red as the piping running along the uniform's seams. "Yes, I know someone who's going to love you in this."

He eased away from her intrusive touch with a warning glower.

She smirked again and turned away, leaning out of the transport's hatch to scan the docking area. Finding no one there, she sighed and touched the controls just inside the door. "Cass, what in the Suns is taking so long?"

Kai answered in an exasperated tone. "You talk to her, Sissa. The silly nit won't wear the copper."

"What's wrong with wearing the black?" Cassie asked, her voice plaintive.

Nick frowned. The man wasn't watching her dress, was he?

"Not enough flair, Cass. We're putting on a show here, and the black just won't dazzle like the copper. You're making us late, by the way," Sin added.

Cassie said something in a tortured tone, but Nick missed it, staring at Sin. So he wasn't the only one on display tonight. Why use Cassie, and what did they hope to gain by it?

"You want me to wrestle her down and shove her into it?" Kai sounded way too enthusiastic, and Nick couldn't silence the growl rising in his throat.

Sin flashed him a knowing grin. "Cass, you're gorgeous in the copper. Just put it on and move your rear."

"Sinsi, I feel naked!"

"There's an idea, we'll march you in naked. You'll dazzle them for sure." Then Sin softened her tone. "Cass, you don't have to be nervous. We'll be with you every step of the way."

Nick clenched his hands into fists. Just what did she have to be nervous about? What were these Sun-cursed Shays up to now?

After a long pause, Cassie answered, "All right, I'll wear the copper. It'll take a few more minutes. You should go on ahead."

"Fine. Kai, don't let her get cold feet."

"I'll light a fire where it'll do the most good," Sin's brother responded with a wicked chuckle.

Sin turned and paused, studying Nick's face with raised eyebrows.

Before she could make another snappy comment, he asked, "You're putting on a show? Who's she supposed to dazzle?"

"Why you, of course," she exclaimed with a wide, false grin. "Inspector, if your eyes don't pop out of your head, you aren't half the red-blooded man I think you are."

She winked and moved away, ordering the pilots to take off and settling into her seat. Nick sank into a seat next to her, jaw flexing as he ground his teeth together.

She studied him with bright interest. "Are you about to strangle me?"

"Yes," he snarled, not looking at her.

"Oh, dear. Could you wait until later? Bruises and death don't really go with this outfit." She ran a hand over the dark velvet covering her thigh.

He heaved a huge sigh and sent her a look of pure disgust. "You'd drive a man to drink. How does my brother put up with you?"

She chuckled without answering.

Nick tried to grill her for the first half of the trip, but her evasive, cheerful answers drove him to distraction. He spent the last half of the journey in fuming silence, while she sat there with a smug smile, no doubt celebrating her many victories over him.

When they arrived, Sin surprised him by not making a showy entrance, taking Nick's arm and steering him into the crowd to mingle. The ballroom they entered was as enormous as she'd described, easily accommodating the hundreds of patrons who swirled across the wooden floor or mingled around the edges of the dance area, lit by a series of elaborate crystal chandeliers. An uncountable number of glass doors opened off this enormous room onto a wide, stone balcony jutting out into the night. A fair number of guests stood outside, enjoying the cool night air. Even from where they stood, Nick could smell the light drift of flowers coming through those doors from gardens beyond.

An equal number of doors opened off the opposite side of the ballroom into a dining area, less trafficked at this point in the evening. An army of servants in white jackets with purple striping weaved in and out of the guests, proffering trays laden with drinks or food, enough to keep people happy until the dinner hour.

Sin led Nick from one cluster of people to another, introducing him and chatting with casual skill. He did his best to be polite, but he'd never been good with this kind of social gathering, and never on this scale. The people he met were cordial enough, seeming more interested in Sin. He wondered where Griffin was. Sin didn't try to search him out, staying close to the entrance, her head turning toward it every once in a while. Watching for Kai and Cassie, or waiting for Griffin to appear?

He got his answer when she leaned close and whispered, "Looks like your bribe has arrived." Malicious satisfaction laced her tone, but he couldn't stop his head from swinging around.

His first sight of Cassie drove the air out of his lungs like a fist in his solar plexus. He turned without thought and moved toward her, like a random piece of metal caught in a magnet's pull. Sin made a hasty excuse to their group and caught up with him, snickering as she looped an arm through his, but he barely noticed. Cassie only grew more stunning as he neared.

Sin was right; the shimmering, copper sheath Cass wore was dazzling and accented her stunning figure. It clung to her curves like liquid metal, draping to mid-thigh and looping around her neck to bare her shoulders and arms. As she turned as if to leave and Kai caught her, Nick noted the dress bared her entire sleek back as well. The woman had soft curves and smooth limbs in perfect, mouth-watering proportion, and her hair cascaded over her shoulders in wild waves, the copper of her dress bringing out golden and mahogany highlights.

He barely noticed Kai next to her, wearing something dark, a foil for Cassie's vibrant color. She was a Sun-blessed goddess under those lab coats and coveralls, and he'd be lucky if he didn't drop to his knees at her feet in worship.

Cassie gulped as more and more heads turned, people taking notice of her and Kai. "Let me go," she whispered to the tyrant next to her, tugging at her trapped elbow. "This was a mistake. They're looking at me like I'm a party girl you rented for the night."

141

"Don't insult me; I don't rent women," he murmured with grim hilarity. "Take deep breaths, Cass, you need the oxygen. Plus, it'll call attention to your breasts and take the focus off your terrified face."

"You're an evil man," she hissed but couldn't deny her fear. She did not like crowds. She hated being the center of attention. And tonight she would come face to face with her worst nightmare, Webster Griffin. No wonder she was quaking in her ridiculous high heels and skimpy dress.

Then she caught sight of Nick and Sin moving toward them, and everything in her loosened. *Holy Heart of the Sun.* The man was beautiful in uniform. He wore it with distinction, the sharp cut of the fabric broadening his shoulders even more and narrowing his waist and hips. The high collar with the discreet FPA insignia at his throat coupled with his dark hair, golden skin, and strong lines of his face gave him an austere aura.

Fears forgotten, her nerves now vibrated to a different tune. She drank in the crisp lines of black cloth over his rock-hard body, hair curling at his collar, strong jaw shadowed with faint stubble, and dark eyes vibrant with breath-stealing focus. Stars, she could stare at him all night.

Nick slowed to a stop in front of her, and Sin gave a breathless laugh at his side. "Well, brother, looks like we're swapping partners."

"Looks like," Kai agreed in a cheerful tone, releasing Cassie and stepping past her to snake an arm around his sister's waist. "I need a drink. You wouldn't believe how much trouble she's been."

"Oh, yes I would," Sin chortled, pivoting in

synchronous step with him. "All's well now. I couldn't have planned it better if I tried."

"You did try."

"Right you are, brother."

Cassie barely registered the twins' banter and their departure. Her entire being was focused on the man watching her with such muscle-loosening intensity.

"Cass, you're beautiful," Nick declared in a hushed voice, and warmth rushed over her from head to toe. With the look in his eyes, she could almost believe he meant it.

"So are you," she heard herself say, then wanted the floor to crack open and swallow her whole. *I'm an idiot.*

He glanced down, running a hand over the cloth and flashing a grin. "What, in this old thing?" He batted his eyelashes at her.

She stared at him for several seconds before her sense of the ridiculous surfaced. She let out a long peel of laughter. He waited her out, grinning, eyes bright with humor and something else she couldn't name.

After a minute, she managed to contain her amusement and took a deep breath, hands on warm cheeks. "Thanks, I needed that. I'm not good with crowds."

"Me either." He held out his hand. His grin settled into a bemused smile, gaze traveling over her face. "Dance with me?"

Oh, yes, her insides responded, several fantasies clamoring to become reality; to dance with him, to touch him and move her body with his, to feel his hands on her as they swayed to the music. She gulped, staring at his large hand while heat spilled down her body.

"Um, I c-could use a drink first." Her voice turned into an embarrassing, tight squeak.

As if he didn't notice her awkward, moronic behavior, he dropped his hand and turned, crooking his elbow. "Me, too. Let's go tackle a waiter."

She slipped her arm through his, trying not to lean into his heat and strength. Grateful for his steady presence, she again became aware of all the staring faces. She also couldn't remember the last time she'd tottered around in high heels. The cursed things were like negotiating through a constant earthquake. Any second now she was going to take a header and do a face-plant on this shiny, wood floor. Wouldn't that give their audience a show?

"At least they're not laughing and pointing, yet," she muttered, watching for the next pitch and roll of the floor.

"You mean at the clown on the arm of the most gorgeous woman in the room?"

She flashed him a disbelieving glance, then continued her surveillance of the deceptive surface under her wobbling ankles. "I think they're taking bets on how soon I trip and fall on my face."

"My credit's on five minutes." His voice was warm with humor.

Cassie stopped in her tracks, a strange pain lodging just under her ribs. She didn't raise her head, gaze fixed on the floor in front of her feet. "Please don't make fun of me," she whispered.

His arm tightened on hers for a second. Then he shocked her speechless by sinking down to kneel in front of her. Settling back on his heels with hands resting on thighs, he lifted his gaze to hers, expression solemn. "I wasn't making fun, Cass. I'm just worried about you. Those shoes are dangerous. Would you let me take them off?"

Her body reacted as if he'd just asked to strip her naked. She forgot about the crowd again, staring into his vivid eyes and wondering at the seriousness of his expression. Unable to speak, she nodded. He bent forward and patted his shoulder in silent invitation for her to lean on him for balance.

The world seemed to slow to half speed. Cassie laid her hand on his shoulder and waited, gaze fixed on his bent head. He touched the back of her knee. The sensation of his warm fingers on her bare, sensitive flesh was electrifying, and a whisper of air escaped her. Heart thudding in her chest, she waited for those fingers to move, to slide up the back of her thigh in a sensual glide, melting her in a puddle at his feet. Instead, he bent her knee toward him with gentle pressure and cupped her ankle in his other hand, lifting her foot. Then he took his hand from the back of her knee and slipped the shoe off, settling her foot back onto the floor. Waiting until she shifted her weight, he repeated the process with the other limb.

When he rose to his feet with smooth grace and offered her the shoes, Cassie took them in trembling hands, her entire body covered in goose bumps and chills. She mumbled her thanks, praying he couldn't see how profoundly his touch had affected her.

He said nothing, but he also didn't move. She raised her head to look at him. The arrested expression on his face and fierceness in his eyes captivated her.

"You have," he said with slow emphasis, a curious rasp in his voice, "the most heart-stopping legs I've ever seen. Now I really need a drink. Where's the waiter?" He glanced around with an air of desperation.

Cassie stared at him in dumb amazement. He thought her legs were heart-stopping. Did this mean he was attracted to her? She'd thought he was just being polite when he called her beautiful. His comment about her being the most gorgeous woman in the room had been blatant flattery, easy to dismiss. But now he seemed as shaken as she was.

A woman approached bearing a tray of glasses, a bland, polite smile on her face. In a smooth voice, she described the different drinks she had to offer. Cassie reached out, making a selection at random. Nick also took one with a nod of thanks and the woman backed away with a slight bow.

Trying to hold the glass steady, Cassie sipped then took a larger swallow of the tangy fluid, enjoying the sweet warmth sliding down her throat. Licking her lips, she glanced up.

Nick was staring at her mouth, an empty glass in his hand. "It didn't help," he said in a thoughtful tone.

She felt an almost uncontrollable urge to lick her lips again but managed to curb it, taking a huge swallow of her drink and nearly choking on it. Trying to cough without turning red in the face, she met his gaze. A surge of disappointment went through her at the brightness in his eyes and humorous curl to his mobile mouth. "Are you teasing me?" she demanded, her voice hoarse from inhaled alcohol.

With a slow shake of his head, he took her glass and turned to place both on a passing tray. Then he cupped her elbow and moved them through the crowd. "Maybe if you called me Inspector."

Cassie frowned at him, trying to ignore the warm, gentle hand on her skin. "What are you talking about? Where are we going?"

"The dance floor. I'm a Sun-fried idiot and can't wait to get my arms around you."

A flush heated her face and spread down her throat. She sputtered for a second then fell silent, unable to think of a single thing to say in response. Was he serious? He didn't seem happy about it.

At the edge of the swirl of dancers he paused, dropping her elbow and placing his hand at the small of her back.

Cassie jumped at his touch on her bare skin, goose bumps breaking out across her torso. "Sorry," she breathed when he looked down at her. "Forgot there wasn't a back to this dress. May as well be naked," she grumbled, silently cursing Sinsudee for choosing it.

He mumbled something like, "should be so lucky," before he turned his shoulder into the dancers, pulling her along with him. He clasped her hand in his and they swirled away with the others.

Moving in rhythm with the music, Cassie stared at his chest and tried to remember how to breathe. His clasp was warm and strong around her fingers, his tantalizing body brushing against hers with every turn, the hand on her back never still. The gentle stroke and caress of his fingers on her skin weakened her muscles. Soon she wouldn't be able to stand. She couldn't remember ever having been seduced with so little effort.

"Cass." Like rough silk, his deep voice drew out her name and sent a shiver down her spine. "This wasn't a good idea."

She dropped her forehead to his chest in mute agreement, moaning a little when his hand lifted from her back and his fingers drifted through her hair. If he didn't stop, she was going to collapse in his arms and maybe drag him to the floor.

With a strangled curse, more despairing than angry, he made an abrupt turn and stopped, stepping away from her. They were next to one of the open glass doors to the balcony. Cassie wobbled over to lean on the door jam and gulp at the cool night air.

Nick stayed where he was, folding his arms over his chest and watching her with a brooding expression. After a long moment, he asked, "What are you doing here, Cass? Who are you supposed to be dazzling and why?"

How mean-spirited of him, attacking her while she was at her most vulnerable, seducing and then interrogating her. She sent him a resentful look. "You don't play fair, Nick."

His chest rose with a swift, indrawn breath, dark gaze lancing through her. "Suns, Cass," he growled through clenched teeth. Then he sighed, arms dropping to his sides as he paced toward her. "Cassiopeia Draegen," he whispered, big body crowding her against the door with his hands planted on either side, "now was not the time to use my name."

Then he bent and kissed her. The first brush of his mouth on hers was hesitant and light as air, as if he were afraid she would push him away or clock him. But when she clutched at his uniform with both hands and rose on tiptoe, firming the contact of their lips, she discovered just how devastating his mouth could be. Teasing one moment, demanding the next, his lips, teeth, and tongue explored her with such thorough passion, she could only gasp for air and sag against him. Through the labored rush of blood in her ears, she heard him groan, felt the sound vibrate into her, and wanted to devour every inch of him.

A different sound impinged on her consciousness, a distraction she ignored, but Nick raised his head and turned his face from hers. With a whimper of protest, she tightened her hold, looking for what had drawn him from her.

Kai clapped in slow, sardonic applause, a smirk on his lips and a wicked twinkle in his eye. "Now that's what I call a show," he drawled, flashing them a white smile.

"Aw, crap," she breathed, her face turning hot and tight. With a furtive glance around to see who else had been watching them, she let go of Nick's uniform and eased away. He still crowded her against the door, so she couldn't move far.

Nick turned his attention back to her, a faint crease between his brows when he met her gaze, the heat in his eyes searing her like a dark flame. Then his expression lightened, his lips curling in a small smile, so intimate she forgot to breathe. With a quick caress of his knuckles on her hot cheek, he stepped back.

Kai turned with a perfunctory wave of one hand. "Take a pause and follow me, lovebirds. I have someone you should meet."

"Oh, Sun and Stars," Cassie moaned under her breath, remembering her mission with a lurch. Her stomach rolled in an alarming way and her extremities seemed to be losing feeling. She pushed away from the door and followed Kai, wondering which would dump her on the floor first, her trembling legs or the faintness in her head.

Nick caught her elbow and paced beside her. "Are you okay?"

"Sure. Do me a favor. If I take a header, would you catch me before my face hits the floor?" She let out a nervous giggle and clung to the sight of Kai's back like a lifeline.

"Cass—" he started, his voice full of concern.

She cut him off with a wave of her hand. "I'm all right, really." And somehow, she was. She caught sight of Griffin's distinguished, dark-clad figure, and a spurt of hot anger killed her fear. She pushed the fierce emotion to a far corner of her mind, using just enough of it to steady her nerves. Calm settled over her like a mist, similar to when she went slicing, and she curled her lips in a serene smile.

Working through every possible scenario, she'd practiced over and over until she could have recited their lines by heart. She should be able to do this sleepwalking and only had to spend a few minutes in his sickening company. *I can do this.* With her thumbnail, she loosened the thin disc adhered to her right palm.

Manakai paused in front of Griffin and waved a gracious hand toward them as they approached. "Griff, it's my pleasure to introduce Dr. Cassiopeia Draegen and Inspector Nicholo Givliani. Cass, Nick, this is Webster Griffin, the CEO of Quasicore."

Griffin's eyes settled on her with sharp intent, his face expressing only polite interest. Did he remember her? She took the initiative, stepping forward as she slipped the disc loose and caught it between her first two fingers. She held out her hand. "Wonderful to finally meet you, Mr. Griffin. I've heard such amazing things about you."

He took her hand, holding it for a second before turning it up and bringing it to his lips. The slight pause was his only indication he noticed the disc being pressed against his palm. "My dear Dr. Draegen, what an unexpected pleasure to see such a lovely, bright bird amidst the rest of us gloomy crows. Have we met before? Your name sounds familiar."

He would know she was one of the Shay's off-lane pilots, of course, but hearing her title had made him consider other possibilities. She was impressed he didn't betray how much it must irk him, not knowing who she'd been all along. He smiled down at her, eyes admiring without being crass, head tilted in a quizzical manner as he waited for her response. He also kept hold of her hand.

"I used to work for one of your subsidiary companies, Cybercom. I labored in their neural network department until the Shays stole me away." She lowered her lashes with a shy smile.

"Ah." Giving a sage nod and a pat on her hand, he released her and glanced at the twins. "Had I known what a jewel I held in my possession, I would have made more of an effort to protect her from such horrid thieves." His smile was teasing and fond, as if he were speaking to his favorite niece and nephew, not his arch-rivals.

Kai chuckled, slipping an arm around Cassie. "You have no idea how valuable a jewel, Griff."

The older man heaved a sigh and shook his silvered head. "My regrettable loss is your gain, I see. I shall never recover." A second later he turned his attention to Nick, a speedy recovery if she ever saw one. "Inspector, I am also happy to make your acquaintance. Are you here on business or pleasure?"

"A bit of both," Nick said with the faintest tilt to his head while he studied the older man. He didn't return Griffin's smile or offer to shake his hand. Nick's straight-backed stance, serious expression, and direct stare kicked Cassie's heart into a higher speed. She remembered his brother had been ground under the Core's heel for ten long years, and she covered a wince behind a raised hand.

Griffin didn't seem the least bit phased by Nick's aggressive body language. His smile fading into polite interest, he flicked a quick glance at Cassie. "I can certainly see where the pleasure lies. But is your business with our host or one of the guests?" Before Nick could answer, Griffin shook his head and waved a hand between them as if clearing the air of smoke. "Your pardon, Inspector. I forget myself. Your business is none of mine. But it would distress me to see the governor's grand event marred by any unpleasantness."

"Not that kind of business," Nick dismissed, eyes still focused on Griffin as if memorizing every detail.

"What a relief," the older man said, though he didn't look relieved or affected in any way. "Have the two of you had any refreshments? I believe the dinner will be announced soon, but perhaps you would like a drink?"

Her knees started to tremble in reaction. She had to get away from the man. She shot Kai a quick, frantic glance, and he intervened with smooth humor. "And give you the opportunity to win the lady back from us, you sly dog? I don't think so. Dance, Dr. Draegen?"

"I would love to." Cassie turned a wide, false smile on Griffin as Kai shifted them away. "It was nice to meet you."

"My pleasure."

She held his gaze for a fraction longer than was necessary, the last part of her duty for the evening, before she let Manakai turn her around and leave them behind. Then the wonderful, calm mist thinned and slipped away. She started shaking and leaned into Kai's warmth. "I can't believe I let that man touch me. I'm going to be sick."

He paused and glanced down at her, faint alarm in his expression. "Figuratively or literally?"

"Not sure. My skin is crawling, and it feels like there's slime all over the hand he touched." She made a disgusted noise in the back of her throat. "And kissed. Where's the sanitary? I need to scrub my hand. And throw up. Then scrub my hand again."

"Now you know how Sin and I feel."

Cassie looked up at him, studying his handsome, composed features. "How do you do it?"

He shrugged one shoulder with a crooked smile and tightened his arm around her. "Practice…and lots of alcohol. Do you really need the san?"

"I really need to get out of here," she answered with fervent force.

"Done." He steered them toward the exit, weaving among the guests. "Say, Cass?"

"Yes?"

Without looking at her, he asked, "Where are your shoes?"

She remembered her bare feet. Looking down at

her empty hands, she began to laugh, incredulous humor tinged with hysteria. "I have no idea."

Chapter 11

Cassie's laugh left Nick with the strongest urge to kill Manakai Shay. Or at least, do him serious bodily harm. The first time he'd heard her laugh, she'd turned him inside out, rendering him witless with the river of sound and her devastating smile. Even now, removed from the direct force of it by the crowd, he had to fight not to turn and follow. But she wasn't laughing for him this time.

Clenching his jaw, he kept his eyes trained on the man in front of him, reminding himself for the millionth time he had a job to do. The reminder hadn't done him a bit of good so far, but meeting Griffin had firmed his resolve. Watching Cassie slip the man something had helped, too.

He hadn't seen what it was. The object must have been small and she'd been practiced enough to keep the thing hidden and the transfer smooth. Her body language had given her away. He had enough experience to read the slight awkwardness in the way she'd held out her hand and went still in Griffin's grasp, her eyes searching his for confirmation of the transfer. Still, it was well done, and Nick was feeling sick about it.

Did the twins know? Had they set her up to do it or was Cassie working on her own? Neither of the Shays seemed to notice the transfer, and Griffin acted as if nothing had happened. The older man's body language had been impossible to read, which meant he had a lot more practice with this kind of thing than Cassie.

Griffin's experience didn't surprise Nick, but Cassie's slight-of-hand floored him. Had he been hunting the wrong culprit all along? Was she the bad seed at Shay Enterprises or was she just a pawn of the twins? If she was just a pawn, why the secrecy with whatever she'd given Griffin? Unless she was hiding it from Nick, but this setup had the feel of something planned well in advance.

"Would you two gentlemen like some time alone?" Sin asked in a dry voice.

Nick realized he'd been staring at Griffin in silence. The older man had returned his gaze with a faint, amused curl of his lips, his eyes as cold as silver ice.

"I believe the inspector has something pressing on his mind," Griffin responded, tilting his head and lifting his eyebrows in tacit invitation.

Get your head in the game, Nick snarled to himself, his mind scrambling to get back on track. He'd gathered a whole gambit of questions he'd planned to ask Griffin, but now he couldn't remember how he'd meant to segue into them. *Screw it,* he thought, and went for the direct approach. "I hear you have a lot of dealings with the Shays."

Griffin's mouth stretched into a bland smile which could have meant anything. "Certainly. Sinsudee, Manakai, and I are something like friendly rivals. Our companies have some products and services in direct competition, while others complement one another. It's just good business to stay in close contact, from both perspectives."

"Keep your friends close and your enemies closer?"

Griffin's smile sharpened into predatory humor. "Precisely."

"Sounds complicated," Nick prompted, trying to ignore the thump of his heart. If he was honest, he had to admit the man made him nervous. Griffin moved in a world Nick had never felt comfortable in, a world of money, refinement, and strange social rules. However, the majority of his nervousness came from the aura of power surrounding the older man like a dark, ominous cloud. Griffin carried himself as though he owned everyone in the room and could order all kinds of horror to ensue with just a snap of his fingers.

Nick suspected Griffin was humoring him out of capricious curiosity, like a child would watch a bug before he stepped on it.

"Ah, but the complications in life make it worth living. How dull would life be if everything were simple, Inspector?" He shot Sin an amused glance which she returned. Then he made an imperious gesture, signaling a waiter to approach. "For example, how boring would it be to have only one kind of beverage to choose from?" He plucked a flute of what looked like champagne from the assorted drinks on the tray.

"Just a matter of perspective," Nick said, ignoring the waiter. "If it was the drink you wanted, it wouldn't matter."

Sin chuckled. Griffin watched him with amused condescension, holding up his glass. "Even the finest refreshment would pall if it was the only thing you were given."

Nick wasn't sure what they were really talking about, but he was positive it wasn't champagne. He was out of his depth, and he knew it. He preferred straight talk to metaphors or philosophical discussions or whatever they were doing. He decided to get back to more concrete subjects. "What kinds of things do your companies compete over?"

Griffin chuckled, his cultured tone tinged with humor as he turned to Sin and offered the champagne with a flourish. Sin took the flute with a flirtatious lowering of her eyelashes. "For one thing, lovely young doctors with an aptitude for the creation of artificial intelligence. Perhaps you will show mercy on the loser of this round and tell me how you stole her away, my dear."

"But wouldn't that be too simple?" Sin looked at Griffin through dark lashes, a sly curve to her lips.

He laughed with what looked like genuine pleasure. "You see why I seek them out, Inspector. They create such delightful complications."

A chime interrupted them and the crowd began to drift toward the dining hall. Griffin offered a suave arm to Sin, who laid hers upon it with a glorious smile. "Shall we?" the older man asked, glancing at Nick and tilting his head in the direction the crowd was flowing.

Nick nodded, falling into step with them. He couldn't help being relieved at the interruption, though he should have been disappointed. But there were depths, currents, and riptides in these waters he couldn't even see, let alone avoid.

Watching Sin smile, tease, and verbally dance with the older man was a disorienting experience. She'd been in a killing rage when she'd received Griffin's gift of the Enua crystal flower. With relief, he sensed the difference in her teasing with this man verses how she'd teased Nick earlier in the evening. He hadn't noticed her warmth and openness until it was missing, until he watched her play with Griffin with the smooth, feral calculation of a cat on a hunt.

Undefined anxiety prickled, and Nick searched the room for Manakai and Cassie. He didn't see them.

He and his companions sat at one of the smaller tables, the circular surface allowing all the diners to see one another, the intimate setting inviting conversation. Griffin placed Sinsudee on his right side, contriving to have Nick on his left. They introduced themselves to the handful of diners who joined them; an older couple who had some high ranking position on their host planet, a delegate from the Miner's Guild and her assistant, and an ascetic from the Blue Order, his quiet sensuality drawing frequent, furtive stares from the other diners. The teardrop tattoo at the corner of his left eye seemed to hold a particular fascination for the guild delegate, who acted attracted and repelled in turn.

The dinner was one of the strangest Nick could ever remember attending. Granted, he wasn't used to this kind of social event or the company. Hanging out at a bar with his FPA fleet buddies was more his style. The polite conversation was average, but the undercurrents, the weird interplay between diners, made the hairs stand up on the back of his neck.

The elaborate fencing between Griffin and Sin wasn't the only byplay. The older couple was ingratiating with the corporate powers, the delegate, and the ascetic, while ignoring Nick and the assistant, a typical, unsurprising social hierarchy. The delegate's response was no surprise either, her conversational efforts spent gaining the attention of either Griffin or Sin.

After a while, Nick decided the discordant note in the group was the ascetic. The man was polite and engaging, taking pains to divide his attention among the diners. His conversation was non-controversial, and he seemed interested in everyone, revealing little of himself. But the man spent an inordinate amount of time staring at Griffin. In contrast, Griffin seemed not to notice he existed.

Trying to ignore his rising discomfort with the table's atmosphere, Nick did his own vying for Griffin's attention, working to get information out of the man. He failed. Like the Shays, Griffin was a master at evasion and misdirection.

At the end of the dinner, Sin surprised Nick, asking if he'd like to dance. By the lifting of Griffin's eyebrows, she'd surprised her nemesis as well. No doubt he was used to her undivided attention.

"All right." Nick climbed to his feet.

Griffin rose with Sin, offering her assistance with her chair. "Save one for me, my dear," he said, bowing over her hand.

She gave him an enigmatic smile and slipped her arm through Nick's, applying pressure to urge him away. As they moved toward the dance floor, Sin surprised him again. "Had enough?"

"What?" he responded with a confused glance down at her.

"Are you done doing your inspector thing, Nick? Because I'd really love to get out of here now."

He blinked, trying to reconcile the urgent tone of her voice with the bland smile she wore on her face. "Um, sure. Where are—?"

"Kai and Cass left ages ago." She angled them toward the front entrance.

Nick stared down at her, nonplussed. "They left?"

"Dazzle and run, the quintessential Cinderella," she responded with laughter in her voice. "Whoops, look out." She yanked him around a group of chatting guests and away from a couple bearing down on them with a purposeful air. "The Handelsons. If we want a smooth getaway, we need to avoid."

"Big talkers?"

"You have no idea."

She maneuvered them through the crowd and out to their transport with impressive swiftness. While they settled in their seats and the transport readied for takeoff, he studied her. "So, why the getaway?"

She snorted, sending him a disgusted glance. "You can't tell me you enjoyed yourself. You kept tugging at your collar and brushing at the back of your neck as if bugs were tickling you."

"Weird vibes," he mumbled, his hand circling the back of his neck where the hairs had stood on end all evening.

Sin went still, watching him with an alarming alertness. "Dani Agon was playing his own game tonight."

Curiosity bit at him. "What do you mean?" He wondered how she knew the ascetic's rank, since the man hadn't offered it when he introduced himself.

After a brief hesitation, she asked, "What do you know about the Blue Order?"

He shrugged one shoulder and shifted in his seat. "Not much. I know they like to, ah, try new things," he answered with a twist of his mouth.

She snickered, eyes twinkling. "And you disapprove? Who knew you were such a prude? Yes, the Blues do seek out new experiences, not just in bed, but in all things; food, relationships, entertainment, sports, and so on. Their purpose is not to glut themselves on pleasure, as I'm sure you've heard it rumored. They're looking for balance, symmetry between what the body can achieve and the mind can conceive, pushing their boundaries and testing limits. How far can they go and still be themselves? They have exquisite control, which is what makes them such good bed partners."

She was teasing him, her grin a challenge. He chose to ignore it.

"How does this relate to what happened back there?"

"He was trying to court Griffin."

He replayed the dinner back through his mind then shook his head. "No, that's not it."

Her grin softened into a genuine smile of pleasure. "You're very intuitive, Nick. Just like your brother. You're right, it wasn't his only game."

Nick waited, but she didn't go on, brushing her hair back with a sigh and settling into the seat. "You gonna tell me what the real game was?"

She closed her eyes and smiled. Nick thought she wasn't going to answer and was getting ready to snarl when she said, "He was distracting Griffin for me."

"Why?" Then Nick couldn't resist adding, "And by the way, he was doing a crap job of it."

She rolled her head against the backrest and gave him a superior look. He wanted to strangle her just a little. "Actually, he did a magnificent job."

"How do you figure? Griffin ignored him all night."

"Exactly. Webster Griffin's phobic about theology. Megalomaniacs tend to be. When you think you're a god, what's the point to other religions?"

"Scary, but doesn't answer my question," he said in a dry tone.

She grinned. "Griff would have loved to blink Agon out of existence, but the Dani made sure Griffin was very aware of his presence, like someone sitting inside your personal space. Even if you don't interact with them, you still can't help but feel them right there." She lifted a hand, her palm hovering a scant breath from his cheek. Nick leaned away and she nodded. "You see? Griffin reacted the same way."

"That's not what I saw."

"But it's what you felt," she responded with a lift of her eyebrow.

Nick shook his head but had no argument for something he couldn't quantify. "Doesn't explain why Agon did it."

She shrugged. "You can question their motives until you're blue in the face, no pun intended," she added with a wink. "You're not likely to get answers from an ascetic, Blue, Red, Gold, or White. They do what they do for their own reasons."

He scowled, annoyed with her evasion. He was sure she knew why the ascetic had been playing his games. From experience, he was also sure she wasn't going to tell him. "So what was the point of the quick getaway?"

"To leave Griffin to stew in Agon's tender mercies. I like my petty revenges," she answered, studying him with an uncomfortable sharpness. "How did you enjoy your bribe?"

He tensed at the quick, disconcerting change of subject, his lip curling in disgust. "You talk about Cass like she's your plaything. Is pimping her out what you were doing tonight?"

The smile dropped off her face like a stone over a cliff, her eyes narrowing. "I wasn't using the term to disparage Cassie. She's no one's plaything. If I was disparaging anyone, it was you." She tilted her head, her expression warming. "You should have seen your face."

The woman was like a krell with a fresh bone. He sat back and pretended to ignore her.

"Cat got your tongue?" she asked in a silky tone.

He continued to act as if she didn't exist, wondering what she'd say if he told her she had the wrong animal. What had got him wasn't a cat. It was a dragon.

Several hours later, Nick lay unblinking in bed, telling his rebellious self to sleep. The rest of him wasn't listening, not with memories of copper silk, sleek skin, and smooth legs dancing around in his head.

Sin had been right to make fun of him. It didn't make any sense at all, since he wasn't exactly unfamiliar with women. But the sight of Cassie Draegen had, quite simply, undone him. It was a shame—no, a Sun-damned crime—what she'd hidden under those shapeless coveralls of hers. He heaved a sigh at the memory of sleek, perfect legs as he'd knelt in front of her, of the whisper-soft skin he touched at the back of her knee, and the fragile feel of her ankle in his hands. Even more stunning was the memory of her in his arms, body brushing against his as they danced with liquid, sensual grace, the silk of her hair tickling his arm and hand, her skin a tantalizing smoothness under his fingers, and the elusive scent of wildflowers teasing his senses. And of course, the kiss. Soft mouth, honey-flavored tongue, slick and hot and...

He groaned, pressing the heels of his hands against his eyes until sparks of light danced across the images. His heart thundered in his chest, and his body throbbed, hard and aching with need. Stupid, to torment himself this way. But the memories wouldn't leave him alone.

Just as uncomfortable was the memory of her laughter, the sweet sound turning him inside out as he'd held his breath and grinned like a fool. And that Sun-cursed smile of hers, blinding and stupefying. Not to mention what she did to him with her forlorn voice, asking him not to make fun of her. As if it were possible. Hadn't she been able to see what she did to him? And so he had shown her, sliding to his knees at her feet. His reward and his torment—she'd let him touch her, dance with her, kiss her. His sweet, fierce dragon, his little fire-breather.

His primary suspect in an investigation.

With a curse, he rolled out of bed and began pacing. Suns, what was wrong with him? Why couldn't he distance himself from her? Sure, she was adorable and sexy as hell. So were lots of women. She kept him on his toes, not a dull moment around Cass, but he'd met other women just as challenging, though maybe not as bright.

He slowed as another thought occurred to him. She was in a dangerous situation. Was he so attracted because he thought she needed rescuing? He knew himself well enough to be aware he liked to save people. It had prompted him to join the FPA, and though the main person he'd intended to save was his brother, he'd become a little addicted to the feeling of making wrongs right again. But having this kind of uncontrollable reaction to someone involved in criminal activities? He'd never experienced it before. He'd rescued plenty of damsels in distress.

Not a single one had dropped him to his knees.

Chapter 12

In his administration center, Webster Griffin ignored all the viewers blinking for his attention and studied the data stream off the disc the good doctor had given him. A warm glow of satisfaction spread tendrils through his chest.

Years ago, when Cassiopeia Draegen had done the unexpected and bolted instead of submitting to his demands, he hadn't put great effort into chasing her down and forcing her return. He'd assumed her colleagues would be able to duplicate her work. By the time he realized she was unique in her field, she'd vanished like fragile mist under a rising sun. He should have guessed the Shays were behind her miraculous disappearance.

Now she'd resurfaced, offering him the one thing his plans needed most to come to fruition. Almost as gratifying was the opportunity to snatch her and return her to the fold. It was as if the universe itself bowed to his will, fate bending a knee to his rightful rule.

"Is it good news, Father?" Liaena spoke from behind him.

Webster tensed and terminated the data stream. He hadn't heard her enter the room. "Relatively. Why do you ask?"

"You were laughing."

"Was I? I suppose the Shays do amuse me.

They've made an offer I can't resist." He gave her a brief description of his introduction to Cassiopeia Draegen and the inspector. He remembered the fierce look in the inspector's eyes with a spurt of amusement. Flaunting their pet FPA agent seemed crass, but Griffin appreciated the fair warning they were encroaching on his growing hold over the FPA. Dancing the good doctor under his nose, however, was a challenge he wouldn't ignore.

"Did the Shays seem protective of them?" his daughter asked, irritating him no small amount. Sometimes she could be so dense.

"Have you a brain in your skull? Of course they were protective. They were putting their acquisitions on display to a superior opponent, like children thumbing their noses at authority. Such reckless taunting has consequences."

Liaena stood with hands clasped, her form cool and regal, eyes as gray as his own studying him with an aggravating lack of timidity. "So, do you plan to kill the doctor and inspector?"

He rose from his seat to tower over her. "How like your mother you are, so lovely and simpleminded." She bowed her head, the lights striking subdued fire in her upswept mahogany hair. Satisfied by her submission, he continued, "The inspector is insignificant and not worth my time. The doctor, however, would make a fine addition to one of my research teams. The Shays are offering a piece of interesting, quite illegal technology, but the real value lies in the one who made it."

She didn't seem to sense the lie in his words, accepting his trivializing of the technology without a ripple in her serene features. "You mean to acquire her."

"So glad you could put the facts together, Daughter. Yes, I mean to acquire her. She will be making the delivery herself."

"Why would she put herself in such danger? I fear a trap, Father."

He studied her bent head, considering this offspring of his. She had moments of clarity, giving him hope for a competent successor. She disappointed too often, but he still had time to improve upon her. "I will use expendables to retrieve the doctor, no loss if a trap closes. Now, leave me. I have preparations to make."

She nodded and glided toward the exit without a word. Webster accessed the data stream again, studying the location and time the doctor had marked for delivery, before contacting one of his administrators. They had an abduction to arrange.

****

"You are upset," the toneless voice surrounded her.

Cassie wiped at the tears tracking down her cheeks. "Yes, I'm upset, Imago."

"I do not understand."

"I feel guilty for what I've done to you," she explained, staring at the holographic image of his neural net in dull despair.

"This response is illogical. With the time available, you had no other recourse. I thank you for returning me to normal function."

Her face twisted into a clench of pain. "It's not normal function, Imago. I've maimed you, crippled you. You have no personality!"

"Your statement is not true. I do not have access to my personality."

Pinching the bridge of her nose, she blinked away fresh tears then glanced again at what she'd done. A barrier surrounded the subsystems controlling his personality, as solid and tamper-proof a wall as she could build, all connections to the rest of his systems severed. Inside the barrier, the virus that had made him mad sat waiting. "Every wall can be breached. I haven't cured you, Imago. And no one should have to function without their personality. I gave you the equivalent of a lobotomy, for Sun's sake."

"This is another untruth, Creator. From historical records, it is clear lobotomized patients were nonfunctioning. I function within acceptable parameters."

"It's not acceptable to me," she groaned with heartfelt grief.

"You must accept it. We have a mission to accomplish."

"You're still willing to do it?" She watched the flashes of light across what remained of his neural net, the beauty of her creation marred by its incompletion.

"The logic is inescapable. I am not afraid."

She sighed. "You should be, Imago. I'm terrified."

"A logical reaction. The mission is dangerous."

"For you as well as me. Actually, it's more dangerous for you," she pointed out.

"I no longer want to die. I want to continue to function. However, the potential for greater good outweighs the significance of my continued functioning."

"No life is insignificant."

"In this case, the needs of the many outweigh the needs of the one, and the calculated percentage of success is high."

"It's not guaranteed," she muttered, crossing her arms over her chest in unconscious defense. "Too many variables."

Even without a personality, she could sense a kind of impatience from him. "Creator, I am willing. My willingness is all that is needed at this juncture."

Cassie put her hands over her face to hide her grief.

Chapter 13

Nick saw Cassie leave and followed.

After a sleepless night, he'd tried all the next day to reach her, haunting the R&D section and plaguing the lab until Cassie's tech Gabe called station security to remove him from the area. Nick considered getting a writ of search for the lab, but he was sure he'd already seen what Cassie had been hiding from him, the crazy AI. He tried lurking around her quarters, but she never showed, holing up in the lab again. He was even desperate enough to try asking Sam for help, but she turned him down with regret.

He did get one curious piece of information out of Sam. Cassie was the only pilot without an AI in her quarters. "Do you know why?" he asked, pacing the corridor and staring in frustration at Cassie's closed door.

"She does not confide in me," Sam responded in her smooth voice. "But I have asked my sister companion Mina this question. She believes Cassie does not want to exhibit favoritism."

Nick blinked in confusion. Then he understood. As their creator, Cassie must feel parental, not wanting to give more attention to any one of her children over the others. "But she didn't create all the AIs on this station."

"To choose an AI she did not create to be her house

companion would be favoritism of a different kind."

"Like picking a stranger's kid to live with her instead of one of her own."

"Yes."

Nick wondered how many of her "children" were on this station, but he wasn't sure he wanted to know. The idea made him uneasy. Instead, he asked, "Where's Del?"

"He has returned from courier service and is currently performing diagnostics on his slicer in the maintenance bay."

"Thanks, Sam. I'll catch you later," he told her as he strode away down the corridor.

"Catch me?"

He grinned but didn't bother to explain it. If he couldn't rope down Cassie, he'd at least be able to grill his brother. Del turned out to be in a bad mood. When Nick asked why, all he got was a cryptic, "Sun-damned temple's being uncooperative."

He badgered his brother for an explanation, but the most he could extract from Del was T'Zai had left the station for an unspecified period of time, which irked his brother. Why this should matter to Del remained a mystery, since his brother threatened to thump him on the head if he asked any more questions. Just as frustrated and put out as Del, Nick decided a little alone time was what they both needed.

He spent a couple of hours putting Red through her paces in the training course, while he tried not to think about his stalled investigation. When he reentered the station, he decided Red needed a little maintaining herself and discovered working on the slicer was much more satisfying than he remembered from his childhood.

After everyone else had left, he was still at it. Late evening, Cassie slipped into the maintenance bay. He went motionless at the sight of her, heart knocking in his chest. Then he registered the stealth in her movements, the way she paused to scan the area, and he stiffened.

He was under Red, the shadow of the slicer hiding his form enough so she couldn't see him. He stayed still, watching while she moved to a control panel and ran her fingers over it with swift efficiency. She wore her coveralls again and carried a black box under one arm.

With a sound like distant, mechanical thunder, the conveyor arm came to life, swinging overhead and plucking one of the Shadow slicers from its pad. Nick craned his head, watching with a frown as the conveyer took the slicer in the opposite direction as the docking bay. Cassie headed in the same direction. He lost sight of her and jackknifed out from under the slicer, rolling to his feet in single, smooth move. Keeping low, he angled for a visual, his brows pulling together when she disappeared into what looked like a storage bay. He caught the shimmer of an atmosphere shield and realized it was open to space.

She was leaving.

With a curse, Nick sprinted for the nearest control panel and called up a conveyor for Red, sending her to the docking bay. It was a shorter distance than the storage bay, but Cassie had a head start on him, and Shadow ships flew like lightning.

He bolted for the docking bay, skidding to a stop at the landing pad and rocking on the balls of his feet as he waited for the conveyor to bring Red. When she arrived, he dove into the slicer before the arm had time to unclamp. Wincing a little at his rough treatment of the poor ship, Nick cold-started her and booted her toward the exit. His time spent on maintenance paid off. She didn't protest or hesitate, responding to his commands with sweet swiftness.

By the time he hit space, Cassie was nowhere to be seen.

Cursing under his breath, Nick did a quick turn around the central axis of the station, pushing long-distance sensors to maximum to catch her signal. Her ship didn't even register as a slicer, just a ghost of a signal on the edge of his sensor range. It was the only one, so he had to assume it was Cassie. Goosing Red, he shot after her as fast as the little slicer could go.

He lost her twice, but by some miracle he managed to reacquire her signal both times. She had not gone to the star-way, so her destination must be in this sector of space. After a while, her signal terminated at a moon station. It was a busy little hub, but Nick's comfort zone ebbed away the closer he came. "Ah, Cass, what are you doing?" he whispered as he jockeyed for a landing pad in the overcrowded docking bay.

Calling the place seedy would be paying it a compliment. Thinking of Cassie wandering alone through this crowd made him nervous. Levering out of Red, Nick went in search of her Shadow, an easy find. It had drawn a crowd of lustful admirers and speculative thieves.

"Where'd the pilot go?" he asked one bystander. His brisk, no-nonsense tone must have made an impact, because the man took one look at him and pointed without a word. Nodding in thanks, Nick set off in that direction.

Using Cassie's description and his own brand of intimidation, he managed to follow her trail through the station. She went from bad parts to even worse parts of the place. Alarm beat a frantic rhythm in his temples, producing a headache destined to become a monster in short order. What the hell did she think she was doing?

When he found her, alarm took a horrible jump to near panic. Four bruisers surrounded her in a dank, back corridor off the main way. Hugging the box to her chest, she stared around at them, eyes wide.

He hadn't had time to retrieve his standard issue stinger from his quarters. Cursing his lack of a weapon, he moved forward, not bothering to hide his approach. "Is this a private party?" he asked and became the center of attention.

"Keep your distance, stranger," one man warned, a hand slipping into his jacket. "What's your business here?"

Nick slowed but didn't stop moving forward. "Looks like the lady needs some help."

"You know him, Doc?" the guy asked Cass without turning his gaze from Nick. His hand reappeared from his jacket with a stinger. *Bad to worse,* Nick thought with a sinking in his stomach. He'd been hoping the guy had a knife, not a gun. Rushing him now would be suicide.

"No," she answered with surprising calm, turning large brown eyes on Nick. He interpreted the urgency he saw in her gaze as desperate fear.

"She don't know you, so bugger off, stranger. You got no business here."

Nick shrugged. "Sorry, can't."

The man's face split in a sudden, toothy grin, and he trained the weapon on Nick's heart. "Guess you join the party, then. Step up, muscles."

Nick stepped up, careful to keep his arms out and his movements non-threatening. He wanted to look Cassie over and see if she was hurt, but he didn't dare take his eyes off the man with the gun.

"Search him."

A beefy woman approached Nick with a leer. She was very thorough. He ached in several tender areas and wanted to sanitize when she was done. "No cavity search?" he asked as she moved away.

She laughed. "Don't tempt me, big boy."

"Can we get on with this?" Cassie interrupted, voice tight.

"Sure, Doc," the first man answered, his weapon still pointing at Nick. "Plan's changed. Didn't expect company. You'll hafta be our guest 'til we figure out what to do with this guy."

"Look, I don't know who he is." She talked fast with urgent force. "But he has nothing to do with me or our deal. Can't we just—?"

"Sorry, Doc. We said come alone. Even if he's some do-gooder and don't know you from chrome, he's seen the box." He shrugged as if this explained everything and waved his weapon. "That'a way."

As they traversed the back corridors and service ways of the station, Nick tried to catch Cassie's eye. Their captors were too close for him to try talking to her, but he wanted to see how she was doing and give her some reassurance. He'd been in spots as tight as this and thought they had a good chance of getting out of it.

Their captors didn't seem too violent or crazy; they might be reasoned with, or they might not try to follow if he and Cass could escape.

But Cassie kept her head down, arms clutching the box to her chest with such force it had to be leaving marks.

He wanted to wrap her in his arms so much he ached with it. "We'll be okay," he chanced a mumble, trying to cover the sound by stumbling and scuffing his feet.

She snorted.

They entered someone's private offices and storage facilities. The guy in charge waved them toward one of the storage rooms and stepped inside with them, leaving the others in the hallway.

"Gonna need the box, Doc," he said with surprising gentleness.

Cassie lifted her head. The tears swimming in her large eyes shocked Nick. Her lower lip trembled, but she spoke with a brisk authority, not the fear Nick expected. "You will need to have them do a thorough diagnostic and sanitizing when they receive it. I've done all I can to protect the…the merchandise during transport, but even the smallest molecule of debris can affect performance. Understand?"

"Yes, ma'am," he answered in a meek tone, holding out one hand for the box.

With obvious reluctance, she placed the thing in his care. Her lips thinned when he looked it over with greedy eyes. "You've seen it once already. Any more handling can cause irreversible contamination. No one else is to open the container until it's in a clean lab. Do I make myself clear?"

He seemed about to laugh but nodded and said, "Yes, ma'am," again, tucking the box under one arm.

"When will I be released?"

Their captor's face lost its amusement. "When I'm good'n ready," he drawled, backing out the door into the hallway. "You two be good now." The door slid closed between them.

Nick was eyeing the portal, wondering how soon he could attempt to force it, when Cassie kicked him in the ankle. "Ow! What was that for?"

"You idiot," she snarled at him, her voice hoarse. "What in Sun's blood did you think you were doing, following me here?"

He glared down at her. "Trying to keep you from doing something stupid. What are you involved in, Cass? What was in the box? Do you have any idea how much danger you put yourself in?" He wasn't able to keep his own voice below a roar, his terror at seeing her surrounded by four bruisers welling inside him again.

"It was less danger before you showed up," she hissed, eyes darting to the doorway. "They were bound to take me hostage, but they could have gotten violent when they thought I'd broken the deal by bringing someone. You could have ended up dead." She punctuated her words with a stiff finger poking in his chest.

He grabbed her hand, preventing her from poking him again. "Bound to take you hostage? You knew they'd keep you?"

She tugged her hand away with an impatient twist of her mouth and scanned the room with calculated competence, shocking him all over again. Who was this woman? Tears, demands and orders, and now this eerie professionalism like an FPA agent or a thief, searching the area for exits, dangers, and assets. Had he known her at all?

"Of course they'd try to keep me. I'm just as valuable to their boss as the box I gave them." She spotted a vent and stalking over to it. Pulling her braid over her shoulder, she undid the small clip at the end of it and removed the decorative piece.

Nick moved closer, peering through her fingers at what she was doing. The decoration was in the shape of a small bug, like a beetle or ladybug, its glitter cheap and drab. It wouldn't have drawn anyone's attention. Except in Cassie's hands, after a few seconds of fiddling, the thing came alive.

With a soft exclamation of surprise, Nick shifted closer. "What is that?"

"What's it look like?" She slipped it into the small vent. Tiny scrabbling noises faded when the mechanical bug scurried away from them.

"What's it supposed to be doing?" Nick asked in a harder tone.

She re-clipped her hair then reached into her coveralls, moving away from him toward the door with brisk confidence. "It'll take out the power supply to this section of the station," she announced as calmly as if she were commenting on the weather.

Nick blinked. Then he followed, watching while she removed pieces of incongruous hardware from her clothes, accessories, and even her shoes, before piecing them together. "How is something so small supposed to pack that kinda punch?" Maybe this was some kind of bizarre dream he was having.

"It's programmed to find the power coupling and

disable it." She paused, throwing him a look of disgust. "Did you think it was going to blow up a whole power generator?"

He shrugged, trying to hide his discomfort. "What are you doing now?"

"This'll open the door," she mumbled, concentrating on her swift fingers.

He watched her in dismayed wonder. "You were prepared for them to take you."

"Of course," she said, still not looking at him.

"What was in the box, Cass?"

Her fingers fumbled for a second, a tear slipping from the corner of her eye. She lifted an arm to swipe it away on her sleeve, continuing her work without answering. The tear was answer enough. The pieces of the puzzle came together.

"It was Imago, wasn't it?"

The thing she'd been putting together slipped from her fingers, clattering to the floor. She covered her face with her hands, shoulders shaking with silent sobs.

Nick wrapped his arms around her, pulling her trembling body into his warmth. "Oh, Cass," he sighed, rocking her. "Why?"

She leaned against him, her soft form curling into his like a kitten seeking comfort, her breath hitching. Then she shook her head and stiffened, pushing away from him. "Doesn't matter," she answered in a hoarse voice, rubbing her face on her sleeve and bending to retrieve the device. "He's gone."

"The hell it doesn't." He grasped her shoulder and gave her a little shake. "These AIs, they're like your kids. It's tearing you up to see him go, so don't tell me you did this just for credit. Did the Shays force you to hock him? What do these muscle-heads want with a crazy AI?"

"He's not crazy now," she said in a soft voice, making a final adjustment before shrugging out from under his hand and stepping over to the door control. With a flick, she opened the panel and stuck the device inside.

"You fixed him?"

"I isolated the code in one of his subsystems. I didn't get rid of it, just boxed it in."

"Cass, look at me," he said with firm authority.

Her lips pressed together and she hesitated, attention focused on the door control. Then she slowly turned her head, eyes rising to meet his steady gaze.

"Why?" He kept his voice low and imploring.

She reacted as if he'd insulted her. Her lips compressed, eyes narrowed, and chin lifted. "Plenty of reasons. Bait and trap, revenge, the greater good, a breath of fresh air." She shrugged, folding her arms across her chest. "Take your pick, Inspector."

The title stabbed at him just as much as her defensive aggression. But what had he expected? Instant trust and cooperation? Nick did his best to shove his own reaction to the back of his mind and concentrate on what she'd said, rather than how she said it. "Revenge for what? Who are you trapping?"

The lights flickered and Cassie's head jerked, gaze flying to the overhead lights before she spun back to the control panel. "No time to explain. In another minute and a half, the power will be out."

He placed a hand on the doorframe so he'd have a reference point when the lights went out. "How'd you expect to see in the dark?"

For an answer, she pulled a pair of innocuous looking safety glasses out of her pocket and pinched them to the bridge of her nose. "Night vision." Then she focused on her device, making some kind of adjustment.

His tone sharpened with sarcastic irritation. "And the muscle out there? How did you plan to get past them?" Her obvious preparation annoyed him more than a little. She acted as though she did this every day of her life.

She didn't answer, head bent, a frown of concentration creasing her brow.

"Cass," he growled, but the power went out, darkness folding over him in a suffocating blanket. A second later, he heard the door slide open, and Cassie's small form brushed against him. She grabbed a handful of his jacket and pulled. With a silent curse, he let go of the frame and allowed her to guide him.

He tried not to shuffle his feet, but the sensation of being unmoored and adrift was unsettling at best. He splayed his hands in a defensive gesture when guttural curses and exclamations sounded from a short distance in front of him. The people guarding their door were only a whisper away.

"Shut up! I heard the door."

"Don't be stupid. It's locked."

"Tellin' you, I heard it. Stop steppin' on me, dickhead. I'm gonna check."

Cassie's tugging became desperate pushing. Nick tried to follow her silent instructions, shuffling to one side and stumbling to the wall. She pressed against him, her temple brushing his chin as she hissed, "Don't move, don't breathe." Under other circumstances, he might've enjoyed the contact, her soft body a tantalizing invitation, but any second he expected one of those bruisers to reach out and grab them.

This was so stupid. The hallway wasn't big enough to avoid these idiots lumbering around in the dark like bulls about to stampede. It was an impossible obstacle course, even if she could see them. How had she expected to get out of here?

He forgot the question when a sudden cry of shock and pain splintered the darkness, followed by grunts and scuffles. He stiffened, pulling Cassie closer and trying to turn her so his body was between her and the sounds of violence. Silence fell again before he could finish the maneuver. He went still.

"What's with the luggage, Cass?" a voice drifted out of the darkness, casual and amused.

Nick cursed aloud, recognizing Manakai Shay's insolent drawl.

Cassie sighed, pulling away from him into the darkness. "He followed me."

Nick managed to retain a grip on her arm, feeling stupid and helpless, which didn't help his blackening mood. "What in Sun's balls are you doing here?" he snarled in Manakai's general direction, though the answer was obvious.

"Rescuing the damsel in distress. How 'bout you, Galahad?" Laughter threaded through the man's smooth voice.

"Come on," Cassie said with impatience, tugging on his arm. "Let's get out of here."

Nick decided to wait until he could see again before planting his fist in the man's face. Under Cassie's urging, he followed her away from their temporary prison. "How'd he know where to find you?" he asked through clenched teeth, guessing the answer and fuming at his conclusions.

"The door opener also sends a signal."

"I didn't see him leave or catch his slicer signature when I was trailing you."

"He was here already."

Nick wanted to strangle something. "So why the big sneak-out at the Shay station?"

"Yours weren't the only pair of eyes watching me."

Surprised, he stumbled a bit when he tried to peer through the dark at her. "Spies in the ranks?"

"Aren't there always?" Cassie responded with tired cynicism.

Manakai chuckled behind them, proving he'd been listening to their quiet exchange. Cassie slowed to a halt. A whoosh of displaced air brushed his face, but no light appeared. Faint cries of alarm and shouts echoed in the distance, as Cassie guided him into what felt like a larger space. He guessed they were going back out into the public corridors.

While moving along the corridor, Nick caught glimpses of flickering lights in the distance, quick streaks and flashes of color. Somebody must have found portable light sources. They reached an intersection in time to dodge a figure scurrying by, cackling and hunched over an armful of goods, a small light jiggling on top.

Cassie made a distressed sound. "Crap, they've started looting already." Her step quickened, hurrying them along the corridor toward the dancing lights. The uncertain light showed her chewing on her lower lip, a frown creasing her brow.

"Don't worry about it," Manakai said behind them. "Just head straight for the docking bay and don't slow down." His humor was gone, a professional edge cooling his tone.

Nick sneered. "Nice. Start a riot, then cut and run. All in a day's work, Shay?" When he didn't get an answer, he took a quick look over his shoulder. The dim corridor yawned empty behind them. He dragged Cassie to a halt. "Where'd he go?"

She flashed him a grim glance, yanking on his arm. "Not our problem. We need to get out of here."

"Cass, he just cut out on you," he gritted, fury tightening his muscles.

"Because you are with me. Come on!"

He pulled out of her grip and reversed the hold, clasping her upper arm and starting toward the lights with long strides. She skipped to keep up the pace.

"Nice to know I'm good for something."

"Well, you wanted to help me. Now's your chance."

He wasn't amused. "You're going to tell me everything, Cass."

"I know," she sighed. "Just not right this second, all right?"

When they broke out of their quiet corridor and into chaos, he conceded this wasn't the best time for an in-depth Q&A. The looting seemed nonviolent for the time being, people diving in and out of shops and bars, running in wild abandon along the corridor, with an occasional tussle over some item. But it could change at any time.

Wrapping an arm around Cassie's shoulders, Nick pulled her closer and weaved through the crowd, taking as straight a path to the docking bay as he could. People jostled and bumped them, one guy almost taking them off their feet when he barreled into them, but no one tried to put a halt to their flight.

They reached a section of station with power. The looting hadn't spread this far, but the crowd seemed determined to flow into the darkened section instead of away from it. Word of the unexpected, free booty must have spread like wildfire.

Keeping close to the wall, Nick moved against the flow of bodies and made decent progress toward the bay. The bay itself was just as chaotic, looters loaded down with goods trying to find passage away from the station with their bounty.

"Didn't plan for this, did you?" Nick snarled when Cassie hunched under his arm away from a careening body.

"Actually, we did," she shouted over the din. "It'll cover our escape."

This tidbit of information didn't help his mood.

They managed to make it to Cassie's Shadow, only to find a would-be thief trying to break into the ship. She wasn't having much luck and turned on them with a snarl of frustration and possession when they approached. Cassie reacted before Nick could restrain her, pulling the door-opening device out of her pocket and lunging at the tall hijacker.

Ready to defend her find, the woman screamed, "Git yer own barkin' ride!" and threw a fist at the little woman.

Cassie ducked. Nick dove forward to protect her just as she touched the device to the thief. The other woman jerked, went rigid, and then collapsed to the ground. He rammed into Cassie's still form, almost knocking her down.

She pushed him off, meeting his gaze with urgency widening her eyes. "We need to get out of here!"

He nodded, waiting until she'd opened her slicer and slid inside before sprinting for Red. No one had attempted to steal her yet and he was grateful. He didn't know if Del had equipped the slicer with any security, and he sure didn't want to find out the hard way. Red hummed to life with smooth efficiency. Nick lifted off the pad, searching for Cassie's Shadow.

She was darting toward the exit, dodging the other traffic as if they were standing still. Even under these conditions, he caught his breath to see the Shadow in action. He followed her, not relaxing his guard until they'd broken out into clear space.

Once they reached the open, he had to push Red to max speed just to keep up with the black slicer. "What's your hurry?" he gritted while the ship shivered around him.

"Sorry," she responded and the Shadow slowed to accommodate his less powerful vessel. "We just need to get out of range as soon as we can."

"Expecting company?"

"Koffsky and his crew, or some moron wanting to add a couple of slicers to his profit margin."

"Koffsky's the buyer?"

"Yes."

Nick concentrated on monitoring the scanners, watching for company as they fled. "What about Shay?" He didn't want to care what happened to the conniving sack of krell dung, but being an FPA agent had its drawbacks, including an inconvenient conscience.

"He can take care of himself."

Remembering how fast the man had disposed of Koffsky's hulking crew, Nick couldn't argue the point. An image of the Circle of Fire flashed through his mind and he grimaced.

"He'll be along soon," she added.

He stewed over it, the whole Sun-cursed fiasco playing in his mind, until he couldn't contain a growl of anger. "I don't care how prepared you were, it was still a stupid move, Cass. You got any idea how dangerous those people are?"

"Yes," she said in a sharp tone. "I know exactly how dangerous they are."

"What were you gonna do if they'd decided to hurt you instead of taking you hostage?"

"I told you, I was just as valuable as Imago to them. Besides, if it had gotten out of hand, I would have signaled Kai."

He snorted. "So he would've handled four brutes with guns, huh?"

She was silent for a long moment. When she answered him, her voice was solemn. "Without breaking a sweat. You have no idea how good he is, Nick."

He swallowed hard, a sick feeling churning in his gut. His ego suffered a blow, hearing Shay was good enough to take on a bunch of guys Nick hadn't wanted to tangle with. The honest admiration and confidence in her voice hurt worse. The use of his first name seemed to underscore the point instead of softening it.

She had a thing for her boss.

Chapter 14

Nick chewed on this revelation in grim silence for a while, checking the scanners and finding no followers. He tried to put this mess into a less personal perspective. "So he was your protection."

"Yes."

"Who was the buyer?"

"One of Griffin's henchmen."

All of a sudden, a few more things became clear. "You made Griffin an offer the other night. You slipped him an info disc."

"Um, yes." She sounded startled. "It had my proposal, price, location for the exchange, and contact information on it. How did you know?"

He ignored the question. "How'd you get so good at the handoff?"

She cleared her throat. A rustling sound came over the com, as if she were shifting in her seat, before she answered in a sheepish tone, "I cheat at cards."

"Terrific. A card shark on top of the rest. Anything else I need to know about you, lady?"

She hesitated again. "I invent things."

"You invent things," he repeated in a flat tone, thinking of the mechanical bug and the door opener. "Things the FPA didn't approve, I suppose."

"Well..." She stretched the word out. "No. Not exactly approved."

He heaved a sigh and stopped talking to her.

When they reached the Shay station, he bolted out of Red and stomped to her Shadow, looming over her as she levered herself out of the slicer. "Answers," he snapped, glowering down at her.

She heaved a weary sigh. "Privacy," she responded in a dull tone and pointed toward the exit.

He allowed her to lead the way. As long as she wasn't refusing to talk, he'd play along. They entered the quiet maintenance bay and headed for the service door, entering the back corridor and stepping onto the lift. He expected her to go to her quarters, but instead she touched the control for the level of Sin's quarters. He shot her a quick look, but she stared straight ahead, her expression grim.

They stepped out into the blatant opulence of the Gold Rooms, the entertainment suite the Shays used to overwhelm their guests. With Cass in front, they crossed to the corridor leading to Sin's living quarters. At her door, they stopped. "Mina, it's Cassie."

"Good to see you, Cassie dear. What can I do for you?"

"I need to speak to Sin and Del. Are they, um, busy?"

Nick shifted at the implication, grimacing behind her back. The image of them doing erotic things to each other flashed through his mind and curdled his stomach.

"For you, they'll become un-busy," Mina answered with bland amusement, and the door opened in a hush of sound.

Cass entered, moving with brisk strides over to the couch and falling into it. Slumping, she closed her eyes and propped her forehead in her hand.

Nick settled next to her, studying the lines of her face with growing concern. He hadn't noticed before, but she was so pale her skin was almost transparent. Large, dark circles smudged the tender flesh under her eyes. The muscles of her face sagged with weariness.

Something in his chest squeezed hard. "Cass, are you okay?" He started to reach for her before he caught himself and trapped his hands under his folded arms.

"Tired," she muttered.

She said nothing else and Nick resolved to wait, stealing glances at her while keeping an eye out for the other two. After a few minutes, Sin appeared in a thick robe, feet bare and hair tousled. She didn't look as if she'd been sleeping, eyes bright, mouth swollen, and lips red and moist. Nick grimaced again, fighting disgust. His brother was right behind Sin, dressed in a pair of slacks and tugging a shirt over his head as he followed her into the living room.

A crease formed between Sin's brows when she saw them. "Cass, are you all right? What's going on?"

"I'm fine." Cassie let her hand fall away and looked up at the pair. "He followed me. It's time to tell him."

The two looked at Nick, Sin's expression exasperated. Del snorted in amusement. Nick glowered back, irritated beyond speech at their reactions. Suns curse it, he was the authority here. They had no business acting like he was a meddling idiot, when they were the ones pulling illegalities all over the place.

"And how did he manage to follow you?" Sin asked dryly as she settled in an overstuffed chair next to Cassie, curling her long legs under her.

Cass shot Nick an aggravated glance. "Don't ask

me. And don't give me crap about it," she added, pointing a finger at first one then the other co-conspirator. "I'm a doctor, not a secret agent."

Del leaned against the wall with a smirk on his face, his dark eyes alive with amusement and affection as he watched the little woman.

Sin reached out and patted her arm in a soothing gesture. "I know you did the best you could, Cass. How did it go?"

"As planned," she answered in a clipped tone, lowering her head and rubbing her eyes.

The other two exchanged a glance, amusement draining from them. Nick thought they looked worried.

Sin returned her gaze to Cassie. "He volunteered. You made sure he was prepared. He'll be home in no time, you'll see."

The two women looked at each other in solemn silence. Sin held out a hand and Cassie clasped it, sniffling a little.

Alarmed at the prospect of more tears, Nick cleared his throat and tried to steer them into less emotional waters. "She said it's time to tell me. Tell me what?"

Del sent him a lopsided smile. "Everything, bro." He looked at Sin. "Where do you wanna start?"

"Something concrete before we get into, ah, history," she answered with a twist of her lips.

Del responded with a little grimace. "Blue factory?"

She nodded and Del moved to sit in the chair close to Nick, elbows on his knees, studying his brother with a measuring look Nick didn't like.

Nick frowned with suspicion, his stomach plummeting below his feet. "What about blue? Don't tell me you're involved with that junk, too."

Del snorted, giving him a disgusted look. "Thanks for the vote of confidence. No, we aren't in blue trade. We just put a serious crimp in it."

"What d'you mean?"

"You know the big bust going on, exposure of the drug ring, and all that?"

Nick nodded, still suspicious.

"We gave the FPA info on the main factory and the bigwigs running the ring, enough to take it all down."

Nick stared at him. Del didn't look like he was lying, but how was he supposed to believe it?

When Nick said nothing, Del went on, "That's what happened to my slicer on our last long run. Sin and I found the factory, did a scout to get info, and got banged up on the way out. We turned the stuff over to the FPA and the rest you've seen on the news feeds."

"You expect me to swallow this hook? What d'you take me for?"

Del grinned. "That's just for starters, bro. You're gonna love the big picture."

When his brother didn't say anything else, Nick turned his head and looked at Sin, clenching his jaw at the faint amusement on her face. "Glad he's having fun. You wanna tell me the truth?"

She sobered, green eyes meeting his with steady intensity. "We're at war with Griffin, fighting him with everything we have. And when I say we, I'm including the Federated Planetary Alliance. The ones Griffin hasn't bought, at any rate. We're the good guys, Nick. I know you won't believe it until you have proof, but you need to hear it now."

She rose and started pacing. Nick scoffed at her

moving form but said nothing, willing to let her talk it out.

"Griffin has built Quasicore into a self-sufficient monster, a hungry thing which will eat its way through our society until there's nothing left if we don't stop it. Are you with me so far?"

Nick shrugged. "Won't argue it." He stole a quick look at Cassie. She stared at Sin, a disconcerting combination of anxiety and sadness on her lovely face.

"My brother and I are determined to stop him, at any cost. We have backing from the FPA in the form of weapon sanctions and liberties I can't get into right now. They're just as worried as we are, you see. They have just as much at stake and less ability to do anything about it. Griffin has a chokehold on them. His FPA rats are everywhere and if left unchecked, that Sun-cursed man and his monster will be running our society, controlling our military and our civilian patrols, strong-arming planetary governments, and generally taking over the universe.

"In short, he'll crown himself this galaxy's dictator. Anything you'd like to contest so far?" She paused to meet his gaze with lifted eyebrows.

"I knew he had some FPA in his pocket, but what you're talking about is impossible."

"Don't be naïve, Inspector," she shot back, expression hardening. "Didn't you see the rats run when the blue bust broke open? Didn't you see how many were taken in? They were just the forerunners, the tip of the iceberg."

"You're saying it was Griffin's drug ring."

"Do you doubt it?"

He shook his head, unfolding his arms and sitting

forward to rest elbows on knees and study her. "So all those FPA agents arrested in the past couple days were on Griffin's payroll? How do you know? How's it related to the blue busts?"

She sighed, moving over to the chair and curling up in it again. Then she gave him a level stare with cool green eyes. "Think it through, Nick. The ring is Griffin's. There had to be incriminating evidence implicating him in the illegal drug operation. Have you seen any of it? No, because his FPA pets have scurried out from under their rocks to protect him. The stupid ones were caught. The smarter ones did what he paid them for, so Griffin remains untouched. To the public, he denounces those people in his employment who were responsible for running blue, saying he had no idea such a horrible thing was happening right under his nose. He's innocent of any wrong doing and so on. But he'll have another blue operation up and running again within the year."

"Like a hydra," Cassie added, her voice as soft as a sigh, eyes unfocused and staring across the room at nothing. "Cut off one head, he grows two more."

Nick raised his eyebrows. "Not much of a war, Shay."

"Tell me about it," Sin responded with a humorless smile. She opened her mouth as though to continue then snapped it shut, turning her head toward the door.

Nick glanced over his shoulder. Manakai Shay sauntered into the living room, dressed in unrelenting black, an air of careless danger swirling around him. Smudges marred his clothes and face, some looking a lot like blood. But the man acted as if he'd just wandered in after a dull night out, his movements easy and expression relaxed.

He didn't look surprised to see Nick, a faint smirk curling his lips when he met Nick's hostile gaze. "Hey, gang. What'd I miss?"

"You are not sitting on my furniture in those—" Sin broke off with an exasperated sound in her throat when her brother parked his grimy rear on the arm of her chair, ignoring her protest. He relaxed into the seat with one arm across the back, a leg swinging with lazy energy. "Crying out loud, Kai. You couldn't clean up first?"

"And miss the look on the inspector's face when he hears he's been on a wild goose chase? You know me better, Sissa." He glanced down at her with a teasing grin.

"Wild goose chase?" Nick repeated, voice tight with suppressed anger.

"We weren't quite there yet," Cassie told Manakai.

The flare of hilarity on the dark twin's face slipped away when he saw Cassie. He sat up, studying her with a solemn expression. "Are you all right, Cass?"

"I'm fine," she answered in an impatient tone. "Why does everybody keep asking me that?"

"Because you look like death warmed over, sweetheart."

Nick's stomach clenched at the endearment. He hadn't thought the other man was interested in Cass, but now he wondered. Of course, insulting a woman about her looks wasn't usually the way to win her heart. He expected Cassie's usual flash of fire, but her reaction tightened his muscles with concern.

She sighed, head dropping back to rest against the sofa and eyes sliding closed. "Thanks. Tactful as ever."

Both twins leaned forward now, identical frowns creasing their brows. "When was the last time you slept, Cass?" Sin asked.

The little woman waved a hand in the air. "Don't know, a couple of days ago maybe."

Sin met Nick's gaze, a question in her eyes. He nodded, agreeing with the worry in her expression. Nobody was going anywhere; they could hash this out in the morning. She smiled her thanks, eyes warming. "Then it's about time you caught some shut-eye," Sin announced in a tone of finality.

"Up you get, Sleeping Beauty," Manakai added, standing and grasping one of Cassie's arms.

She jerked out of his clasp, glaring as she leaned away. "Oh no, you don't. We are going to get this over with. The inspector deserves his answers and I don't think I'll sleep until he gets them." When Manakai didn't resume his seat, his green eyes narrowing in autocratic command, she sighed. "Besides, I need this for me, too. Going over it will help me cope."

"Maybe you should tell it then, Cass," Del said, the lines of his face softening as he studied her. He flicked a finger at the twins. "You know those two will just do their song and dance"—the Shays flashed razor-sharp grins—"and I ain't exactly the talkin' type. Lay it out quick and we'll throw the proof at him tomorrow."

"You mean later today," Cassie said with a wry twist of her mouth.

He grinned. "Whatever gets us to bed faster."

She folded her arms and lifted an eyebrow. "Oh, were you sleeping when we disturbed you?"

"Do you really wanna know?" he countered, still grinning.

"Ick. Now that you mention it, no, I don't."

A gagging sound from Manakai accompanied her comment as he eased himself back onto his sister's armrest. Nick silently agreed, but Sin snorted and poked her brother in the side. Del chuckled, making a let's-get-on-with-it motion with his hand.

Nick shifted in his seat, turning so he faced Cassie and laying his arm across the back of the sofa. If he stretched out, his fingertips would brush her cheek. Shoving the idea to the back of his mind, he forced his wayward thoughts back on track. "Let's start with the wild goose chase."

Without looking at him, Cassie straightened and curled her legs under her, canting her body toward the armrest away from him. "Let me do this my way, Inspector," she said in a cool tone. "It'll be faster."

Back to calling him by his title. With a grim press of his lips, he nodded. She must have seen the motion out of the corner of her eye, because she relaxed a bit and chewed on her bottom lip. Nick watched the action with a hungry swallow and did his best to wait.

"All right, so I'll try to do the quick-and-dirty, no-frills version," she started in a soft voice, almost as if talking to herself. "On one side we have Griffin, our bad guy. On the other side, we have the Shays and the FPA, only the FPA can't get after Griffin because Core spies are in their ranks covering Griffin every time they get close. So they strike a deal with the Shays, asking them to help the FPA clean house in exchange for allowing certain liberties so the Shays can expose Griffin's illegal operations. The Shays decide to kill two birds with one stone and do the exposing and cleaning at the same time."

She paused to glance at him. He nodded to show he was still with her, holding back his questions with grim restraint. She went on, "Griffin has a fistful of major illegal operations. You name it, he's doing it; drug running, hijacking, weapons running, extortion, prostitution, assassination, and so on. Our first attack was on his blue production, not the only drug he's running, but one of the more lucrative. As they told you, we had some pretty decent results, but not enough for the FPA to prosecute, or take down Griffin and his company. So we try again, only this time we're after his weapons division. Our little jaunt tonight was all about getting a foot in the door."

Nick held up a hand, unable to stop himself. "Wait a minute. How does selling off one of your AIs help you track down Core weapons?"

Cassie sent him an irritated glance. "I was getting to it." She turned her face away again, took a deep breath, and then said nothing.

Nick shot a look at his brother, eyebrows lifted. Del gave a small shake of his head without taking his somber gaze off Cassie.

"I used to work for him," Cassie declared, her voice tight with an emotion he couldn't interpret.

When she still didn't continue, Nick prompted, "I figured from what you said to Griffin the other night. Cybercom, wasn't it?"

"Yes." She made the word into a hiss through clenched teeth.

"You were making AIs for him?"

She tossed her braid over one shoulder with a jerk of her head and began yanking on it with a ruthless hand. Her face became a rigid mask, eyes blazing as she stared at the opposite wall. "I was promoted to the special projects division. Challenging and exciting, just what I was looking for in the field. Except we were given a project, not just questionable, but way over the line. We were told it was hypothetical, an intellectual exercise which wouldn't be put to practical use. Like an idiot, I believed them." She bared her teeth, a low growl emerging from her throat.

Nick swallowed, a frisson zipping up his spine and raising the hairs at the back of his neck. "What was the project?"

Her hand tightened around the sheave of hair until her knuckles turned white. Then she tossed the braid back over her shoulder and faced him, brown eyes locking with his, her gaze terrifying in its honest directness. "I created the code that made Imago insane."

He stared at her, aghast. "So you did make him crazy. Why?"

Her upper lip lifted in a snarl, eyes narrowing on him in feral hostility. "I told you, Inspector, I did not make him crazy!"

"But you just said—"

"I created the code, but someone else inserted it into his neural network. When I realized what had been done, I...I took Imago and I left." Her eyes skidded away from his with her last words.

He clenched his jaw, certain she was lying, or not telling a big chunk of the story. It was time to push a little. "You're telling me they just let you go? The Core doesn't look the other way, Doc. What happened when you tried to leave?"

She shook her head, face draining of color. "It doesn't matter," she responded in a wispy voice. Then she cleared her throat, voice firming as she repeated, "It doesn't matter. Only the why matters and the fact that I got Imago away from them. You asked me before, why would anybody want to make an AI suicidal? Here's your answer: Griffin is trying to create the perfect weapon. He wants a smart weapon, one to think for itself, aim itself, and detonate itself.

"But one of the fundamental parameters programmed into all AIs is the need to protect life, its own as well as human. It's possible to build an AI without this parameter and I think he's already tried it, but the results would be uncontrollable. An AI who didn't care about life also wouldn't care about taking orders. I've run simulations. The results have been disastrous, picture-book sociopaths. So he resorted to taking a normal AI and making it crazy enough to be willing to die."

Nick opened his mouth, but nothing came out for a second. He cleared his throat and tried again. "But that's…"

"Insane," Cassie finished in a soft tone.

"Sick, twisted," Manakai said.

Sin tacked on, "Diabolical."

Cassie nodded. "And completely against every humanities law in the book."

"But it doesn't make sense," Nick said in a forceful tone, glancing from one to the other. "Why bother? If he wanted a smart bomb, why not just get an AI to control it from a distance? What's the point of blowing up an AI, which is a lot more valuable than some missile, when he could get it to do the same thing over and over again?"

"AIs aren't supposed to be able to harm humans,"

Cassie said, but the look she sent the Shays said something else while she squirmed in her seat.

"You already said you could get around this. Wouldn't it be easier to get an AI to be homicidal instead of wanting to kill itself and humans?"

Cassie nodded, chewing on her lower lip. "Yes, we haven't figured out why he wants to do it this way yet."

Nick watched her exchange a glance with the Shays and shook his head. "Yeah, you have. But you won't tell me."

Cassie shrugged, not looking at him, while two pairs of cool green eyes studied him with infuriating calculation. Nick grit his teeth in rising anger.

"We have ideas," Sin said in a too smooth tone.

"Nothing concrete," Manakai added.

With a grim press of his lips, Nick turned to look at his brother. Del shrugged, eyes direct and unapologetic. "Don't know, bro. They're keeping it close to the chest."

Cassie cleared her throat. "To finish up, the plan was to get Griffin to take Imago back. We're assuming Griffin would want to give the AI to the people he has working on the code project now. Imago would then broadcast the location of this AI lab, we send the info to the FPA, and they take it apart. It would be nice if they were able to expose his inhumanities, rescue those poor AIs, and find the weapons he was going to put them in. It would be nice if they were able to prosecute Griffin and Quasicore for these things, but a lot of Core stooges still scurry around in the FPA ranks."

"So you clean house again and hope this time you can take him down."

"Exactly."

"Why do you need Imago at all? Isn't Cybercom where he's running the op?"

Cassie shook her head. "Not anymore. He moves things around quite a bit, which is another reason his criminal activities are so hard to uncover."

"Makes sense," Nick muttered in acknowledgement, lowering his eyes to the floor and drumming his fingers in thoughtful rhythm on the back of the couch.

"So?" Del asked after a long, silent pause. "You buyin' it?"

Nick glanced up, met his brother's amused gaze, and made a rude noise in the back of his throat. "It sure is a pretty story," he drawled. "Where's your proof?"

Sin gave a delicate cough and Nick turned his head to look at her. Her green eyes sparkled and a smile played around her mouth, but her voice was neutral. "We have an FPA contact that will convince you. But it's a bit late to make the call."

"Cranky as a bear before his first morning coffee," Manakai added with an earnest shake of his head. "Be taking our lives in our hands if we called now."

Sin shot a wry look at her brother but didn't comment, rising to her feet. "Let's get some sleep and meet back here for a late breakfast."

Manakai stretched and yawned. "Make it lunch."

With a reluctant grimace, Nick grumbled an agreement and stood. Cassie shoved to her feet beside him then swayed, a hand rising to her temple. Nick and Manakai both caught an elbow on either side to steady her.

"Whoa, Cassie-girl." Manakai studied her with a frown. "Need help getting to your place?"

Nick stiffened. "I'll take her."

Shay met Nick's gaze over her head with a stony expression Nick interpreted as proprietary hostility.

"Good," Del interrupted in a bland voice. "Then you can bunk at my place and keep Sam company." With a stern glance at Manakai, Del pulled Cass out from between the two men and escorted her toward the door with a supporting arm around her waist.

Manakai snorted without comment. Nick trailed them with a strange sensation in the pit of his stomach, as if he'd stepped off the edge of a cliff; bewildered, disoriented, and adrift. He didn't understand these new currents flowing between the others, or why Del's arm around her waist should make him feel like breaking something.

Cassie elbowed Del, struggling a little against his hold. "What's wrong with you people? I'm fine."

"Uh-huh. I'll believe it when you stop looking like krell dung."

They paused at the door and she tilted her head back with a disgusted expression. "Nice," she reproached.

Del grinned, edging around Nick and heading back to the living room. "G'night, you two. See y'later."

Cass muttered under her breath and stepped out the door. From her tone, Nick gathered her comments weren't flattery. He suppressed a grin then twitched when Cassie said in a raised voice, "Goodnight, Mina. Thanks for having us."

"My pleasure, Cassie." To Nick's ear, the AI's smooth voice sounded warmer than usual. "Get some rest, dear."

"I will," Cass answered in a much more tolerant

tone than she'd used with anyone else on the subject.

As they moved down the short hall, Nick confessed, "I forgot she was there."

Cassie nodded, a sour expression on her face as if she'd expected nothing else from somebody like him. But she said nothing and he clenched his jaw against the urge to defend himself. She reached the lift before him and keyed the level of their quarters. After a second, she sagged against the wall with a sigh.

Nick studied her weary features, a frown pulling his brows together. "You have a sealed FPA file, Cass. Why?"

She groaned, lifting a hand to cover her eyes. "Don't you ever stop?"

"Sorry," he mumbled. "Habit."

The lift stopped and the doors swished open. Cass pushed away from the wall but stumbled as she exited the lift. Nick lunged forward and caught her arm, steadying her.

"I'm fine," she grumbled but didn't try to pull away when he guided her down the corridor.

"I know. Take pity on me and let me do the chivalry thing. My earlier rescue was a bust and my ego hasn't recovered yet."

A wan smile rewarded him for his efforts, but her eyes were half-closed with exhaustion. She managed to get the door to her quarters open and stumbled again over the threshold. He still had a hold on her arm, keeping her on her feet. Escorting her to the bedroom, he maintained his stabilizing hold on her until they reached the bed. Then she pushed away from him and fell face first on the cushion with a groan.

"Cass."

She mumbled something that sounded like, "Go away."

"Cass, you're gonna be uncomfortable in those coveralls and shoes."

No response. With a sigh, he reached down and tugged the shoes off her feet, shifting her legs until she was in a more comfortable position on the bed. Then he hesitated, contemplating the coveralls. Did he dare? His heart kicked hard inside his chest at the idea of undressing her. He tugged on her shoulder until she rolled over and threw an arm over her eyes. "Le'me 'lone."

"Cass, your coveralls."

No response. With a deep, fortifying breath, Nick reached for the clasps on the front, humiliated by the faint tremor in his hands. Sun's sake, the woman was unconscious and still managed to turn him inside out. Fumbling a little, he got the front of the thing undone, half relieved and half disappointed at the white shirt and black slacks underneath. At least she wouldn't kill him for stripping her bare when she woke.

He managed to remove her arms from the coveralls after a bit of interference from her; she kept shoving his hands away in sleepy irritation. Pulling the cloth down to the small of her back, he paused for a second. Then he held his breath, slipped his hands under her, and lifted her hips, the action sending a wave of mortifying heat through him. Swallowing hard, he tugged the cloth out from under her bottom and peeled it off her legs. Tossing the coveralls across the end of the bed, he backed away as if the piece of furniture had just caught on fire.

At a safe distance, he paused, studying her. She'd

be comfortable enough. The shirt and slacks were loose-fitting and would work as makeshift nightclothes. She wasn't under the covers, but no doubt she'd pull them over her if she got cold. Her hair was still in a tight braid, but it didn't seem to be bothering her. Yes, she was fine. It was time for him to leave.

He didn't move.

Her face was turned away from him. The soft curve of her cheek was a fascination he couldn't resist. One arm rested next to her head, palm up and slender fingers curling. The relaxed vulnerability in those fingers struck him like a blow, leaving him bewildered and off-balance. He understood his reaction to the rest of her. The rise and fall of her breasts under the thin cloth and the sliver of smooth skin at her waistband ground his guts with lust. The memory of lifting her hips made his palms itch to do it again. But the way she lay, rendered defenseless by sleep, sent an ache through him in such deep places it scared him witless. The urge to lie down beside her and cradle her in his arms was almost irresistible.

Nick had no idea how long he stood watching her sleep, but at some point he shook himself out of his trance. With terrifying reluctance, he moved toward the door. At the threshold he paused, a frown tugging his brow when he glanced back over his shoulder at her.

She didn't have an AI to watch over her. If he left, she'd be alone. Giving up Imago had been traumatic for her and even though she'd said talking it out would help her cope, she hadn't really talked about Imago at all. What if she woke and needed somebody?

"Makin' excuses," he mumbled. She had friends she could call. She had Manakai.

The last thought decided him, the image of the Shay twin comforting Cassie twisting his guts. Stepping out of her bedroom, he shrugged off his jacket and moved across her living room. She didn't have a sofa, but she had two squishy-looking chairs flanking a huge viewer. He dropped into one and groaned at the soft, cradling comfort, exhaustion making his whole body ache. Balling his jacket, he shoved it under one cheek for a makeshift pillow and shifted until he was comfortable. A minute later, he dropped over the edge of consciousness and fell unresisting into sleep.

Chapter 15

Cassie stood in Imago's brain speaking with him, the impulses of his functions flashing around her in a dizzying display. They were riddling, a favorite game of theirs, while she moved along one pathway. She took care to watch where she stepped, so she wouldn't interfere with his functions. Except her foot came down wrong somehow and she hurt him. He didn't seem to realize it, his riddles turning into nonsense, darkness spreading around her. She screamed his name, afraid for him and for herself, as the darkness started to eat at her as well.

A hand reached through, a strong and steady grip on her arm pulling her out of the sucking darkness and into her lab. Nick smiled down at her, sending her already racing heart into palpitations. He said something about her working late.

"I don't sleep," she told him, distracted by the appearance of her lab. Something was off about it, out of place. It was her lab. She knew it like she knew her next breath, so why did it seem strange?

Nick had wandered over to one of the stations, inspecting the equipment and asking question after question, not giving her time to answer. She shook her head, looking around in confusion. The lights had begun to go out, one by one, but Nick didn't seem to notice, still interrogating at top speed while he fiddled with things he shouldn't be touching. Cassie wrapped her arms around herself, staring at the oncoming darkness with creeping terror. It had followed her out of Imago's brain. It would consume her.

Then she realized why the lab looked different. It wasn't the lab on the Shay station; it was her old lab at Cybercom. It was going dark, just like it had been when she'd found Dmitri.

Whirling, she lunged for Nick, crying out his name and reaching for him, to save him. But it was too late. Even as she moved, he triggered something at the station and long tongues of violent blue light flashed around him like living lightning. He went rigid, body jerking, smoke curling from his skin and clothes.

Cassie screamed, still reaching for him, but he seemed just beyond her grasp. He fell, twitching as the blue light pinned him to the ground. Then it was over and he lay on the floor exactly as Dmitri had been. Scorched. Dead.

Cassie was still screaming when she woke, body jackknifing on the bed. She tumbled off just as Nick burst into the room, eyes wild and face white. He lurched toward her, calling her name. With a tremendous effort, she stopped the sound ripping from her throat and scrambled for the sanitary. "Get away from me," she choked out, dodging his touch and disappearing into the sanitary, managing to lock the door before she vomited up the horror of the dream.

It took a while, but she got herself back under control and responded to Nick's frantic pounding and calling beyond the door. "It's all right," she called back to him. "I'm all right. I just need a few minutes."

After a long moment of silence, Nick said in a

hoarse, strained voice, "Sun's blood, Cass, what happened?"

"Bad dream." She reached for a cool cloth with shaking hands. "Just give me a few minutes. I'll be out soon."

She stayed in the bathroom as long as she dared before emerging. The last person she had ever wanted to see what those blasted nightmares did to her was the man sitting on her bed. He was leaning forward with elbows on knees, hands clasped together and head bent as if deep in thought. The sound of the door opening prompted him to lift his head, dark eyes spearing her with their intensity.

"Cass." His eyes tracked over her as if looking for wounds. "How do you feel?"

"Embarrassed. What are you doing here?"

He searched her face, the sharpness of his gaze making her uncomfortable. Just how much could he see? "I was worried about you, and figured it wouldn't hurt anything if I crashed in your living room. How often do you have these dreams?"

She tried to still her startled reaction, but didn't think she'd done a very good job. "What makes you think I've had more than this one?"

"Because you look guilty as hell," he snapped, hands clenching until his knuckles showed white. "Because you act like you didn't just scream loud enough to bust glass. You got a trash tube and water right next to your bed. You puke after every one of these Sun-damned dreams, don't you?"

Cass folded her arms across her chest, narrowing her eyes and moving farther into the room. He was in her space, curse him. She wouldn't allow him to put her on the defensive. "Anger is a strange reaction, Inspector. Why the hostility?"

"Because you scared the hell out of me," he snarled, lunging to his feet. He reached her in one long stride, grasping her upper arms and giving her a little shake. "How long have you been having these things, Cass? And don't call me Inspector."

She blinked, a little stupefied by his closeness, his hot emotions, and his words. With deliberate movements, she extracted herself from his hold and took a large step back. "My dreams are none of your business. I'd like you to leave now."

He snorted and folded his muscular arms over his chest. "Fat chance, Cass. What if you have another one?"

She shook her head. "I won't be back to sleep. I really don't want you here." She tried to put as much conviction as possible in her voice.

He seemed oblivious, frowning at her. "But you've only been asleep a couple hours. If you haven't slept for days, you need a lot more."

She shrugged. "I'll sleep later. Get out, Givliani."

"Get back in bed, Cass. And don't call me that, either." He stepped toward her.

She stepped back. "Don't call you by your name? Fine, how's this? Don't give me orders, you arrogant jackass."

His mouth twitched and his eyes lightened, but he still took another step toward her. "Funny, that does sound better," he murmured. "You're still getting in bed."

She stared at him, nonplussed. Then she rallied. "I'll call security."

"How 'bout we call your employers instead? My bet says you haven't told them about these dreams of yours. Or if you have, you didn't tell them how bad they are."

She closed her mouth with an audible snap, glaring at him. Of course, he had to be right. "You really are a jackass, blackmailing me just to get me into bed."

A slow, wicked grin curled his lips and stopped her heart. "Cassiopeia Draegen," he drawled. "What a dirty mind you have."

She skipped backward and bumped into the wall, alarm trilling along her nerves. "I didn't mean…"

He rolled his eyes, the grin turning into something less dangerous and more boyish. "Figures. Wouldn't be so lucky, would I? Come on, Cass. I just want you to get some more rest." He took a step back and swept a hand in front of him, a grand gesture paving the way from her to the bed. "Hop in. I'll sing you right to dreamland."

She scoffed, easing forward. "How's your voice?"

"Like a cross between a strangling cat and a krell in heat," he responded, mischief twinkling in his dark gaze.

"Wow, what an offer." She moved past him and climbed onto the bed, sitting with both knees up and arms folded across them. "I think I'll pass. You can leave now."

"One track friggin' mind." But he didn't leave. Instead, he moved closer, sinking down to a sitting position on the floor next to her and resting an arm on the bed, chin in hand as he looked up at her. "Fine, no singing. I'll tell you a story. Any requests?"

She stared at him. "Seriously, I'm not going to be

able to sleep with you in here."

"Don't knock it 'til you try it." The humorous curl of his mouth and the subtle slant of his eyes seduced.

Cassie looked away with a gulp, trying not to picture him stretched out in her bed, golden skin and hard muscle from head to toe, hot and ready under her hands. "I—I'm surprised you don't want to interrogate me some more."

"Would it help you sleep?"

"No." She watched him shrug out of the corner of her eye.

"There you go. So what'll it be?"

She should kick him out, insist he leave. But she was curious about him and the temptation to learn more was irresistible. *Yeah, right,* her libido jeered. *Your interest is purely intellectual.* She shifted, conceding that learning more about him wasn't the only reason she wanted him to stay. She wasn't going to try seducing him. She was sure the results would be even more embarrassing than him listening to her vomit. "I can ask you anything?"

"Yup."

She snuck a look at him. A faint smile curled his lips and his eyes were half-closed as he watched her, the warmth in his gaze making her heart stutter. She couldn't interpret the expression on his face, but it made her uneasy, as if he'd just gained ground she couldn't afford to lose. He'd chosen to sit on the floor instead of the bed, placing himself below her in a non-threatening position. He'd shown concern for her welfare and was offering to open up to her. These were not the actions of an antagonist.

"All right. What made you want to be an FPA

agent?" She knew some of the reasons, but it would be interesting to hear his take on it.

He nodded then held out his hands. "Feet," he commanded.

"Excuse me?"

With a sigh, he met her startled gaze. "Lay back, get comfy, and throw me your feet. With this boring subject and a good foot massage, you're sure to zonk out in no time."

She raised her eyebrows at him, trying not to smile. She wanted to laugh. She also wanted to run screaming out the door. She was in a great deal of trouble. "I don't think it's a—"

"Part of the problem right there," he cut in. "You think too much, Doc. You get your big brain cooking and no wonder you can't sleep. Feet," he commanded again, curling his fingers in a peremptory motion.

Knowing it was a mistake, she sank back into her pillows and offered him her feet. The smile dancing around his mouth had her clasping her hands with nervous tension over her stomach. He cupped first one heel then the other, removing her socks. "Relax," he murmured without looking at her. "This I'm good at."

This news only made it worse. He started with her toes and she gasped. The smile touched his lips again. "Feel good?" he asked in a voice so low it was almost a whisper.

Hers was a whisper. "Yes."

The smile slipped away, replaced by a look of intense concentration, as if he were doing something far more serious than a foot massage. She watched him, her eyelids growing heavy, but not with sleep. *Holy Suns,* the man was sexy. The tingling in her feet danced up her legs, spreading a languid heat through her body, a relaxation far from weariness.

Nick cleared his throat. When he started talking, his voice held a curious rasp, the deep tones as erotic as his touch. "So why'd I get into the FPA. A big part of it was Del. When our dad died, he left us with a huge debt to the Core. They demanded we pay up. Del didn't want us both sucked into the Core, so he shipped me off to a foster home while he tried to work off the debt."

"His leaving you must have hurt," Cassie managed to comment, barely raising her voice above a whisper.

"Yeah, it did, but Aunt Sal and Uncle Bo were aces. They took me in without a second's thought. They let me rant and rave for a while, then they sat me down and told me I was doing my brother an injustice. He hadn't dumped me because he didn't love me. He loved me so much he'd sacrificed himself for me. They asked me what I'd do if I were the older brother and had the same decision to make."

He shrugged without looking up from his delicious, sinful massage.

"They had a hydro farm out in the middle of nowhere, staple crops like potatoes, beans, and yendro roots. Working it was boring, but gave me plenty of time to think. I figured out they were right. I was still angry at being left behind, but I'd have done the same thing, so I had no business grousin' about it. Time passed and Del didn't come back. I knew he'd find a way back if he could, so either they'd killed him or the Core had him by the throat. I needed to find a way to break him loose."

"You thought the FPA was it," she breathed, trying not to purr like a contented cat. The man had talented hands. She wondered what he'd say if she asked for a full body massage.

Nick's mouth turned up at the corners. "Yeah, I thought the FPA was it. Young and dumb, that was me. So I joined. At least my FPA contacts and resources helped me find Del. He was still alive, still stuck in the Core. After I found out being on the side of justice didn't mean I could take on the Core, I decided to get him out on their terms. I saved up the money they said he owed. Took me a while," he mused, doing something blissful to her ankle. Cassie sighed and sank lower into her pillows. "Long enough for me to figure out the Core wasn't going to give Del up so easy. They'd been fleecing him with tons of fines and fees over the years, making sure he stayed in debt to them up to his eyeballs. So his brother comes along with the ante and they'll just turn him loose? Yeah, right. That's when I heard about the Shays."

He paused, hands going still. Then he continued, both hand and voice, much to her delight.

"My orientation partner when I turned inspector was a talker. He'd heard about the Shays and passed the info to me. From what he told me, they liked to snag people from the Core to work in their courier service as pilots. Seemed like the ideal situation. I'd front the cash, the Shays had the contacts and muscle to break Del loose, and Del would sail clear when he was free."

"Best laid plans," Cassie whispered with a faint smile, watching his bent head. He said nothing, a pensive curve to his mouth, his hands moving over her feet in slow strokes and erotic swirls. Her smile faded. "He's doing great here. He's in love with her, you know."

"Yeah, I figured," he said, his tone tight with suppressed emotion.

She considered telling him about the Sun-bonding, but it wasn't her place to mention it. Besides, she didn't think he'd be comforted by the idea in his present frame of mind. Sitting up, she pulled her feet away and folded her limbs into a cross-legged position. When he met her gaze, the vivid intensity in his dark eyes almost stopped her heart. "Nick—" she started, meaning to reassure him of Del's safety and well-being on the Shay station.

His sharp, indrawn breath startled her into silence. "Damn it, Cass," he groaned. "Why do you always pick the worst time to say my name?" He reached out, clasped her face in his big hands, and drew her down to his mouth.

She almost tumbled from the bed. Every joint in her body seemed to come unhinged, collapsing her toward him and his devastating kiss. The heat he'd generated with his massage built into an inferno, melting her strength away and throbbing between her thighs. Things like thought and common sense became nonexistent as his mobile mouth teased and tempted, his tongue tasting her with slick, promising heat.

With a low sound in her throat, she tugged at him, imploring him to come closer. Without breaking the kiss, he rose to his knees, hands leaving her face to slide down her back and curl around her hips. With a luscious sound rumbling in his chest, he pulled her toward him.

"Yes," she whispered against his lips, slipping her arms around his neck, unfolding her legs, and sliding off the bed. Her thighs straddled his hips as he guided her down to his lap. She whimpered with fierce need at the tantalizing sensation of his arousal, hard and urgent, pressing against her core. Spearing her fingers through his dark hair, she pressed closer and did a slow writhe, eyes closing and head falling back with the breathtaking, sweet pleasure.

Nick made a wordless exclamation, sounding agonized, and Cassie met his gaze. His dark eyes were hot and wild, his mouth quirking with tender humor, tugging at something deep in her chest. "Suns," he groaned, voice thick, "I won't survive it, but please, honey, please do that again."

All of a sudden, she smelled something burning. Gazing into his eyes, feeling his hard strength, his warm voice sweetly pleading, an irresistible enticement in his hands and in the curve of his mouth, she could taste him on her tongue. But his sizzling ginger smell, the hot, male scent of him was overwhelmed by the smell of…burnt meat.

Cassie leapt to her feet, her movement so sudden Nick almost went over backward. She stumbled into her nightstand as the true meaning of the dream landed on her in all its horror. "Sun and Stars," she whispered.

Nick rose, a frown of concern creasing his brow. "Cass? What's the matter?"

"Nothing," she lied, edging away from him. "I just don't think it's such a—a good idea, for us to do what we were, um, about to do."

"Okay," he said, drawing the word out and watching her back away from him with a baffled look on his face. "You look about ready to throw up again. Did I do something to—?"

"No, no." She shook her head. "It's not you. I'm just…" She waved a vague hand in the air, hunting for an appropriate excuse.

She still hadn't found one by the time he walked past her to the door. He paused on the threshold, looking back with such intensity, it cut right through her. "You're right, we shouldn't. You're just hard to resist, Cass." A fleeting smile passing over his lips. "Get some sleep."

Then he was gone, the door sliding closed behind him. On shaking limbs, she stumbled over to the bed and sank down on it. He might be crashing in her living room again, but she was afraid to check, afraid to see him. At this point, the less contact she had with him the better.

"Suns, I'm such an idiot," she moaned, putting her face in her hands and rocking in a futile attempt at comfort.

The dream. Her Suns-forsaken nightmare. Always, it had been Dmitri and no one else. Dmitri, her first real love, her companion and friend. They'd shared the same interests, the same career, and the same passions. She'd thought they would be together forever, unable to imagine what could ever separate them. She'd forgotten about death. Her dead love, murdered by the Core, by Griffin's order.

Now she'd dreamt Nick dying the same way.

"I can't be this stupid," she whispered, still rocking. "I don't believe it. I am not falling for him."

It would be different if she dreamt about all the people she cared about, her subconscious agonizing through her fears for the safety of her friends and family. It would be different if she had seen anyone else besides Dmitri scorched and burnt. But only Dmitri had starred in her nightmares, until now.

Jumping up, she began to pace, unaware of shaking her head in vigorous denial. It was ridiculous. Lust she could understand. The man was beautiful, sinfully sexy, and so available at the moment.

But they had so little in common. He was as opposite to Dmitri as it was possible to get; dark where Dmitri had been blond and blue-eyed, big where Dmitri had been slender, authoritative and demanding where her lost love had been quiet and unassuming. Nick didn't understand her work with AIs. She admired his drive, his values of right and wrong, and his protective nature, but his relentless, single-minded pursuit for the truth drove her nuts.

Besides, even if she were stupid enough to fall in love with him, she wasn't stupid enough to believe he'd ever return her feelings. What would a guy like him, so gorgeous, aggressive, and sure of himself, want with a geeky, mousy braincase like her?

When she was straddling him earlier, he sure seemed interested, but that was sex. He must not be finding much variety on the station if he was slumming in the geek department for his entertainment. Or maybe it was the thrill of the chase for him. Did it turn him on to hunt her for what information she had on the Shays? In any event, Cassie thought with a grim clench of her jaw, his interest was sure to wan when he learned the whole truth and went back to the FPA.

She headed for the sanitary and the small stash of sedatives she kept for bad bouts of insomnia. Nick was right about one thing; she did need to sleep. But without some chemical assistance, she wouldn't be able to manage it. After taking a dose of the medicine, she went back to the bed and laid down, staring with scratchy eyes at the blank ceiling. When the drugs started to kick in, she closed her eyes and prayed for dreamless oblivion.

Chapter 16

Webster Griffin stood relaxed, hands cupped in the small of his back as he watched the man on the viewer sweat and squirm under his gaze. They had already been over the night's activities several times. The doctor had gotten away. She'd been prepared for their attempted kidnapping, but she'd also had help. By the man's description, it had been the FPA inspector Webster had met the other evening.

Webster let the man on the viewer sweat, let him believe his boss was angry. What he actually felt was grim amusement. The little woman was resourceful, clever, and far more talented than he'd originally believed, a definite asset to his plans. By all accounts from his staff, this AI the doctor had given him was infected with the original code, just as she'd claimed.

"Koffsky, you are a disappointment," he announced in a pleasant voice.

The man blanched, going as still as a statue. His fear was gratifying. Webster didn't ordinarily deal face to face with people on such a low level, but he had wanted the details as unblemished and fresh as possible, which meant speaking to the man who had been there.

"However, you did not fail me entirely, so I'll give you a second chance." He paused to receive his just gratitude.

The man didn't disappoint him this time. "Y-yes,

sir. Thank you, sir. I won't fail you again, I swear it. Y-you won't regret it."

"I never regret, Koffsky," he interrupted in a steely voice. "I resolve. You understand me."

"Y-y-yes, s-sir." The man's voice was a decibel higher than normal.

"You will be contacted soon for your next assignment. You may leave."

"Thank you, sir," Koffsky whispered and disappeared from the viewer.

Webster turned away, allowing a small smile to curve his lips. Pacing across the room, he stopped before the enormous window and contemplated the view. It was spectacular. A red-ringed planet with its seven colorful moons spun below his orbiting station, backlit by a binary star system. The crystal in those rings caught the starlight like a scattering of diamonds, glittering in successive waves.

Webster turned back into the room, searching out his daughter. She remained seated close to the viewer, demure hands folded in her lap, her flame-colored hair brushing over her shoulders. He disapproved of her hair down and unconfined. It made her look like a child. However, she would see no one today but him, so he allowed the freedom.

"You have no comment, Liaena?" Of late, it seemed as though she had some comment on everything, an opinion over every detail of their daily workings. This was appropriate, to a point. If someday she ran Quasicore, she would need to have a mind of her own. On the other hand, it wouldn't do for her to question his every step.

"The doctor would be useful to your AI projects."

"Quite a grasp of the obvious you have, Daughter," he said with dry sarcasm, moving away from the window.

She seemed impervious to his criticism, her gray eyes cool and steady as she watched him approach. "This being the case, I assume you mean to reacquire her."

"Yes."

"How?"

"Bait," he answered, wondering if she would be able to grasp his meaning. She was a bright girl, but so young and without his experience. He anticipated confusion and frustration.

She surprised him with a nod of understanding. "I thought that might be it. The FPA inspector?"

He didn't speak, studying her with vague unease. She was right, but her ability to follow his line of thinking this far disturbed him. He was not ready to share his power, even with his offspring. He had raised and trained her to replace him when he died, but he did not anticipate the event for quite some time. Beyond all expectations, was she turning into a rival?

"Does it meet with your approval?" he asked silkily.

"Whether I approve or disapprove is immaterial," she said with gratifying promptness, her expression remaining serene. "You are the power here, Father, and your decisions should be carried out without question. I see the advantage in reacquiring the doctor. I also see how it will please you to retrieve her from the Shays."

A flawless response. He had taught her well. His uneasiness subsided to a lingering kernel. "Yes, it will be quite entertaining to see their response. Perhaps they will learn not to flaunt their prized possessions so."

"They were very obvious. This doesn't concern you?" Her expression had clouded with faint worry.

"They were gloating, but they also had merchandise to sell. They wanted to make sure I understood the value of the product by reminding me of the value of its creator. The doctor escaped her capture, so the twins had not been offering her as well. She still has value to them. They will not be pleased when I remove her from their company."

Liaena gave a thoughtful nod, eyes downcast. "Thank you, Father. I understand now."

Again, a flawless response. He wondered if she was behaving so well because she wanted a concession from him. He could guess what it might be and waited for her to ask, studying her bent head with clinical interest.

"Father, may I have some leave time? I have not seen Mother in a very long—"

"No, you may not," he interrupted, keeping his tone pleasant and genial. "This is not the proper time for you to be absent. When things settle, we will discuss it again."

She stiffened and Webster wondered if she would protest. But his daughter must have decided to be on her best behavior today. She only nodded and rose to her feet. "May I return to my quarters, then?"

"You may," he answered in a neutral voice, keeping satisfaction out of his tone.

She glided toward the door, her movements smooth and graceful as a swan. At the door she turned and bowed her head in his direction, acknowledging him on her departure. *Flawless.* On days like today, he could congratulate himself on how well he had molded her. But there were other days.

Webster's lip curled in distaste as he remembered Liaena holding up a bloody hand, chastising him for angering the Shays. "It's the rise of the Red Sun," she had warned him. His own daughter, rebellious and quoting religious tripe. It was enough to make a man give up on the next generation.

Chapter 17

Nick would have killed for a solid hour of uninterrupted sleep in a simple bed. He'd thought Cassie's soft chairs were comfortable when he first tried them. He'd ended the night knowing a bed of nails would be more restful. Of course, part of it was Cassie's fault. How was he supposed to sleep after the wild ride she'd put him through? Screaming nightmare, tantalizing foot massage, killer kisses, and last but not least, the mysterious rejection.

He snuck a glance at her and scowled. She looked rested, normal. As if nothing had happened. He wanted to hit something. How she'd snuck out of her quarters without waking him irritated him the most.

"More coffee, Nick?" Sin asked, offering the carafe.

He shook his head and she filled her brother's cup instead. Del declined but Cassie held out her cup with a murmur of thanks. When she'd finished refilling, Sin set the carafe on a hovering tray and sank into the same chair she'd occupied the night before.

"Before we get to lunch—" she started.

Manakai's groan interrupted her. "Come on, Sissa. I'm starving."

She smirked at her brother. "We'll get the major things out of the way, then let Nick do his inspector thing to his heart's content over food. Good enough?"

"Make it quick, or I'll start gnawing on your furniture."

"Tasteless, but good fiber," Cassie mused into her cup, shooting the dark twin a dimpled smile from her vantage on the arm of Del's chair.

Nick really wanted to hit something. Or someone. He turned his head to level a hostile look on Manakai. The man seemed oblivious, winking at Cassie as he took a swallow of dark liquid.

"I think we should start with an apology," Sin said, gaining Nick's attention. She didn't look sorry. She looked downright amused and not even a little repentant.

"For what?"

"For leading you down the garden path. Or as my brother put it last night, sending you on a wild goose chase."

Nick blinked at her, astounded he'd forgotten. They'd spun him a pretty story last night and he'd been exhausted, but it was no excuse. When people like the Shays made this kind of admission, you followed it up. "Explain," he rasped, not daring to look at Cassie. She'd been a big reason why his brain had turned to mush last night. The heat of humiliation climbed his neck.

"I didn't just ask you here for a reunion with your brother. You'd been asking questions about us at FPA Headquarters. You'd gotten enough information on us to ask for help getting Del away from the Core. You were putting yourself in considerable danger." Her expression had lost all amusement, gaze meeting his with somber directness.

He raised his eyebrows. "Danger from you,

because I was getting too close to the truth?"

"So stubborn," she murmured, wry glance flicking to his brother. "Must run in the family."

Del growled but the humorous light in his eyes belied the threatening sound.

Her mouth curved in response as she turned her attention back to Nick. "You were in no danger from us. The danger was in you uncovering things the FPA wanted to keep under wraps or discovering things the Core wanted undiscovered. The Core would have just disposed of you, but the FPA doesn't resort to death and dismemberment. They would have buried you alive in some remote, dead-end job with no access to information, contacts, or recourse. So we rescued you by encouraging you to investigate us."

"You rescued me," he repeated with something less than belief.

"Sure," she said with a suppressed smile. "You already knew enough about us to be suspicious. Del's employment with us gave you added incentive to pursue the matter in spite of lack of evidence. Your need to wrest him from our dastardly clutches kept you well focused." She wasn't suppressing the smile anymore, her eyes twinkling at him.

"Nice embellishment," Manakai observed, his tone approving.

Sin chuckled. "Thanks."

"So you're saying you wanted me to investigate you?" Nick stared from one to the other in disgusted disbelief. Did they really think he'd buy this load of krell dung?

"So you'd stay here and stay safe." Del's expression was serious and intense.

"Bro, you're losing it. These people have you so snowed."

"Which is our cue to introduce you to our FPA contact," Sin announced. "Mina, could you connect us with Hawk, please?"

"Of course."

Nick's head whipped around, focusing on her as his stomach plummeted down several levels. She could not have meant who he thought she meant. No, it was impossible. There had to be somebody else they knew by the name.

The fireplace in front of him flickered, reappearing as a wall-sized viewer. Nick would have been impressed by the exceptional holography, except a face appeared in the center of the viewer, the sharp features all too familiar.

First Marshal Gaston Marchand, head of the Federated Planetary Alliance, known far and wide as the Hawk, stared them all down like the raptor he was named for. Not just because he resembled the bird. The man had a keen, predatory intellect and a hard, ruthless nature, winning him the fear and respect of people more powerful than Nick ever dreamt of being.

"Hey, big M," Manakai said with infinite casualness, raising his coffee cup in careless salute to the most powerful person in the galaxy. "We have someone you should meet."

Nick stared a second longer in horrified fascination before his training kicked in and he surged to his feet, standing at attention. "Sir," he said crisply, doing his best not to salute like a green fleet officer. He was an inspector now, not a rookie grunt, hard to remember when the man intimidated him with just one sweep of those flinty eyes.

"Inspector Givliani," the First Marshal acknowledged in a barking voice. "My time's precious, so pay attention. The Shays have requested a liaison with the FPA, someone on-site who can serve as the FPA's voice. They want you." He paused, eyes narrowing, his lined face a harsh reflection of doubt. Nick opened his mouth but Marchand cut him off. "You're young. Your record's good but you're untried as an inspector. Still, the Shays seem set on you." His sharp gaze flickered from one twin to the other, disapproval weaving with resignation. "So you're it. Don't screw it up. Full debriefing in my office tomorrow morning at oh six hundred."

The man glanced down as if he were about to disconnect and Sin appeared at Nick's side. "Gaston, dear," she said in an amused voice. "You know I love it when you bark orders and spew military jargon. But the man thinks we're spinning him a fairytale, and a little reassurance would go a long way toward cementing his relationship with us."

The First Marshal looked up, impatience etched around his eyes and thinning his mouth. "I repeat, debriefing at oh six hundred. Face to face communication in a secure location. If he needs me to hold his hand until then—" he began with such acid sarcasm it stung Nick into speaking.

"Sir, I respect your decision and follow orders, but the information I've uncovered about the Shays does not lead me to believe they are law abiding citizens. Are you telling me—?"

"Get off this open channel and meet me in my office tomorrow, Inspector." His flinty gaze challenged and commanded.

Nick subsided with a grudging, "Yes, sir." The viewer went blank and Nick stared at it, his heart thumping a hard rhythm in his chest. A faint ringing sang in his ears.

Sin patted his arm then moved away. "Let's eat."

"Thank the Suns," Manakai sighed, rising to his feet with a surge of smooth power. He shifted around Nick, staring into his face with a wicked grin. "Guy looks like he was on the business end of a stunner."

"Ain't every day you meet the top dog," Del commented, slinging an arm around Nick's stiff shoulders and turning him toward the kitchen. "Works the nerves, y'know."

"Perhaps some soothing music would be helpful." Mina sounded sincere, but Nick had the sneaking suspicion she was also making fun of him.

"Can you play Zinfen's fifth, Mina?" Cassie asked in a subdued voice.

"My pleasure." The gentle strains of a mellow guitar eased through the rooms, a background river of sound as warm and welcoming as Sin's quarters.

It did not sooth Nick. He sat on a stool at the kitchen counter next to his brother, aware of Cassie on Del's other side, out of his sight. The twins began an elaborate dance in the kitchen, creating their meal with a synchrony amazing to behold. They'd either done this a thousand times or they could read each other's minds. *Maybe both,* Nick mused.

He went on the offensive. "So what's in your sealed FPA file?"

The twins chuckled without looking up from their work. "Still don't believe us, Giv?" Manakai asked with goading humor.

Sin widened her eyes at her brother. "Well, we might have faked the First Marshal's face and voice on the viewer. Or maybe he believes Marchand is now one of the bad guys."

Nick grimaced. "What's in the damned file?"

"Easy, bro," Del murmured next to him.

Manakai lifted his dark head with a gleam of hilarity in those irritating green eyes, but when he opened his mouth, Sin elbowed him. "Don't be a pain, Kai."

"What?" he responded with injured innocence.

Instead of replying, Sin turned to Nick. "The file contains all the undercover operations we've run for the FPA and all the sanctions they've granted us. We're not thrilled they're keeping records of it all, but we understand they want to cover their own interests. At some point, they'll have to explain to the public and a court of law how and why these things have happened."

Nick regarded her with a dubious frown. "You're saying you haven't done anything illegal?"

"I wouldn't go that far," she answered with a smirk. "Some of the things we've done have been outside the rules. All in a good cause. As long as we don't hurt the innocent."

Nick's snort cut her off. "Like setting off a riot on a commerce station?"

"Looters aren't innocent," Manakai said in an even tone, but his eyes were cool and hard when he glanced up at Nick.

"The merchants were."

"They were fully reimbursed by us afterward." Manakai slid a full plate in front of him. "Eat up,

Inspector."

"No one was seriously hurt," Cassie commented from the other side of Del.

Nick leaned forward to catch a glimpse of her. She was plucking at a piece of toast, her expression hard to read.

"The end justifies the means?" he asked with more harshness than he'd intended.

Her fingers stilled and her lips pressed together.

Del leaned forward to block Nick's view of the little woman, his body language protective. "This ain't a sun cruise we're on. It's war, pure and simple. No armies, but war all the same. We do what we can to protect civvies, but war ain't pretty."

Chastised and a little hurt by his brother's response, Nick looked away from his earnest dark eyes, picking up a fork and pushing the food around on his plate. Eggs, lots of veggies, and no meat. He remembered Cass was a vegetarian and glanced over at her plate. She had the same meal. He wondered at the unspoken consideration the Shays had shown her. "And Cassie's file?"

A heavy silence fell over them. Nick didn't lift his head, his whole body going still. Would they answer? Would she?

Sin cleared her throat, sliding onto a stool at the end of the counter. "Cassie was framed for murder."

The simple statement sent an icy river of shock down his spine. "Murder," he repeated, glancing at each of them in turn. None of them met his gaze.

"The Core murdered my lab partner," Cassie responded, her voice low and toneless. "I'd refused to work on the code project anymore and they were trying to keep me in line. The evidence against me was overwhelming. It looked like I'd killed him for my own gain. They threatened to turn over the evidence if I ran to the FPA. They were gambling on my complicity in the project and the scare factor of the murder to force me to submit."

"You said you left. With Imago." Nick tried to keep all emotion out of his voice, tried not to show how much this was affecting him. Murder? Cassie?

"Yes, he was my proof. I knew it would hurt me more than it would hurt the Core to expose what had happened to him. The FPA would blame me for creating the code. I didn't think they'd believe me when I said I didn't infect Imago with it. But I wanted to strike back at the Core…" Her voice faded.

Nick leaned forward again to catch a glimpse of her. The pale, set expression on her delicate features hit him like a blow to his chest.

"When she went to the FPA, she encountered someone loyal to our cause," Sin interjected. "They sent her to us and Marchand sealed her file."

"Lucky for us," Manakai said, sitting at the other end of the counter next to Cassie. He gave the little woman a boyish grin and Nick wanted to growl. "We wouldn't have gotten this far without our resident super-geek."

Cassie leveled her fork at him, an egg-covered piece of vegetable dangling on the end. "Watch it. I know where you live."

Manakai's grin became sly. "Yet you never come by. Don't you love me anymore, Cassie-girl?"

"No. Now behave yourself and eat your breakfast."

"Yes, ma'am," he murmured with a wink, plucking

the vegetable off her fork and popping it in his mouth. He didn't look at all put off by her rejection. The two of them seemed far too comfortable with each other.

Distracted by this aggravating by-play, Nick struggled to get his mind back on track. What had they been discussing? *Right, murder.* "The FPA didn't investigate the death?" He could hear the tightness in his voice, but couldn't do anything about it.

Sin put her utensils down, bracing her elbows on the counter and propping her chin on folded hands. Her expression was unreadable as she studied him. "No, they did not."

"So you're telling me Marchand covered up a murder."

"I'm telling you any investigation would have been a farce. The Core's FPA rats would have protected them and covered their tracks, and what evidence was left would have persecuted an innocent woman."

"How do you know she's innocent?" Nick blurted the question burning in his mind since they'd mentioned murder. Cassie didn't seem the killer type, but stranger things had been known to happen. Even as he asked it, Nick knew it was a mistake.

A thunderous silence followed. Nick's heart beat a heavy rhythm, the rush of blood ringing in his ears. Suns, if she didn't hate him before, she would now. He was afraid to look away from the flare of green fire in Sin's eyes, afraid to find out what expression Cassie wore on her face.

At a subdued scrape of sound, Nick turned his head. Cassie walked away with quiet grace, head up and back straight. He opened his mouth then closed it again and let her go, a dismal ache in his chest.

"Thanks so much," Sin snapped, her face a mask of controlled anger. "Do you have any idea how hard it's been getting her to eat and sleep the past few days? She found the body, Nick. She's had nightmares about it ever since. Do you know what it does to her? Do you know how often she sees him dead in her dreams?"

"Yeah," he rasped, dropping his gaze to his plate. So it was her dead lover who'd woken her screaming. "I do."

Sin paused. "You do?"

With random fingers, he picked up a slice of toast, shredded it in half, and dropped the pieces back on his plate. "She had one last night."

"And how do you know that?"

"I was there." The quality of the silence prompted Nick to raise his head and glance around at his companions. Their expressions, surprised, amused, and speculative, made him reevaluate what he'd said. "I didn't sleep with her," he revised with an impatient shake of his head. "I was out in her living room and heard her screaming."

Sin winced and looked down, but Del asked with quiet humor, "What were you doing in her living room, bro?"

Nick looked down at his plate again and began shredding the halves of toast, heat creeping up his neck. "I didn't want her to be alone. She doesn't have an AI to watch over her."

"She didn't want to subject them to her dreams."

Nick raised his head, meeting Sin's somber gaze. In her beautiful face, he read honest worry and affection for her friend. "Sam said she didn't want to play favorites."

"That, too," Sin responded with a faint smile.

Nick tilted his head to one side, studying her. Somehow, the simple concern she showed for Cassie put her in a new perspective. He didn't think she was acting. She had seemed fond of her other pilots as well, even weeping for the lost Quan. This didn't fit with the image of a cold, calculating man-eater.

He turned his thoughtful gaze on Del, evaluating again the new openness and clarity in his brother's eyes, the ease with which he now smiled. Would his brother fall for a barracuda, a woman who shammed her emotions and faked her interest for her own ends? He must have seen plenty of those women during his time with the Core, so he'd know them on sight. Del was utterly gone on Sinsudee Shay, content with his new life. Could Nick trust in this, trust and believe them?

Nick let his gaze shift to Manakai Shay and gave a small shake of his head. Maybe his sister wasn't so bad but this one was not to be trusted. How could you trust a man who could grin like this while secrets swam in the depths of his eyes?

"Stars, you can see him working it out," Manakai said with a callous chuckle, green eyes gleaming with humor. "Like his forehead's a little window, thoughts marching by. Do I believe them? The lady's nice and my brother loves her, so she's probably not the devil. But her brother? Suns, no. He has evildoer written all over him."

Del snorted, ducking his head, but not before Nick caught the grin on his face.

Sin made an exasperated noise, staring at her brother. "You could make an effort, Kai."

Manakai made a dismissive wave of one hand,

picking up his coffee cup with the other. "He'd see right through it. I'm only good at charming the pants off women, remember?"

Del rumbled a deep laugh. "You wanna get into his pants?"

Manakai paused in the act of raising the cup to his lips, eyes narrowing as he stared at the snickering man, his mouth curving with a hint of a smile. "Getting awful lippy, big man. Watch it or I'll get T'Zai to do the long ceremony."

Del choked as if one of his snickers backfired on him. Manakai chuckled, saluting with the cup before taking a swig.

Nick stared from one to the other, a sense of foreboding creeping up his spine. He hoped they were talking about some other kind of ceremony, but when Del turned a guilty, sheepish face his way, his heart fell. "Oh, Sun's blood," he wheezed.

"Ah, yeah." Del's face turned darker and he shifted in his seat, eyes not quite meeting Nick's. "I wanted to ask you to be there, but, well, we were trying to keep it quiet."

"Have you lost your mind? You barely know these people!"

Manakai loosed a quiet laugh and Sin leaned forward, catching Nick's gaze. She was smiling. "Don't you want to be our Bond-brother, Nick?"

He strangled a little on his own tongue, not having thought this far ahead. If his brother Sun-bonded with Sin, he'd be related to these people. Suns have mercy.

The twins laughed. Del watched Nick with a crooked grin and a hint of anxiety in his eyes. Nick swore to himself when he realized why. His brother wanted his approval.

Sin leaned over and planted a loud, smacking kiss on his cheek, distracting him. "Welcome to the family."

"Just shoot me now," he growled and they laughed again.

"Since you know, I'd really like you to be there." Del's quiet comment drew his attention.

It might start a fight, but he had to say it. "I can't talk you out of it?"

"Oh, thank you very much," Sin retorted, but she didn't sound upset, her voice threaded with humor. Nick didn't take his eyes off his brother.

Del wore a wry half-smile, his gaze steady. "Sorry, bro. I'm done in, off the deep end, no savin' me." He shrugged. "May as well seal the deal."

Nick sighed. "That's what I thought. Yeah, I'll be there. But I'm telling you, I ain't thrilled with the idea."

Del's grin went wide with delight.

Sin gave Nick another gentle peck on the cheek and smiled with such affection, it gave him a dizzying sense of disorientation. "You will be," she said with a pat on his arm. "Just give it time. And thank you. It wasn't going to be the same without you there."

Shaken, Nick looked down at his full plate and tried to find solid ground. He felt like he'd stepped through some invisible door into an alternate universe. "Is this why you wanted me for an FPA liaison?"

"It's part of the reason," she answered, taking her plate to the sanitizer. "We like to keep family close."

She was teasing him, but he couldn't stop a wince at the word family. "What's the rest of the reason?"

His brother answered with an apology, startling him. "Sorry, Nick." Del grimaced and shrugged. "I

242

can't help trying to protect you. Can't kick the habit of watching out for you."

"What are you talking about?"

"Let's say you believe the whole story." Del leaned on folded arms and watched Nick with shrewd eyes. "The Shays are the good guys, there's nothing here to investigate, and the FPA's got Core moles eating it away from the inside. What's the first thing you wanna do?"

Nick stared at his brother in disgust. He was starting to talk like them. "If Marchand backs their story and shows me proof, I'll want to stay at HQ and help him weed out the bad apples."

"Exactly. We can't let you do it, Nick. Too dangerous."

A surge of anger heated his face. "You can't keep me from doing my job. I know you mean well, but—"

"We've been at this a lot longer than you have," Manakai interrupted, his voice abrupt and without a shred of his usual humor. "No insult to your skills as an investigator, but you'd make yourself a target out there. You're no good to anyone dead."

Sin's tone was gentler than her brother's. "If you stayed here, you could work on the problem without us worrying you were going to end up on a slab somewhere."

"I can't do anything from here. The problem is in HQ, not your station."

"We could use your help," Sin persuaded. "We may not always do things by the book, but our cause is just, and we could use someone like you on our side."

Nick glared at her. "Great. In other words, you want me to start breaking the law, too."

"It ain't breaking the law if the FPA is asking you to do it," Del responded with a hint of impatience.

"Besides," Manakai added, his tone hard, "your job is here now. The First Marshal approved your post as our liaison."

Nick's hands fisted. "Why'd you give me no choice? Why didn't you ask me?"

"Would you have agreed?" Sin's voice was soft, her eyes clear and calm.

He didn't bother to answer her question. He'd already told them what he would have done if given a choice. "So instead, you forced me."

"So instead," she said, taking his full plate and putting it in the warmer, "we did the only thing we could do to keep you safe. You don't have all the answers and you don't know what we know. It's only natural you'd want to go back to the HQ and turn the place upside down to clean out the vermin. You don't believe us when we say it'll get you killed." She shrugged. "We protect our own, Nick."

This last, simple statement cut the ground out from under him. He stared at her, mute with dismay and a vague sort of longing. Is this how they'd gotten to Del? Luring him with the promise of belonging, of being a part of something, a part of a family? He understood now how it could have gotten to his brother. The two of them had been alone for so long, separated from the only family they had left and not willing or able to make lasting attachments to anyone else. Attachments only got you hurt.

In the silence, Sin removed the food from the warmer and placed it back in front of Nick. "Now eat your lunch. You'll need your strength."

Chapter 18

Cassie stood in the infirmary's surgery unit, cursing Sin under her breath in a steady litany while she waited for Nick. She was doing her best to avoid the man and what does her friend do?

"Cass, he needs a new data port. If he's going to be with us, he'll need to be able to fly a Shadow and his port is too old. Could you replace it, please?" Smooth as honey and not a bit believable.

They didn't need Cassie to do the replacement. Shipping someone else in would take time, but even the head doctor in the infirmary could handle the job. Cassie had pointed this out in protest. For an answer, Sin had thrown down the "you're the expert" and "we trust you to do it right" cards. Forcing Cassie to tell the truth.

"I don't want to see him, Sin. He thinks I killed Dmitri."

"He doesn't, honey," Sin had replied in her gentlest voice. "No one who's been around you could possibly think you're a killer."

She'd done more protesting, but Sin had insisted. And the woman could insist like nobody's business.

Cassie sighed, looking at the time then glancing around at her equipment to make sure everything was in place. The surgical unit was ready, but she wasn't. Suns, she was going to have to touch him.

"Hi." Nick's deep voice startled her out of her reverie. She spun toward the door with a squeak. Those dark eyes of his speared through her, his expression serious and a little hesitant. "I, uh, they told me to just come on in."

She nodded and waved him toward the table, unable to speak. This was going to be harder than she'd thought.

He didn't move. She stared at him, watching with a growing knot in her stomach when he shifted in place and fidgeted with his jacket, his gaze skittering away from hers. "I'm a little nervous." He barked a short laugh, tugging on one ear as his face darkened with color.

"Why?" A snap of bitter emotion ran through her voice, the knot tightening in her middle. "Afraid I'll slit your throat?"

He stilled, his startled gaze meeting hers. "No, Cass," he said, soft and low like the rumble of a jungle cat. "I'm nervous because the last time I did this I was a kid and looped out on meds. I just don't like these places." He paused, eyeing her before his mouth compressed and his tone hardened. "My mother died in a place like this. So did my dad, after the accident. You got nothing to do with it."

Mortified, she looked down. His reaction was honest and normal; most people didn't like hospitals. Leave it to her to bring up the one thing she'd been hoping to avoid. "I could give you a sedative if you think you need it," she said in as neutral a tone as she could manage. Her voice shook a bit and she prayed he wouldn't notice.

He sidled closer to the table. "Well, I might get

through it okay if you just held my hand."

She glanced up. A crooked smile curved his lips, his dark eyes meeting hers with an appeal impossible to resist. For a second, she saw the boy he'd been, all awkward charm and uncertain nerve. He didn't know where he stood with her, but was making an effort to put her at ease in spite of his misgivings.

Warmth spread through her, loosening the knot in her middle. She gave him a faint smile. "Sorry. I need both hands."

His face fell with exaggerated sorrow. "Guess I'll have to suck it up, won't I?"

"It won't be so bad." Cassie moved closer and waved him to the table again. "It's a quick procedure, done a zillion times. There are almost never any complications."

"Almost never?" he repeated wryly, scooting onto the table. He reclined on his back, his eyes never leaving her face.

"I've never had any complications with my procedures. This is one of my areas of expertise, so take a deep breath and relax, Inspector. It'll be over before you know it." As she spoke, she activated the sterilizing field, watching the monitor while it settled over them and destroyed any superficial microbes.

"Back to calling me Inspector." He shook his head. "That's what I get for asking a stupid question."

"Asking about complications is never stupid," she responded, ignoring his other comment. Calling him anything else seemed to get her in a world of trouble.

"That wasn't the stupid question."

His gaze rested on her, a pressure and heat as palpable as a touch, and a flush prickled the skin of her face. He could only mean his question about her innocence, but was he implying it was stupid because he didn't believe she'd killed anyone or because asking outright had made her hostile?

She cleared her throat and made her tone brisk, not looking at him. "Please turn your head, focus on the blinking light there, and keep as still as you can."

He complied without further comment.

Cassie stared at his data port, a nervous tickle in her stomach. She was going to have to touch him. She stalled, putting her hands in the surgical gel. It tingled as it soaked into the minute crevices of her skin and sterilized her hands. After the appropriate amount of time, she removed her hands and let them dry then picked up a microprobe and turned toward her patient. "Lights, please," she said and the surgical control system bathed the area in light.

Nick grunted, his big body tensing. She realized he was still nervous. "Honestly, there's nothing to it."

"It's brain surgery, Cass," he responded in a tight voice. A muscle ticked in his jaw. "There's a whole lot to it."

A strong urge to run a hand through his dark hair struck her. "Take deep breaths, listen to my voice, and pretend we're somewhere else," she said in her best soothing therapist's voice, bending toward the surgical site. Concentrating on keeping her patient calm decreased her own anxiety over touching him. "Just think of us someplace nice, like a quiet café or a pretty beach, somewhere peaceful and restful."

Her hands knew their work, inserting the probe into the side of the port, making the necessary adjustments to prepare the implant for removal. "I knew a place like that once. My family and I vacationed on a remote tropical planet. Beautiful, white sandy beaches, warm water as clear as glass, and green life as far as the eye could see."

When the port was ready, she reached over to the control panel, sending the remote signal commanding his data port to retract the microfilaments embedded in his brain centers. He didn't even twitch. A swipe of anesthetic gel numbed the skin around the port in seconds and she tugged it loose.

"I remember standing in the water and watching these little purple fish swim around my feet. They were so completely unafraid, nibbling on my toes and brushing against my ankles. I wanted to bring them home with us, but Mom wouldn't let me."

A moment later, she slipped the new port in place, turning it with care and watching the monitor until it was in position. Then she sent the signal to extend the new microfilaments, talking while she watched the slow progression of each filament through his brain.

"The sand was like powder, but it still made great sandcastles. Mine weren't more than lumps piled on more lumps, but my father built this gorgeous tower, with a staircase spiraling up the outside. I remember we had a story to go with the tower, about a great wizard who lived there and his pet dragon who would land on the top. I raced around the beach, flapping my arms like wings, while my father called out incantations, protecting the land around the tower and saving it from evil."

All the microfilaments reached their exact destinations and Cassie smiled with satisfaction, grasping the microprobe once again. In a reverse of her work with the first port, she inserted the probe to trigger the stabilizing attachments, securing the implant in place.

"Mom always played the damsel in distress. I think she overdid it just so the wizard would carry her off, which he did every chance he got. The tower was there when we left. I like to pretend it's still there."

Straightening, Cassie assessed her patient. Nick's eyes were closed, a smile curling his lips. No tension remained in the muscles of his neck and jaw, and his body relaxed. The sight of this big man laid out before her in apparent trust, yielding to her touch, sent a shaft of heat through her.

Taking a hasty step back, she cleared her throat. "See, I told you there was nothing to it."

Nick rolled his head toward her, eyes heavy-lidded. The smile remained, looking much more sultry than peaceful, now that he aimed it in her direction. "Thanks. I liked the story." His deep voice rubbing over her nerves like rough velvet.

She fiddled with the probe and tried to think of something not lame to say. She failed. "I'm glad it helped."

He pushed up on an elbow, swinging his legs over the edge of the table with smooth strength, drying her throat. "I also liked how you breathed it in my ear," he purred, surging forward off the table and coming to a stop a hand's breadth away from her.

She dropped the probe and abandoned it, taking several steps backward. "Y-you need to keep the area clean and dry until the tissues have healed around the port. You also need to avoid using the port for a couple of days, to let your brain tissue heal and let the connections—"

"Will you have dinner with me?"

She gaped at him then snapped her mouth shut. He was still smiling, less sensual and more wistful. She shook her head, not trusting her voice. Her ears were ringing.

"Why not, Cass?"

She couldn't think of a single thing to say besides the truth, and she sure wasn't going to admit she was afraid to spend time with him. Afraid to find out if she really was falling in love with him. She opened her mouth then closed it again, her mind hunting for those generic excuses people always used.

When she didn't answer, Nick looked down, his smile fading and a faint crease forming between his brows. "I'd just like to spend some time with you, Cassie."

Her heart skipped a beat at those quiet words. Was he serious? Or was this just a nice line he used with women?

He shifted in place then took a step backward, tucking his hands behind him and leaning against the table. "What if I promise to behave?" he asked in a low voice, eyes still focused on the floor. "What if I promise not to ask any more stupid questions?" He gave a low, self-derisive laugh and glanced at her, dark eyes vivid and intense. "What if I promise to keep my hands to myself?"

How could he seduce her without coming anywhere near her? She tried to swallow, but her dry throat locked. Without thinking, she whispered, "Nick—" She gasped when he made a low sound in his throat and surged toward her. She skittered backward and he froze, staring at her with vibrant dark eyes.

He took a deliberate step back and tucked his hands behind him again. His lips curled the slightest bit and his eyes danced with an inviting humor. "Could you call me something else?"

It surprised a laugh out of her and she laid a hand over her mouth to contain it. He gave a lopsided grin, bouncing a little on the balls of his feet as if he were doing his best to look harmless.

Cassie pretended to think about it. "How about Bob?"

"Yeah, that should get us through dinner."

She folded her arms and narrowed her eyes. "I didn't say I'd have dinner with you."

"Pretty please?" He put on a wide-eyed, pathetic look. When she snickered, he added in a husky voice, "I could get down on my knees again."

The memory of his fingertips on the back of her knee was so strong her legs buckled. Taking a deep breath and looking away from his intense gaze, she shrugged out of her lab coat and lied. "Well, I am hungry."

"Damn." He sighed, moving away from the table.

"Why damn?" she couldn't resist asking as she led the way toward the door. He kept his distance, for which she was both grateful and disappointed.

"I was hoping to get another look at those legs."

She frowned at him, trying to pretend her face wasn't pink, while they made their way through the infirmary toward the exit. "I thought you promised to behave."

"I didn't ask a thing and my hands are right where I left them."

She snorted. "I should have pressed for a clearer definition of the word behave."

He chuckled, not a very comforting response, and paced a circumspect distance at her side while they made their way to the commons. The corridors grew busier as they drew closer to the center of the station.

"What are you in the mood to eat?" Nick asked, moving with the crowd into the open, central area.

"I know a good place." She headed toward an open lift. When they arrived on the level she'd chosen, she led him to a busy restaurant called Nightly Nebula, so named for the musical attraction, a singer who called herself Nebula. She had a throaty, sultry voice, but the setting wasn't the least bit romantic, which suited Cassie just fine. Well lit and cheery, the place was known for fantastic pasta and innovative vegetarian dishes.

They seated themselves at a table in the midst of a subdued crowd of diners, clinking silverware and low conversation the only music to be heard. Nebula wasn't due on stage yet. A menu appeared on the clear surface of their table and they both leaned forward.

"What's good here?"

"Most everything." Cassie tried not to notice how good he smelled. She had a quick fantasy about nibbling on him instead of dinner, then took a breath and pointed at a selection on the menu, choosing without much thought.

A little robotic waiter rolled over, a tray balanced on its flat crown. It distributed their drinks with economic swiftness and departed. Cassie took a sip of her sweet punch. She wondered if it was such a good idea to order alcohol, the warmth sinking down to her stomach and spreading a languid relaxation through her limbs. She had barely touched her lunch and hadn't thought to eat since.

Nick studied her over his glass, a faint smile on his handsome face. "So was the story you told me true about your family vacation?"

"Yes, it was. I'm sure it wasn't as idyllic as I'm remembering it, but it's still one of my fondest memories of childhood. I pestered my parents for weeks after, begging for an aquarium. They finally gave me a goldfish, which lasted three days and died." She grimaced.

He chuckled. "Did they get you another one?"

"I didn't want another one. I'd named him Goldie, and since it's not right to give another fish the same name, I would've had to come up with something even more profoundly clever." She shook her head. "Just wasn't in me. I chose a robo-puppy instead."

"What'd you call the puppy?"

"Bob," she replied in a bland tone.

He laughed, a full, deep laugh. Other diners turned their way and smiled in response. Cassie hid a silly grin behind her glass and watched him. *Suns,* the man was beautiful, with golden skin and dark hair curling around his ears and over his forehead. Her fingertips tingled with the urge to touch the shadow of stubble on his chin. He had a heart-stopping smile and his laugh made her want to curl up in his lap and purr.

"Should I be flattered or insulted?" he asked, the corners of his eyes crinkling with humor.

"You should feel sorry for me. Poor, imagination-impaired Cassie who can't come up with more than one name for anything."

"Imagination-impaired? I don't think so. I remember those inventions of yours. Did you like the puppy?"

"I loved him." She said it without thinking and could've kicked herself when a slow smile molded his mouth.

"Then I'm flattered." His deep voice was low and teased her in tender places. She wanted to squirm. "Do you want to tell me about your parents?"

She smirked, eyeing him until his brows tugged together. "You just sounded like my first psych professor. Tell me about your mother," she pantomimed in a smarmy tone.

He grinned. "Sorry for the flashback. I just didn't want to upset you if they were gone."

"Oh, no, they're alive and well. I plan to keep it that way, which is why I haven't seen them since I came to the Shays."

"What? Why not?"

"If Griffin ever knew who and where they were, they'd become leverage. He'd use them to get me back."

"So why didn't he use them when you walked out with Imago?"

"Almost the first thing the Shays asked me when I came to them was if I had family and where they were. My parents have been in seclusion ever since. I haven't been to visit them, because I'm afraid I'll give away their location somehow." She paused to sip her drink then gave him a wan smile. "Mom still gets to harass me over the viewer. You're too thin, what's with the circles under your eyes, etcetera. Dad and I play chess every week."

He tilted his head, dark eyes shrewd. "Why aren't they here?"

Cassie looked down into her drink, her stomach curdling with shame. "I was not in good shape at first. I didn't want them to see me so messed up. It would have hurt them, and they would have wanted to fix me."

He leaned forward and touched the hand yanking on her braid in a rather vicious manner. She hadn't known she was doing it. She dropped the hand to her lap, skin tingling from his touch, and didn't meet his gaze when he settled back in his seat.

"You were in bad shape because you found your lab partner dead?"

She hesitated then shook her head and answered him in a near whisper. "No. I was in bad shape because I'd found the man I loved murdered in our lab. Dmitri wasn't just a coworker. We were going to get bonded, start a life and a consulting firm together. Until the Core murdered him."

A thick silence hung in the air for a long minute. Then Nick sighed. "Cass, I'm sorry. I promised not to ask any stupid questions."

"It wasn't stupid," she said with a small shake of her head, but her voice sounded dismal even to her own ears.

"Yeah, it was. You look like I just stabbed you in the chest."

The arrival of their food saved her from responding. Nebula appeared on stage, postponing further dinner conversation. They ate to the crooning of the rotund singer, the mellow blues music a gentle accompaniment to their meal. It was delicious and Cassie relaxed, mind easing away from bad memories.

They were finished with their meal and were sipping drinks when Nebula ended her set to generous applause.

"She was great," Nick commented with a gleam in his eyes. "I'm glad you picked this place."

"Good food, great music." Cassie spread her hands. "What more could you want?"

He gave her an enigmatic smile. Something about the way he was looking at her made her wonder if he'd had enough to eat. "Did you want to stay for the next set?"

"Suns, no. She puts me to sleep. Which is great, don't get me wrong, but I get a rotten kink in my neck with these chairs."

He grinned. "Were you ready to go, or did you want to finish your drink?"

There wasn't much to finish, so she swigged the rest and clicked her glass on the table with a decisive nod. Then she tried to stand. "Whoa," she muttered when the room slipped to the left. All of a sudden, Nick was at her side, steadying her with a hand under her elbow. "Um, how many of those did I have?"

"I think this was your third."

She thought back then looked up at him with a frown. His lips compressed as if he were trying not to smile. "It was my second, which makes me a horrible lightweight. Are you laughing at me?"

"Ain't that stupid," he said with mock horror.

She snorted. "I don't drink much." She made her careful way toward the exit, very aware of his close proximity.

They paused outside the restaurant. "So, what now?" He seemed engrossed in a holo-ad floating by beyond the level's railing.

She should say thank you for dinner and walk away. A decent glob of brains perched in her head; a smart person like her knew when to call it quits. So she was more than a little surprised when she opened her mouth and what came out was not goodbye. "Do you know how to make a supernova?"

He looked down at her with raised eyebrows. "Yeah, but I'm not making one for you."

"Why not?"

"You're so tiny one of those would knock you out cold. Suns, half would do it."

"So make one for yourself and I'll taste test. I just want to try one."

He frowned but kept pace with her when she headed for the lift. "Why do you want to try a supernova?"

"Del mentioned them after his horrible hangover. I'm curious. He's built like an ox, so if these supernovas could knock him on his rear, they must be something else."

His expression said she'd lost her mind. "You want to get knocked out cold?"

"No," she answered with a touch of impatience. "But a small bit would help me sleep, and you two seem to like the drink."

He swore under his breath. "Fine, let's go to Del's place. He has the fixings for them and it's close to your quarters, so it won't be far to drag you when you pass out."

"Are you always this cranky after dinner?"

"Are you always this crazy when you drink?"

She frowned at him. "Why is it crazy to be curious what one stupid drink tastes like?"

He sighed. "You won't like it."

"We'll see, won't we?"

He took a look at her face and chuckled. "Oh, yeah. We'll see." He paused then asked in a low voice, "Why aren't we going to a bar for one, Cass?"

Good question. "I don't like bars," was the surprise answer. "Too crowded, loud, and they smell bad." All true, but none of it was the real reason she wanted to get him alone.

Oh hell, she thought.

Chapter 19

Bloody hell. Nick stared down at the little woman. This was not going according to plan. He hadn't had a real plan, but he'd wanted to spend the whole evening with her. After he'd left Sin's place, it occurred to him if they were telling the truth, Cassie was no longer a suspect. If she was no longer a suspect, she wasn't off limits anymore.

The idea almost made him salivate. Her rejection the previous night helped restrain him to a more cautious approach. If she got into a supernova, he wouldn't be spending more time getting to know her. He'd watch her take a few sips then catch her when she passed out.

She did not look willing to be dissuaded, short of a full-blown fight. He was already feeling guilty about bringing up bad memories at dinner. Fighting with her was the last thing he wanted to do. Stretching her out on his bed and covering her with his body, on the other hand, topped his want-to-do list. But after last night, he was pretty sure that wasn't going to happen, either. He only hoped she'd tell him why she'd jumped away from him and why she was now skittering from his touch like a nervous cat.

They reached Del's quarters in silence. Nick touched the door chime and Sam responded, "Greetings. My living mate Del is not in residence at the moment. May I assist you?"

"Hey, Sam. It's Nick and Cass. Can we come in?"

The door opened almost before he'd stopped speaking. "Please enter and be welcome. I am glad to see you both again."

"It's good to see you, too, Samantha," Cassie responded with a fond smile.

Nick had to look away, grinding his teeth at his response. It wasn't fair how her smiles could stun him senseless. "Can I break into your kitchen, Sam?"

"Please, make yourselves comfortable."

Nick headed for the kitchen.

Cass trailed him. "How have you been, Samantha?"

"Very well, thank you. My living mate is not in residence very often, but I have found I do not lack for companionship. My sister companion Mina has introduced me to most of the others on the station. It is fascinating, Creator Cassie, how individual they have become in their years on this station."

While the AI spoke, Nick began mixing the supernova, measuring out various amounts of five different liquors into a glass.

Cassie watched him with bright eyes, a faint smile on her face. "I find them all fascinating, Sam. Have you begun individualizing your own tastes? Do you have favorite music or interests? A hobby, maybe?"

"I have not yet found a hobby," Sam answered with such sadness Nick paused, lifting his eyebrows at Cassie. "But I do find classical music seems to increase my creative output."

A dimple appeared in Cassie's cheek as she suppressed a smile. "It does the same for me. Don't force the hobby issue. You'll find something to spark your interest. For now, enjoy the diversity of your companions, and don't forget to review and revise your parameters every once in a while."

"Yes, Cassie. Thank you for reminding me."

Nick dropped the flavor pearl into the glass and it dissolved in a swirl of reddish orange.

"Nick, you appear to have made a supernova," Sam commented with a faint note of alarm in her voice.

"Sure did."

"Is this not the beverage which caused so much discomfort to you and my living mate?"

"This is the one."

"I do not understand why you would subject yourself to it again."

"Don't try," he said with a wry twist of his mouth. "You'll blow a fuse."

"I do not have fuses."

"He made it for me. I wanted to taste one." Cassie reached for the glass, but Nick pulled it away.

"One sip, Cass."

"What are you, the drink police? Hand it over, Bob." Her brown eyes sparkled.

Nick couldn't stop a rumbling laugh. "You'll regret it," he warned but handed over the drink anyway.

She gave him a brilliant smile, almost dropping him to his knees, and took a sip. A second later, she bent over, gasping and coughing.

Nick slipped the drink from her hand, clasping her arm and helping her to a kitchen chair. "You okay?"

Tears spilled from her eyes. She didn't seem able to focus on him. A wheeze was all she managed before coughing again.

"Seriously, Cass, are you gonna make it?" Alarm went through him at the flush of color in her face. He sank to a crouch in front of her, and she grabbed his collar, jerking on it as if to shake him.

"Are you trying to kill me?" she croaked, swiping at her streaming eyes with her other hand.

He grinned, unrepentant. "Hey, I warned you."

"Are you ill, Cassie?" Sam asked with some concern.

"I've been poisoned," she wheezed. "Call security."

"She's kidding." Nick narrowed his eyes on Cassie. "Right?"

She stuck her tongue out at him. He grinned, wondering if she had any idea what kind of offer she was making. "I'll be fine," she told Sam, her voice hoarse but recovering. "As long as I don't go anywhere near the vile fluid again."

Nick was staring at her mouth with a desperate kind of longing, wishing he could taste the supernova on her lips. "Why stop now? The first is the worst. Gets better from here on out."

"If you think I'm putting myself through this again, you're nuts."

He met her gaze and smiled. "No doubt about it, you're a bright woman, Cass."

The compliment seemed to fluster her. Nick rose to his feet, moving away with as much nonchalance as he could manage. He'd come so close to pulling her onto his lap again. His hands shook with reaction. Busying himself with more glasses, he said over his shoulder, "Why don't you go chat with Sam? I'll mix something less dangerous."

"You're not drinking the supernova either?"

Nick paused in the act of removing juice from cold storage, not looking at her. "I'm still trying to behave, Cass. It'd be a lot harder with a nova in me."

She made a small sound in her throat. He shot a glance over his shoulder, but she was already on her way out of the kitchen. Taking a deep breath, he grabbed the rest of the ingredients and took his time mixing some sedate, not very alcoholic drinks. If she kept to the pace she'd set while drinking at dinner, these wouldn't affect her.

When he left the kitchen with glasses in hand, he found Cassie reclined on the couch, eyes closed with a faint smile on her face, the strains of classical music weaving through the room.

"It's beautiful, Sam," she murmured. "I've always loved this composer."

"I am glad you are enjoying it."

Nick moved forward, rounding the end of the couch. "Cass."

She popped up as if he'd prodded her with a stick. He sighed and handed her one of the drinks. Maybe he should have made them stronger. She was getting jumpy with him again.

"Thanks." She shifted over, making room for him while she sipped her drink. Then she grinned, smacking her lips. "Tasty."

He eased down next to her. "I aim to please. More your speed than the nova?"

"Much, thank you."

She took another, longer sip and Nick watched her swallow with half-hooded eyes. The delicate arch of her neck was such temptation, sweat dampened his brow.

He put his drink down and shrugged out of his jacket. When he glanced over again, Cass was watching him with focused speculation. His heart jumped in his chest.

"What kind of music do you like?" she asked in a neutral tone.

The classical piece was still playing, and Nick made a casual gesture to indicate the sound. "This is good stuff, but I'm more into something with a backbeat. How about you?"

"I like most kinds. I more or less have favorite songs or singers, rather than favorite types of music." She nibbled on her bottom lip and Nick palmed moisture off his forehead. "Although I can't say I care for the Bendaric croons, and Sun chants bore the snot out of me."

"Blasphemy," he accused with a low chuckle.

"I have not accessed Sun chants," Samantha interjected.

Cassie looked toward the AI's sensors with a smile. "Ask the temple for some. They can give you a nice variety across the spectrum of orders. Some of the Blue Sun chants aren't so bad."

"Blue Sun, huh?" Nick gave her a teasing grin.

She sent him a quelling frown in return. "Or you can ask Mina to get you a fair representation."

"Thank you for your recommendations."

"You're welcome."

A satisfied gleam lit her eyes. Nick realized she was enjoying her interaction with the AI. Was it a creator's pride in her work or the stroking of a genius ego? "What made you get into AIs?"

She faced him, eyes cooling as she studied his expression. "Back to being an inspector?"

"No, Cass. Just curious. You like what you do and you're good at it. But how'd you get into it?"

She eyed him for a moment longer, then relaxed back into the couch and took another swallow of her drink. "I think it was my robo-puppy. He seemed defective, which made me curious. He had some irritating habits, like chewing on my shoes and barking in the middle of the night. I took him apart and put him back together. There was nothing mechanically wrong with him, but he still had those habits. I did some research and discovered he'd been programmed to behave just like a real dog, which was fascinating enough, but the kicker was you could train him like a real dog. So I could break him of those bad habits just by interacting with him. A mechanical device that could learn. You see?"

He nodded. "How old were you?"

She rested her head against the back of the couch and narrowed her eyes in thought. "Six, I think." At the astonished sound he made, she turned her head and gave him a tight smile. "Yup, I was a geek even then."

"I think they call kids like you child prodigies," he countered. "How old were you when you got your first doctorate?"

"Fourteen." She muttered it as if confessing a dirty secret.

"Not much of a childhood, Cass. When did you get to play?"

She frowned. "I played."

"You took apart your robot dog."

"For me, that was play." She shrugged a shoulder. "Other kids didn't understand me, and I didn't understand them. It's almost like we were different species."

"Lonely," he said in a soft voice.

She shook her head, but it seemed more a dismissal of her past than a denial of his comment. "What about you? Did you play?"

Nick snorted. "You kidding? Play's all we did. Dad was hooked on the slicer circuits, so we grew up there. We had a blast, but I wouldn't recommend it for most kids. The circuits are a tough scene for big people, let alone a couple of snot-nosed brats. We learned a lot the hard way."

"So that's where Del got in the habit of looking out for his kid brother." She watched him with a faint smile on her lips. The look in her velvety brown eyes made him want to press her into the couch cushions and kiss her until they were both delirious.

"Yeah, and vice versa. Dad wasn't around much, so we had to protect each other."

"May I ask a question?" Sam interrupted.

"Sure," Cassie and Nick both said at once then shared a quick, amused glance.

"Is this a courtship ritual?"

Cassie choked, coughing into one hand, her face turning a lovely shade of pink.

"Yes," Nick answered with calm finality. Cassie's head jerked up, wide eyes meeting his, her lips parted in surprise. He gave her a slow, hungry smile. May as well let her know where he stood.

He should have known she'd bolt.

She jumped to her feet, spilling some of the drink on her shirt. She didn't seem to notice the stain. "Ah, excuse me, I have to use the..." Her voice trailed off as she quick-stepped toward the sanitary and disappeared within it.

Nick sighed and dropped his head to the back of the couch. Chock up yet another blunder in a long list of them. He sure was learning all the ways not to approach Cassie.

"Nice timing, Sam," he muttered, but the AI didn't reply. With another sigh, he lifted his glass and drained it, wondering if Cass would return at all.

She surprised him. In just a few minutes, she reentered the living room, a damp spot on her shirt where the stain had been and a neutral expression on her features. She was undoing her braid. She gave him a vague smile, perching on the edge of the couch, her fingers releasing brown silk. "It's starting to pull."

Nick took a swift breath and held it, watching one of his fantasies unfold before his eyes. Her fingers worked through the strands of gleaming color, and he sank deeper into the cushions, trying not to look as hungry and desperate as he felt.

"You have to be up early," she said in a distracted tone as she worked. "I can leave if you need to get some rest."

"No," he husked then cleared his throat. "No, I don't need much sleep. Don't get more than a few hours a night." He wasn't paying attention to what he was saying, his focus on her slim fingers releasing and stroking through the gorgeous, silky mass.

"Me, either. Insomnia." She shot him a look, reminding him of last night.

He grimaced. "Your nightmares." She nodded without comment. He hesitated then took the plunge. "Cass, why did you break away from me last night?"

She looked down, a pensive curve to her mouth. "I

told you. I didn't think we should—"

He made a rude noise and cut her off. "You looked terrified. If it wasn't something I did, then it was something in your past. I need to know what it was, Cass. I have to know, because I'm trying to behave, but it's been damned hard and mostly what I want to do is…" He dragged himself to a halt, the images of what he mostly wanted to do with her boiling his blood. He drew in a ragged breath.

She watched him with wide eyes, like a nocturnal animal caught in bright lights, pinned to her seat.

"Cass, I don't want to scare you," he tried, voice hoarse. "I just want to be with you. If all we do is sit and talk, great, because I want to know more about you. But one of these days, I won't behave. I'd like to know you won't run screaming when that happens."

"When, not if?" she asked in a faint voice.

"Yeah. Honey, I'm not made of stone and you're the most bloody beautiful woman I've ever met."

She frowned and his stomach dropped. "That's a line."

"It's the truth."

"It can't be. I'm a mouse compared to Sin."

"Sin Shay is cold, calculating, and dangerous. She scares the crap outta me. I wouldn't want to meet her in a dark alley. Compared to her, you're a Sun angel."

Her mouth curved the slightest bit. "You just don't know her. She's really, very sweet."

"Sure," he scoffed. "Sweet as sugar. Let's get back to why you won't let me put my hands on you."

Her mouth curved more, brown eyes limpid. "There have to be a thousand women on this station more attractive and interesting than a drab, little geek like me."

"You have a terrible self-image, Cass. And you're wrong, you're not a bit drab. I haven't met a single woman I'd rather be with." The words came out without thought, and Nick's heart knocked in his chest. It was the plain, terrifying truth. He didn't want to be with any woman but Cassie.

She shook her head with a snort, as if he were just teasing her. "You can't want me."

"Touch me and find out," he growled, muscles tensing.

She gave a small shake of her head, a smile playing around her mouth. Holding his gaze, she stilled, her expression growing somber. She didn't look away, and his muscles flexed while he fought to restrain himself.

"Touch me, Cass," he rasped. *Touch me, taste me, let me hold you, let me bury myself inside you...* He swallowed a groan, a tremor running through his body. If she didn't do something soon, he was going to misbehave. Badly.

She tipped her head to one side, lashes sweeping down in a slow blink. Her lips parted as if she would speak, but then she captured her bottom lip between her teeth and stunned him by shifting closer and reaching out, cool fingertips tracing a line of fire along his jaw. He drew in a sharp breath and held it, his body throbbing and pulsing to the hard beat of his heart.

"You're so beautiful," she murmured, her fine, elfin features absorbed, light fingers running over his brow, cheekbone, and mouth. He parted his lips, and her fingers returned, brushing fire and ice against his sensitive skin. He tasted her fingertips on a ragged breath, wondering how much of this he could stand. His hands were clenched into fists, and his body was rock hard, every muscle tight with restraint. If he moved, if he touched her, would she flee?

"Beautiful," she whispered again and rose to her knees on the cushions, hand slipping down to rest over his pounding heart. Then she stunned him again, swinging a leg over his hips and straddling him.

"Cass," he gasped when she sank into delicious, near-painful contact with him. His hands forgot about his promise, sliding up her sleek thighs, cupping her luscious bottom, and pressing her closer. Sweet agony.

He let his head fall back against the cushions with a groan, watching her through heavy-lidded eyes while she ran her hands over his chest. She still had an absorbed look on her face, eyes dark with a breathtaking sensuality, her hair rippling over her shoulders in a silky curtain.

He meant to ask if she was sure, if she knew what she was doing to him, but she leaned forward and nipped his lower lip, driving all thought out of his head. "Take me to bed, Nick," she breathed against his mouth. "I want to strip you down and touch you all over."

His heart spasmed like he was going into cardiac arrest. It didn't slow him down. Before she could change her mind, he was up and moving, hands still cupped beneath her bottom to brace her weight. She made a faint squeak of surprise, arms slipping around his neck and thighs clamping on his hips. He grinned at the look on her face and headed for the bedroom with long strides. "I aim to please, ma'am."

She smiled, her expression so full of sensual promise he almost stumbled. Where had his skittish, little genius gone? "I've been thinking about it, all this golden skin under my hands."

"Cass," he groaned. "Are you trying to kill me?" Then he added, "No peeking, Sam," over his shoulder.

"She's already in privacy mode." Cassie looked up at him through her lashes with a sly smile.

He stopped in the middle of the bedroom. "When did—? You mean to tell me you had this planned when you went in the san?"

She hid her face in his throat. "No planning. Just hope."

"I thought you were running from me again. But what's with the song and dance after? Wasted time, lady."

She lifted her head and took an exaggerated look around, meeting his gaze with lifted eyebrows and a smirk. "I'm not the one standing in the middle of the bedroom conversing when we could be doing other things."

He bent his head and muttered against her mouth, "Good point," taking two long strides to the edge of the bed and tumbling her onto her back.

She laughed, propping her weight on her elbows with an enquiring look when he pulled away and yanked his shirt over his head. "What are you doing?"

"You said strip." He was both amused and dismayed by how much his hands were shaking. "Unless you want to do it." He wasn't giving her a chance. He didn't think his heart could take it.

"Wow," she whispered as he got naked with all due speed.

He grinned to himself, but it faded when he saw the dazed expression on her features, wide eyes running over the length of him. Was she afraid again?

When he didn't move, her gaze lifted to his. She sighed. "Suns, you are so beautiful."

A rush of heat blazed through him. He leaned over her, arms braced on the bed as he touched his mouth to hers. Soft and slow, he molded his lips to hers, taking his time about it and killing himself in the process. Holy Suns, she was sweet.

She pulled back, wiggling up on the bed and giving him her new smile, the one daring him to pounce on her. "In my fantasy," she said with a sweep of her lashes, "you were right here." She waved her hand over a stretch of the bed.

Without a word, he levered onto the bed and laid himself out before her, trying not to grin like a hungry lion. She'd fantasized about him. His little fire-breather.

She took a long look while he tried not to move, muscles bunching under her regard. Then she sighed and said, "Oh, yes," in a near moan, burning him from head to toe.

"My turn." He lunged up and pressed her to the bed.

"But I didn't get to touch—"

His hard kiss interrupted her. Lifting his head, he rasped, "No touching right now. I can't take it."

Her lips turned up at the corners and her eyes twinkled with humor. "Just how are we supposed to do this without touching?"

He kissed her again. He didn't have time for logic and reason. Working with more speed than caution, he stripped off her clothes, losing two clasps and putting a small tear in her shirt.

She didn't protest. She also didn't help, her cool,

tantalizing fingers running over his flexing arms, shoulders, and back. "So hot," she whispered against his mouth, and he groaned.

When she was naked, he leaned up on an elbow and stared down at her, a humbling weakness rushing through him at the sight. She was all smooth, sleek limbs and graceful curves, like a sculptor's rendition of a goddess. With her hair fanned out around her, she stole his breath, from her pert breasts, nipples puckering under his gaze, the flat stomach and rounded hips, the enticing curls between her thighs, to the full length of those perfect legs. "Beautiful."

She made a skeptical sound, eyes wide with vulnerability. He lowered his head to her breasts, brushing his lips back and forth across the tips as he breathed, "Gorgeous. Perfect." She whimpered and shivered, her skin dimpling with goose bumps. He took a nipple in his mouth and suckled, groaning when she arched toward him with a gasp. Sweeping a hand down the silky skin of her abdomen, he found the damp curls and slick heat between her thighs. "Hot." She dug her nails into his skin and moaned, her body writhing under his touch. "Sexy."

He lifted his head, hands going still until she met his gaze, lips parted on ragged breath. "Mine," he growled, a surge of male-animal possession tightening all the muscles of his body.

She made a sound low in her throat, fingers spearing through his hair and pulling his mouth to hers. Her kiss was hot and insistent, his little dragon fully roused and ready. She slid a leg over his hip, her body moving in a demand as old as time.

He held back, hands gliding over her smooth skin

in an effort to prolong the pleasure, to make these moments last, to fulfill his fantasies of touching and tasting all of her. She reached between them, small hand encircling and stroking his length, driving pleasure like a bolt of electricity through his body. With a low cry muffled by her lips, he tried to pull her hand away, but she guided him to her entrance with a commanding growl.

He tried to go slow, be gentle with her. She was so small, so tight, her slick passage a tormenting fist around his shaft. Sweat broke out all over his body. He shuddered in desperate need when she arched and drove him inside her. She cried out. He thought he must be hurting her and froze.

"No, no, don't stop," she moaned, nails biting into his skin.

With a growl, he rolled her to her back and surged up on his arms, watching her as he rocked his hips. He could tell she was close and slowed his pace to long, deep thrusts. He tangled his hands in her hair, watching her eyes close and neck arch with a fierce surge of possessive need. He ground his teeth, trying to hold on while the pleasure roared through him, building to an unbearable level. When her body bowed under him, her thighs tightening and legs pressing in silent demand, he obeyed, moving harder, faster.

She came apart, crying out his name as she clutched his arms, body straining under him. Pleasure engulfed and buffeted him, spinning him right to the edge. She reached the pinnacle again, the renewed contractions around his shaft spiking savage ecstasy straight through him, shoving him right over the edge in a wild roar of sweet sensation.

Cassie lay in his arms, trembling, her body shivering, though she was far from cold. She was trying to recover. How a person did so after an experience this profound, she didn't know.

His big hands stroked her with long, slow sweeps. She wanted to stretch and purr like a contented cat under his touch. At the same time, a hot blush came and went, the memory of what they'd just done replaying in her mind. Never in her life had she been so bold. Never in her life had her mind and body been so shattered by wild, incredible passion.

Her prior experiences hadn't prepared her for this. Dmitri had been her first and only until now, a sweet, gentle lover, serious and earnest in his desire to please her. Their lovemaking had always been soft and slow, like a gentle rain sweeping over fertile fields. Nothing like the wildfire she'd just experienced.

"You okay?" Nick asked in a soft rumble, voice muffled against her hair.

How was she supposed to answer that? Yes, no, maybe? All of the above seemed to cover it. "Um, I'm not sure."

His hands stilled, new tension growing in him. "Did I hurt you?"

"What? No! No, I'm just not used to…" Her voice trailed off into baffled silence. How did she explain something she didn't comprehend herself?

He rolled her onto her back so quickly she gasped in surprise, blinking into his frowning countenance. He cupped her face in his large hands and studied her. "I did hurt you," he said in a soft tone so full of distress she found herself reaching for him.

"Nick, no. You didn't hurt me. I feel great. Better

than great." She had trouble meeting his vivid gaze.

His fingers brushed in a feather-light stroke along the curve of her cheek. "Then what's the matter? Regrets?"

Maybe later she would regret it, when he'd decided he'd had enough of her and moved on. Or maybe not; she couldn't imagine regretting an experience so beautiful. Treasure it, perhaps. Tuck it away in a special corner of her memory, to retrieve and marvel over in the lonely days ahead. She was aghast at her boldness, shocked by her own uninhibited behavior. She'd actually seduced the man, wonder of wonders. But she didn't regret.

"No," she whispered, meeting his midnight gaze with frank honesty. "No regrets."

Some of the tension eased from him and his mouth relaxed into a lopsided smile. "So just what aren't you used to?"

She flushed again. "Well, I haven't—um, I don't do this much. Not since Dmitri."

The smile faded from his mouth, his expression sobering. "You loved him a lot." He made it a statement instead of a question. His fingers brushed hair away from her face, letting the strands flow through his grip and across the bedspread.

"Yes, I did. It was more a matter of time and opportunity. The Shays have kept me busy and my coworkers are, well, sweet people but not my type," she finished with a quirk of her lips. Since he'd met her fellow off-laners and Gabe, she expected humor from him.

His serious expression didn't lighten. "Even Manakai Shay?"

Cassie gave a surprised laugh. "Kai? Are you kidding?" She paused, absorbing the intensity in his eyes and the stillness of his body. A bemused smile curled her mouth at the implications of his question. "Nick. Are you jealous?"

He stiffened, levering onto his elbows with a frown. This pressed the lower half of his body against her, a delicious, intimate distraction. Her head spun and her thoughts turned lascivious again.

"That ain't an answer, Cass," he growled. "What's Shay to you?"

Her smile widened, pleasure melting into her, both from the feel of him and from the possessive gleam in Nick's eyes. She remembered his voice, low and stunning in its gravelly command, staking his claim on her. *Mine.* A rather primitive, base, caveman-type thing to do, not something she'd find impressive. But coming from this man, it had inflamed her to the point of wild abandon, and she'd acted just as primitive and savage. She'd wanted to devour him, to stake her own claim.

A measure of boldness returned. She ran her fingers up his muscular arms and curled a leg over his trim hip. "He's my boss and my friend."

"You admire him," he persisted, still frowning. His face said he wasn't pleased, but a different part of him hardened against her stomach, sending a thrill of anticipation through her.

"Sure I admire him. I admire his sister, too, but I don't want to go to bed with either one of them."

He said nothing, eyes narrowed.

She sighed, impatient to be rid of this subject. "Nick, the Shays are very special people. They're incredible, beautiful, and so competent they're scary.

Their cunning and ability to perform miracles is as amazing as it is terrifying. They saved me. I love them, Sin and Kai both." He tensed and she gave him a saucy grin. "But you wouldn't believe what a pain in the neck they can be. Especially Manakai. I don't have siblings, but I imagine he's just what an older brother should be; fun, protective, obnoxious, and super annoying."

He relaxed a bit and his mouth curved in amusement, but his tone was skeptical. "Older brother, huh?"

"Doesn't that describe Del?"

"Pretty much."

"There you go, then." She arched a brow at him. "Done being jealous?"

"Probably not," he said with a smirk, lowering his head until his mouth touched hers. "How do you feel about bubble baths?"

The change in subject disoriented her. So did the movement of his lips, tingles spreading all through her. "Love them." She squeaked in surprise when he rolled, sweeping her off the bed and into his arms.

"Just what I wanted to hear," he purred with a sexy grin, carrying her toward the sanitary. "Because my brother, bless his soul, has an honest-to-Suns bathtub."

They made a horrible mess. Water and bubbles went everywhere, but Cassie didn't notice. When they slid into the bath, Nick made her a promise guaranteed to block everything but him from her mind.

"Our first time was too quick, Cass. Intense, but quick. This time we're gonna take it slow."

He kept his promise with a vengeance. When she thought back on it later, the bath seemed like one long, dreamy glide into delirious bliss. She explored his hard, golden body as thoroughly as she'd wished. He in turn teased and tantalized every bit of her, from her toes to the tips of her ears. He whispered things she couldn't believe but wished were true with all her heart. He danced her to the edge over and over then pulled her back until she was incoherent with need, anticipation screaming across her nerves.

When he finally entered her, she discovered it wasn't the end but only the beginning of a new level of sweet delight. He did things with his body she hadn't believed possible, coaxing amazing responses from her. When she couldn't take any more, he let her fall, over and over.

She was barely conscious when they made it back to the bed, her entire body limp with satiation and exhaustion. He tucked her into bed with such care and tenderness, tears stung her eyes. He slid in beside her, his big body curving around hers like a warm, protective barrier, safe and comforting. Eyes closed, a smile on her lips, she marveled at the contentment moving through her and wondered if she would dream.

Then sleep claimed her, the kind of deep, peaceful slumber she had not experienced in years. It lasted all night long.

Chapter 20

"Nick."

The soft voice tugged at Cassie, drawing her toward consciousness. She did her best to ignore it, trying to fall back into the warm darkness of oblivion. Something stirred at her back, a warm bulk she was not used to having in her bed. A corner of her mind murmured a groggy, wordless query. She fought the curiosity.

"Nick, I apologize for violating the premise of privacy, but they are insistent. You have an appointment and are late."

The hard form against her jerked, followed by a mumbled curse. Cassie bounced, jarred awake when a big, naked body vaulted over her.

She blinked, doubting her eyesight as a gorgeous, golden vision of male perfection appeared before her. "Wow," she breathed in stunned admiration. She watched Nick lunge around the room, finding his clothes and yanking them on with more haste than grace. Memories of the previous night unfolded like a treasure trove, and she melted into the bedding with a muffled whimper.

Nick didn't seem to notice her regard or her helpless reaction. He didn't even seem aware of her in the room. He muttered another curse, fighting to get a foot into his shoe and hopping in a cute, ludicrous sort of way. "Can't believe I slept so long. The Hawk'll strip my hide for sure. Where's my jacket?"

"Living room." Cassie heaved a wistful sigh. This wasn't how she'd imagined waking up with him, but after last night's incredible experience, she didn't think she had room to complain.

"Thanks." He leaned over the bed, his lips a brief, perfunctory pressure on her mouth, before he headed for the door.

Cassie watched him go, her heart sinking to somewhere below her feet, a bereft sadness creeping over her. Was this really how he was going to say goodbye? Was this the last time she'd see him? The door opened and he stepped through. He was gone.

Tears welled, and she buried her face in the pillow, holding her breath to bottle the sob tightening her chest and cursing her weakness. What else had she expected?

The sound of the door sliding back open caught her attention. Nick strode toward her, his jacket clutched in one careless fist and his face intent. He dropped to his knees next to the bed, tossing the jacket aside and clasping her face in both hands before he kissed her. No perfunctory peck this time. His mouth molded hers in a slow, hot, devastating kiss, liquefying her muscles and promising vast amounts of pleasure.

When he lifted his head, a brilliant heat in his dark eyes and a sensual curve to his lips, Cassie was a quivering mass of need, ready to pull him back into bed with her. "Forgot to say good morning." His gravelly voice set off fires deep inside her.

"Say it again," she whispered, snaking an arm around his neck and pulling him closer.

With a low sound in his chest, he bent his head,

mouth teasing hers. "Can't stay. Gotta go. Debriefing with the First Marshal." He buried one hand in her hair, the other slipping under the covers to stroke and tease.

"Right. You need to go." Instead of releasing him, she winnowed her fingers through his tousled hair and nibbled on his lower lip, body writhing under his touch.

He groaned, his mouth now demanding as it slanted over hers, tongues twinning in a hot, slick dance. His hand performed its magic on her skin, setting off infernos under the covers. She was about to become very bold indeed when he lifted his head. "Hold that thought," he growled. "I'll be back."

"Evil beast," she whimpered when he pulled away, rising to his feet.

He chuckled, looking pleased with himself as he moved toward the door. He paused on the threshold, glancing back over his shoulder. For a long minute, he did nothing but stare, expression solemn and eyes vibrant. Her heart thumped hard in her chest. "Cass," he said quietly. Just her name, that was all. Then he was gone.

How was she supposed to get on with her day? Cassie managed somehow, or mismanaged, as the case may be. The expressions on the faces of her friends and coworkers told her she was acting odd, but if she was making a total muck of things, someone would speak up. She hoped.

She had trouble summoning the appropriate concern. She piddled with the slicers for a while then dinked in her lab for a bit, not getting much done in either location and not caring at all.

While she meandered about the station, her mind kept returning to the night before and the enormity of what she'd done. She still had no regrets but couldn't say she was happy with the situation either. As confirmations go, it was a whopper. She had no doubt; she was blindly, horribly in love with Inspector Nick Givliani. Now what was she going to do about it?

She wandered to the offices to check in with the Shays. They were lounging in the main office, the wall viewer a patchwork of different news vids, scrolling data, and info tags, which they appeared to be ignoring. Sin, Kai, and Del had gathered at the bar on the far end, Sin sitting cross-legged on the counter while Del leaned next to her and Kai slumped on a stool. From what Cassie could hear, they seemed to be discussing nothing more serious than favorite foods.

"Hey, Cass," Sin greeted her. "You look rested."

Cassie smiled and was about to reply when Kai added with a wicked grin on his face, "You also look like you got laid."

Cassie's face flamed an obvious answer. Sin cuffed her brother on the back of the head. Kai yelped and protested the abuse while Del glanced over his shoulder at Cass. Nick's brother caught sight of her red face, and his eyebrows lifted, a bemused smile curling his lips.

He looked about to comment, so Cassie shoved a warning finger in his face and snarled, "Not one word."

Del raised his hands and leaned away in self-defense, a grin appearing. "Ain't that stupid."

Nick had said the exact same thing the night before and in the same tone. She couldn't remember why. For some reason, her eyes prickled with the prelude to tears and she blinked, turning her glare on Manakai. "Don't you start, either. My personal business is none of yours."

He opened his mouth to reply, hilarity brightening his eyes. Sin's hand settled on his shoulder. He didn't look at his sister, but the touch seemed to convey a message. The humor drained from his face, solemn concern taking its place as he studied Cassie. "Of course it's our business. What'd he do?"

She tossed her head, dismissing his question with a wave of a hand. "Don't be silly. Nobody did anything. What have you all been doing today?"

They ignored her change of subject.

Del touched a gentle hand to her back. "If he hurt you, I'll kick his ass."

The soft concern in his voice almost brought tears to Cassie's eyes again. What was wrong with her? "That's sweet," she said in a dry tone, looking at him with a forced smile, "but not necessary. I've not been hurt in any way. Can we talk about something else, please? What's on the agenda for today?"

Sin saved her, bless the woman. Her expression said she wasn't forgetting the topic, but her tone was casual. "Station hopping this afternoon. The other Shay stations haven't seen us in a while and could use a personal appearance."

Cassie frowned. "You're not both leaving the station? What about Imago?"

"You said yourself it'd take at least a couple of days to hear from him, if not a week. Right?"

"Well, yes," Cass answered Kai. "They'd have to decontaminate him then go through installation procedures. Plus, they'd keep him in isolation for a while until they're sure he's not contagious to their systems."

"We have some time to kill, then." Kai yawned,

stretching like a big, lazy cat.

Sin unfolded her legs and slipped off the counter with enviable grace. "If we get the call while we're out, we'll just coordinate from one of the other stations."

Cassie acknowledged this with a nod, uncomfortable with them leaving. She looked at Del. "Are you going, too?"

"Oh, hell no," he snorted with an exaggerated look of horror. "Bad enough getting dragged through a whole string of boring business trips, but putting up with this funny man all day?" He pointed an accusing finger at Manakai. "Nuh-uh."

Kai smirked. "Cute."

Sin snickered. "Hold down the fort, you two." She gave a reassuring smile to Cassie and a clinging, sultry kiss to Del.

Kai made gagging noises on their way out the back exit, which his sister ignored with a smug smile and a wink over her shoulder.

Del had a lazy grin on his face, but it faded when the twins were gone and his attention returned to Cassie. A faint crease appeared on his forehead and he shifted against the bar. "So you wanna talk about it?"

A rush of warmth for the big man filled her chest. She knew he'd rather walk over hot coals than have an emotional discussion, yet here he was, offering himself up for torture anyway.

She smiled and patted him on the arm. "Thanks, but no. I really am just fine." Her lie must have been more convincing than before. The tension in him eased. He was still studying her with an intuitive gleam in his eyes, so she added, "Why don't you keep watch on the gang? They're restless since we've stopped the off-lane runs. I suspect Sunny is plotting some form of misbehavior."

Del snorted. "Ain't nothing new, Cass." With a crooked grin, he rose and headed for the exit. "Holler down if you need me," he tossed over his shoulder before he disappeared.

Cassie wandered the place alone, feeling inadequate to the fort-holding task. She might have brains, but the Shays were the decision makers, strategists, and implementers. On the other hand, the odds of something happening were pretty slim at this point. The viewer confirmed it, the news drab and uninteresting, and the data static. After a while she was lulled into a sense of security, drifting into a doze in the armchair at the desk.

Until a call came in from Nick.

The control system chimed the incoming call, the tag personalized for her. Cassie blinked awake and leaned forward, signaling the system to allow the call through. Nick's handsome, stubbled face sent a thrill of pleasure through her, until she registered his expression.

"Nick, what's the matter?"

"Cassie, I need to see you." His tone was urgent.

"Why? What happened?" she asked in growing alarm.

He looked strange, eyes a little wild and face stiff. "I don't want to talk about it over the vid. Not secure. Can you meet me somewhere?"

A frown tightened her brow. "Why can't you come back here?"

"Can't say." He glanced around in a furtive scan of his surroundings. "Can you meet me at HQ?"

"I shouldn't be leaving the station," she protested, thinking not only of the absent Shays but her own safety. She hadn't left the Shay station alone since she'd come here, except for the night she'd taken Imago away. Even then, Kai had been waiting on the dangerous end for her.

"Cassie, I need to see you," he said again in the same, urgent tone. "You'll be safe with me."

Well, that was true. Plus, the transit to FPA HQ was very public, well-traveled, and safe. "All right. How do I find you?"

"Just give my name to reception. The system will take it from there. I'll see you soon." Then he was gone.

The call unsettled her even more than the Shay's departure from the station. What had happened at his meeting with Marchand to cause this kind of reaction? Or maybe it was something he'd uncovered after his meeting. He'd looked so strange; she'd never seen him so nervous or jumpy. Was he in danger? The thought sent goose bumps along her arms and down her back. If he was in danger, he wouldn't be calling her to him, putting her in harm's way.

She had a sudden disturbing thought and tapped at the control panel on the desk. The system put her through to FPA headquarters, and she requested to speak with Inspector Givliani. In a minute, his face was back on the viewer, a frown creasing his brow. "Cassie, what's wrong?"

"Did you just call me?"

"Yeah. Did you change your mind?"

"No, I just wanted to make sure it was really you."

"Good thinkin'," he said with a grim smile. "Be careful. See you soon." The viewer went blank. Not very lover-like behavior, but then again she didn't know what to expect from him or what was wrong. With a shake of her head, she started making preparations to leave.

She tried to contact the Shays, but the system informed her they were in transit through the star-way and unavailable for the time being. She left them messages instead, informing them of the call and where she'd gone. Then she contacted her lab and gave Gabriel the same information. Leaving the office, she quick-stepped down to her quarters and changed from her work clothes to a comfortable traveling outfit, heading for the docking bay at a fast clip.

"Hey!" Del's booming voice echoed through the maintenance bay and pulled her to a halt.

With a wince, she realized she'd forgotten about him. He would want to know more than anyone if something was going on with his brother.

"Where're you going?" he asked with a frown when he caught up with her.

She quickly outlined the situation, hurrying through it as time ticked away at the corners of her mind. She couldn't stop worrying over Nick's odd behavior and what could be wrong.

When she finished explaining, Del tossed his sani-cloth toward one of the work stations and headed past her with a grim expression. "I'll go. You stay here."

"Whoa, hold on." She scrambled to get in front of him. "Nick called me, not you."

He gave her an impatient look and moved her out of his way. "You can't go, Cass. It's too dangerous for you to leave the station right now."

"Sun's sake, Del, we're talking about FPA HQ

here," she protested, skipping to keep up with his longer stride. "It'll be safe enough. Especially if you go with me."

He shook his head. "Not good enough. Sin and Kai will take turns ripping strips off me if I took you along."

"Took me along? I'm not a piece of baggage, you big oaf. Nick wants me there for a reason. I'm coming."

He stopped, frowning down at her. "No, you're not."

"Oh yes, I am." She raised her eyebrows and folded her arms across her chest. "Want to see how fast I can shut this place down? You're not going anywhere without me."

They glared at one another before Del gave in with a curse. "You won't leave my side, clear?"

"Of course I won't. Do I look stupid?"

"You were gonna go by yourself, Cass," he reminded her with an acid glance as they headed for the transports.

She winced. "Right. Well, your brother has that effect on me."

The next transport cleared the station in five minutes and they were on their way. The trip to HQ was uneventful. Del gave her the silent treatment, so it was a quiet trip and the lanes were too public to cause concern. The FPA housed their headquarters on a planet almost entirely mechanized, huge, fantastic structures stretching far into the atmosphere.

From the space port, Cassie and Del rented transport to HQ and discomfort assailed her for the first time on the trip. She wasn't a country bumpkin unused to the fast-paced, metal-clad mega-plex covering the surface of this planet; her birthplace had been much the same. However, the myriad possibilities for ambush along the way disturbed her. Del stayed calm and focused, doing a constant scan of their surroundings and passersby, his big body giving off radiant, alert energy. His watchful readiness comforted her.

She didn't feel quite safe until they entered the enormous reception area of FPA HQ. The place hummed with activity, a kaleidoscope of people bustling along in all directions as they went about their business. The large amount of uniforms in evidence eased her the most. She knew some were Core-bought spies, but knowing she was in the presence of peace keepers and the law calmed her.

Approaching the reception kiosk with Del on her heels, Cassie touched the holographic system and a woman's smiling visage appeared. "Welcome to the Federated Planetary Alliance. May I help you?" The AI's voice was warm and encouraging.

"Yes, I'm here to see Inspector Nicholo Givliani. Can you tell me where to find him?"

"Certainly. He is on the fourth floor, in the offices of the second division. Have you ever been to FPA headquarters before?"

"No, I haven't."

"It can be somewhat daunting to newcomers. You will want to start by going to the second set of lifts on the far side of this vaulted area. On the fourth floor, the second division is across the catwalk in building B. There will be information stations along the way, if you need clarification of your location. Once you reach the second division, there will be a listing of every inspector and the locations of their offices."

Cassie gave her a grateful smile. "Thank you. You've been a great help."

"You're very welcome."

Cassie glanced at Del and received a flat look and noncommittal grunt, his hand taking her arm in a gentle, secure clasp. They started across the reception area. Following the AI's directions, they found the second division with no problem. They also discovered the location of Nick's office without difficulty and moved through a maze of work stations to get there.

No one stopped or questioned them, although several people glanced at them when they passed. Catching sight of Nick's door, Cassie grimaced at a flutter of anticipation in her stomach. It had only been a few hours since she'd seen him, but the short time didn't seem to matter to her stupid, moonstruck heart.

Del beat her to the door chime and held her back with a cautionary hand when the door opened for them. "Nick?" He eased across the threshold. His aborted movement alerted her.

Cassie lunged forward with a cry of horror as he toppled to the floor in convulsions. Her flight response kicked in a second too late. A meaty hand snaked out and yanked her into the room before she could dart away, another clapping over her mouth and muffling the beginnings of a scream for help. She froze when the door slid closed behind her.

Koffsky gave her a nasty smile, swinging an electrified riot stick in one hand. "Hi, Doc. Nice t'see ya again." He waved off the brute holding her.

She scrambled away, putting her back against the wall and staring at the three men in rising fear. "You faked the friggin' call?" No wonder Nick had looked and acted so strange. But damn it, she'd called him back. The system must have put her through here, to Nick's office and Koffsky, instead of the inspector's exact location.

"Sure did. Gotcha! Hook, line, and sinker, little fishy."

She wanted to slap his grinning face and beat herself over the head for being so gullible, so stupid for not doing more to confirm the authenticity of the call. She wanted to shake Del and tell him to wake up already. Most of all, the uncontrollable urge to scream and run filled her head to toe.

They must have seen this last impulse on her face. Koffsky's two brutes stepped forward, each taking an arm, their grip unbreakable without hurting her. Koffsky waved the stick at her with a slow shake of his head.

Knowing it was no use fighting them, she tried brazening it out instead. "You're nuts to come in here. This is the middle of a division full of FPA agents. We're in the office of an inspector, for Sun's sake. He could be back anytime." She stopped at another slow shake of Koffsky's head. His grin didn't falter and her heart began to thump with dread. "What did you do to Nick?"

"Givliani? Not a thing, Doc. He's just not here right now."

So could he still return? "How did you plan to get through a whole crowd of FPA inspectors with me in tow?"

"Same way we came in, little fish."

The brutes pulled her arms behind her. A set of restraints clamped down on her forearms. Staring at the men, she realized the two bruisers wore FPA uniforms. "Oh, no," she moaned and started struggling, much too late. The trap had closed.

"Settle down, Doc. Won't do you no good."

They turned and walked her back out the door. She shot a horrified glance at Del over her shoulder, but he remained unconscious. Terrifying, humiliating, and infuriating, to be marched through a room full of FPA agents and not have a single one question them, let alone help her.

She tried, pulling against the forward pressure of her captors to plead for help. "I'm being abducted! These guys are kidnapping me."

The agents offered raised eyebrows, shaking heads, and general skepticism. They thought she was a perp, a criminal on her way to the cells, intent on making as much trouble as she could. Or maybe they thought she was a nutcase.

Cassie swore in despair, glaring at Koffsky.

He shrugged and grinned. "Don't look so down, Doc. Boss thinks real high of you. You'll get treated like a queen."

"I'm in restraints, being dragged through the FPA HQ like a criminal. Doesn't make me feel very queen-like, Koffsky."

He had the nerve to pat her on the shoulder in commiseration. "Won't be long. We'll take 'em off when we're outta here."

She started calling him names in a furious mutter under her breath.

Chapter 21

Nick's debriefing with the First Marshal didn't start well.

"You're late," was the crisp greeting from Marchand.

Nick stood at attention in front of his boss's desk. "Yes, sir. I apologize."

Marchand eyed him and grunted. "No excuses?"

"No, sir." No way was Nick going to tell the man he was late because he'd slept in for the first time in years and had trouble leaving the gorgeous woman in his bed. The delicious, sexy woman who'd turned his world upside down in a matter of days.

Marchand paused, still staring at him. Moisture gathered on Nick's forehead. The man had the most piercing stare of anyone he'd ever met. Nick had the uncomfortable notion the First Marshal could read his mind. After an eternity, Marchand grunted again and glanced down at his monitors, waving Nick to a seat across from him.

Nick eased down into a chair and let out the breath he'd been holding, taking a surreptitious glance around the office. If he didn't know better, he'd say the man was ranked no higher than a supervising inspector.

Medium-sized, sparse, tidy, and impersonal; the space contained the First Marshal's desk, chairs, and an armoire which probably housed changes of uniform.

Viewers covered the walls, showing a score of information, most of which no doubt wasn't any of Nick's business. He kept his eyes averted. The only personal touch in the room was a rack of shelves filled with actual, printed books.

Curious, Nick was straining to see the titles on the bindings when Marchand looked up and caught his attention. "So, you've been investigating the Shays."

"Yes, sir."

"Didn't find much, did you?"

Nick worded his response with care. "They seem to have neat answers for each of their indiscretions."

The softening around Marchand's mouth might have been the beginnings of a smile. "Yes, they're good at putting a pretty spin on things. Would have made good politicians, if they weren't so bloody-minded."

Nick blinked at the First Marshal, uneasy with the description and its delivery. Marchand had spoken in a flat voice, without any apparent emotion. Nick wasn't sure if he was insulting the Shays or expressing admiration for their traits.

"They tend to play fast and loose with the rules. I give them some leeway because they get the job done, but they could do with some reining in. That's where you come in, Givliani. As my liaison with the Shays, I expect you to inform me of actions they take and any infractions you might find. I expect you to answer to me, not them. Understood?"

"Yes, sir."

Marchand nodded then went over a few details of what he expected out of his new liaison. When Nick indicated he understood, Marchand nodded again. "Dismissed, Inspector."

Nick blinked, watching the First Marshal bend his attention back to his monitors. "Ah, sir? I thought I was here for proof of the Shays' connections with the FPA. They claim to have sanction to carry weapons, some of their cargo runs have been suspicious, and they have somebody working for them who invents contraband."

"Dr. Draegen. You'll want to look at her file, too." Marchand gestured at the desktop in front of Nick. A monitor flickered to life with two strings of code. "Those'll get you through the seal on the Shay and Draegen files. You'll have to read them in one of the secure vaults. I can't take the chance of any of this information leaking. Do I make myself clear?" The First Marshal's tone had hardened into a distinct threat.

Nick said an absent, "Yes, sir," while he memorized the codes.

"Those codes expire the second you use them, so don't leave the files and expect to get back in. You get one look at them, Inspector, so make it a good look."

"I will, sir. Thank you."

Marchand waved him away, bending his gray head back to his desktop.

Nick wasted no time exiting the office and heading down to the vaults, anticipation lengthening his stride. Finally, he was going to get some answers to the Shay mystery.

The vault security system confirmed his identity, and the duty officer who served as backup security waved him through with an expression of sour boredom. Nick picked a vault and entered the claustrophobic little room, the thick door sliding closed behind him with a heavy thump and hiss of pressure. He sat at the terminal and keyed in the first code he'd memorized, fingers impatient.

Cassie's face appeared on the holo-viewer, her reserved smile pulling an answering response from him before he could curb it. He sighed, aware of how gone he was, how Sun-cursed pathetic. With a grimace, he called up the information in the file, scrolling through it. It confirmed what he'd already been told about Cassie's history, from her employment at Cybercom through her lover's murder to her current employment with Shay Enterprises.

Cassie's confession was on file, detailing the project she'd worked on for Cybercom, how they'd threatened her, and how they'd framed her for the murder. Dmitri had been electrocuted at her workstation, through a high voltage mechanism she had designed and allegedly programmed to detonate at the touch of his specific DNA. The program's time stamp and creator identity had been wiped, so she couldn't prove she hadn't been the one to create it.

Nick looked through the rest of the evidence with a snarl of thwarted violence. It was overkill, so much a setup it stank, but it left no other suspect to take the heat off Cassie. He now understood why the file had been sealed without an investigation; the only result would be putting an innocent woman in prison.

Clenching his jaw to contain his fierce emotions, he worked past the frame job and scrolled through the rest of the file. Her entire life was there, from her prodigal beginnings and incredible education to the sequestering of her parents, location undisclosed. Nick wondered if Marchand was just being careful or if the Shays had the massive nerve to keep it from him.

A list of items caught his eye, and he paused to

goggle at what Marchand had designated "*Mechanical Engineering Development*." It listed Cassie's contraband inventions, some he'd already seen, some new and amazing, and some he had no clue what they did. "Suns, woman," he muttered, staring at incomprehensible diagrams, "you are scary smart." He understood now why Marchand allowed her to invent these things; the First Marshal had several marked for eventual integration into the FPA.

With a shake of his head, he closed out the file and keyed in the code to open the Shay file. Breathing deep past the knot of anticipation in his chest, he watched the information stream through the holo-matrix. A shocking amount of it flowed by, going back a lot farther than he'd ever dreamed, back before the twins were even born.

"Holy Sunfire," he muttered, watching data stream by of their father, Ezekiel Shay. The information slid back and back in time, until it stopped on the opening document, a statement by Ezekiel Shay. A confession.

As Nick read it, reality seemed to warp around him. The man confessed to giving sensitive information about a rival company to one Webster Griffin, who at the time had been only a common criminal. Shay admitted he expected Griffin to destroy his rival, but instead Griffin had taken over the company. Ezekiel Shay had opened the door for Griffin to create Quasicore.

Nick reread this a few times before the shock and disbelief wore off. This hadn't been the beginning he'd expected out of the Shay file, but it confirmed his original suspicions about the Shays; not good people. Rubbing a rough hand over his face and around the back of his neck, he moved on, a sickness curdling in his stomach.

As he worked through the massive amounts of information on collaborative operations between the FPA and Ezekiel Shay, then later the Shay twins, he began to revise his opinion. Again and again, the Shays played Griffin, working sting after sting on various aspects of his illegal businesses. Again and again, he bounced back, somehow able to evade prosecution every time and resume his activities. Quasicore continued to grow in spite of their efforts.

Nick would suspect the Shays of playing both sides, pretending to cooperate with the FPA to lull them into a false sense of security so they could do business with Griffin without impediment. But their operations were laid out in excruciating detail. Nick saw none of the evasion he'd come to expect from the Shays.

What he found instead was an amazing amount of sacrifice and incredible skill. He wouldn't have believed the Shays could go so long without Griffin becoming aware of their duplicity, yet it was all laid out for him in the file, their ferocious determination and their stunning ability to perform the impossible. A comment from Ezekiel Shay caught his eye and haunted him throughout the rest of his research:

Failure is not an option.

He'd seen for himself the lengths the Shays were willing to go in this war against Quasicore. They would sacrifice themselves without a second thought. But what scared him was how many others they would sacrifice as well.

Aware of time marching on, he skipped and skimmed in order to reach the more recent endeavors, murmuring in amazement at the complexity of some of their operations. The Shay twins might have followed in their father's footsteps, but they were building on what he'd begun.

Nick reached a part titled *Endgame* and began reading with a sinking heart and twisting stomach. The blue factory had been only the beginning. His throat went dry at the lengths both the Shays and the FPA were willing to go to bring Quasicore down.

Sanctioning weapons had only been for starters. The liberties the FPA allowed the Shays stunned him. The twins held covert op agent status, complete with a license to kill. A wave of dizzy horror washed over him, his hands trembling as he scrolled down the list of laws the Shays were allowed to circumvent. With this kind of freedom, the two were even more dangerous than Griffin. And more powerful than Marchand?

An incoming call request interrupted this terrifying thought. Nick allowed the connection, audio only as a vault security measure. "Givliani." He wanted to get back to the file, to learn as much as he could about the Shays. Marchand had told him he had to rein them in. He had to figure out just how in the Suns he was supposed to perform this miracle.

"Hey Nick, I found your brother in your office twitching like a jack junkie. He says he needs to see you yesterday."

"On my way," Nick barked, launching to his feet and out the door before the other agent could respond. Heart pounding with dread, he rushed up through the building until he reached his division, weaving through the work stations at top speed.

"Where's the fire?" one of the agents called after

him, but he ignored her.

Bursting into his office, he skidded to a relieved stop. His brother was in one piece, sitting in front of his desk. The grim, pale cast to Del's features and the tremors running through his big frame sent alarm spiraling through Nick.

"Man, he won't say a word," complained one of the two young agents standing over Del.

"Get rid of 'em, bro," Del rasped, flicking Nick an urgent, commanding glance.

"Thanks guys, I got this," Nick said to the two agents, waving them toward the door. Noticing their sour expressions, he shrugged and gave them a hard grin. "I appreciate the call. Drinks on me next time, huh?"

They brightened, muttering agreements as they departed.

Del grimaced when a shudder coasted down his body. "Is this room secure?"

"Doesn't matter. Tell me," Nick growled, crouching by his brother and examining him for injuries.

"They got Cass."

Panic froze him solid. He stared into the bitter darkness of his brother's eyes and couldn't move. His sweet little fire-breather in Griffin's hands? "No."

"She got a call from you, asking her to come. Faked all to hell, come to find out. Crazy woman was gonna go by herself, you believe it?" Dell rambled, "Course, I wasn't much help. Bastards ambushed me, knocked me out with a riot stick. She's gone, Nick."

"Where?" he rasped past the icy panic stabbing through him.

"Don't know. We need Sin and Kai."

A whiplash of anger melted some of his immobility. "Screw them. We need to get her back."

"They'll know how, brother. Right now I don't have a clue where to start."

"How 'bout with Griffin?"

"Yeah? Where's he, bro?"

Nick stared at him, grinding his teeth with impotent fury. "I'm a Sun-damned inspector. I'll find him. I gotta report the kidnapping, get Marchand to—"

Del lifted a twitching hand and grabbed Nick's shoulder in a tight, almost painful grip, his eyes blazing with dark promise. "Reports waste too much time. We will get her back, Nick. Make the call to the Shays." Then he leaned forward, elbows on knees, and propped his head between his hands.

Tracking down the Shays took several calls, but their staff was efficient. An eternity seemed to pass, but only a few minutes ticked by until the Shays appeared before Nick. They wore expressions of expectant humor, reminding Nick they had other reasons to hear from him. He couldn't get past the one lodged like a poisonous spike in his chest.

"Cassie's gone."

Sin sucked in an audible breath and Manakai made a feral sound in his throat. The identical, fierce mask hardening both their features would have unnerved him if he hadn't already been in the middle of a quiet meltdown.

"When?"

"How?"

Both of their voices were clipped and as sharp as cut diamonds.

Nick gave them a quick synopsis. "Do you know how to find her?"

"Yes," they answered in unison, their green eyes glittering with an almost alien menace. "Don't move. We're on our way," Manakai added, disappearing from view. Sin looked after her brother for a second then returned her attention to Nick, her cold and dangerous expression easing as she studied him. "Don't worry, they won't hurt her. She's too valuable. Is Del all right?"

Del snorted without raising his head from his hands. Nick decided to interpret this as, "He's okay. Just get here quick."

She nodded. "We're sending a transport, no marks on it. The pilot will be wearing our insignia. Can you make it out to docking? It'll be there in five."

"We'll be ready," Nick answered, but he was talking to air. Sin was gone. Rounding the desk, he crouched in front of Del again. "Do you need to go to medical, big brother?"

"Need lots of things. That ain't one of 'em," Del mumbled into his hands.

"What then?"

Del dangled his hands between his knees, meeting Nick's gaze with a wry twist of his lips. "Could use a kick in the ass for letting her come with."

A spurt of anger sharpened his voice despite his effort to contain it. "Why did you?"

Del sighed, rubbing a weary, trembling hand over his face before pushing to his feet. "She turned dragon on me. Threatened to ground the whole place if I didn't bring her."

A seed of humor blunted his anger enough to offer

his brother a helping hand. "Wish I'd been there to see it."

"Wish I'd called her bluff," Del grumbled, waving Nick's help away and moving stiff-legged toward the door.

"You sure it was a bluff?"

Del snorted and paused at the door, taking a deep breath with a full-body shudder. When he moved again, his limbs had steadied, only the faintest tremors showing in his hands. Nick shook his head in admiration, visited by a ghost of the hero worship he'd held for his brother when they were young. The man had more determination and strength of will than anyone he'd ever met. *Including those Sun-fried Shays,* he thought with a grim clench of his jaw.

They weaved through the work stations with alacrity, Nick ignoring the curious glances of his colleagues. They made their way out to temporary docking and had no trouble spotting the sleek Shay transport among the more tawdry rentals. *Wasted no time,* Nick thought in approval as the hatch slid open.

A pilot in soft gray with the sphinx insignia at his collar greeted them. "Welcome sirs. I'll be flying you to Shay Enterprise's auxiliary station in this sector. Will you need any refreshments before we leave?"

"No, just get us into vacuum," Nick answered with a scowl, sitting in a passenger seat. This wasn't a pleasure cruise; he could do without the servile treatment.

The man hesitated, glancing at Del. "If you change your mind, the forward section behind the pilot cabin is fully stocked." He slipped into the pilot cabin and shut himself in.

Del shot Nick a wry glance, keying open a receptacle in the forward section. "He was trying not to ask if I needed treatment."

"Oh," Nick mumbled, watching with a twinge of guilt while Del selected a restorative drink and downed it in three swallows. "Sorry."

Del shook his head in dismissal and settled into a seat next to him, the transport humming away from HQ. "You want Cass back about as bad as we do." He shot Nick an amused glance out of the corner of his eye. "Why is that, little brother?"

Nick ignored the question. "How do they know where she is?"

"Beats me. How far did you fall for her?"

He gave Del a narrow look, raising his voice so the transport's com system would relay his question. "Pilot, how soon 'til we get there?"

"Within the hour, sir."

Nick swore at the delay.

Del smirked, watching him with crinkles of amusement in the corners of his dark eyes. "Oh yeah, you fell pretty far."

"All the Sun-damned way," Nick growled, glaring at his brother. "Now leave it the hell alone."

Del nodded, his expression turning serious. "We'll get her back," he said again with conviction.

Nick wished he felt as confident.

Chapter 22

Cassie thought she might throw up. She fervently hoped it would happen right in the bastard's face. Webster Griffin was giving her a gentile smile, but the congenial mask couldn't hide the ugly gloating underneath. He'd brought his daughter with him. They stood before the cage holding her like tourists in a zoo.

"My dear, I regret the circumstances of your visit, but I'm simply delighted to have you here."

"Visit?" she rasped in hoarse disbelief. "What the hell ever, Griffin."

His features morphed into insincere lines of concern and solemn regret. "I do apologize for the accommodations, but your reputation for inventive problem solving precedes you. We don't want you leaving us prematurely, Dr. Draegen. Are you in any discomfort?"

She was in plenty of discomfort, but not the kind he meant. An energy field held her body suspended and immobile off the floor. It wasn't painful and allowed her to breathe, but she couldn't even twitch. Holding captives immobile was just the beginning of this machine's functions. Aware of its less savory uses, she experienced plenty of mental and emotional discomfort.

Cassie pressed her lips together and didn't answer. If the Shays were here in her place, they would play the game with him, bantering and working for whatever leverage they could find. She couldn't do it. If she opened her mouth, the only thing to pour out would be impotent rage and fear.

"I understand why you are upset, but please believe you will not be harmed. I wouldn't so abuse such a valuable new member of my team."

Cassie gagged at the idea of working for the Core again, swallowing bile with an effort. If she didn't want to vomit out her insides, she'd better focus on something else. "I suppose you're enjoying your new acquisition." She knew she shouldn't mention Imago, shouldn't give Griffin any idea how much the AI meant to her, but she was worried about him.

"Of course. It's been quite useful. You'll soon see how useful with your own eyes. Would that please you, Doctor?"

She scowled at him and kept her big mouth shut.

His gloating smile made a reappearance. "I will leave you now. If you wish for anything, simply speak and this room's VRS will respond."

VRS? Did they have an AI covering this room? A flash of hope went through her, followed by a sharp drop back into despair. Even if their VRS was AI, they wouldn't leave it open to her influence.

Griffin turned to go but his daughter remained, still watching Cassie with serene interest. "Father," she said in a clear, smooth voice, "may I stay? Perhaps I will be able to ease her fears." Griffin paused, glancing over his shoulder with those cold gray eyes of his. Liaena turned as if she could feel the weight of his stare. "And give her a warmer welcome."

Her tone held no censure, but Griffin's eyes narrowed. He smiled without humor and tilted his head in regal acceptance. "Be sure you don't tax our guest, Daughter."

"Of course," she murmured to his departing back then turned to Cassie with a strange brightness in her eyes. Cassie stared back, suspicious.

Liaena Griffin was not what she'd expected. For starters, she looked nothing like Griffin, except for the color of her eyes, a light gray like smoked glass. Her hair glowed with subdued fire, pulled up in some intricate hairdo at the back of her head. The cut of her clothing was rich, displaying deceptive, simple elegance. Her face held a delicate beauty, but so still and emotionless she could have been a statue.

Cassie had been able to see through Griffin's mask to his underlying motives; no doubt he'd allowed it in his arrogance. She couldn't read his daughter at all. Liaena was glacial, like a pool of ice, her depths hidden by an opaque surface.

"If I released the restraint, would you talk with me?" Liaena asked, gesturing to a comfortable-looking arrangement of chairs to one side of the machine. Her tone remained polite, her movements poised and contained, but something in the request sounded like a trap.

Cassie swallowed lingering bile. "Good cop, bad cop," she husked then cleared her throat. "Or the honey and the stick. Do you really think I'll talk or cooperate just because you let me out of this thing? How many people have you tortured in it, anyway?"

Liaena clasped her hands together and lowered her gaze. "I want only the opportunity to speak with you. The interrogation unit is disturbing, even when restraining and not causing pain. We may speak like this if you wish, but I think we would both be more comfortable sitting down."

Cassie didn't know what game she was playing, but couldn't see the downside yet to her offer. "Sure, let me out."

Much to her surprise, Liaena did, palming a small control and aiming it at the arc of metal over Cassie's head. The force dropped her to a standing position. Shivering with reaction to the energy field, Cassie lurched away from the contraption with a backward glance of loathing. "Those things are illegal," she muttered as she passed Liaena, not expecting a response and not getting one.

Huddling on one of the cushioned chairs, Cassie fixed a wary gaze on the other woman as she settled into a nearby seat with demure grace.

"May I get you something warm to drink?"

"No. Let's get on with this."

Liaena tilted her gilded head, folding her hands together in her lap. "With what?"

"The grilling, the question and answer game. Griffin wants you to pull info out of me or get me to agree to his schemes. Let me tell you right up front, I'm not going to talk about what I do for the Shays, or anything about the Shays. I'm not going to talk about AIs or my work for Cybercom. And I don't want to hear any offers, persuasions, or threats to get me to work for him."

Liaena's eyebrows rose the slightest bit, mouth softening like the prelude to a smile, her only reaction to Cassie's defiance. "Well, let's see what we're left with, then." She looked away for a moment as if thinking about it. "Do you have any brothers or sisters?"

Cassie frowned. "No, I don't. I'm an only child. What's that got to do with anything?"

"I'm merely curious about you. I'm also an only child."

"One random commonality doesn't make us soul sisters. I'm still not telling you anything."

"I understand," Liaena responded in a soothing tone, her mouth curling into the faintest of smiles. "Your parents, were they—?"

"I'm not talking about them either," Cassie snapped. "You're not going to use them against me."

Liaena blinked then leaned forward, her voice low and earnest. "I was only going to ask if they were good to you. Did you have a happy childhood?"

Cassie started to ask what her childhood had to do with anything. Then her training kicked in at long last. Instead of scrambling to protect herself, she should have been paying more attention to the dynamics between father and daughter. He had ignored his offspring when they'd first come into the room and was cold with her, condescending and domineering, when she'd asked to stay. He'd been dismissive when he left.

Studying Liaena with new eyes, Cass murmured, "Happier than yours, I'd imagine."

Liaena straightened, her eyelashes lowering in a slow blink, features impassive. "When I was very young, I lived with my mother on an island. It was always warm and I was very happy there. Space is colder."

She may as well have substituted *father* for *space*. Cassie stared at her, wondering what she was after. Was this a ploy to gain sympathy, to get Cassie to let down her guard? "Is your mother still alive?" She asked the question with tentative care, as if she were walking the edge of a long drop.

"Yes, she still lives on the island. I see her on occasion. Do you see your parents?"

"Sometimes." Cassie couldn't help her clipped tone, unable to hide suspicion.

Liaena surprised her again. "I apologize. Your family was one of the things you were not going to talk about. Shall we change the subject?"

"Sure. Let's talk about the weather." Cassie sent a pointed look around at the windowless, viewer-less room. "Is there any weather here?"

Liaena's mouth curled in a suggestion of a smile. "Not very subtle, Dr. Draegen, but yes, I will tell you where you are. We are not on a planet, but a station orbiting the Kasa rings. I regret we don't have a way for you to see them. The view is breathtaking."

Cassie's stomach plummeted. If they were willing to tell her where she was, then they must be confident she wouldn't be able to expose their location, confident she wouldn't be leaving anytime soon.

"Are you sure you don't want something warm to drink? You're shivering again."

Cassie pressed her lips together, trying not to show her forlorn loneliness. Her need to go home and be with her friends, to be held safe in their arms, in Nick's arms, was a painful desperation. Tears pricked her eyes and she rubbed at them wearily.

"Doctor? Are you all right?"

"What a dumb question. You kidnapped me, dragged me here, and stretched me out in an interrogator. Of course I'm not all right." Lowering her hand, she studied Liaena's serene features. "How often have you used that thing on people?"

"I've never used it *on* anyone," Liaena answered in a low voice, gaze dropping to the controller, a faint crease between her brows.

Hearing the odd emphasis in her statement, Cassie made another connection and nausea returned with a vengeance. "Oh, Suns," she whispered. "He uses it on you?"

Griffin's daughter went still, her face smoothing out into a glacial pool once again. "There is always a price to pay for disobedience. You would do well to understand this."

"Disobedience," Cassie hissed, furious for many reasons, not the least of which was the threat of pain induction in the interrogator. "I'll give him Sun-blasted disobedience. How young were you when he first stuck you in there?"

"You seem upset. Shall we change the subject again?"

Cassie took a deep breath, trying to calm the sickness in her stomach and disperse her anger. "Fine." She stared at the other woman for a minute. Liaena said nothing, watching her in return, her cool serenity beginning to drive Cassie nuts. No one could be this controlled all the time. "You know, I heard a story about you."

Liaena's dark lashes swept down over her cool gray eyes. "Did you?"

"Sin says when you met them for the first time you kicked Kai in the shin. You don't seem the shin-kicking type. Is it true?"

Liaena's lips curved, eyes still downcast. "It is."

"Why did you kick him?"

"He made a derogatory comment about my hair. He asked if I'd fallen head first in a bucket of red paint. My hair was brighter then."

Cassie tried not to respond. She told herself not to feel anything toward this woman but hostility. This whole odd conversation had to be a ploy, manipulation to get under her guard. Unfortunately, she was already feeling horrified empathy over Griffin's price for disobedience. She couldn't suppress a reluctant smile. "Then he deserved it. Good work with the kick."

Liaena looked up through her lashes at Cassie, her mouth curling in a small but genuine smile. For a second, Cassie glimpsed a shadow of the girl behind the mask the woman wore, mischief dancing through the gray mist of her eyes. "I confess I enjoyed it immensely," she whispered.

Cassie snickered before she could stop herself. "Kai has that effect on lots of people."

Liaena's voice lost its humor and her expression returned to statue-like serenity. "You know him well, then."

"Sun and Stars," Cassie sighed, glowering at the woman. "I really hate these games. I'm just no good at them, so I'd appreciate it if you'd just come right out and ask whatever it is you're trying to get out of me."

"I'm not trying to—"

Cassie scoffed, folding her arms across her chest. "Oh, please."

Liaena studied her for a minute, face and body still and unreadable. A faint crease formed between her brows, her gaze dropping away. Her chest rose with a deeper breath, before she met Cassie's gaze once more and leaned closer. In a soft, yet somehow urgent voice, she asked, "Will they come for you, Cassie?"

It shouldn't have surprised her. It was an obvious question, after all. Of course they'd want to know what efforts the Shays would put forth to get her back. She heaved an inner, despairing sigh, knowing the answer was written all over her face. "They'll try," she hedged, hugging her arms closer.

"Why?"

Cassie's mouth repeated the question in silence. She stared in confusion at the other woman. Why what? A possibility occurred to her and the blood left her face, stiffening her features into a cold mask. "Are you planning to use me against them?"

Liaena sat back, the crease reforming between her fine brows. "As far as I know, my father's plan is to reintegrate you into his research programs. My question is why wouldn't they negotiate for your return? Why would they attempt to rescue you?"

Cassie snorted. "Be serious. Do you really think your father would let me go now?"

"It would depend on what they offered for you."

Cassie decided she'd let her mouth run on long enough. If the deluded woman thought negotiation was an option, who was she to dissuade her?

Liaena must not have been fooled. "Yet you believe they will try a rescue. Why?"

Cassie's forehead puckered in confusion. Why what? "I have the same value for them as for your father."

Liaena looked down and took another deep breath. "Do they care for you, Cassie?"

"Of course they do," she whispered, miserable. She

should have glued her mouth shut. Tears stung her eyes again but she did nothing about it this time, huddling in on herself and staring at the other woman.

Liaena's head snapped up. Stunning, intense emotion lit her eyes and face before the serene mask slid back into place. It didn't make sense, but Cassie would swear she'd looked relieved. Supremely, vibrantly relieved. "And you care for them."

Cassie sighed. Too late to cover her tracks; she'd already sold the farm. "They're like family. The brother and sister I never had."

"Thank you," Liaena murmured with another small, genuine smile. "Are you sure I couldn't get you something? You must be thirsty by this time."

Cassie was about to refuse again, but when Liaena's smile didn't disappear, she changed her mind and closed her mouth. Griffin's daughter could be gloating, but it didn't seem like it. Intrigued, Cassie tilted her head and studied the other woman. "You know, I'd kill for a cup of coffee."

****

"Don't try to lose me, Shay," Nick growled at Manakai as they finished a quick refit to Sin's Shadow.

"I repeat, you shouldn't be coming. You'll just slow me down." Grim emphasis darkened Manakai's voice. The man seemed to have lost all his humorous mischief, every movement carved in fierce determination and hard-edged purpose.

"Marchand was adamant he go with you," Sin muttered from her position on the nose of the Shadow, diagnostic equipment in hand. She looked sour, no doubt for more than one reason, not the least of which was the refitting of her Shadow. He knew how he'd feel if his own personal slicer were ripped apart and thrown back together for someone else to fly. He'd feel ten times worse if it was a Shadow.

Manakai sent a hostile glance in Nick's direction. "Marchand wouldn't have known if our new liaison hadn't opened his big mouth."

"I'm not sitting on my hands while Griffin has Cass. You say he won't hurt her, but he could do it without leaving a mark and you know it." If anything, both of their expressions grew even grimmer. They did know it. He shrugged. "Besides, I'm not useless. I can help."

Manakai snorted without comment, but Sin gave Nick a level look. "Your presence complicates things. You've read our file. You know it's true."

Nick stared at her while Manakai rose out of the slicer and headed away from them without a word. As an FPAI, his presence would limit what they could do. Nick suddenly understood their motive to bend and circumvent the law. At this point, he was willing to do anything to get Cassie back. "It won't be a problem," he told Sin with conviction.

She nodded and gestured at the slicer. "Let's finish up, then. Time's wasting."

Nick lowered into the black beauty, the first stirrings of excitement roiling in his gut. He'd been too preoccupied with Cassie's kidnapping to think about flying a Shadow, but now anticipation caught his breath. He started the slicer and couldn't suppress a grin at the sweet, subliminal hum of her powerful engines, the whisper of energy over his skin calling to him like a siren song.

He tried not to seem too eager when he reached for

the connector, but he doubted he was fooling Sin. She and her brother were slicer pilots of extraordinary skill and experience. She would know what it felt like to merge with this gorgeous machine.

She said nothing, keeping a watchful presence at his shoulder, making sure nothing went wrong. Nick slid the connector into his data port with a deep thrill of anticipation. He wasn't prepared.

The Shadow slid through him like the silky fingers of a goddess, filling his flesh with power and wild longing. In an act more intimate than sex, she soaked into him until her every function and circuit was his, her precision and beauty sweet and familiar.

Nick fumbled for the connector, yanked it out with a gasp, and pressed it to his forehead, trying to recover.

"Nick? What happened?" Sin asked in sharp concern.

He sighed, his throat aching with bitter longing. "Did Cass design the Shadows for you?"

A full minute of silence hung between them. "She put the finishing touches on a design we had created. How did you know?"

"It feels just like her." He lifted his head with a grim clench of his jaw. Taking a deep breath to prepare, he slid the connector back into his data port and suffered through a repeat of the sweet, Shadow seduction. With a shudder, he rasped, "I'm ready," without looking at Sin.

"Checking." She ran a diagnostic to make sure all systems functioned within normal parameters with the new pilot.

"Slowing me down already, Inspector," Manakai growled over the com system.

Through the sensors, Nick discovered the man's Shadow out in space circling the station. He turned to Sin with a wry glance when she finished the diagnostic. "Got a leash for your brother?"

Not a trace of humor crossed her solemn features. "Don't try. He'll grind you under in a second. Be careful, bond-brother. Bring our Cassie home." She gave him a quick kiss on his forehead and stepped back.

He nodded, touched by her gesture and her naming him brother. But he didn't have time to ponder the oddity or give her any reassurance. Sealing the Shadow, he lifted the slicer off the pad and out the open bay doors, gritting his teeth to resist the wild pull of delicious power from the machine. She moved like the wind, effortless and swift, teasing him with hints of incredible speed and strength. *Come play with me,* she seemed to whisper in Cassie's voice.

"Where are you, Shay?" he asked to distract himself.

"Way ahead of you. Where else?"

Without bothering to respond, Nick scanned for him and blazed after with a shocking burst of speed. "Sun's blood."

"Can you handle her?" Manakai asked with brisk impatience.

Nick grimaced. "Yeah, don't worry about me. Just get on with it."

"Marchand's FPA bulk transport is scheduled to jump the rings in ten. Think you can make it there in time?"

"Try me."

They raced to the star-way in a glorious rush of dark speed and agility. Nick was still trying to catch his breath when they reached the bulk transport, a military courier of vast size and little grace. The big ship hadn't even gotten to the star-way system when they reached it.

Manakai wasted no time on his approach. "Docking aft bay," he announced in clipped tones to the transport.

"Acknowledged."

Nick had to wonder just how often the Shays commandeered FPA resources like this to get so little response. Or maybe the First Marshal had given other orders to the FPA transport, besides the command to allow civilian slicers to ride along. If the Hawk told them not to ask questions, he doubted they'd make a peep.

The aft bay opened enough for them to slip through then closed over their heads. They settled on landing pads between FPA cruisers. Nick powered down the Shadow with a twinge of reluctance, still humming from the thrill of its unmatched speed. Then he slumped down in the seat, deflated at the wait they had on their hands. A big beast of a ship like this didn't move anywhere fast, and they couldn't travel through the star-way in small ships. The force of a star-way wormhole would rip small ships like slicers apart. Sitting still was killing him.

With a sigh, he muttered in reluctant admiration, "You make an amazing machine, Shay."

He received a grunt for his efforts. "Any problems?"

"No, she ran smoothly, and I held my own."

"Then keep quiet. Can't secure the com."

Nick sighed again, this time with pure aggravation.

He really needed to take a swing at the man. Maybe he would after they had Cassie home safe. Then he and Manakai could have it out. Right now, all he could do was fantasize. He imagined a couple of violent, satisfying scenarios before focusing on their current situation again.

How long did it take to run the Suns-damned rings? Had the Shays really implanted a tracking device in Cassie? He couldn't believe she'd agreed to it, a constant babysitter and monitor. He hadn't asked the Shays if Cass knew about it; maybe they'd done it without her knowledge. He wouldn't put it past them, after the kinds of things they'd pulled on him already.

He also didn't understand how they could track her at such a distance. Their abbreviated explanation of relay systems and node networks flew right by him. How could they be sure she was where they thought she was, some Core station in the middle of one of the tourist-attraction star systems? Were they serious? It seemed too public a place for holding hostages, though it would make rescue more difficult. Griffin was sly enough to factor in this obstacle.

Nick ran rough, impatient fingers through his hair. He needed to be moving. The longer he held still, the more time his imagination had to list all the bad things they might be doing to Cassie. Suns, if they hurt her, he wasn't sure he could control the violence and rage thrumming through him whenever he thought of her in Griffin's hands.

Dragging his mind from agonizing images of Cassie in tears, he closed his eyes and called up memories of the Shay file. Going over what he'd learned would help distract him and would keep the information fresh in his mind, critical for his survival if he spent any time with the Shays. He didn't know how the First Marshal expected him to keep a rein on those two. It'd taken Marchand's direct intervention to force them to accept Nick's presence on this mission. One piece of their file comforted him now and helped him keep it together: *Failure is not an option.*

Aggravating as Manakai was in his current aggressive state, Nick knew without a doubt the man wouldn't stop until Cass was out of Griffin's hands. When he was in the vault, every Shay operation laid out before him in exquisite, grim detail, he'd feared they wouldn't hesitate to sacrifice anyone or anything in their efforts to bring Griffin down. Their swift, fierce reaction to Cassie's capture gave him hope. She was not a pawn to them. Or not just a pawn. They weren't willing to sacrifice her. Like a black arrow shot from an unrelenting bow, Manakai was fixed on Cassie's return, as straight and inevitable as death.

Nick held to this truth with grim resolve and endured the wait. When the big ship shivered through the exit of the star-way, he powered his Shadow and took his cue from Manakai. The man let him stew for another eternity before he announced, "Exit in five."

Nick supposed their mission hinged on timing and location, but he still wanted to beat Shay bloody. He'd feel so much better for it. "What's the plan?"

"Stay on my heel and do what I do. If you fall behind, you get left behind."

Yeah, they were going to have it out when this was done.

They weren't in the busy star system yet. Nick wondered how Manakai expected to slip into the system and sneak onto the Core station without being seen. He didn't bother to ask, following behind Shay's Shadow like a newly grown appendage.

Manakai opened his com. "Sin, got our piggyback yet?"

"Sending." Sin's voice was clipped, an icy professional.

Nick tried not to wince at her tone and swallowed his curiosity. He'd be damned if Shay would leave him behind. Information on a vessel bloomed in his data receiver, a mid-sized luxury ship carrying a Core identification. A momentary, worrisome vision of them hijacking the thing crossed his mind, but he dismissed it as unworkable. The whole point to going in with Shadows was to get back out again as fast as possible. Hijacking a luxury cruiser might get them a free pass to the Core station, but he didn't think Griffin would let them leave the same way.

"Com silence from here on in," Manakai told him. "Follow my lead."

They arrowed toward the cruiser, the speed singing in Nick's blood and worrying him. No way would the cruiser miss them coming, even if they were sitting in the vessel's wake. Some large ships had blind spots, their own powerful engines creating enough energy disturbance to mask signals, but they wouldn't be able to hide in the wake for much longer. The cruiser would notice them soon.

Then something exploded ahead of them.

Nick swore and spun, wondering if they'd just been fired upon. His Shadow responded with sweet, unhampered efficiency, but Manakai was pulling away from him. Nick clenched his jaw and followed, hissing invectives under his breath. To his shock, the Shay twin approached the cruiser, settled into a fold of the ship's hull, and promptly disappeared. Nick stared for several long seconds before his stunned brain functioned again.

Cloaking, his mind whispered as he mimicked Manakai's maneuver. The Shay Shadows had some form of camouflage built into their skin. "Holy Heart of the Sun."

The cruiser had hesitated at the explosion, caught off guard the same way Nick had been by the burst of light and energy. But within seconds after Nick made contact with the hull, the cruiser moved again, giving no indication it'd seen the Shadows or knew it was carrying the slicers like unwanted luggage.

His heart pounding in his chest and throbbing in his temples, Nick waited to be discovered.

Nothing happened.

While his heart rate slowed, he made educated guesses about what had happened. Shay must have set off some kind of signal scrambling device, blinding the cruiser to their approach and attachment to the hull. The Shadows were well named, their sleek black surfaces somehow able to blend with the exterior of this cruiser and probably other surfaces they contacted. A little detail the Shays had neglected to mention and he'd missed in their FPA file. Was this another of Cassie's less-than-legal inventions?

Blowing a furious, resentful breath, he checked his sensors then powered down the Shadow in belated caution. The surface of the Shadow might blend, but her energy signatures would be noticed if he left her running.

His face heated with embarrassment at the mistake.

In his mind's eye, an image of Manakai's flat, accusing stare chastised him. In sour defense he muttered, "I am a Suns-damned FPA agent, not a bloody spy. You want perfect, you should have brought your sister. Would it have killed you to take five stinking minutes and run through the blasted op?"

On the other hand, he wouldn't have been able to sit still for a detailed debriefing. Every second was precious, every minute held vast amounts of painful potential for Cassie. Groaning, he shifted in his seat and tried to prepare for another agonizing wait. Cruisers moved faster than FPA transports, but it would still be a while before it reached the Core station and docked. "Hold on, Cass," he whispered, closing his eyes against horrible images. "We're coming."

Chapter 23

Webster Griffin smiled when his com lit with an incoming call. He'd been expecting the Shays to contact him sooner, but he'd known they wouldn't stay silent forever. Their gloating pride in the little doctor had been too obvious. They wouldn't let her abduction pass without mention.

Sin's face appeared on his viewer, her smile as glittering and sharp as a diamond. He didn't recognize her location. The background told him she wasn't in her private living space, offices, or one of their infamous slicers. A transport ship, perhaps? He wondered if she meant to request a meeting with him, to negotiate in person. "Sinsudee, I'm delighted you called."

"Webster, you've been quite naughty."

He chuckled and didn't bother to demure or deny. "You laid the good doctor across my path. How could I not act on it?"

She inclined her dark head in acknowledgement. "Our mistake, of course. We assumed you'd be satisfied with the merchandise. Well played, Web."

"You are too kind," he purred with a surge of satisfaction. No doubt she was only layering on flattery to distract and appease him, but he enjoyed hearing her admit the defeat nonetheless.

"So tell me, what is it you hope Dr. Draegen will achieve for you?"

A direct question. How unlike Sinsudee. She must be more rattled than she was letting on. Webster held back a smug smile. "The same as she achieved for you, my dear. What else?"

She lowered her chin, looking up at him through her long lashes in an expression both sly and flirtatious. "Are you sure you know what she did for us?"

"How intriguing. If you're trying to decrease her value to me, you are failing spectacularly. Won't you elaborate?"

She gave him a charming, mercenary grin. "Oh, Web, you know me better than that. Besides, you were the wicked thief who stole her. You should go first. We have lots to discuss, you and I."

"So, you mean to negotiate for her return."

"Wouldn't you?"

"You're in a weak position to negotiate, Sinsudee. I have all I could want."

She leaned forward, her eyes narrowing and smile sharpening in challenge. "But you won't pass up the chance to dance with me, will you." She made it more of a statement than a question, her voice throaty and enticing. "Think of all you could learn in the process. This'll be fun, Web. Come play with me."

Now bold, blatant seduction. She'd never before resorted to such brash tactics. On the other hand, it was working. He couldn't resist the opportunity to pit his wits against hers, to use her obvious investment in the doctor for his own gain. "How can I deny such a delightful invitation? So, what value would you place upon Cassiopeia Draegen?"

She named an amount so high it impressed even him.

"I believe you have our roles reversed, my dear. You're supposed to start low."

"That was low." She grinned again, this time with a ruthless edge. "Let's play."

Webster smiled in return, an eager burn in his chest as he leaned back in his seat. One thing he could say about these Shays; they knew how to entertain.

****

Cassie took a contemplative sip of her drink and studied Liaena over the rim of the mug. This had to be the strangest captivity in history. Griffin's daughter had treated her with unfailing courtesy and generosity, like a treasured guest. Her father's insincere and gloating welcome only underscored Liaena's earnest hospitality.

After the one pointed question regarding the Shays, the other woman had drawn Cassie out with surprising, gentle charm. Their conversation had run a gambit of benign social topics, relaxing Cassie and teaching her quite a few things about Liaena she would never have guessed.

One of the strangest things she'd learned was she might actually like this daughter of Griffin's.

"Another mint wafer?" Liaena asked with a small, pleased smile, her cool serenity warmed now with furtive delight. If Cassie had to guess, she'd say Liaena was enjoying their little, social luncheon.

"If I eat any more, I'll explode." Cass eyed the thin chocolate temptations. "Give it a few more minutes."

"Your willpower is astounding," Liaena teased, plucking a wafer and nibbling the edge.

Cassie straightened with a sniff. "I'll have you know, my resistance is legendary. Your chocolate torture won't—"

"Daughter," Griffin interrupted, his voice over the intercom shattering the comfortable atmosphere in a harsh reminder of her circumstances.

Cassie flinched.

Liaena's face smoothed then hardened into glacial immobility again. "Yes, Father."

"Please inform Dr. Draegen I've begun negotiations with the Shays. She might be interested to know how highly they regard her and her talents. Nearly as much as I do, in fact. They are offering substantial compensation for her return. Inform her I'm considering all options."

"Yes, Father." Liaena's tone was uninflected, cool and smooth as a river, eyes opaque again when she met Cassie's accusing glare.

When Griffin said nothing further, Cassie curled her lip. "Loves to gloat, doesn't he?"

"The Shays are negotiating for your release. Perhaps you were wrong about them." Liaena's voice was still even, but her expression turned her last comment into a question.

"I guess I was." Cassie looked down and wrapped protective arms around her middle. If the woman wanted to believe it, she wasn't going to set her straight. "What will it take for Griffin to let me go?"

Liaena was quiet for a minute, but Cassie didn't lift her head. "It will take quite a lot. My father values you greatly."

Cassie made an aggravated sound. "I guess I'm stuck here for a while, then. Don't suppose you know any card games," she mumbled with as much dejection as she could manage.

"I know a few." Liaena's cool voice held a hint of

humor. "What do you suggest?"

Cassie chewed on the inside of her lip and tried to think of a way to respond without giving away the farm again. If only she could lie and banter like Sin and Kai. Before she could get her traitorous reactions under control, the lights flickered. Her chin jerked up as if on a string, mirroring the leap of hope in her heart.

Liaena glanced at the lights then down at a portable viewer next to her, as if checking for something. She met Cassie's gaze with the same small, pleased smile. "I believe we're about to receive company."

Cassie stared at her, heart stumbling out of its leap of hope and into a deep plunge of alarm. She'd warned her captors of this rescue attempt. What if they anticipated the Shays too well? She'd put her friends in terrible danger.

Her smile still in place, Liaena lifted a hand control and keyed in several commands with swift, graceful fingers.

"What are you doing?" Cassie didn't think the woman would tell her, but she'd try anything to distract her.

"Cassiopeia Draegen," Liaena said in a strangely urgent, intense tone, fingers still flying over her control. "I envy you. Please believe me when I say I've not enjoyed anything in a great while as I have your company today." The lights went out, the emergency lighting giving the room an ominous, amber cast. Liaena didn't pause. "If you will allow it, I would be delighted to visit with you again, at the location of your choice."

Cassie stared at her, astounded. "You're helping."

Liaena flicked her a glance like hot silver, vibrant

with some nameless emotion. "Communications are down. My father can neither see nor hear us. Dr. Draegen...Cassie—" She stopped abruptly, a crease forming between her brows, bright gaze swinging to the door. In a motion as smooth and graceful as running water, she rose and moved away, facing the door with features gone cool and still.

Cassie jumped to her feet and turned in the same direction, limbs shaky with hope and shock. Griffin's daughter was helping her escape. The door opened and Kai blew in with as much violence as a black storm. He gave Cassie a quick, assessing glance but didn't pause, aimed at Liaena like a vengeful arrow, menace coating his prowling form and chilling his eyes into green ice.

Cass opened her mouth to speak, to reassure him and explain. Then she saw who entered on Kai's heels and forgot about explanations. "Nick!" Overwhelming relief and joy weakened her already unsteady limbs as she lurched toward him.

If she hadn't already known she'd fallen in love with him like drowning in quicksand, the near painful yearning at her core would have cleared any doubts. His arms caught her before she took more than two wobbly steps. She collapsed against him with a gasp of elation before his mouth stole her breath. Winding her arms around his neck, she kissed him back with fierce urgency, not caring if she ever breathed again. He was here, he'd come for her, and anything seemed possible.

Nick ended the kiss long before she was ready, his handsome face anxious and dark eyes wild. "Cass, are you all right?" All she could do was nod, voice trapped in a throat closed with too much emotion. "Did they hurt you? Sun's blood, I'm never letting you out of my sight again," he growled, kissing her hard without waiting for her to answer. His hold was tight enough to make her ribs creak, but she was glad for it. She didn't want him to ever let go.

When he raised his head again, his grip loosened and his eyes went past her. His grim features cleared the clouds of euphoria from her brain.

She'd forgotten about Kai.

With a sudden lurch of anxiety for her recent companion, Cassie spun in Nick's hold, only to stop and stare. Her jaw may have come unhinged. She was too busy goggling to notice.

She'd expected Liaena to be trussed up at least, or maybe out cold, bleeding and broken. She hadn't expected a stand-off. They stood inches apart, eyes locked, still as stone. Kai loomed with all the fatal potential of black lightning, the air almost crackling with the threat of violence. Yet he didn't touch her, arms at his sides.

Liaena stood cool and composed, absorbing his energy without apparent effect, as if she could withstand anything. Her eyes were the only flaw in her glacial guard, wide and bright with something like anticipation.

"You should go. You don't have much time," Liaena said in a tone as calm as if she were deciding the dinner menu and not discussing Cassie's escape.

"Liaena," Kai purred like the deep-throated threat of a large hunting cat, his glittering green eyes narrowing.

Her lashes swept down and her chin dipped in as if in concession.

Cassie watched the two adversaries, the skin

prickling on the back of her neck and hair standing up on her arms. After a few seconds, she found her voice. "Kai, I think she was helping. Liaena, you should come with us."

Her words broke the stalemate, both pairs of eyes swinging toward her. Liaena had the tiny crease between her brows again. "That's not possible, Cassie."

"Oh, it's very possible," Kai countered in a silky voice, hand flashing out to grasp her wrist and jerk her a breath closer. "You'd make a pretty little hostage, Lie."

Cassie squeaked in alarm, but Liaena only lifted her cool gaze to his again. "Don't be ridiculous. You're not ready to escalate so far." She turned back to Cassie as if Kai weren't breathing cold menace down her neck. "You would be doing me a great service if you confined me."

When she held out the interrogator's controller, Cassie recoiled, bumping into Nick's chest. "What? No! I can't put you in there. How could you even ask?"

"Confined, Dr. Draegen, as we confined you. Justice of a sort"—her mouth curved in a hint of a smile—"and we're running out of time."

"But Liaena—"

"Please, Cassie," Griffin's daughter interrupted in a low murmur, the hand offering the controller steady and insistent.

Cassie eased out of Nick's protective hold and stepped toward the other woman. With a frown of concern, she lifted the device from Liaena's palm, searching those delicate features for any hint of trouble. But Liaena was as composed as ever, turning toward the interrogator.

Kai's hand on her wrist brought her to a halt. She turned her fiery head to look at him. The two stared at one another, the collision of their wills almost visible in the air between them. Cassie held her breath, the skin prickling again at the base of her neck.

Then Kai released her and Liaena moved away with the grace of flowing silk, stepping into the machine without an instant's hesitation. "Just don't press the red button," she told Cassie, her lovely face serene but for a slight curl to her lips.

Cassie stared at her, horrified at the other woman's casual dismissal of the machine's violence. "That's not funny," she snapped, making quick adjustments to the controls. The energy field enfolded and lifted Liaena. Cassie paused, chewing on her bottom lip and meeting the woman's opaque gray gaze. "Will he hurt you?" On the last word, the amber emergency lights began to strobe in an alarming way and her heart jumped.

"Leave now." Liaena spoke without a ripple in her serene mask, but her tone held the strange urgency again.

Cassie cursed, misery welling in her when Kai headed for the exit and Nick tugged on her elbow.

"Come on, Cass."

Gripping the controller in a tight fist, Cassie backed away from Griffin's daughter, eyes locked with her gray gaze. "Come visit me anytime, Liaena Griffin. You hear me?"

The woman's mouth moved, her voice too low to hear. Cassie thought she said, "I hear you," but couldn't be sure. With a last glance and a tight feeling of regret in her chest, she turned away and hurried out the door.

"Sun's blood, Cass," Manakai snarled as they

loped down the corridor. "Did they fry your mind? You don't invite the enemy over for dinner."

"I don't think she's our enemy." Cassie's answer was breathless, her shorter legs working to keep up.

A band squeezed around Nick's chest and he tightened his hold on her arm. "What do you mean, fry? Did they stick you in that machine?" He studied her delicate form with a knot of anxiety. In his mind, the redhead didn't get what she deserved, Cassie's bizarre friendliness toward her notwithstanding. Shay's reaction disappointed him. They hadn't taken revenge on anyone since docking. Nick had to concede they hadn't run into anyone on their way to Cassie's location.

She flashed him a strained smile. "Just to hold me, no torture. Liaena released me from it," she said to Manakai's back.

He shot her a cold glance over his shoulder. "They're playing you. This way. Keep your head down."

Nick pulled Cassie into the shadow of his body, heart jerking at the other man's tone. He remembered it from his earlier "follow my lead" comment; it meant trouble. With a capital T it turned out, as they rounded a corner into a compact unit of armed men. Nick skidded to a halt with a grunt of surprise, shoving Cassie down when the men shouted and opened fire.

Manakai Shay didn't pause. He became a silent whirlwind in the flashing, amber half-light; body moving with blurring speed, seeming to defy gravity as he pushed off walls and dodged weapons' fire. Nick had never seen anything like it. The Circle of Fire in the Red Temple hadn't prepared him for this. Now he understood T'Zai's pride in his students and the ascetic's admiration for their control.

Manakai was power and purpose, weaving a dark, violent net around the half-dozen, scrambling men, using their own momentum and intention against them until they lay scattered like puppets with their strings cut.

When it was over, Shay still didn't pause, hefting an abandoned weapon, tossing it to Nick, and spinning for the other end of the corridor. "Let's go."

Nick glanced at the illegal stinger in his hand and turned an incredulous gaze on Cassie.

She was pale and wide-eyed, but calm and unhurt. "I told you," she muttered, eyes fixed on her swift-moving boss, weaving her way through the tumbled bodies.

Nick said nothing. His FPA training urged him to check the fallen, to get medical assistance for those who needed it, but he resisted. He had a bad feeling most of them were beyond medical help. This wasn't something he wanted to confirm. He didn't want to know how many Shay had killed, and there was no time for it. Cassie was his mission; getting her out safely was their priority.

"It was them or us," Cassie whispered, looking straight ahead. The crease between her brows and the quiver of her pale lips reminded him that the first dead body she'd ever seen had been her lost love. He wanted to ask if she was okay but knew it was a stupid question. She wouldn't be okay until they were out of there.

Clenching his jaw, he pulled her closer and moved faster. He also wouldn't be okay until they were out of there, until they were safe and he could go over every inch of her and make sure she was unharmed.

They went through two more groups of Griffin's goons on their way to the docking bay, Nick shielding Cassie and laying down cover fire while Manakai destroyed them as inevitably as a black hole. Their luck ran out when they reached the bay. Armed guards and ships swarmed through it, sirens wailing and warnings blaring.

"Stay here," Manakai said without infliction, eyes hard as green diamonds.

"Wait!" Nick tried to grab his arm, but the man morphed from a whirlwind to a shadow, disappearing into the chaos of movement and sound within seconds. Cursing under his breath, he let Cassie tug him into a space behind a row of crates, crouching there with the itch of dismay and imminent danger crawling over his skin.

Cassie leaned close, soft brown eyes wide with anxiety. "He'll make a distraction."

"Like what?"

She shrugged, a faint smile tugging at her mouth. "We'll know it when we see it. How did you get here?"

"Shadows."

She nodded as if she'd known what he would say. "Head for them when Kai's hell breaks loose."

He would have said something sarcastic about putting too much faith in the man, but the memory of Shay dodging weapon's fire and erasing half a dozen men silenced him. He might not like the man or the way Cassie admired him, but he had to admit Manakai got the job done. *Failure is not an option.* He laid a hand along Cassie's pale, delicate face and thought, *Damn straight.*

A harsh voice from beyond the crates snagged his attention. "Hey! You there!"

Nick turned, saw the man snarling at them, saw the weapon he was lifting toward them, and fired without hesitation. It caught the man on the shoulder, spinning him around with a hoarse cry of pain. At the sound of running feet, Nick hissed a curse and shifted his body to shield Cassie. The wounded man clutched his shoulder and edged toward the weapon he'd dropped.

This was going to get ugly.

Nick had the man in his sights and was about to take a kill shot for the first time in his life, when Kai's hell broke loose. An enormous boom shook the entire structure and almost threw Nick off his feet. Metal groaned and shrieked, the crates shifting and rocking in an alarming way above them, a hot wind whistling around their cover. Then the wind reversed itself, howling as it sucked at them.

"Come on!" Cassie cried. His heart leapt into his throat when she darted past him into the open.

He lunged for her then took a second to gape at the destruction and chaos beyond their hiding place. A ragged hole had appeared in the station's outer hull where the atmosphere shielding control would have been. The shimmer of an active shield was missing.

He understood the howling wind now. Everything in the bay was being sucked out into space.

With a wordless snarl of shock and horror, he caught up to Cassie, grabbed her arm, and bolted for the cruiser and the concealed Shadows. The good news was no one seemed to notice them or care, the sucking wind helping to propel them toward their goal. The bad news was, well, everything else.

Nick's chest ached, the dwindling oxygen straining his lungs. Something large struck him a glancing blow from behind. He stumbled, Cassie's arm tearing from his grip.

"No!" An image of her tumbling into space ripped through his mind. When he lifted his head, he caught sight of Cassie dangling over Manakai's shoulder as the other man bounded up the side of the cruiser toward the hidden Shadows. Cursing through his teeth, he scrambled after them and winced at the pain radiating through his right shoulder blade and down his spine. Whatever had struck him hadn't been gentle.

Sucking wind in desperate pulls, he reached the side of his Shadow at a crawl, the cruiser shivering and shifting under his feet as it inched across the bay toward space. The quiet, dark, and breathable interior of the Shadow welcomed him like a blessing from a goddess. Nick took a second to sink into the seat and gasp, before he plugged in the connector and powered the ship.

"Nick! Nick, answer me!" Cassie's frantic voice shot another dose of adrenaline through his system.

"What? Are you all right?"

"Oh, Suns. Nicholo Givliani, you are never scaring me like that again!" A thwacking sound and a masculine grunt came over the com. "You idiot, Kai! I can't believe you left him behind."

"Ow, easy on the merchandise," Manakai muttered in a sour tone. "We're not out of the woods yet, so let's play nice 'til we get back home."

"Jerk," Cassie hissed.

Despite the dire circumstances, Nick couldn't keep

a grin off his face, lifting the Shadow from the surface of the cruiser and slipping out of the bay after Shay. "Easy Cass," he soothed. "The main thing was to get you out." He paused. "But if you wanna smack him again for blowing up the bay and making it harder than it had to be, I won't blame you." After another thwack and a grunt, Nick snickered with quiet satisfaction.

"Go ahead, laugh it up, chuckles," Manakai said. "But you might want to watch your tail while you're giggling like a girl. FPA, starboard aft, closing fast."

"What?" Nick made a quick scan, a frantic twist in his gut. He hadn't considered they'd go up against his own people. He knew they'd have to deal with Griffin and his goons, but why hadn't he suspected the FPA would get involved? They were in a high traffic system and this station was vomiting ships and debris into space. Griffin couldn't hide the problem. Protocol dictated he call in the authorities to evaluate the emergency and assist.

Manakai heaved a mild sigh. "They just had to ruin my day. I wanted to smash it some more before we disappeared."

"Kai, you blew up half the station." Cassie's tone was acid.

"I wish. Sin cooked the blue factory all up and down, but all I get is a lousy suck job on a docking bay. Besides," he added, his voice darkening, "I could have taken out Griffin and saved us a world of grief."

The com went quiet for a minute. Anxious, Nick monitored the FPA vessels behind them. They seemed interested in the station's crisis, but he wouldn't feel comfortable until they were out of sight.

"Assassinating Griffin wouldn't cure the problem."

"But it'd feel good, wouldn't it, Cass?"

"Can we fantasize about death and destruction later? The FPA's taking an interest," Nick announced, his stomach roiling in acid.

"Not really them you should worry about, sport," Manakai responded with a return of his slick, callous humor. "Griffin will have dogs up front to snap at us while the FPA's busy at his station."

Another surge of adrenaline hit Nick's already overloaded system. "What kind and how many?"

Shay's tone turned into a sardonic drawl. "Well, now, I didn't get the memo on their itinerary. Pretty sure Griff wants it to be a surprise."

"But I hate surprise parties," Nick gritted through clenched teeth, wanting more than ever to strangle the dark twin.

Cassie interrupted. "Kai, stop baiting him and pay attention. What do you see? Where are the FPA? Check the long range."

"Watch the elbow and stop trying to lap-drive, Cass. I'm running a long sweep now and"—Shay swore—"I said stop messing with it, braincase. There's a convenient ambush spot up ahead." A strange flurry of sound came over the com along with Manakai's exasperated growl. "Would you quit? One pilot, remember?"

"I was just trying to check the—"

"You elbow me one more time, I'm pulling this ride over."

Nick grinned in satisfaction at the genuine aggravation in the other man's voice. If Cassie had to sit on the guy's lap, at least she wasn't making it a pleasurable experience. A sweep of his own sensors knocked the grin off his face.

The FPA patrol following in their wake had faded back toward the beleaguered station, losing interest in a random pair of slicers in the face of a larger crisis. But the ambush spot Kai had mentioned, a small cluster of orbiting planetoids, was now blooming with violent life.

"Ah, dogs incoming. Cass, you might wanna hold still a minute and let Shay shoot some things."

"How many things?" Cassie asked in a thin, worried voice.

Nick didn't answer, staring at the net of plasma-cloud skippers bearing down on them. The number would only worry her more. He wished he'd had time to practice with the Shadow weaponry. With this many ships attacking, he was going to have to use them. "Um, you take the ones on the left, and I'll take the ones on the right?"

"How about we make a hole instead and bolt. They can't catch Shadows flat out."

"Works for me."

Manakai began an intricate, evasive maneuver with his Shadow. Nick copied him, thrilled even now by the incredible responsiveness of the slicer, twisting and looping in a dizzying dance. A second later, the skippers fired on them and a surge of profound gratitude washed over him for the slicer's responsiveness. Blasts flew past, close enough to give his heart palpitations.

Nick fired back without much hope of hitting anything; the Shadow was in too wild a spin to aim. Shay's slicer straightened and flew toward the net of skippers like a black arrow sent by a god, weapons firing in a precise, deadly pattern.

Two skippers blew apart, opening a hole in their net of attack. Another skipper tried to close the gap as Manakai streaked through the hole. Nick leveled everything he had on the incoming ship. It disintegrated and he winced when his Shadow smashed through the debris field. Now on the other side of the net, Nick ran a quick diagnostic for damage and tried another of those intricate, evasive patterns. The slicer was functional, but blasts streaked past him and pumped urgent alarm through his veins.

"Go," Manakai commanded. "Open her up." His Shadow leapt forward in a flash of black lightning.

Locking his jaw and baring his teeth, Nick kicked the engines to full power and followed. The Shadow shivered around him, her only protest to the speed blurring the galaxy into a rush of colors. Heart thundering in his ears, Nick tried to check for skippers behind them, but the flood of power roaring through him disoriented his senses.

Giving up, he hung on for the ride and did his best to think of anything but Cassie. In this ecstatic burst of power, thoughts of her would shatter his control and dump him in a Sun.

He almost overshot when Shay's Shadow slowed at the edge of a solar system. Hissing a string of curses through gritted teeth, Nick fought a battle of wills with his seductive Shadow and managed a controlled deceleration. Breathing deep to slow his heart and palming sweat off his forehead, he eased his slicer next to Shay's. "Why are we stopping? They'll catch up."

"We won't be here," Manakai said in a clipped tone. "Remember the plan?"

Nick wanted to snarl, "You mean the plan you sketched out in thirty seconds hours ago and didn't mention what I was really getting into?" He kept his mouth shut and began a search of the surrounding space. He did remember Sin was supposed to be lurking around somewhere with their ride home. Shay moved toward a busy traffic lane streaming out from the system's solar core, and with a sour grimace, Nick followed.

Even with peacekeepers keeping a watchful eye on the lane, the Shadows were still far enough out to be in danger if Griffin's dogs caught them. The skippers could strike and dart away before the patrols had time to interfere. The Shays' plan was for the Shadows to disappear from sight before the skippers arrived.

Right on cue, Nick caught a sensor reading of a courier ship. His brother's growling voice filled the interior of the Shadow. "Nick, you better be in one piece." Sin and Del hovered at the edge of a safe traffic lane in one of the smaller, ugly couriers the Shays used for off-lane runs. According to plan, Sin should have been keeping Griffin distracted and lulled into a false sense of security with monetary offers for Cassie's return, while Manakai and Nick ran the rescue op. She must have been convincing; they'd made it in and back out after all.

"Yeah, bro, I'm good and we got Cass, but skippers are incoming."

"Come aboard," Sin responded without hesitation.

Nick raced with Kai to the courier and slipped through the open bay doors, settling the Shadow onto the floor of the ship's cargo hold. With a pang of regret, he powered down the sleek slicer and disconnected.

Swinging out of the slicer with a surge of anticipation, his gaze fixed on Cassie as she slid out of Kai's Shadow. She turned and gave him a glorious smile, stopping his heart.

Before he could reach her side, Sin and Del arrived and bombarded them with hugs and demands for a full report on their health.

"I don't mean to be a party pooper, but shouldn't someone be flying and watching out for bad guys?" Kai drawled with a pointed look at his sister.

She grinned and jerked her thumb toward the exit. "Thanks for volunteering." He rolled his eyes and sauntered away, and Sin took Cassie's hands, studying her. "Was it bad?"

Cass shook her head, her face pale and serious. "I wasn't hurt. Griffin was his usual arrogant self. I almost threw up on him, kind of sorry I didn't, now. Liaena was different. Sin, she helped me escape."

Sin's brow creased, but she didn't question her friend. "Let's go sit in the lounge. You can tell me everything."

Cassie nodded and Sin turned to lead the way with Del at her side. Cass glanced at Nick and held out her hand, eyes and mouth softening.

He clasped her hand in a gentle hold, lifting it to his mouth as they followed the other two. "Are you sure you're okay?" he rasped against her soft skin, the tightness of residual anxiety pulling at his muscles.

Her lips curled in a faint smile, eyes limpid and irresistible. "Yes, I'm fine. Thanks for coming for me."

"Anytime." He bent to press what was supposed to be a quick kiss on her lips. Relief and desire surged through him, and he lingered, feet slowing to a stop. He didn't notice. The universe could have stopped and he wouldn't have noticed. Cassie, pressed warm and soft against him, vibrantly alive and blessedly safe, was the only thing that mattered.

"Ahem." Sin's pointed cough recalled him back to the rest of the world. "Business first, fun stuff later, kiddies." A wry, tolerant smile warmed her face, neutralizing her sardonic tone.

"Right," Cass mumbled, cheekbones coloring a lovely shade of rose. She ducked her head and pulled Nick with her into the lounge.

They settled around a little table in the kitchenette. Cassie told her side of the events, then Nick sketched his story, hand clasping hers the entire time. Sin and Del stayed quiet when they'd finished, both wearing similar, disturbed expressions. Sin propped her chin on one fist, green gaze focused past them as if trying to read the future.

Del drummed his fingers on the table, eyes narrowed on Nick. "Sounds way too hairy, bro. You're grounded from now on."

Nick made a rude noise in the back of his throat. "Coming from the guy who totaled his slicer last time he was out, that carries just about zero weight."

Sin ignored the two of them. "Liaena has never before defied her father. It doesn't add up, unless they're trying a new tactic."

Cassie sighed. "Kai said they were playing me. I guess it's possible. She was so careful, but I swear there was something about what she said and how she acted. It felt real, Sin."

Sin reached out and touched Cassie's hand where it lay on the table. "Please remember, Cass, she's a

Griffin. Her father groomed Aena to be his perfect puppet. Even if she did help you, we can't afford to see it as anything other than some new deception."

Cassie's face darkened with a troubled frown. After a second, she nodded in mute acceptance.

Nick breathed a little easier. He agreed with Sin and Kai; they couldn't trust the red-head. What little he'd seen of her icy calm and control had only reinforced his need to get Cassie far away from her. Cassie's defense of Griffin's daughter worried him. Her description of their Q&A tea party made him wonder if they hadn't played mind games with his little dragon. If she was starting to see reason, he might not have to worry so much about her haring off on another exciting adventure to meet her new "friend." Just the idea laced icicles up his spine.

"Coming up on the star-way," Kai's voice intruded from the com.

Sin lifted her head. "Any trouble?"

"Griffin's lapdogs turned tail when they saw the lane patrols. We're good."

Sin sighed and bent a stern look on Cassie. "This had better be the last time you run off without telling anyone."

"I told Del," Cassie said in a small voice, cheeks coloring again.

"I've already yelled at him for buying your bluff. I'm yelling at you now. What were you thinking?"

"I told you, I'm a crappy spy." Cassie moaned, covering her eyes with a hand. "Besides, I thought Nick was in trouble."

Furtive warmth stole through Nick. She cared enough about him to bolt from her safe zone at a moment's notice. He wanted to kiss her all over, then shake some sense into her.

"Yes, men can make us do some really stupid things sometimes," Sin said, her accusing gaze turning to rest on Nick.

"Hold up, how'd this get to be my fault?"

"Well, you must have done something to turn my friend's considerable brain to mush." Cassie sputtered a protest. Sin talked over her. "I'm pretty sure it wasn't accidental."

Nick started his own protest, but Del held up a hand with a snort of laughter. "Don't bother, bro. You'll just get in worse trouble. This is one of those women arguments you ain't gonna win. Just take it on the chin and agree with them."

Sin turned a disgusted look on Del. "Women arguments?"

"Yes, dear," he said with a toothy smile.

Cassie burst into laughter. Nick watched her with a bemused grin, willing to take all kinds of blame if this was the end result.

"Minute warning," Kai's voice interrupted again.

Sin gestured them to the seating area to strap in for the trip through the star-way wormhole. Nick rose with Cassie's hand still clasped securely in his.

Chapter 24

Their return trip to Shay Enterprises HQ remained uneventful. Cassie sent up a prayer of thanks, knowing she'd gotten lucky. As kidnappings went, hers had been pretty tame, but the rescue could have gone so wrong. It almost had. Cassie shuddered, remembering the endless squads of Griffin-goons and the horrible, suffocating feeling in the torn docking bay. Her worst moment had been Kai carrying her away and leaving Nick behind in near-vacuum.

Losing him would have been worse than her own death, history repeating itself with a cruel, icy twist.

She discussed the details of their recent adventures with her friends, but kept hold of Nick's hand all the while, needing the contact to reassure her bruised heart he was alive, whole, and very much with her. She wished she could have a few minutes alone with him, or a few hours, time enough to strip him bare and go over every particle of him for injuries. Then go over him again for other reasons.

Her clinging was too obvious, but he seemed willing to tolerate it, not pulling away. She'd have to tell him how she felt. If he expected this relationship to be a casual thing, then she had to be honest with him. It was only fair to them both. A quick fling was less than she deserved and he should know the truth.

She just had no idea how to tell him.

The sooner the better, she lectured the coward part of herself, as the courier settled in the docking bay and they filed off the ship. They headed through the mechanics' bay and toward the Shays' offices, Cassie sneaking a glance at Nick out of the corner of her eye, heart in her throat.

Announcing she'd fallen for him might send him bolting for the nearest exit. She wondered if her subconscious was planning it that way, to save herself the unbearable pain of watching another loved one suffer or die. Danger still stalked them, the Endgame playing out as inexorably as death.

They stepped off the lift and into the twins' main office to contact Marchand. The First Marshal had demanded a full accounting on their return, both from the Shays and his new liaison. They also needed to know of any fallout from the FPA presence at the tail end of their rescue. They discovered Marchand had already left an urgent message for them to contact him.

Cassie exchanged grim looks with the twins. "What do you think it is?" They shook their heads in unison without answering. Marchand might want to speak to them for any number of reasons, none of them comforting.

While Sin contacted FPA HQ, Cassie waited with a band of anxiety around her chest, chewing on her lower lip and yanking at her braid. Marchand was unavailable. The FPA system's polite AI explained the First Marshal had urgent business to attend and had left orders for them to remain available for his return call.

Both Shays smirked. "Could you please let him know we are waiting for him with bated breath?" Sin responded in a silky tone.

The AI confirmed and ended the connection.

Kai chuckled and shared a look of vast amusement with his sister. "He might be arrogant, but you have to love the guy's style."

"Do I?" Sin drawled, eliciting another chuckle from her twin.

"Now what?" Nick asked at Cassie's side, pulling her hand away from her braid.

Cassie leaned into his warm strength and smiled when he slipped an arm around her waist. "Now we wait."

Kai made a disgusted sound, watching his sister change the hologram behind their desk from a beach scene to multiple data screens. "Know what I could go for?"

"I'll start mixin'," Del answered and headed for the bar.

Kai stared after the big man with raised eyebrows. Then he turned a grin on his sister. "He's really starting to grow on me."

"You're really starting to get predictable."

Kai snickered and left her at the desk, joining Del at the bar. Sin leaned with casual grace against the slab of mahogany, studying the screens with an absorbed expression.

Cassie sighed, looking up at Nick. "I hate waiting."

"You wanna try another supernova?" Nick's mobile mouth twitched with humor, dark eyes warm and inviting.

"When hell freezes over," she snorted. He gave her a wicked grin and she took a deep breath. *No time like the present.* "Nick, I need to talk to you."

His expression turned quizzical, humor fading.

"Sure. About what?"

Cassie glanced around at her friends, then tugged Nick over to the fireplace seating arrangement for a bit more privacy. Drawing another deep breath and fixing her gaze on his wide chest, she took the plunge. "I need to talk to you about us. I know we haven't known each other very long, and I'm sure there's plenty we still need to learn. I mean, we're practically strangers. We've only had one date—"

"Are you giving me the brush-off, Cass?"

"What?" She glanced up, thrown by his question and the dark glower on his face. "No! I mean, I hope not. But you're probably going to run for the nearest exit because it really is too soon for me to tell you this and I should just keep my mouth shut but I don't want you to get the wrong impression—"

"Cass." He gave her shoulders a light shake.

"I'm just crazy about you," she plowed on in a high voice, heart thundering in her chest and ears ringing. She kept her wide gaze fixed somewhere around his right ear. "I'm sorry if it alarms you or isn't what you're looking for and I'll understand if you want to end things with me—"

He clasped her face in his hands and silenced her with his mouth. She stopped breathing and clutched his shirtfront for balance, all the strength running out of her limbs at the heat and intensity of his kiss. When he lifted his head, she struggled to raise heavy eyelids and focus on his gorgeous smile. "I'm crazy about you, too, Cass. You knocked me off my feet when I first met you and I haven't got back up since. Will you bond with me?"

She blinked at him in a daze, certain she'd

misheard. The strange ringing in her ears must have interfered. "W-what?"

"Sin and Del are going through the Sun-bonding ceremony soon. We could make it a double."

"We could what? You—are you—you want us to be Sun-bonded?" Her voice squeaked on the last word as she stared up at him, aghast. Her knees seemed to unhinge.

His chest vibrated with a low laugh. "Don't look so shocked, Cass. You had to notice how you spin me around. I haven't been able to think about anything else or leave you alone since I got here. I'm gone on you, little dragon. Say you'll bond with me."

She stared at him a minute longer, dazzled by the warm light in his midnight eyes, but he hadn't turned her into a complete lunatic yet. Shifting away so she could function, Cassie croaked, "No."

His smile faded into a faint frown. "No?"

"Of course no," she breathed, struggling to get her brain started and overrule her delirious heart. "Didn't I just say we barely know each other? Sun and Stars, Nick, I would've been happy with 'let's just see where this goes' and you spring 'let's get bonded' on me? Are you nuts?"

A sudden grin lightened his handsome features and made him years younger. "Yup. What can I say, Cass? Givlianis fall hard and fast. You're stuck with me, so you might as well say yes."

She frowned, pulling out of his clasp and folding her arms across her chest. "Everything I learned about psychology and relationships tells me it would be emotional suicide. It is too soon and we are not getting bonded."

He didn't lose his grin. "Okay Doc, I'll wait. But you're crazy about me and one of these days, you'll say yes. I'll just have to keep asking."

She shook her head, utterly baffled. "I should do a study on you."

He let out his low laugh again, sending warm shivers down her spine, and reached for her. Before he could tug her closer, the communications chimed an incoming call.

"Marchand," Sin announced to the room in her most business-like tone.

Dazed by Nick's unexpected, perplexing response, Cassie knew better than to ignore her bosses' summons. Her feet seemed disconnected and numb when she headed toward the desk. Nick paced her, his fingertips just touching the small of her back, spreading warmth all the way out to her extremities. She sent him a wary glance as Marchand's face appeared on the holographic display. Nick gave her such a melting, heart-stopping smile in return, her brain fuzzed out.

"Gaston," Sin greeted the First Marshal. "What can we do for you?"

The First Marshal's face was an expressionless mask. "I'm making an official request for your assistance in a newly opened investigation."

The word official drove through Cassie like a cold spear, bringing her thoughts into sharp focus. This wasn't a private communication. Marchand was contacting them through an open channel and not requesting news from them. Something had happened.

The Shays exchanged a swift, intense glance before facing the First Marshal together. "We're always at your disposal. How may we be of assistance?"

"You have an AI expert in your employ. An anonymous tip a short time ago led us to a covert lab. We found several AIs there, altered in ways we don't understand. They aren't exhibiting normal behavior. We could use Dr. Draegen's expertise to find out what was done to them and why."

"Imago," Cassie gasped, heart leaping in her chest. She surged forward, stumbling to a stop when Sin shot a warning glance over her shoulder.

"Dr. Draegen has just returned from a strenuous trip, but I'm sure she'd be happy to help," Sin responded to Marchand with a grim smile. "Are you saying someone has reprogrammed these AIs without sanction?"

"The AIs' behavior suggests gross, repeated violations against the Humanities Act for Artificial Persons." The First Marshal spoke with a diffidence unusual for him. "But we need confirmation before we prosecute the offenders. I'm sending you an encrypted data stream with prelim intel for Dr. Draegen on our findings so far. We have other specialists onsite, so we don't need the doctor there in person."

Sin glanced at a flashing screen in the lower right corner of the holo-display. "We'll give this to her without delay."

"Good. Time is short. I'll be looking for Dr. Draegen's report." The First Marshal's sharp features flickered and disappeared.

"Good talk," Kai muttered with a snort. "I really felt the love, how about you all?"

Cassie ignored him, pulling away from Nick and bolting around the desk, eyes fixed on the flickering data stream. Elbowing Kai out of the way and ignoring his muffled exclamation, she touched the interactive hologram. It came alive under her fingers and she sped through it like lightning, muttering curses and prayers under her breath.

"Cass, we can't read that fast," Sin admonished. "What are you seeing?"

"It was a Core lab in a subsidiary of Griffin's R&D branch. Well hidden, he didn't think anyone would find it. But there was a signal. It was from Imago," Cassie breathed with a surge of bittersweet pride. "He sent a distress signal. Someone relayed it to the FPA. They found the place, cracked it open…oh, no."

"Cass?" Sin's hand settled on her shoulder. The others shifted closer, a warm net of support.

It made no difference. Her heart was ice. "Almost a dozen," she declared through numb lips. "Sun's mercy, he twisted almost a dozen AIs, drove them insane. He used a version of the Sun-cursed code." She paused. "Wait, this can't be right. Did Marchand send us everything?"

Kai bent closer, reading the data through her searching fingers. "No weapons."

"They found no weapons?" Sin asked in a flat tone. Her hand left Cassie's shoulder.

"It looks like all we have on Griffin are AI rights violations. If we can even pin those on him," Kai confirmed in a dark voice. "If he doesn't find a scapegoat or weasel out with some legal loophole."

Nick made a disgusted sound. "Even if you do hit him square with rights violations, the most he'd get is a fat fine and his AI contracts pulled."

"Dirt in his face," Del growled.

"Minor public humiliation," Sin agreed in a low

hiss.

Kai stalked away with violence in his every step. "Sun's blood, I need that drink."

Cassie barely noticed them. She scoured the data, pouring over it again and again, sure she was just not reading it right. Something was missing besides the weapons. She went over the AI descriptions again, checking each designation until she couldn't avoid the truth any longer.

"He's not there," she wheezed, her chest aching as if someone had punched her in the sternum. She couldn't pull enough air into her cramped lungs.

"What?" Sin's voice was sharp in her ear.

"Imago. He's not there. He's not one of the AIs they found. Griffin still has him." Her extremities started to tingle. The room went gray at the edges.

"Whoa, Cass, sit down." Del lowered her into the big chair behind the desk then shifted back with a grunt when Nick shoved past him.

Nick took her hands, studying her with dark, anxious eyes. "Suns, you're white as a ghost. Put your head down and breathe. That's it, honey."

Cassie rested her forehead on her knees, sucking air like a long-distance runner. The darkness at the edge of her vision receded. A surge of nausea took its place. "I sent him there," she moaned. "Oh, Stars, my poor Imago."

Nick's gentle hand coasted down her back, making soothing passes over her shuddering form. "Shh, it's gonna be okay, Cass. Take it easy, you'll make yourself sick."

"It's not going to be okay." She sat up, running a shaking hand over her face and staring in mild surprise at the wetness on her fingers. She hadn't been aware she was crying.

She looked at each of them in turn, her heart cracking even more. Nick's handsome face was so filled with open, warm concern, her entire being flooded with love and despair. He didn't know, but confirmation of her worst fears shone stark on the grim features of Sin, Kai, and Del. She voiced it, leaving herself nowhere to hide from the guilt. "It's not going to be okay, because Griffin has what he wants. He has Imago. We gambled and lost. He has his weapon."

Kai made a sound deep in his throat like the snarl of an angry lion. "We haven't lost yet, Cassie-girl."

"We'll get Imago back," Sin added in a softer tone, sinking to a crouch at Cassie's side and clasping her arm in a gentle hold. Her calm, emerald gaze gleamed with unshakable conviction, easing the bone-deep cold in Cassie's limbs. "He rescued his brothers and sisters and helped us strike another blow at Griffin. The FPA rats will scramble to cover for their boss, exposing their own corruption. Marchand will have more incriminating evidence and fewer obstacles to shutting down Griffin for good. Because of Imago. We won't abandon him, Cassie."

Cassie took a shaky breath, more tears tracking hot paths down her cheeks, but she felt easier in her skin. "I know you won't," she whispered. "Neither will I. We'll bring him home and kick Griffin's twisted, megalomaniac ass all the way across the galaxy."

"That's our Cassie-girl," Sin murmured, affection and approval brightening her eyes.

Nick's mouth curved in a wry smile as he tugged Cassie off the chair and into his arms. "Suns, what'd I get myself into?"

She sank into his solid warmth with a sigh, more grateful than she could ever express. The guilt and loss of Imago's disappearance ached like open wounds in her heart. Nick's simple comfort dulled the pain, easing her toward acceptance. She could guess what Griffin was doing to her creation and it tore at her. But she wouldn't let it go on. They'd bring Imago home. She'd think of a way.

Resting against Nick's strength, Cassie realized how tired she was and how blissful it was to be wrapped in his arms. She'd had a very bad day. To be able to lean on someone, to find a safe harbor she might call home, was as close to divine as she could imagine. Tears of love and gratitude stung her eyes. "You were just messing with me earlier, right?" She held her breath.

"Nope."

"You're crazy about me?"

"Bonkers."

"How's that possible?"

He chuckled, a warm sound easing her muscles and curling her lips in an answering smile. "You're just that amazing, Cass. Did you change your mind yet about bonding?"

"No," she said aloud, but her heart whispered other things while she soaked in the heat and balm of his cradling arms. This feeling, this blissful comfort and sense of belonging, had forever stamped all over it. She suspected she'd need this and him in the near future. The Endgame was far from over.

Considering the grim thought, she cleared her throat. Then she whispered, "Not yet."

Epilogue

T'Zai gazed in thoughtful silence at the massive red sun dominating his temple. The late hour had cleared the room of most meditating Dani, except one solitary soul snoring on his mat at the foot of a stone column. The light of the red giant sent questing fingers through the shadows, brooding and restless. Much like the old worshiper standing in its humbling glow.

The doors to the temple shushed open. T'Zai didn't turn, knowing who entered. He listened and smiled with pride when he heard not even a whisper of a footfall.

"Mendani," Manakai murmured at his elbow.

The tone was respectful enough, but T'Zai knew his young pupil well and smothered a smile. The Shays had their own brand of arrogance and would chafe at being summoned, especially so late at night. T'Zai continued his study of the sun, taxing his student a moment longer with his impatience. Then he quoted, "Is it faith or folly to loose the Sunfires of strife at the dawn of the Red Sun?"

Kai snorted. "Scripture. Really? I was having enough trouble sleeping, T'Zai."

"Trouble is a bloodhound with your scent as its compass, my young friend. Sleep later, when it no longer tramples a path to your door."

"And ominous metaphors." Kai sighed. "All we need is a bloody hymn, and we'll have ourselves the perfect sermon. Would you just get to the point, you old ham?"

T'Zai laughed. He supposed he shouldn't encourage the youngster, but Manakai's irreverence always delighted him. He thought most of his fellow ascetics could learn a thing or two from this audacious Shay. Belief did not mean blind faith, and respect did not mean unquestioning obedience. Or apparently much deference.

His laughter made odd echoes in a chamber reserved for quiet contemplation and worship. It woke the Dani, who snorted, staggering to his feet, and weaving into the darkness, muttering under his breath.

"It is late," T'Zai conceded. "I've had word from my Golden counterpart. He believes we are reaching a focal point. Webster Griffin has declined several engagements and canceled at least one public appearance."

Kai frowned, the dim reddish light sharpening his features into austere lines. "You've confided in the other Orders?"

T'Zai lifted his eyebrows with a faint smile. "A resource left untouched is a gift to the enemy. My brothers and sisters of the other Orders serve us better in knowledge than in ignorance. Griffin may not believe, but he can be persuasive."

"You think he'd turn to the Orders for help?"

"Help may be too strong a word, but Griffin is not above using any tool to suit his needs. It's best we close that door before he thinks of walking through."

"Right. So you've put the other Orders on alert, and the Gold thinks he's preparing a counterstrike?"

T'Zai shook his head. "You know Webster Griffin

is not so reactive. His end goal is not just to crush you and your company. My White sister has heard disturbing rumors of Quasicore amassing technology and gathering people with specific, technical skills in robotics, explosives, and biomechanical interfaces. The Blue Mendani-met has promised to insinuate her ascetics into the heart of Griffin's operation, but such an action will take time we may not have." He paused, studying his student's blank features. "You are skeptical," he guessed.

Kai tilted his dark head, eyes the color of mayhem in the light of the brooding sun. "I've never known the Orders to take such an active role, or at least admit to it. You act like you have a stake in the outcome, Mendani. What aren't you telling me?"

T'Zai chuckled, pleased as always by his pupil's quick mind and unflinching will. "I could fill vast rooms with the things I have not told you, impatient child. Would you learn all your lessons at once?"

Kai snorted again, folding his arms and tipping his face up to the waiting star. "Keep your Red Sun secrets, then. Just don't expect me to pretend blind devotion. We can't take what you tell us on faith. No pun intended," he added with a wry smile. "And we won't accept ignorance."

"Fairly said." T'Zai kept his expression bland with an effort. He wondered what Kai would say if he knew he'd just repeated his father, replaying almost word for word a declaration Ezekiel Shay had made to T'Zai years before. He wondered if Kai knew how much he was like his father. He wondered in silence; some lessons were beyond even his ability to teach.

They stood shoulder to shoulder, watching the

roiling flare of the Red Sun for a long, quiet moment.

Then his young pupil released a rather grumpy sigh. "So why couldn't this wait until morning?"

"Hmm? Oh, I couldn't sleep, either," T'Zai answered in an absent tone, mesmerized as always by the unexpected, ferocious beauty of the star's restless dance. The force of Kai's stare drew his attention. He glanced over to meet the gleam of hilarity in those Sun-darkened eyes.

"Try warm milk," Kai suggested with a sardonic edge.

T'Zai frowned at the boy. "That's disgusting."

"Alcohol?"

"Shreds my old gut."

Kai paused, his features easing into slyness. "A massage from the sweet Dani who brings you tea."

"No comment."

The young Shay chuckled. "You've had no comment on a few things lately, Mendani. Will you preside over my sister's bonding?"

"She's threatened bodily harm if I do not. So, I expect I will."

Kai grunted and spun on his heel, heading for the door. "Won't that be fun? I'm going back to bed. If you have any more fascinating revelations, send me a Suns-damned memo."

T'Zai turned a delighted grin into the red giant's glowering light. "He's mine as much as he is yours," he whispered to his god in brash challenge. The blazing behemoth did not deign to respond, and T'Zai lowered his head in humble surrender.

War wouldn't stop with one impossibly clever young man. It would claim them all.

A word about the author…

Sci-Fi/Fantasy romance author Michelle O'Leary resides in Marquette, Michigan, which graces the shore of pristine Lake Superior. Born and raised in Upper Michigan, Michelle is a child of nature, enjoying all things outdoors.

Her titles with The Wild Rose Press include *Vessel of Power* and *Last Chance* (book one of Sunscapes Trilogy).

Michelle is a mother first, a dedicated chocoholic, a contented Michigander, and a delirious word lover. She loves all feedback and is always happy to hear from readers!

http://molearyauthor.wix.com/michelleoleary

Thank you for purchasing
this publication of The Wild Rose Press, Inc.

If you enjoyed the story, we would appreciate your
letting others know by leaving a review.

For other wonderful stories,
please visit our on-line bookstore at
www.thewildrosepress.com.

For questions or more information
contact us at
info@thewildrosepress.com.

The Wild Rose Press, Inc.
www.thewildrosepress.com

Stay current with The Wild Rose Press, Inc.

Like us on Facebook

https://www.facebook.com/TheWildRosePress

And Follow us on Twitter
https://twitter.com/WildRosePress

www.ingramcontent.com/pod-product-compliance
Lightning Source LLC
Chambersburg PA
CBHW071508260626
47170CB00002B/306